THE DEVIL'S SIGNATURE:

The Devil's Signature

J. E. ELEND

THE DEVIL'S SIGNATURE: THE ABIDING PACT

Copyright © 2024 by Jane E. Elend

This book is protected under the copyright laws of the United Kingdom. Any reproduction or other unauthorised use of the material or artwork is prohibited.

This book is a work of fiction. Names, characters, places, brands, media and incidents either are a product of the author's imagination or are used fictionally.

All rights reserved.

ISBN: 9798872281696

THE DEVIL'S SIGNATURE: THE ABIDING PACT

<u>Trigger warnings:</u>

Racism

Witch Prosecution

Homophobia

Suicide

Trauma

Sexual scenes

Violence

Strong language

Death

Murder

Kidnapping

… THE DEVIL'S SIGNATURE: THE ABIDING PACT

THE DEVIL'S SIGNATURE: THE ABIDING PACT

For Kristian,

My brightest star.

THE DEVIL'S SIGNATURE: THE ABIDING PACT

ACKNOWLEDGMENTS

I am forever grateful to the following people:

To my best friend, my soulmate and number one fan Tata, thank you for all your patience, support and inspiration.

To my mother and nan, two strongest women I know, for being there when I needed you the most and supporting my dream; you have been inspirational.

To Carl, for motivating me to go beyond my comfort zone.

To my precious readers, I hope this story will take you into my own personal, intimate world of an emotional rollercoaster. I hope all of you find a character to your liking, someone who will represent your fears, worries, anger, and love. Let this palette of characters inspire, lead and help you through difficult times.

THE DEVIL'S SIGNATURE: THE ABIDING PACT

THE DEVIL'S SIGNATURE: THE ABIDING PACT

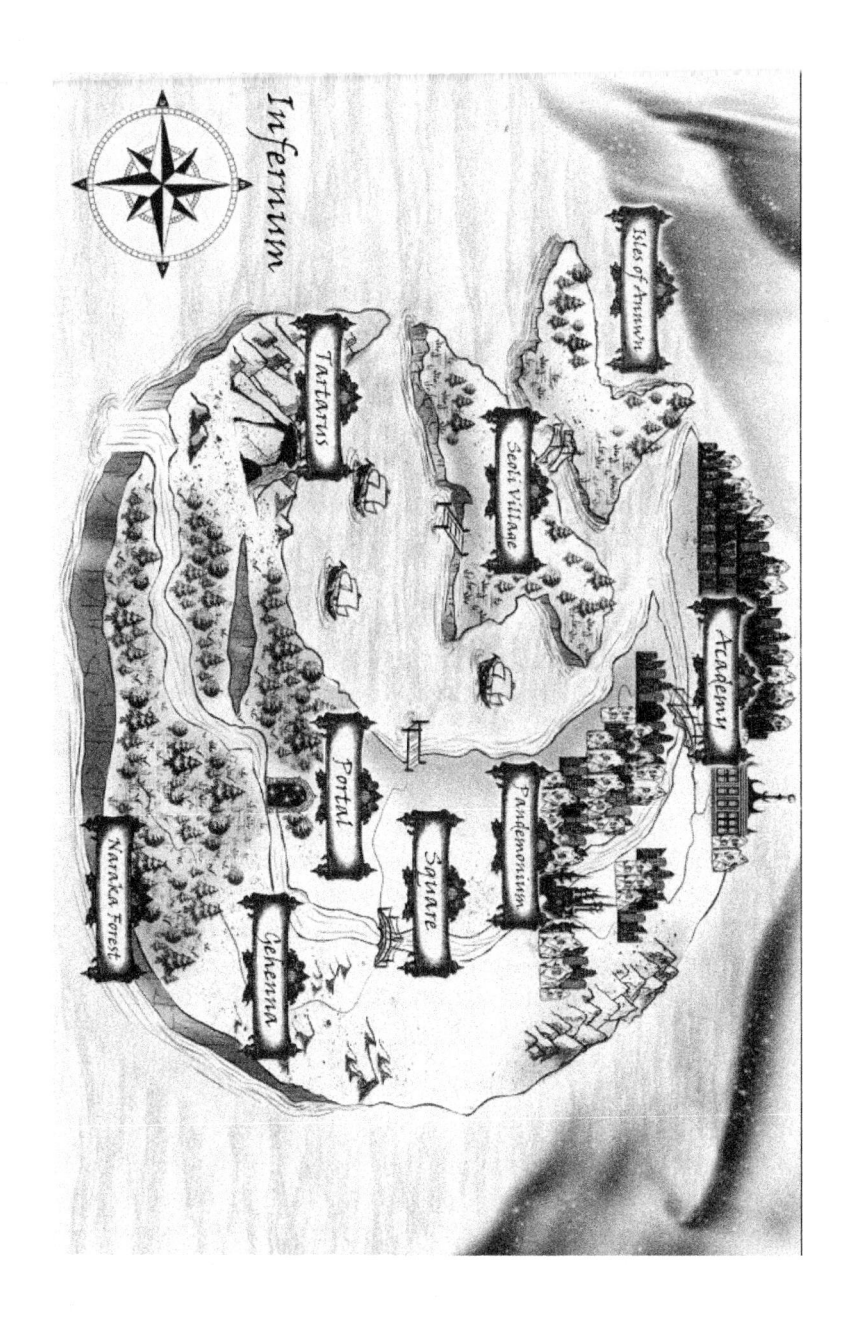

PROLOGUE

The wheezing sound of a thin, rusty, grinding fan echoed from a far corner of the room. It fused with the slow tapping of my wristwatch that resonated with the loud beating of an aching heart in my tight chest. The pulse transmitted throughout my body and pain was reflected in my temples.

Deep, slow breathing intermittently passed through my lips as my eyes searched for a way out in the darkness of the poorly illuminated room. Goosebumps pimpled my cold skin as the howling wind outside shook the walls of the steel container I was trapped inside. With my hands tied at my front, I ran my fingers through my hair in an obsessive manner. The ropes were tight on my wrists, stinging my skin. I was swaying from side to side, feeling as if there was a massive rock on my chest. I sobbed loud. Slowly exhaling and trying to keep myself in control, I got up and looked back into the dark. A wave of anxiety completely enveloped me . My palms were sweaty, my body shook, and the lack of air was making me dizzy.

'*I am all right...*' I whispered to myself, and my heart missed the beat again . '*I am OK.*' Control breathing. Save oxygen.

A panic attack began to replace my anxiety. Feeling my heart speed up and worsening pain in my wrists , I felt like I was suffocating. '*I can't breathe*', my mind was shouting. '*I can't breathe.*' It seemed as if I was drowning inside a boundless ocean. The walls were pressing in on me.

In a desperate attempt to escape the darkness, I hysterically punched my fists against the steel walls, hoping to burst my way to freedom. Fear filled me. I knew I would never again see the light of day if I didn't get out of this dark, horrible place now. I was terrified.

Cold water dripped through the rusty pipes onto the concrete floor, and rat claws scratched outside the walls, making me shiver. My wrists were sore from tight knots, and my fingertips had turned blue. I prayed for my captors to never return as I was sure they would kill me, but I was also eager for someone to find me.

I shed tears and fell to my knees, touching the surface of the steel door with my forehead, losing my last hope.

Why am I here? I wondered. What have I done? Where are my mother and father? Who are those people, and what will happen to me next?

My thoughts were slowly drifting away. Dusty air filled my lungs, exhaustion taking me over, and my mind entered a whirlpool. I slowly opened my eyes and stared at my reflection in the floor's puddle. Tired eyes looked back at me. Cracked lips trembled, and I noticed a slight grin in my reflection just before my eyes shut. Flinching, I gulped and frowned. Was I so exhausted that my imagination was playing tricks on me?

Hearing footsteps outside the door, I crawled back and shook my head in denial, preparing for the worst. Would these be the last moments of my life? Was I going to die?

'Sophie!' The door swung open, and a bright light hit my face, blinding me for a moment. Squinting, I held my breath. Warm hands touched my wrists and untied the rope, first releasing and then embracing me. A familiar scent and a beloved voice gave me hope , and I firmly surrendered into the man's arms, sobbing with relief and looking at the torch on the ground.

'Dad!' I cried when my father lifted me up and carried me out of the container, hurriedly running through the hallways of an abandoned storage building. In my eleven years, I'd never been so scared. I was shaking, and my chest was tight; the panic attack threatened to rise again. I felt sick as my stomach churned.

After running out into the pouring rain onto a dark alley, my father put me down and squatted in front of me, looking into my face with his glistening blue eyes and stroking my head. His wavy brown hair was wet from the downpour, and his bright and beautiful features seemed pale under the single street light.

'Sophie, listen to me,' he wheezed, looking back. I heard distant footsteps and started to panic even more.

'Jeremy!' a stranger's voice called, and I immediately approached my father, grabbing his shirt and looking at the stranger. A young man was standing before us, soaked to the skin in his dark jeans and silky shirt. His jet black hair was dishivelled, and glowing golden eyes with a flaming spark in them looked straight at me with surprise and relief. His hands caught my attention. The stranger's veins were shining bright with a blue flame that slipped through his skin as if kissing his hands. He was magical, and mysterious.

'Take her!' My father pushed me to the stranger. I was about to object, but father wouldn't let me say a word. 'Sophie, go! He'll protect you!'

'Jeremy, are you out of your mind?!' the stranger hissed, baring his canines and taking a step towards my father.

'You can't stand up to them right now!' Father insisted, arguing back and threatening the young man with his finger.

'Don't forget who you're talking to!' the stranger smirked and showed an evil, arrogant grin.

'Don't be stupid, boy! Think clearly,' Father objected. 'You haven't been to Infernum in over a month! Your energy is on the verge of explosion, and if you go against them all, you'll destroy this city and every single one of us! So please, take her away! You can't teleport; save your power. My car's around the corner. Take it to Astrid's, and I will handle the rest! They're just spirits! I still have some power left!'

'Damn it!' the young man snorted at him, grabbing my arm and holding me uptight.

'Sophie—' my father stepped towards us and placed a silver chain around my neck with a crescent-shaped pendant and a star '—be strong! You can do this, honey!'

'Dad…' I whispered with tears in my eyes. Something was telling me that I wouldn't see him again.

'Don't forget who you are! Sophie!' He kissed

my forehead and smiled gently. 'You are the key to the light! Remember, the deepest darkness holds the brightest of lights!'

'Daddy!' I cried when the stranger fled around the corner, taking me with him.

Holding tight to his neck , I held my tears and bit my lip, trying my best not to scream . I was so tired, so scared but, somehow, a gentle fragrance of burning fire and pine soothed my trembling body; it seemed so familiar.

Once at the car, my protector opened the door, sat me down in the back seat, jumped in front, and pressed the pedal all the way down, making the car screech and move. As he manoeuvred the steering wheel and cut the corner, the vehicle dashed away. I grabbed on to the back of the seat and looked behind, watching my father's figure seem further and further away until a group of strangers surrounded him and a tall man approached my father; his face hidden by the dark. A bright flash blinded me for a moment, the earth trembled, and my father's silhouette was no longer visible. Only a faint light streamed upwards, soon shattering into millions of pieces.

'Hold on tight!' my driver suddenly exclaimed, turning the car around and leaving the chase. Only then did I notice two other cars trying to catch up with us. Heavy rain made our car slide from side to side in the rain. We pulled away from the pursuers and hit the main road, but the wheels slipped on the wet tarmac, and the car hit a tree. My body suddenly lifted off the seat, and I flew forward, feeling a sharp pain in my head as the windscreen crashed into pieces. Cold air burst into my lungs, and the shattering of broken glass was the last thing I remembered.

ID# THE DEVIL'S SIGNATURE: THE ABIDING PACT

THE DEVIL'S SIGNATURE: THE ABIDING PACT

CHAPTER ONE

Graceful brush movements were followed by a bright line of blood-red paint, crossing the warm, soft tones of the canvas. Going upwards, descending and performing a gracious, artistic dance. The brush was then laid on a wooden table's rough surface, which was stained with a bright palette.

A warm breeze gently touched the shabby wind chimes hanging at the edge of the curtain pole, and they started their morning song. Distracted from my deep thoughts, I turned my head towards the open window and smiled at the beginnings of a new day. My lungs were filled with fresh air, the breeze chilled my skin, and a feeling of something unusual and intriguing enveloped me. That strange dream, or memory, once again crossed my mind.

Setting aside all the art tools, I grabbed my worn grey tote bag from a flimsy chair and hurriedly threw it over my shoulder, glancing at the finished portrait of a stranger that was painted on my easel. It wasn't new to me – my mind had often been visited by unusual ideas lately. My hands moving on their own, I would paint the faces of people I'd never met. It was especially odd that, after such detailed effort, I was embraced by an indescribable desire to cross all the portraits off with a bloody red line. And, each time, this desire grew stronger. Perhaps it was my desperate attempt to get away from my deep anxiety, which had haunted me and suffocated me for years.

As I turned the door handle, I glanced into the corner of my little art studio. There was a vast canvas covered with dark, cold colours. Bright amber eyes shone right in the middle of a smoky background, reflecting a fire spark. I often dreamed of these familiar, extraordinary eyes. They were attracting, hypnotizing and drowning me in their eternal flames.

It was my only unfinished portrait; I had redrawn it many times, but I could never achieve the desired results – the man remained a stranger to me. I somehow remembered him from the past but could never make his appearance exact – who was he? Still, I imagined his eyes clear as they burned into my memory. Inspiration visited me occasionally, then left indefinitely, and the unfinished portrait, or rather its sketches, remained dusty in the corner of this room.

I took my keys from the chest of drawers at the entrance. With a sigh, I shook my head unhappily, seeing a pile of unwashed dishes and takeaway boxes on the dining table. As always, my dear mother had not bothered to clean up even a little. Her absent-mindedness, frivolity and childish personality never ceased to amaze me. It would seem that I would never get used to my mother's attitude. She had repeatedly presented me with surprises for twenty-six years, bringing my inner self to rage and utter chaos.

My mother was overly friendly, an oversharer and

often irresponsible. Perhaps many would think these qualities must have been highly negative elements in her relationships with people. However, everyone loved her madly, including my father. She loved to flirt occasionally, to show herself in all her glory at the age of forty-three. However, despite such playful behaviour, she loved only my father. All her life she was faithful to him... even after his death. Left with her alone, I took over our family's main house chores and finances, as I could not trust her with a penny without fear that she would spend it all. Unfortunately, we could not afford any luxury. Due to my father's death, his company went bankrupt, and we were left with huge debts. Even selling our other property, an expensive car, and most of the company's shares did not help us. All we had left was our little house.

However, I was ready to pay tribute to my mother for her eternal positivity and faith in herself and me. To help with my university education, she opened a small café in central London on our remaining savings . It wasn't an easy decision, but it certainly helped paying most of our debts as soon as profit started to come in. She successfully kept it under control, thanks to me, and pleased regular visitors and customers with her divine coffee.

The front door of my house slammed, and I quickly jumped on the seat of my old blue bicycle, which had a basket of flowers at the front. Breathing in the morning air, I pushed the pedal, and my prestigious vehicle moved forward.

My name is Sophie Angela Mortis. I live in central London and work in my mother's cosy little café. I never had any special features, and one might not even notice me when passing by. Everyone is the main character of *their* story, subject to the trials of their destiny and obstacles. But this… is my story. It's a story about my life that was turned upside down in an instant when fate threw a burden on my shoulders that was beyond my control.

☆

Perhaps not everyone would agree with me, but I had always considered London one of the world's most magnificent cities. And it wasn't just because it was my hometown and the capital of England, soaked in history. For me, London was a diversity of cultures, a centre of active life and a separate world filled with a vibrant atmosphere. Anyone could find comfort here. The introvert absorbed the cosy, small, secret alleys, full of bright flowery shrubs, colourful houses, evergreen lawns, and private, hidden-way spots. An extrovert could enjoy busy high streets, crowds, pubs and restaurants to suit all tastes.

I loved my daily bike rides around the city in the morning. The light fog enveloped it like a heavy blanket mixed with the first sunrays. It was the smell of rain and morning dew for me. The smell of new beginnings.

London was still asleep during my early morning rides, and sometimes I could meet sleepy shopkeepers or tired truck drivers delivering scented scones. The smell of freshly brewed coffee filled the air, and my mind cheered as I cycled past another coffee shop.

I lived on St. Mary Road, inside one of the little houses with the blue door. Our house was old and shabby, but it was still dear to me. It was my abode, where all our memories of my father were kept as a precious treasure.

I remember the first time my dad brought me to my little art studio. He smiled gently and told me what extraordinary achievements awaited me in this cosy room that used to be his office. He sincerely believed that I would succeed and become an outstanding artist. My passion had subsided since then, and my inspiration visited less. And if I took up the brush, I only painted portraits of people I didn't know, crossing them all out in the end. Fifteen years had passed since my father's death, but I still heard his voice in my mind sometimes, which lulled me and brought warmth to my heart.

As I drove past London Stadium and turned towards Victoria Park, I glanced through a window of a red double-decker bus. Its windows reflected my shredded brown hair, which barely touched my shoulders and pink cheeks with freckles. My ivory blouse was blowing in the wind, and my worn black jeans were surviving their last moments, starting to rip at the seams and the edges. I moved my blue eyes on the road and smiled, turning to the city canal and heading for City Road.

Approaching the centre after almost forty minutes of my trip, I noticed the bright sign of my mother's café. The thin columns, embraced with vine, were shiny and tall. 'Astarta' was written on the sign hanging above the door with vintage glass. I always found the name strange for a café, but my mother justified it by saying it was the best name for her workplace. Astarta was a demon of lust, pleasure, motherhood and fertility, according to some legends of folklore and mythology. And in my parent's opinion, there's nothing closer to such qualities than sweet cakes and pastries, and coffee freshly brewed by the hands of the most divine mother in the world… Astrid was always big-headed and completely random.

After driving into the alley and leaving my bike in

the café's backyard, I opened the door and walked into an empty room. I opened the windows, letting in the fresh morning air. The coffee machine made a funny noise as I switched it on, and the oven rumbled in anticipation of baking sweet treats.

The café interior was made in the style of Provence. Paints of gold and grey, decorative panels made of different types of wood, furniture with vintage elements, and other interior details were made by professional artisans. And the harmonious combination of colours and materials gave a sense of comfort. It made anyone staying in this café feel incredibly cosy.

I heard footsteps from above and smiled a little, greeting my colleague, Martin, who was slowly walking downstairs.

'Morning! Did you stay up all night gaming again?' I laughed as I looked at the man's sleepy face.

'Hi! I tried to complete the Warzone challenge, like a hundred times. I lost track of time.' He stretched out, sitting in a chair and spreading like jelly all over the table. Martin was a genuinely kind and sweet guy. Still, his addiction to online games and computer technology often disrupted his regular human schedule. By nature, Martin was a relatively relaxed, friendly, lazy nerd who had to be kicked in the butt to get him to work sometimes. However, he was always ready to help, support and comfort. That is exactly why my mother let him live upstairs in a one-bedroom apartment above a café to keep an eye on the place if we were busy.

After ruffling the man's short wheat-coloured hair, I put a cup of freshly brewed coffee on the table in front of my friend, noticing his blissful smile, and I smirked. Martin was a couple of years older than me, but I always thought of him as my little brother who needed constant supervision. Even now, when I noticed the torn sleeve of the T-shirt he seemed to be wearing for the third day, I just shook my head and sighed.

'Have you seen my mother?' I asked while placing the brownies on the café display shelf.

'Yes, she came in for a minute but then disappeared in a car with some stranger,' Martin smiled charmingly. I looked at him in surprise. His glasses were shining in the sunlight.

'She left?' I was confused. 'With whom?'

'Who knows!' The man laughed, scratching his head and stretching out again, his muscles tensed. 'Astrid is an attractive lady; maybe she has picked up another boyfriend?'

'How strange,' I answered quietly, frowning. 'Mum never left the cafe without telling me…'

'And the guy following her was pretty good-looking,' Martin continued. 'Very elegant and posh. He was Asian, didn't talk much, but was a gentleman. He was wearing a black suit with a bright-red shirt, very sophisticated – I bet it was branded, 'cause it looked expensive as hell. He's weird, though, I'll tell you that. Silent and very serious. Looked more like a bodyguard than a friend.'

'Did she say when she was coming back?' I asked anxiously, surprised at such a detailed description of the stranger. The worry rose slowly. I knew my mother; she rarely left without warning, especially with people from a higher class. After my father's company went bankrupt, I hardly saw anyone from that part of society. Maybe it was one of the shareholders we owed money to.

'No.' Martin shrugged. 'But she was visibly nervous.'

Watching my colleague pull up his shabby jeans

and finish a cup of hot coffee, I couldn't stop thinking that my dear mother was in trouble.

My anxiety rose when I couldn't reach her by noon, torturing my smartphone every couple of minutes, hoping my mother would call me back.

☆

The streets of London overflowed; our café got extremely busy. For a few minutes, I was able to distract myself by serving customers. Packing baked goods and gently smiling at the visitors, I noticed a long-awaited guest from the corner of my eye.

The bell on the door rang, and a man in a white T-shirt and dark skinny jeans entered the café. His tall figure, broad shoulders and strong hands made my cheeks blush. I noticed a wide shining smile and glistening light-blue eyes. Getting a grip of myself and battling my shyness, I said hello.

'Oh, Mike!' Martin exclaimed, waving our guest over to the front till.

'Hello,' said the blond man in a silky voice, as if reflecting the bright sunrays in his curls. 'Wow, you are busy today!'

'Yes, it's Saturday!' Martin nodded cheerfully, handing out a cup of coffee to another client.

'How are you, Sophie?' my friend asked, looking at me with his beautiful eyes, the colours of the bright sky. My heart jumped for a second, and a warm wave ran through my body, making me smile wider.

'I'm all right, thanks,' I nodded, raising my eyes to him, 'and you?'

Michael Haniel was a very good-natured, humble man. I met him in a café about five years ago when he brought his client to us. Mike worked in a retirement home and took frequent walks with cheerful old ladies around town to perk up their dull days. He was very educated, and it was the trait that entertained his clients the most because my friend could talk about anything. You could often see a book or a science magazine in his hands. He had a pure soul, and he was a man who always wanted to give rather than receive. He cared for people in the noblest way possible .

And naturally, I was strongly attracted to him. I didn't even try to fight these feelings. To me, he was an unreachable idol that I wanted to watch from afar and bask in the light of his grace.

Mike was so beautiful in his nature that he spent all his free time at the local church helping to organise charity events and watch over the place. He often helped to hold masses, baptisms, and other holy celebrations. He volunteered at a homeless shelter and regularly donated to orphanages. To an ordinary person like me, Michael was a saint.

Mike's father worked as a police detective. James Haniel was the exact opposite of Michael, though it was no surprise because my friend had been adopted at an early age. The detective was a pretty strict, serious and introverted man. He often went to work with his head full of thoughts and rarely understood any humour. Unfortunately, Michael's mother had become unwell and died not so long ago, and James became very closed up after she passed. I often noticed how Michael distanced himself from his father.

I first met Detective Haniel the day he was standing on our doorstep, patting my mother on the shoulder and comforting her after he'd announced my father's death, fifteen years ago. James had dedicated all these years to finding my father's killer, but with no result. At some point, my mother and I had accepted the fact that we wouldn't find the truth.

James had fought to the end, though, but accepted our decision to move forward.

I vaguely remembered that day. I woke up in the hospital after a car accident. The impact was so severe because I'd flown out of the car through the front window, getting a concussion. That crash was still something hazy and distant in my memories. All I remembered was my dad giving me the necklace and ordering the driver to go. Dad stayed in a dark alley, surrounded by a group of people. My memory was getting foggy as I looked out the back window and watched my father's figure sink into the darkness. And only the bright golden eyes, anxiously looking at me in the rear-view mirror, haunted me since in my sleep. Who those beautiful amber eyes belonged to – I never knew.

My mother always spoke about that night with pain in her voice, explaining that it was most likely another kidnapping for ransom from my father. He was running his high-tech company then. The competition was rough, and his rivals often resorted to dirty tricks. Even now, I was often under surveillance or attack, without knowing the reason. The driver was never found, and I miraculously survived.

Such incidents became a regular occurrence; that's why my mother signed me up for self-defence lessons shortly after. Now, I was often able to fight back against my abusers.

Michael sat at the nearest table, and said, interrupting my thoughts, 'I'm good, thanks.'

I handed him a cup of hot lemon tea, receiving thanks in return. As I returned to the counter, I bumped into a stranger before me. I frowned as he studied me with his dark-green emerald eyes. This tall, brown-haired man with a thin scar on his cheek seemed to dislike me at once. He looked at me as if I had crossed his whole life out. For some reason I felt sure he wasn't to be trusted.

'How can I help you?' I asked as calmly as possible, waiting for the guest to answer.

'Are you Sophie?' he asked quietly in a low voice that gave me the creeps. I only nodded, watching the stranger squint as he saw Michael nearby, receiving a greeting nod from my friend. Do they know each other?

'And you, I'm sorry, are who?' I raised my eyebrow at this rude man. He didn't answer, instead noticing a pendant around my neck and grabbing it with his clinging fingers. I stepped back and was ready to give him a slap on the face, but I – and Michael, who had gotten up from the chair – were interrupted.

'Young man,' a smooth and resounding voice of a woman was heard say behind my assailant, 'it is not appropriate to get touchy with someone on the first date.'

'What?' The stranger snorted, turning to the woman, and I immediately noticed his surprised, even frightened, look. My saviour was none other than Thana, a frequent visitor to our café. A lovely woman with a great sense of humour.

She raised her nose proudly, touching her long, wavy brown hair and turning her face with chubby pink cheeks towards me. Her full figure was wrapped in a tight black dress. White dangling earrings in a shape of the skulls matched a long shiny necklace with an unfamiliar symbol reminding a cross. Squeezing an expensive branded clutch bag in her hand and tapping her heel on the floor, the charming woman smiled. She seemed to send a whole stream of ruthless thoughts to the intruder of my peace, for he immediately snorted, pressed his lips, and looked at me again.

'See you later, Sophie...' he said mysteriously, smiling cunningly, before leaving the café.

'What a day!' I sighed, running my hand through my hair and shaking my head. I suddenly started to feel this familiar pain in my chest. My palms got sweaty, and my heartbeat started to increase. I felt like I was stuck in the box with no way out. Anxiety was back.

'Some people surely forget their manners, don't they? Sophie, sweetie—' Thana smiled, touching my shoulder, and I twitched '—can you get me some jasmine tea, please?'

'Yes, of course, Thana,' I replied, smiling kindly. Somehow, her voice was always so calming.

This woman was an insurance company CEO and also owned several funeral branches. Hence, her specific taste in black attire and sophisticated jewellery. She always dressed very elegantly and tastefully. I wasn't sure of her age, but looked like about forty years old; Thana did not let people address her as 'Miss' or 'Madam'; she preferred her own name. Failure to obey could result in one's visit to her funeral branch in a casket.

'You're such a precious child.' The woman smiled once again, sitting beside Michael and starting a friendly conversation with him.

My worries never went away. Could the stranger who just left have something to do with my mother's escape from the workplace? What did he want?

After rechecking my phone, I sighed. Where did she go, that wretched woman?! God forbid I should find her; I'd lock her in the house!

When I heard the entrance bell ring, I gathered my patience. I greeted the guest with a smile, surprised. Strangely, this guest gave me an unsettling feeling.

A tall, dark-haired Asian man with cold eyes was looking straight at me, holding his hands behind his back while standing at the threshold in a black suit. His sharp, confident gaze of almond-shaped dark, silver eyes penetrated to the bone.

'Oh!' Martin exclaimed, making me shudder and glance away from the man. 'It's him! That's the dude who left with Astrid this morning!'

'Huh?' I was surprised, looking at the man again and nodding at him uncertainly, trying to figure out how not to be rude and find out about my mother.

'Miss Mortis?' he gallantly called me in a foreign accent, bowing. I knew first-hand about the polite manners of Eastern culture, as my best friend Lizzie was from Tokyo, and her family was very traditional and strict in their manners.

'Yes…' I wasn't sure how to react.

'My name is Alastor—' he bowed again, embarrassing me. I looked away as a couple of clients began to stare in our direction '—and I came to get you to take you to your mother.'

'What?' I was surprised. I saw Mike come up to me and look at the man with distrust.

'Sophie, is everything OK?' he said coldly, standing before me and protecting me from a stranger.

'Miss Mortis, they'll explain everything to you on the spot; I've only been instructed to bring you in,' said the man, ignoring Michael. Strangely, despite his icy look, his alienation, and his incomprehensible aura, I felt that he was a man I could trust. My sixth sense forced me to lower Mike's hand, which blocked my way and take a step forward.

'OK,' I answered quietly, not letting my friend argue. 'It's OK, Michael; if anything happens, there are plenty of witnesses. Would you look after the café, please?'

He shrugged his shoulders. 'Sure thing,' he said, watching me leave then sit into a black Mercedes.

Mike looked at me with worry, and I smiled only slightly, feeling the joy of being cared about.

☆

The road was long and tense. Sitting behind the wheel, Alastor didn't share a word with me. The silence only amplified my worry, but my self-protection instinct forced me to watch the road carefully, desperate to remember every detail of the trip. My anxiety was ready to burst out. However, my sixth sense was adamant about trusting Alastor. Something about him was so... tranquil. Terrified thoughts never left me, though. What if I was being kidnapped again?! Who knew... It wouldn't be the first time I'd been in danger. Maybe my mother and I would find ourselves in a dark, dusty barn, tied to a pole and sold for organs. Ugh, shit...

'We have arrived, Miss Mortis,' said Alastor, for the first time in almost an hour's journey. My phone's GPS showed the area on the edge of London. Sighing , I got out of the car when the door was opened by my driver, and I felt a sense of awe.

There was an indescribable beauty of a residence before me. The two-storey Palladian-style house spread over several hundred feet. It was decorated with grey bricks, had brightly illuminated white columns and was surrounded by flowerbeds, topiary trees and palm trees.

There was a large garden and expanses of endless land behind the mansion. At the entrance, there was a fountain illuminated by colourful lights. The view was magnificent. Such houses could be found only on the outskirts of London and belonged to wealthy owners, foreigners, and tycoons.

The idea that my kidnapper could only be a fabulous millionaire, who would become my fated love, immediately appeared. Or he could be a cruel drug lord that wanted to get an impressive sum for my head. Although, none of the options was possible, given that I lived in the real world and such things only happened to girls in smutty novels or romantic films. And this certainly doesn't appear to be kidnapping. *Wake up, Sophie, and focus...*

'This way.' My personal driver led me inside, opening the doors and letting me into the spacious rooms. Marble floors, high ceilings – a dream house for so many. White and blue colours dominated the theme; tall windows and wide doors created the illusion of limitless space. The window apertures were draped, and furniture and interior items were distinguished by their quality. Furniture details were made of cherry wood, preserving the elegant texture and colours shaded by overlays of expensive stone and ancient ornaments carved with gold.

I found it strange that, despite the chic interior and noticeably expensive decor details, the house still seemed cosy and warm, which is not often expected from such places. I always imagined that it would be cold, grey and lonely in such a residence. And here... I wanted to make myself a cup of hot tea and sit in a soft armchair surrounded by light-coloured walls and carpets.

As I walked into the living room, with its high ivory silk curtain windows, I stepped on a fluffy grey carpet. I stared at my mother, who was sitting on a wide, lush silver sofa.

'Mother!' I exclaimed, immediately feeling anger and resentment growing inside.

'Sophie, honey!' My mother waved at me, putting

a cup of tea on a glass coffee table and smiling.

'Are you serious?!' I shouted louder, crossing the distance and rising above her with a formidable, murderous look. 'What the fuck? Do you know how worried I was?'

'Language, dear, you're a guest.' Astrid pointed to the sofa and offered me a cup of tea. Realising that it was useless to argue with this woman, I immediately gave up. I sighed nervously, rolling my eyes and shaking my head.

'What's going on, Mum ?' I monotonously asked, watching Alastor stand at the door like a guard.

'It's all right, dear—' the woman waved her hand again '—just met an old acquaintance of mine.'

'An old acquaintance?' I asked again with my eyebrow up. Even though my mother was known for her friendliness, acquaintances with such wealth frightened me.

'Yes, I've got some terrific news for you, Sophie!'

'Oh really?' I asked, incredulous, taking a sip of tea and refusing to believe my mother. Her thoughtlessness and simple-mindedness began to offend me.

'I found you a husband!' Astrid clapped joyfully, looking at my pale face, which must have been filled with misunderstanding, contempt, and disbelief.

'I'm sorry…' I smiled nervously when I spilt tea on the carpet, 'what?'

'You're getting married!' Astrid repeated, as if this was a casual phrase.

I couldn't answer this nonsense because just then I heard a door shutting in the hallway, which distracted me, and I had no words to object at the moment – I was in shock. Watching my mother's happy face, I tried to recall Astrid's various pranks, trying to understand if I was the victim of a bad joke. However, my mother's eyes shone so brightly that I genuinely started to question her sobriety and sanity.

I suddenly felt something strange: a subtle but persistent feeling that I was in the wrong place. Silently staring at my mother, I continued to sit there, pleading with my eyes for her to take back the words.

The blonde woman straightened her long light curls and straightened the pink blouse that didn't hide her feminine, envious features. The black skirt showed her slender legs, and the lacquered classic night sky-coloured heels reflected the sunrays peeking out the window. Astrid looked much younger than her age, and people often thought she was my older sister rather than my mother. I had often wondered what magical beauty products my mother used as she hasn't changed much in the last few years.

Astrid sat absolutely calm, satisfied and happy.

'Mum…' I gulped, hoping for the word 'joke' from her.

'Here he is!' The woman was cheerfully smiling as she looked towards the doorway. Slowly turning my head, I felt a cold sweat cover my skin and my heart went to my stomach. An electrical pulse ran through my body, and I felt it in my ears for a second. Something made me feel really creeped out, scared, terrified.

A tall man entered the hall, wearing a formal black suit, with a velvety half-unbuttoned black shirt that exposed his pronounced collarbone with a gold chain and a pentagram on his neck. His hands were hidden in his pockets, but I could see a silver bracelet on his wrist. The black suit looked elegant on him, adding a twist to his slender body. However, black cowboy ankle boots with golden chain and a ram scull seemed out of place. Tanned skin, black as tar , wavy hair brushed and tied in a short ponytail on the back of the head. One of his eyebrows has a shaved line. There was star earring in his left ear and few other silver earrings in both of his ears. He had sharp features, with stubble cut neatly and stylishly, forming a beautiful face with clear cheekbones. Plump lips, and thick eyebrows complemented the appearance of a stranger that looked at me, squinting.

But the eyes attracted attention most of all... the eyes that looked at me were brown, dark like coffee beans. It felt like I was drowning in the thickness of bitter chocolate, rushing deeper and deeper with no way out. Despite his strict appearance, the stranger expressed excessive kindness, calmness and some mystical wisdom, and fatigue in his eyes . However, something in those eyes frightened me too , but I could not understand what it was.

He wasn't just handsome. This man was so... fucking... hot with a pinch of charm and overflowing charisma. The air seemed to be freezing and heating up around him at the same time.

'Sophie, this is Bale Deemer,' said my mother in a funny way, taking me out of my dark thoughts and making the butterflies in my stomach flutter away. 'Your future husband!'

THE DEVIL'S SIGNATURE: THE ABIDING PACT

CHAPTER TWO

Looking at my old shabby sneakers, I bit my lip and frowned. I crossed my arms on my chest and tried to remember if I had placed another order for several packs of coffee beans for our café. I thought I had uploaded the order to the supplier for sure, although—

'Sophie, honey, are you all right?' my mother asked quietly, looking at me worryingly. I distracted myself from my thoughts and slowly turned my head to my parent, clenching my lips and just nodding. She didn't seem to believe me.

'Yeah, sure, I'm fine.' I shrugged my shoulders, looking at my shoes again. 'I'm just waiting for you to stop fooling around so we can get out of here, because…'

'Because – what?' Astrid asked me quietly.

'Because it's absolute nonsense!!' I jumped to my

feet, grabbed my head and growled. Rage and panic started to build up inside me. 'Do you even know what you're saying? Mum! Come to your senses, what bloody marriage?! You're… you're…'

'Honey, calm down.' Astrid smiled as she looked at the owner of the house , who seemed to be ignoring my hysteria. It annoyed me even more, by the way . 'Let me explain.'

'What's there to explain?!' I whispered, squeezing my fists ina desperate wish to ounch somebody. I wanted it all to end, I had no time for this. 'No, I realise, of course, that I'm twenty-six, and I don't even have a boyfriend…'

There was a light chuckle in the room, and I went silent for a second, slowly turning my head towards the insolent man who supposedly was the owner of this stunning residence . My murderous stare made him raise his eyebrows and look away, embarrassedly coughing. Making sure my tantrum wouldn't be interrupted again, I stared back at my mother and sighed.

'I won't even ask how you came up with this ridiculous idea and why this shady rich bloke is staying quiet! Did he agree to this stupid scam ! Do you really think that, in this day and age, I would agree to an arranged marriage?!' When I sighed, I sat on the couch again and leaned back, feeling uncertain, exhausted, with a growing headache.

'Sophie, hear me out, it's a temporary measure,' my mother replied. I looked at her sternly, sitting upright and showing her with intently through my gaze that dissatisfaction with these words was still present. 'There's a reason for all and it will all make sense. Also, you don't have a boyfriend because you broke up with him a couple of years ago, so you have nothing to lose.'

'I didn't break up with him; he left the city for some unknown reason, without explaining anything!' I raised my hands, remembering my broken relationship. My ex-boyfriend, whom I knew from college, suddenly moved out of London by sending me a message with the words: 'I'm sorry, but I don't think it's going to work'. He wasn't the first person to run away from me. My love life seemed to be disastrous from the beginning, men usually leaving me after the first date .

There was another chuckle from the side, and I was ready to throw a cup at the condescending owner of the estate. Prick.

'Sophie,' Astrid sighed.

'I'm not marrying a man I just met. How do I know he's not a sick pervert or a serial killer?' I answered monotonously, turning to the silent man. 'No offence!'

'Sophie,' my mother sighed again as I gazed at the light wave of the man's hand as he continued to drink his freshly brewed coffee, 'please listen to me before you make assumptions.'

'I can't wait to find out what made you think my marriage to a stranger would be a great idea!' I started rubbing my temples and dreaming of my solitude.

'Do you remember what happened to your father's company?' my mother asked gently. I nodded. Sure, how could I have forgotten those couple of years of our torment when my father's company instantly went bankrupt after his death? Shares went down, and the firm was at risk and went into administration, leaving us with unlimited debts, as my mother was my father's partner. Her name was also mentioned in the contract.

I heard that sometime before the bankruptcy was declared, the company wanted to sell its last shares.

Still, the process was suspended for a reason I did not know. I never knew what happened next. I didn't know much about business, so I didn't ask for much detail. All I cared about was our home, which we were about to lose, as our debts wouldn't let us pay the mortgage.

'It seems that the remaining shares of the company were repurchased.' I sighed as I tried to dig into my memory.

'That's right.' Astrid smile. 'The company was bought out, along with the debts that have been paid off now.'

'What?' I frowned in disbelief. 'What do you mean... paid off?'

'Your father's company merged with an existing corporation, and our debts were paid almost straight after his death,' Mom repeated, hiding her eyes from me. I was holding myself, and for some reason, I felt a fit of nausea. It seemed like the news was good...

'How long ago?' I asked in a husky voice.

'What?'

'How long ago?!' I raised my voice angrily, looking at my mother. 'How long have you known about this?!'

'It was a few days after Jeremy's death.' My mother lowered her eyes. Suddenly, I felt an inexplicable emptiness, anger, frustration, and as well as awareness of my own stupidity. My thoughts immediately took over my mind, and I tried to remember every bill and debt I'd tried to pay.

'All these years I believed that we would never get out of debt,' I said quietly, 'by refusing to continue my studies in France, working like a slave on three jobs during the last years of my student life and making every effort not to lose the house... Sleep-deprived, exhausted.'

'I know,' Astrid gulped, putting her hand on my knee. My rage suddenly overwhelmed my mind, and I jumped up from where I sat, glaring at my mother.

'And after all these lies, you decided to bring me the news about marrying a stranger?! Without talking to me about it?' My voice was rising noticeably, and I made the last effort not to break down and run away from these people.

'Listen to me, Sophie!' For the first time, my mother raised her voice. Still, I only got angrier, opening my mouth to respond rudely, but I was interrupted.

'Let me, Astrid.' My body seemed to freeze. This voice was painfully familiar to me but also new, making my blood boil and my skin fill with goosebumps. It was a low, velvety voice with a deep, heartfelt English accent, so old fashioned that you could barely hear it these days . I still couldn't understand why that stranger was giving me such a reaction – I had very contradictory feelings: interest, embarrassment, fear, and growing horror...

'Of course, Bale,' my mother said, smiling gently, gripping my hand and making me sit back down, curious as I looked at him, while still wandering in my thoughts about him.

'Sophie,' he began, and it was only by him pronouncing my name that I was ready to explode. *What the fuck is this sorcery?!* Not only could I not take my eyes off him, but I couldn't move. As if under hypnosis, I was entirely under the control of his eyes, trying to fight the inner desire to get closer. All those chaotic feelings completely enveloped me, and I came to my senses only when I noticed a slight smile on his lips. If it wasn't for my paranoia, I would have thought he was laughing at my thoughts. 'My name is Belial Deemer. I am the CEO of Infernum Enterprise, a corporation that develops applications for global, government, and other organizations. I'm an old friend of your father's, and I knew him very closely because he was the one to help me with my career and in many other ways.'

'I never heard of you from him,' I said quietly, straining and trying to get into the conversation.

'I'm not surprised,' Bale grinned again, getting up from his seat and walking to the chest of drawers by the door, opening the top drawer and taking out a couple of papers. He came back over to me, reaching out with the old photo.

Distracted for a second by the dizzying familiar scent of pine, I shook my head and lowered my gaze from this man to the photo. My heart trembled. The picture depicted my father smiling broadly as he stood near a noticeably young Bale by a bright, tall building that read 'Infernum Enterprise'. Was it really true?

'Your father often received threats from his competitors,' continued the estate owner, 'as did I. Sometimes, he got into trouble because he competed with his rivals, who liked to play dirty. Time was cruel and dark. Fearing for his family, and knowing he wouldn't be around sooner or later, Jeremy asked me to watch over you and to provide protection. And I believe it's my duty to keep my promise. That's why I bought out the rest of his company, using his projects to grow my corporation.'

'This kind of charity does not explain your desire for an arranged marriage,' I frowned, clutching a photograph in the palm of my hand.

'Of course, I will not agree to it without my own benefit.' Mr Deemer laughed, and I pressed my lips, starting to get irritated by his arrogance. 'Despite my global fame, my reputation with the company sponsors is not the best, given my frequent business trips, secrecy and isolation. Statistically, family people inspire more trust. And without trust, I will not get a grant for my new project from a potential sponsor from South Korea, who is very respectful of family traditions.'

'So you need a fake wife to get a sponsor and rebuild your reputation for a while?' I raised my eyebrow and started to see where this conversation was going.

'I also need part of your shares, which I cannot have without a marriage agreement. A little cunning idea of your father. We both benefit from it,' Bale nodded gallantly.

I only smiled sadly and looked away.

'What's my gain?' I could barely hear myself say it.

'Sophie, how many times have you been in danger?' Mr Deemer asked me, making me shudder and look at him. Naturally, he knew about my abduction. But did he also know of other potential attacks and harassment I'd experienced over the past fifteen years? I never understood it all. Why did these threats continue after my father died? It seemed like the abusers wanted me personally, not my father's money. That's why Mr Haniel tried to find my father's killer, suspecting that the problem was about personal motives rather than business.

'I don't know what these people want or why are you their target.'

'Huh?' I was surprised and experienced déjà vu. He seemed to have read my mind again.

'Your mother doesn't understand it either, but the fact remains that you're not safe. That's why Astrid had to lie to you so you wouldn't go far from home; so that you'd always be near her to avoid getting attacked again. Believing that you had to pay a huge debt, you were under constant supervision. All your payments are kept in a separate account, which you can use at any time.' Bale's look seemed to have softened. It gave my body a warm feeling. 'My people are trying to find information to understand what's going on.'

'Your people?' I laughed. He seemed to own an underground organization of spies and contractors sniffing out the information. This is bullshit!

'I have enough connections to ensure my own and someone else's safety. That's the price of my success, and you should get used to it, too. Competition with other corporations is endless, and often other people will play unfairly. They like getting rid of their rivals quietly and silently if they can't beat them in a fair fight on the international market,' he explained, pulling out his smartphone and checking the time. 'And often such games include threats that force owners to sell their shares or obey the rules of violators.'

'It all sounds very unrealistic and fantastic.' I frowned again, refusing to believe what I was involved in. It made me angry that what I heard sounded like something from a thriller or a well-thought-out movie.

'When you live in a narrow closed world of your own, the world of others always seems unrealistic,' Bale said thoughtfully, looking aside and squinting. He's strange, this Mr Deemer. 'Often, there are things you don't see. But just because you can't see them, it doesn't mean they don't exist…'

'Sophie,' my mother interrupted that speech, 'as I said, it's a temporary measure. Bale will provide our… your protection, and when things calm down and you're safe, you'll go your separate ways. No one is making you do this without your consent.'

'What if it doesn't stop?' I asked irritably. 'What if these people aren't found? What if it takes years? I would have to live with someone I don't love or know?!'

'Love is overrated,' answered Mr Deemer, and I looked at him with a killer look. *Now, that's rude!* Not only does this self-righteous narcissist set his terms, but he also destroys my hopes and dreams of a happy life. You ungrateful, entitled bastard!

Again, a smile was on the man's lips, and that was the last straw of my angelic patience. *Oh, no, he's not! Screw it!* I'd rather experience terror running away from my kidnappers than live under the same roof with this... this... condescending twat! I mean, he's just playing me! *Look at that smirk on his perfect face!*

My anger grew, and I felt a terrible injustice in my situation. Pride whispered that the time had come to leave this unfortunate estate, but the desire for revenge prevailed over pride. Suddenly a crazy idea came to mind, and I thought for a moment about my options. My dislike of new acquaintances also made me rethink it, as did my resentment towards my mother. *Well, you're playing with fire, you self-centred prick! I also knew how to play a game and find benefits for myself!*

'Deal!' I exclaimed, tapping my palm on the coffee table. Astrid shuddered, and Bale raised his eyebrows, not expecting such a turn of events.

'I'm listening.' He smiled gently, hiding his hands in his pockets and coming close to me, looking straight into my eyes and trying to frighten me with his tall figure. With my hands crossed on my chest in a protective gesture, I accepted his challenge and remained standing still.

'I'll settle for this scam. But in return, I have

conditions,' I said.

'Oh?' Mr Deemer mumbled, changing his smile to a grin. It seemed to me that he smirked like a hunter, a predator. Was I in a trap? He looked too confident.

'First, given that this is an arranged marriage, and I do not know how long it will last, I am entitled to get a divorce as soon as I decide to date another person! I'm not gonna lose the chance to have a happy love life.' I raised my eyebrow and examined the estate owner from head to toe, again convinced of his divine perfection.

'Hm, sure,' Bale extended, mocking my demand.

'Secondly, if I am ever to marry such an influential owner of a corporation, then I have the right to pamper myself.' I shrugged my shoulders. 'I want a rich and luxurious lifestyle.'

'You'll have your own unlimited bank account, which you can spend as your soul wishes. You'll have that account even in the event of a divorce, as a "thanks for the trouble",' Bale answered calmly, and I frowned. 'Alastor will be your personal driver and bodyguard, as I am willing to trust him with my life.'

'Um.' Not expecting such generosity, I was even saddened for a second but refused to give up and only gave in to the current. 'Fine!'

'Will there be a "thirdly"?' squinting, Bale leaned a little forward, making me shudder and look away in embarrassment.

'N-No…' I stuttered with my lips pressed.

'Fabulous,' Bale smiled, 'then here are my terms. First, you can look for your lover in all corners of the world but don't forget that the whole press and the public will be watching us, so if I notice that your hunt for romantic endeavours hurts my reputation, I will personally strangle you with my bare hands.'

I opened my mouth, appalled at such an insult, but

I didn't get a chance to talk because Bale continued his monologue.

'Secondly, I need to know your every move – where you are, who you're with. It's for your own safety and my peace of mind. No objections will be accepted. You must attend most business events with me, learn all the details of my company's developments and be regularly present at the main branch of my firm because this marriage must be considered real and not cause any suspicion.'

'All I hope is that this will be over as soon as possible,' I whispered.

'I'm just as excited about it,' Bale said monotonously, stepping away and turning his back to me. 'You've tired me in the last hour. I'm afraid to think about what I'm about to experience in the future.'

'That's a shame,' I snorted with a smile. 'What are you going to do if I never find a man and you never catch the people who are threatening me all this time?'

'Then it's an eternal married life with me that awaits you, sweetheart.' Bale waved goodbye as he left the room. Alastor bowed to him, and my rival disappeared.

My blood was boiling, and my head was humming. My body was overcome with indescribable rage, panic and adrenaline. I couldn't believe I'd agreed to this scam! It hurt me to lose control and give in to my emotions.

'You two seem to be getting along very well!' My mother clapped her hands at my cold murderous look. I was ready to rip her apart and tear her to shreds. Clutching my fists, I tried to figure out how my life could suddenly turn upside down. Was I supposed to fight to the end and say no? *Wouldn't that be stupid, though?!* Anyone in my position would have taken that chance and allowed themselves to live a fancy life, albeit for a while. Especially next to such a devilishly handsome man, though with a lousy character... *I hope I don't have to see him too often.*

Taking a deep breath and soothing my simmering resentment, I shuddered at the vibration in my pocket. The name 'Lizzie' appeared on the screen of my smartphone, and I involuntarily smiled, thinking of my darling friend. She'd be flabbergasted at my news! I could even imagine her asking for a visit to this residence and friendly shopping at my expense thanks to my new funds – or rather my future husband's savings.

Husband... ugh, sounds horrifying! That arrogant prick was making my blood boil! I'd show him what he'd signed up for. Hell would seem like a vacation to him...

☆

I couldn't wait to take a deep breath of fresh air as the car pulled up to our house. All this mess had made me noticeably tired.

'Here is my number, Miss Mortis,' Alastor said, giving me his card, and I nodded silently to thank him. 'I will come tomorrow morning to take you to work.'

'Alastor, will you be by my side all the times?' Surprise must have been visible on my face.

'That's Mr Deemer's order,' he explained, as he got out of the car and opened the door for me. 'I'll be here for you all the time.'

'What about your boss?' The smile dropped from my lips, and I stepped onto the doorstep of my house, watching my mother stumble in, waving her elegant hand to my new bodyguard.

'Mr Deemer is quite capable of standing up for himself. And he's got enough men to be his personal drivers.' Alastor bowed in a sign of respect.

'He's suspicious, this Mr Deemer,' I mumbled, hiding the card in my bag. Alastor's lips just twitched, and the corners of his mouth rose in a weak smile.

'That's what everybody says before they know him.' The man bowed to me again, and I waved, showing that I didn't need such manners. 'You may call me Al if it makes you feel better, Miss.'

'Then don't call me Miss.' I rolled my eyes. 'It's a temporary measure, as far as you know. And I'm not comfortable with you addressing me like that. Call me by my name, please.'

'As you wish, Sophie,' replied my new friend, and I smiled at him, feeling shy.

After saying goodbye to my new babysitter, I closed the front door and slowly sighed, hearing a rustle behind me and gathering strength for a new quarrel with my mother. As I turned around, I tiredly watched her pack her shiny suitcase, quietly humming.

'Are you going somewhere?' my strict question followed, as I caught Astrid's guilty look.

'As we discussed in the car,' the woman began, 'for the duration of this deal, we will live in Bale's residence. I'm, uh, packing up!'

'I see you're most happy about this stupid deal.' I waved my hand, realising it was useless to argue. And I had no strength left to discuss the matter. 'And no matter what, don't you dare sell the café.'

'Sophie, darling,' my mother sighed sadly, 'forgive me for not telling you about it. I really thought about your safety. I knew well that even if I told you the truth, I wouldn't be able to stop you from leaving our home in a desire to reach your artistic goals. You are stubborn and ambitious; you would have moved out even though you were in danger.'

'Yes, you're right!' I raised my voice and threw my bag to the side . 'I should have gone! And I'd have done better; I wouldn't be stuck in a café! I probably would've had my own gallery by now, or have a job I loved! I'd have improved my skills! Pursued my passion! I would have seen the world!'

'Sophie, please understand one thing.' My mother's face became serious for a second. She squeezed a piece of her clothing and frowned. 'Your father's death was a terrible tragedy. And I wouldn't have survived if I had lost you, too. Jeremy trusted Bale, and they were really close; they relied on each other.'

'It's not that,' I gulped as I sat down on the sofa and sighed. 'Why do I think this is just the tip of the iceberg? My gut is telling me that I am being deceived. You and Bale aren't telling me something, which is making me so angry!'

'I'm sorry,' whispered Astrid. 'There are things you don't know, yes. And I can't tell you everything because it concerns your safety and other people's secrets.'

'So I have to take your word for it and blindly accept nonsense like an arranged marriage?' I laughed, amused at the fact. My mother has just admitted to hiding a more terrible secret from me though still expected me to accept what she was proposing.

'The time will come, and you will know everything, Sophie,' Astrid explained, 'and then you will decide for yourself what to do and how to act. Please, give us time. Soon, you'll be free to go anywhere, to become anything you want. I know you won't do anything stupid, and you'll make the right step based on logic and common sense. Isn't that why you agreed to this farce?'

'I won't deny the obvious,' I sniffled looking down, 'I am not stupid. My pride will not prevent me from taking advantage. Running away from a good opportunity to live a luxurious life and denying the chance to take advantage of a rich man, I will not. I am an adult with needs. Only a fool would refuse and allow pride to take control. As you mentioned before, it's a deal. In this situation, both of us win. Bale will get what he needs. And I can make my own progress by relying on his financial support. It might seem selfish and petty, but it's an opportunity.'

Astrid smiled. 'He's not as terrible as you think.'

'He has a shitty personality, I can tell. He's too arrogant, condescending, big-headed. And that's my opinion about him after speaking with him barely!' I shrugged.

'And he's handsome.' My mother winked, causing a smile on my face. Throwing a pair of socks at her, I waved at Astrid and went into the kitchen, hiding from her loud laughter echoing all over the house.

☆

Alastor's devotion really struck me. The man, as promised, was waiting for me at six o'clock in the morning with a car near the house. Getting sad for a second because I couldn't enjoy my morning cycle anymore, I, however, encouraged myself to think that riding a car with my own personal driver was also a pleasant activity. I was also surprised by the fact that the vehicle was different from the one I saw yesterday. This model was more compact; it was a silver Mercedes with a detachable roof.

THE DEVIL'S SIGNATURE: THE ABIDING PACT

Catching my surprised look, Alastor fixed his grey vest, which he wore over a black shirt and opened the passenger door.

'Your mother told me that you like morning rides on your bike. I decided to change the car so that you could still enjoy the trip to work with more fresh air.'

I sat in the passenger seat and smiled when he pressed the button, and the roof of the vehicle lifted up.

'Very thoughtful, Al—' I raised my eyebrow '— I'm surprised Bale didn't send you with a more exquisite and expensive car. I'm sure he can afford it.'

'Mr Deemer doesn't like to brag about his wealth.' Alastor closed the door behind him and started the engine. 'He's a rather modest and quiet man who considers excess inappropriate.'

'Surprising,' I mumbled quietly as I looked away.

Bale Deemer was a mystery to me, as I couldn't gather enough information about him to get a clear portrait. His social media presence was minimal, he never gave interviews or any comments. That was a big red flag for me. However, despite his smug personality, I still found his gaze warm and wise. I respected his modesty, for I also did not like spending money without good reason. His house did not seem to be the home of the richest man in Britain, radiating only cosiness and spaciousness. And, well... some wealth.

On the one hand, I wanted to know more about this mysterious man. However, I realised that the more secrets I revealed, the more I could be pushed away by his personality or the darkness that surely lurked inside his soul. Because everyone has that dark corner inside them. I knew I certainly did...

However, as much as I was attracted to my independence and my own lofty plans, I thought it would be foolish to give up the opportunity to indulge myself in elegant restaurants, expensive cars and limitless shopping. Don't we all dream about it?

This whole situation, of course, seemed very suspicious. But I thought that it couldn't be the worst. I didn't notice any fangs or claws, neither did Bale glow or burn in the sun, so he certainly was not a vampire. All that was left was to hope he didn't have a pair of whips or steel handcuffs for all sorts of fun games… I preferred such kinks only in my collection of smutty books. *God, Sophie, you gotta stop your imagination spoil the reality!*

THE DEVIL'S SIGNATURE: THE ABIDING PACT

CHAPTER THREE

The car parked in the backyard of the café, and Al politely opened the door to let me out while I went through the bag looking for the keys. Mom had refused to come out to work today, justifying her absence with her urgent need to pack up the last things before we moved.

After opening the windows in the café and letting in the fresh breeze of the morning air, I turned on the coffee machine, offering a cup to my bodyguard with a smile. If he was meant to be my babysitter all day long, he certainly deserved a few treats and strong freshly brewed coffee.

I really liked Alastor. He came across as polite, gallant, and courteous. He didn't say anything superfluous, and, in general, he seemed to be trustworthy. I was glad he could at least brighten up my depressing days of an unwanted marriage. Or maybe... unexpected, rather than unwanted? After all, I have agreed to it. I started questioning myself, thinking whether I came across too superficial. Although, I couldn't really explain my desperation. I could always change my mind and take the money I was owed in the first place. But something inside me... something dark, adventurous and scary was pulling me towards Bale. It wasn't love from the first sight, or anything trivial that makes people agree to risky actions. It was his magnetism, as if my soul was sucked in my his gaze. And I wasn't sure where that temptation and desire to get closer came from – Bale, or myself?

Al told me about his devotion to Bale and how my future husband pulled him out of trouble more than once in the past. I understood that Alastor felt indebted to Bale, so he'd dedicated his life to serving the wealthy owner of the corporation.

Alastor was very silent and spoke out rarely, but I was struck by his honesty and straightforward attitude. To avoid embarrassing him with my inquiries, I decided not to ask about his personal life and background because I did not want to seem rude and too curious. I thought that if he wanted to, he would tell me himself.

The bell in the café rang, and I was just about to say, 'we're still closed,' but when I saw Mike, I involuntarily smiled. The man reciprocated and suddenly changed his facial expression , noticing Al in the corner of the café. My bodyguard nodded politely and continued to read the newspaper.

'Good morning,' Michael looked at me incomprehensibly , glaring towards Al. I poured a cup of coffee and gave it to a worried friend.

'I'll explain later.' I smiled again. Mike looked at

my guest suspiciously and shook his head as he handed me the newspaper. 'What is it?'

'Look at this,' Michael replied, turning the front page and pointing to the article. 'Couple days ago a fire broke out in an apartment building nearby and several pieces of debris fell on a fireman trying to save the residents. The poor guy died on the spot. We had his wife in the church earlier for funeral arrangements.'

I looked at the article with interest and froze for a moment looking at the photo of the victim. My heart stopped for a second, throwing me into a cold sweat. I'd always had an excellent memory of faces. Now, I was looking at a photo of a man whom I painted on the canvas in my studio just a couple of days ago before I crossed it out with a red line.

It scared me. It had happened before, when my head was filled with ideas and my hand moved at will, portraying people I didn't know. This was the third person I had drawn and crossed out that had left this world. Last week I painted a portrait of a young woman who looked just like someone who'd ended up getting into a car accident. Was it a coincidence?

'Hey, you intrigant swine!' A high-pitched voice on the doorstep of the café made me and Mike shudder and Alastor jump out of the chair. Forgetting about the newspaper that fell out of my hands for a second, I stared at the disgruntled guest, who put her hands on her sides and stomped her tiny feet in black trainers, which were decorated with a triple moon pattern, on the wooden floor.

'Lizzie!' I exclaimed, with a broad smile, looking at a young woman with long dark hair and hazel eyes. The Japanese girl struck her little nose up and pressed her lips together, allowing her face to take on a childish look and giving away her discontent. Several silver charms on her handbag made a jingling sound, as did her dreamcatcher earrings. Her T-shirt slid off her shoulder, and I smiled at the image of a cauldron on it.

'Do you think it's acceptable for you to write me a message like that and tell me you're gonna explain later?!' She slammed the door to the café, locked it, then grabbed my hand. She poked her phone screen to my nose, showing my text message from yesterday. Her long black nails followed my message. 'You're getting married?!'

'Married?!' Mike exclaimed with concern. I sighed and sat my friends down at the table, pouring myself and Lizzie a cup of tea and preparing myself for a long explanation. Obviously, with each of my sentences, the faces of those present were changing, as in a comedy sketch, expressing either surprise, misunderstanding or delight.

When my report on yesterday's meeting and the deal with the owner of the corporation ended, there was silence. Mike stared at the cup of coffee in shock. Lizzie gleamed with delight. I smiled at that reaction. What would they say when I named this mysterious groom?

'I can't believe you said yes!!' she exclaimed joyfully, almost squealing while taking off her black fedora hat.

'Why not?' I shrugged my shoulders, explaining my point of view and further plans for my success in this challenging life. 'At least I can get something out of it.'

'I wouldn't dare trust a stranger!' My friend took a sip of her tea while shaking her head.

'My mother convinced me that my father trusted him,' I replied sadly, sighing. 'Perhaps I can learn more about my father. It's not like I have a queue of suitors, to be honest.'

'And what's he like, this mysterious rich man?' Lizzie took a cunning look at me while I glanced at Mike.

'Well, quite attractive, I'd say. However, he is odd...' I frowned, and Mike and Lizzie looked silently at each other. 'I don't know how to explain it. There's something strange about him. It's like there's something dark inside him. I'm glad I can turn back anytime I feel like it.'

'Oh, that's never a good sign,' frowned Mike, and I nodded.

'Maybe he has some kind of weird fetish.' Lizzie winked, and I rolled my eyes and waved my hand at her. Laughing, my friend looked at Alastor and smirked. 'You know, the truth is, I know what you mean. Even this one is stressing me out with his aura. He's your new bodyguard, isn't he? There's something about him that's dark...'

'I'll take your word for it. Does your witch radar feels triggered? Don't you see anything suspicious in my future?' My eyes glistened with curiosity. Lizzie only whipped her nose.

'I'm a witch, not a fortune teller!' a friend smiled. Those words did not surprise me at all, for Lizzie was known for her quirky personality.

Lizzie Maio was born in Tokyo, but almost immediately after her birth, the family moved to London, as her father had a good job offer. Mr Maio was from a wealthy Chinese family but moved to Japan after falling in love with Lizzie's mother. Now he owned a real estate network in London. The Maio family has long been famous for its unique abilities in Japan, thanks to the legends of witches and shamans in their clan; therefore, Lizzie's father, Lee Wei, had to accept his wife's family name to show his respect for such an ancient clan. Both Lizzie's grandmother Miyoko and mother Yui were brilliant, eccentric and mysterious women. Yui was a professional medium. Lizzie also inherited the gift and often shared stories about studying various spells, hexes, and unexplained phenomena with me.

Lizzie sometimes whispered magical words to herself and instantly forced karma to pursue my abusers. Thus, the boys pulling my hair in high school sometimes fell flat on the floor, lost their backpacks, had food exploding in their lunch boxes, or heard frightening voices behind their backs. I wouldn't have believed such bizarre tales if I hadn't experienced such sorcery myself when Lizzie tried to prove her abilities to me.

One of cafe's regular clients had passed away, and this poor old lady had whispered her hilarious dirty jokes in my ear while Lizzie had drawn a magical symbol on the pavement. I'd almost passed out.

After learning of her unusual abilities, I considered to stop communicating with this oddball . Still, Lizzie was my closest friend since school years. My only best friend. I was also afraid that if I ever thought of staying away from her, she would send all the evil upon me and, God forbid, hex me. I had no choice. I had to be friends with her... joking. Honestly, I loved this girl. Lizzie was absolutely bonkers and was always there to support and cheer me up, especially during those horrible times after my father's death. She was my soul sister, my sunshine on a cloudy day.

Lizzie always smiled and rarely gave in to her own darkness. Still, I knew she struggled greatly during her childhood due to bullying and social anxiety. We rarely talked about her attempted suicide years ago... But I still remember that emptiness in her eyes when she told me about it shortly after we met.

I was always practical and lived by the principle of 'believe when I see'. And though I was not a religious person and quite sceptical, Lizzie's witchcraft abilities convinced me. She read people like books and was never wrong about them. However, at times, her ability to talk to ghosts, which she seemed to have seen, frightened me. Her frequent ghost channelling became a habit, and I was already used to it after so many years.

'You don't look OK. Is everything all right?' my friend asked worryingly. I just nodded, looking away. 'Did you have an anxiety attack again?'

'That and... I keep dreaming of the accident again, but it's so vague and unclear,' I answered, sighing and hiding my face behind my palms. 'But the dream feels so real lately, like I can't get out of it. It feels as if I am out of my mind, away from this reality. Everything is blurred, and my stomach is clenching. I feel paralysed.'

'Sophie, dear, something is triggering it for you. You feel this way so often now! Have you spoke about it with your therapist?' Lizzie took my hand, and I smiled weakly.

'I stipped going months ago...'

'Why?!'

'I felt that therapy was just a waste of time. Talking about it didn't help, only confused me more. I feel like I'm in constant, unexplainable pain,' I gasped and tightened my hand, feeling my friend's warmth. Mike was silently sitting beside me, looking at me with worry. 'I feel like giving up, even though I have nothing to give up. I feel like I am caving into these feelings, wanting to fall on my knees. I want to scream. I want to cry. I want to just... stop. I can't stay focused. I feel like I don't belong anywhere in this world. Like my existence...'

'Has no meaning?' Lizzie finished my words, and I nodded, holding the tears.

'I try my best to stay positive, to shove it deep into my sould, to just not think about it! And some days it works, and I am back to my happy self. But sometimes... I feel stuck in this darkness inside me. I feel like that dream and memory are trying to tell me something, but I can't understand it. And this strange creative bloxk of mine is getting worse! I sit before canvas for hours with no ideas, and then I suddenlt feel this urge to draw unknown features! Look, another one,' I said quietly, reaching out to a friend and pointing to the picture of the dead fireman. Lizzie looked at me anxiously and sighed.

'Don't you think it's weird that you draw strangers and cross out their portraits before they leave this world?' she asked me.

I shrugged. 'Who knows, maybe I'm a witch too?' My laughter filled the café, and Lizzie smiled back, looking at me kindly. Michael sat silently, occasionally looking at my bodyguard and ignoring our girlish schemes.

'Who knows, maybe you are!' Lizzie smiled and looked at me once again. I knew she wanted to make sure I was okay, but my friend was also aware of my preferences to keep things to myself and talk about troubles only when I felt comfortable. She never dragged information from me.

'Thank you,' – I whispered to her silent support.

'So, tell me, what does he look like? What's his name and all? What else did you find out?' Lizzie asked with anticipation and excitement in her voice.

'The thing is, there's not much information about him on the internet,' I sighed. 'He's a rather secretive person.'

While I was carried away by the story of my

impression of Bale, I did not even notice that café door open and someone enter. Sitting with my back to the entrance, I continued my monologue while Lizzie froze and stared at the guest.

'And he had—'

'Sophie, shut your mouth for a moment,' whispered Lizzie, waving at me and staring at the man who had entered the café with her devouring look. I was surprised to see my friend in awe, then pale Mike, and then the intruder. I cringed, frowned, and sighed a doomed sigh of trouble.

'Oh, great... What are you doing here?' My voice sounded monotonous and unhappy.

'How rude,' the man snorted as he looked around the room with interest and glanced at Mike. It may have seemed to me, but the blond man looked like he was ready to strangle Bale with his bare hands . I was truly surprised by such a strange reaction from my friend. Mr Deemer chuckled as he looked at Mike with an arrogant look and glanced at me again . For a second, I thought his face looked worried when his eyes scanned my teary eyes and anxiously shaking leg. 'I wanted to try your signature coffee, sweetheart. Gotta make sure I won't get poisoned after our wedding.'

'What?' Lizzie reached out with her hands to me, glared at Bale, and again at me. 'Are you for real?! You're fucking with me! Him?'

'Lizzie, this is Belial Deemer, my fiancé,' I said with displeasure, as if I had swallowed something sour.

'Cauldron swallow me! You're not kidding!' the witch cheerfully exclaimed, reaching her hand to Bale. 'Nice to meet you. I'm Lizzie! Sophie's best friend and maid of honour at your wedding!'

'Huh?' I asked, but my friend seemed to have

completely ignored me. Bale extended his hand gallantly, his silver bracelet glistening, and Lizzie's graceful fingers touched his palm. A sigh came out of her, and she stepped back, frightened, staring at the new acquaintance and clutching her hand into a fist. She looked into Mr Deemer's calm eyes with fear. 'Lizzie?'

'Forgive me.' She grinned nervously, shaking her head. 'Something came over me…'

'It's like you've seen a ghost, even though you're not afraid of them!' I laughed when I noticed Bale's surprised look. 'Don't ask, she's a witch. I know it sounds unreal…'

'Why?' Bale smiled faintly, and Lizzie gulped, grabbing her round marble necklace. 'It's quite real. Legends are not born out of thin air, and people's special abilities have not yet been fully proven. Many people can feel the aura of others and see their energy waves.'

'Um,' I said, surprised, not expecting that answer. 'And this is… this is Mike, my good friend.'

'Mike.' Bale stretched out as if savouring the name, looking at the blond man with a squint. Mike looked like he hated my fiancé from the first moment they met. *What's wrong with him?* Was he… jealous? I couldn't believe it.

'Sophie, you didn't say your fiancé was Belial Deemer,' Michael said as he sat down and continued to stare into Bale's eyes while he moved a chair up to our table and sat comfortably. Lizzie slowly lowered to her seat while I stood up and headed for the door to open the café.

I stopped, for a second, looking at the lock and thinking. Strange, I was sure Lizzie had locked the door when she came in. How did he get in?

'Yeah,' I said, still thinking about the door, 'I… I

was going to tell you. I'm sorry, do you two know each other?'

'No!' the men spoke in one voice. For some reason, I didn't believe it.

'In the business area, Mr Deemer is quite a famous person,' Mike said seriously, tapping his fingers on the table. 'When I saw your bodyguard, I suspected who you were dealing with, but wasn't sure. I often saw these two at my dad's office.'

'So, your friend is a witch,' Bale started and took a sip of coffee, looking down with his chocolate-brown eyes, 'and what's Mike's major?'

'Michael works in a retirement home and is also an active member of the church,' I replied proudly as I gave Bale a disgruntled look.

'Ah,' my guest said sceptically, 'God and all that…'

'You're not a man of faith, Bale?' Michael frowned.

Mr Deemer smiled and put a cup of coffee on the table, circling the saucer's edge with his finger thoughtfully. I noticed a beautiful gold ring with a red ruby on it.

'Why, I'm quite a believer,' Bale said, causing me to raise my eyebrows in wonder. I wasn't exactly expecting to hear that. 'Just disagree with some fiction.'

'You mean the facts?' Michael corrected him, and I was ready to throw something big and heavy at him. What had gotten into him? Why was this scoundrel asking for a fight?! Mike had never behaved like that before, and I was baffled.

'The fact must be proven,' replied the owner of Infernum Enterprise, giving Mike an unpleasant look that made me flinch. I swear these brown eyes had a fire burning in them. 'I find religion very misogynistic and hypocritical, but let's not talk about sad stuff. Sophie, are you free tonight?'

'Are you asking me out on a date?' I laughed as I continued to clean the cups.

'Exactly.' Bale stood up, watching my surprised face and putting an empty coffee cup on the bar. I was shocked as the brew was scorching hot; however, he finished it in a minute. 'The wedding plans are in full swing. However, to not arouse suspicion, we need to make an appearance a couple of times as a happy pair of lovebirds.'

'I see you've thought this through.' There was a sour look on my face. I felt like cheating myself by pretending to be in love with someone I barely knew.

'I'll pick you up at seven. Al, I'll drive her myself, so pick up Astrid after Sophie's done.' Bale smiled. Alastor only nodded, and my 'destined' man left the café immediately, leaving the money on the counter.

'A self-righteous peacock!' I whispered as I flipped the towel aside and rolled my eyes. I hated this already.

'Sophie, I have to run to work.' Lizzie smiled softly, hugging me and holding her hand with many silver rings over my hair.

'Are you all right?' I looked at my friend, confused, noticing her worry. She squeezed her fingers into a fist, and her knuckles got white.

'Yes, of course!' she nodded. She was lying. 'Sorry, it's just a habit of mine, you know that! I understand you very well, and I can see why you think he's creepy. There's a part of him that's dark and unreadable. His energy is powerful.'

'You think so?' My eyebrows curved into an arch.

'You take care, most importantly,' whispered Lizzie, 'and the rest does not matter. Just... be careful.'

After saying goodbye to my friend, I felt a niggle of worry. What had she felt when she'd shaken Bale Deemer's hand? Perhaps I made the wrong choice and signed up for something very dangerous? I began to be overwhelmed by doubts and thoughts that maybe it was better to cancel everything and continue with my life as usual.

I knew my mother was hiding something, and despite her promise to tell me when the time was right, my curiosity prevailed. I wanted to know those secrets. Bale had something to do with all this; I could feel it. He may even have been involved in my father's murder. It was only by being around this suspicious man that I hope to find out the truth.

'Sophie,' Mike called me gently, allowing my thoughts to disappear, and a smile touched my lips.

'You surprised me today,' I said, raising my eyebrow and looking at my friend with a grin. 'Are you sure you don't know each other?'

'No,' Mike laughed as he waved his hand, 'I've just heard a lot about him. My father's department deals with powerful corporations and everything related to them. Bale Deemer is the market leader in high technology and application development. And given that your dad knew him, James interrogated him once, too.'

'I didn't know about it.' My heart was shrinking for a second. What else wasn't she aware of?

'But still—' Mike looked at me anxiously '—I can't believe you're marrying him. I understand that you've decided to take advantage of the situation and achieve more in your life. Naturally, the rich husband greatly supports you, but Bale...'

'I just grabbed the opportunity,' I replied. 'Besides, I don't see a line of candidates to be my husband.'

'Hm.' Mike smiled sadly, looking away and making my heart miss a beat.

I was caught up in sudden frustration and irritation. I had never been naive and almost always noticed the smallest detail. Naturally, I knew Mike was interested in me, and I was happy about it. But... that attraction didn't get us anywhere. No matter how many times I tried to get closer, Michael seemed to get further and further away. My hopes for something special between us had shattered, and my love only remained as something forgotten, unanswered. I didn't expect my feelings to be returned, and I stopped dreaming of a happy ending.

Saying a dry 'bye', I changed the café's sign to 'open' and unlocked the door, waiting for a new flow of customers. The day promised to be full and tumultuous, with Sunday just beginning, and I had to think about what I would wear on my date with Bale Deemer.

☆

As expected, all tables at the café were ful l a few hours after my friends left, and Martin and I were tired of never-ending mugs and plates. Alastor obediently continued to sit in the corner, periodically watching me, talking on the phone, recording something in his journal or looking at our customers.

While manoeuvring between the tables, I filled a tray with dirty dishes. I waved to the lovely woman who thanked me for the coffee as she headed for the exit. As I wiped the table, I noticed the golden wallet. I immediately grabbed it, looking in the wake of its departed owner. Leaving the tray on the table, I ran out of the café, rushing towards the brunette.

After receiving a ton of gratitude in return, I

beamed and headed back, distractedly bumping the shoulder of a passer-by. My legs suddenly went numb, my body was covered in an icy sweat, and my head filled with confused thoughts and visions. It happened so fast and chaotic that I didn't immediately understand what I was seeing. My mind was filled with the faces of strangers, red stairs, the tired look of a man I bumped into while he grabbed his chest and fell to his knees, and then only a bright flash and darkness.

'Sophie!' Al's loud voice brought me to my senses, and I felt his strong hands on my shoulders, holding me. My numb legs had regained their strength, and I stared at my bodyguard with a confused look.

'I'm all right,' I answered quietly, nodding. It was the first time this had happened to me. *What was that? A vision? A dream? Memories?* I didn't even have anyone to ask – they'd prescribe me a visit to a shrink! Maybe I had a tumour in my head, and I'd die young and beautiful...

'Please don't leave without me,' Al sighed, letting me go and receiving a smile.

'I'm sorry, it's all right—' I swung my hand away '—just dizzy. It's hot today.'

Moving towards the café, I inadvertently looked back, searching for that man, but couldn't see him. With a sigh, I tried to forget what had happened and focus on the rest of the day's work.

'Have a nice day!' I said, exhausted, closing the café door and undoing my apron. Finally, this long day was almost over. As I plunged into a chair and said goodbye to Martin, who was in a hurry to go back upstairs in order to chuck on his gaming PC, I turned my gaze to Alastor, who continued to sit in a fixed position. 'And how do you not get tired of sitting like a statue?'

'Habit, experience.' Al smiled weakly. 'Are you ready?'

'Hm?' I said, surprised, rubbing my eyes and wishing for my cosy bed. When I heard the sound of a growling motor outside the door, my soul went to my feet. *Oh, right... the date.* My mood was visibly drooping, and my body was lost to fatigue. Still, my legs obediently led me to the door, and I unlocked it. Looking at the gorgeous red Maserati GranCaprio with S8 TAN number plate, I snorted and shook my head. Well, I guess Mr Deemer did enjoy occasional bragging of his wealth.

'Are you ready?' Taking off his sunglasses, Bale pointed to the passenger seat.

'I need to change,' I replied, tired, watching Alastor leave the café and bow respectfully to his superior. After receiving the order to pick up my mother, Al politely said goodbye and wished me a pleasant time.

'Get in. I'll give you a ride home,' said Bale.

'Would you not take me to an expensive store to pick out an elegant dress? That's what they do in the movies...' I raised my eyebrow, locking the café door.

'You're not in the movie, dearie,' my driver said with a sour expression as I got into the car, 'and I don't have time to take you shopping. That's what you've got Alastor for. And regarding your outfit... I don't care if you're wearing a paper bag.'

'Jerk,' I whispered, rolling my eyes and leaning back in the seat. My pride was hurt.

'Buckle up,' the man cut off briefly. 'I don't need you flying off the window again.'

With a surprised look, I buckled my seat belt and

frowned. What did he mean by that? Was that a hint of my previous accident? How much did he know about me?

The car's engine made a loud noise, and Bale Deemer smirked noticeably.

☆

Turning my closet inside out, I sighed and shook my shoulders. As expected, I had nothing to wear. According to my chaperone, the date was actually a birthday party for one of Bale's sponsors. Given the fact that my fiancé's entire circle of friends was made up of sophisticated rich individuals, the presence of journalists was ensured. As I looked at my outfits, I gave a doomed sigh.

So, in what dress was I not ashamed to appear in tomorrow's paper?

'For Heaven's sake, pick something already!' the dark-haired man growled, grabbing one of the hangers and handing me the blue cocktail dress I'd last worn three years ago on a stormy party night. I gave an unpleasant look at the intruder, snorted and threw the hanger aside, kicking the cheeky bastard out of the room and changing my clothes.

'I'm ready,' my tired voice reached the art studio, where Bale observed my portraits with interest.

I crossed my arms on my chest and leaned against the jamb of the door, staring silently at the guest. It was amazing how the atmosphere of calm and mystery had followed him like a trail, stirring up the fire of curiosity in me.

That I couldn't find a lot of information about him concerned me a little. Why was such an influential rich man so poorly represented in social media?

'You paint well,' he said, glancing at me, and

noticing my satisfied grin. You bet. I knew it myself!

'And thanks to you, I'm going to open an art gallery and become a famous painter,' I replied confidently as I walked into the room.

'You're going to be a celebrity from now on regardless,' Bale said thoughtfully, stopping by the large canvas with my unfinished portrait, 'and with the money you get from me, you can open up a whole museum.'

'It sounds tempting,' I answered, following his gaze.

'Why are they crossed out?' Bale asked curiously, looking at the crowded portraits of strangers crossed out with red paint and covered in dust in the corner of the studio.

'I don't know.' I shrugged, biting my lip and frowning. 'Just suddenly felt like it.'

'You were crying today. Did something upset you?' he suddenly asked, and I twitched from such an unexpected question.

'Ehm…' I looked away and frowned, 'just have a lot on my mind.'

'Did my proposal make you so sad?' He looked at me directly, and I felt like I was burning under his stare.

'No, it's not that.' I shook my head and looked at one of the portraits. 'I… I have suffered from occasional anxiety attacks since my childhood. So… you just caught me in a bad moment.'

'What are you anxious about?' he asked, interested, continuing to walk across the room. I gulped and rolled my eyes. 'Come on, you can tell me. I deserve to know at least something about my wife-to-be. Just because this is an arranged marriage, it doesn't mean I can't support you somehow.'

'I don't want to burden you,' I whispered.

'Try me,' he replied, and I looked at his dark-brown eyes.

'Life... in general. It makes me anxious. I feel like I'm stuck. Like everything is so heavy.'

'Hm. Life is hard.' He nodded and sighed. 'It is unfair. It never gets easier, never gets fairer. Just don't let yourself feel like you are a victim. I know it's easier said than done, but it is possible. Embrace your feelings and your fears. Life is all about moments that will pass one day, so take it in fully. Throw yourself into this rollercoaster where every minute, every second of your life, is vital. Don't run away from these emotions and from this anxiety. And Sophie...'

'Yes?' I was mesmerised by his voice and his wisdom.

'Never feel embarrassed by how you feel. Be proud of it. Learn from it, and make it "yours". It's OK to be anxious about life and what is around you, because that makes you human. Do you want to know what your purpose is? It's OK; keep looking for answers. And keep asking yourself that. Trust me, the answer might change with time, and that's fine.' The man stopped in front of me, and I stood still, looking up at him, blushing, and feeling as if my soul was getting lifted. 'It's OK not to know who you are, sweetheart. Just make sure you know who you are not. Only by defining that will you be able to find your true self.'

I was shocked. I felt as if he had read the deepest secrets of my soul. It seemed as if Bale Deemer knew more about what I was anxious about than I did. His words seemed so right, so... needed. My heart gave a loud beat, and I looked down, feeling like I'd just received a much-needed gasp of air while drowning deep in the ocean. How? How did he know? How did he do that? That heavy, unbearable rock slightly moved from my chest.

'What's that?' With a thoughtful look, Bale looked at the image in the opposite corner.

'An unfinished portrait.' I sighed as I approached my interlocutor, and we both stared at the amber eyes on a black background. 'Eyes from my memories.'

There was silence, and after much deliberation, Bale waved his hand and called for me to follow him. Taking a deep sigh, I walked after my future husband, looking back at the amber eyes behind me for a moment. A smile touched my lips, and a sense of something exciting approaching suddenly enveloped me. Perhaps it wasn't so bad, and something interesting would come out of this farce. A date is a date!

THE DEVIL'S SIGNATURE: THE ABIDING PACT

CHAPTER FOUR

The event was in full swing. The chic penthouse of the central London hotel was crowded with people in formal attire, elegant gowns with shiny jewellery and lots of bedazzling accessories.

As soon as the elevator doors opened, inviting Bale and me into the helm of the buzzing event, I was immediately subjected to camera flashes and queries from several journalists who had swirled at my companion and me like bees on honey . Politely refusing to comment, Mr Deemer led me further in, and introduced me to a couple of his acquaintances, who looked at me with interest.

Fighting the awkwardness, I straightened my hair by pulling a strand behind my ear and reached my hand out as a sign of greeting, starting a conversation and smiling affectionately. Surprisingly, I blended with the crowd quickly enough. I let go of the nervousness and began to enjoy the atmosphere and chat with influential strangers. I might have imagined it, but I noticed a slight proud look in Bale's eyes. My companion's reaction only flattered me, so I decided to relax a little.

'Bale, you player, you didn't tell me you'd given your heart to another lady,' a melodic, soft voice suddenly sounded behind my back while I was enjoying a juicy shrimp that had been politely offered by the waiter. The food here was excellent, and I never denied myself anything delicious… especially when it was served for free.

As I looked at the stranger with interest, I finished my delicacy with a sip of white wine, and then glanced at Bale. He interrupted his conversation with one of the sponsors and smiled at the black-haired lady. I noticed his jaw clench. The stranger was walking around in a bright-red gown with an open neckline. Her black curls went down on her tattooed shoulder with a phoenix on it, opening the view to a long thin neck. Green, like emeralds, eyes were devouring Bale with a hungry gaze.

'I didn't know I had to inform you of my personal life events, Mara.' Mr Deemer looked at me with a playful smile as he approached me and lowered his warm hand at my waist, pulling me towards him with a light movement. My body shuddered from the unfamiliar touch, and my skin almost burned from his body temperature as if I were swallowed by the fire. God, was the poor man sick and struggling with a high fever? 'Meet Sophie, my fiancée.'

'Fiancée?!' Mara laughed in shock, raising her voice and attracting the attention of others. I noticed a couple of curious journalists and bloggers slowly taking steps forward, eager to catch an interesting comment.

I looked at Bale incomprehensibly, suddenly feeling shy and uncomfortable.

'She's charming, isn't she?' Mr Deemer smiled gently, turning his head to me and the his lips touched my temple . His hand squeezed my waist, causing me to blush. I gulped and heard 'play along' in my ear. *This cunning buttmunch!* He was putting on a show. I, too, did not want to fall behind, and accepted the challenge, stretching out my wrist to Mara and giving a friendly smile.

'Nice to meet you,' I said, touching Mara's elegant fingers and catching her judgmental look. Her face was so beautiful.

'Sure,' Mara lied, and her nose twitched. 'Wish I'd heard about you before. I was confident that Bale was smitten by me .'

'Oh.' I raised my eyebrow, imitating surprise. 'Really?'

'At least that's what he told me a couple of days ago when he woke up in my bed . Oh, I think I said too much!' Clutching a palm to her scarlet lips, the woman smiled at me triumphantly. The bitch was playing me, but she didn't know she was messing with the wrong woman. 'He never mentioned you!'

'What a humble man he is!' I laughed, surprising Mara and even Bale with my reaction. 'We have quite an open relationship, you see. It was our agreement before marriage. He told me all about his insignificant lovers when he helped me move my belongings to his mansion and begged me to marry him the other day. The poor man swore he'd prefer burning in Hell than be away from me ever again!'

Bale choked on his drink, staring at me with his dark-brown eyes, confused. Mara opened her mouth but didn't dare to respond with impertinence, instead turning around with resentment and moving away. Journalists were writing down something in their notebooks, and the rest of those present only whistled and laughed, congratulating Bale and me and praising my courage, as it turned out that no one had ever challenged fearless Mara before.

The evening was a lot more fun than I had expected. I even began to get used to the constant attention on me, and noticed Bale's keen eye. He seemed to be in mixed emotions. Oh yes, I knew how to play the game.

☆

Time was approaching midnight, and I was tired, looking around, watching some of the departing guests, and waiting for my companion to be ready to leave the party.

I chose to freshen up, and headed for the stairs at the end of the hallway that led to the terrace. Carrying my clutch bag in one hand, put my other on the bannister, and glanced back at the waiter heading in the same direction as me. I paid little attention to him, but his sharp gesture was hard to ignore as the man grabbed his chest and stiffened, bending over and making a barely audible groan.

'Are you all right?' I asked him immediately, putting my hand on his shoulder and feeling shivers down my spine. I recognised that face. In front of me was the same stranger I ran into on the street earlier today. While trying to speak, the waiter fell to his knees and squeezed his hand, attracting the other guests' attention.

Someone shouted, 'He's having a heart attack!', calling for an ambulance. I continued to sit by the poor man, looking into his frightened eyes and getting angry at myself for not being able to help. The panic slowly grew inside, and I stroked the man on the shoulder with my trembling hands as he lay down on the stairs, in agony.

A crowd of people surrounded us, discussing and trying to help, but I was too shocked to look at the immobile body of a waiter, focusing instead on his face . It wasn't the fact that he had stopped moving that frightened me, but that his body had suddenly shone a golden light. A soft, transparent shine left his body, and then it stood before me.

My throat was dry, and my heart's rhythm slowed. I looked straight into the man's eyes. His ghost looked back, confused, muttering something about injustice, pain, and the desire to go back. I felt a chill. Noticing my gaze, the spirit suddenly pulled his hand towards me. I got pale and scared. A panic attack suddenly enveloped me, and I felt as if I was suffocating. My heart was ready to jump out of my chest, and my shaking palms got sweaty and cold. Everything around me got blurry, and the voices echoed in my head. I closed my eyes and hugged myself, wanting to disappear.

'Sophie!' Bale's loud voice made me open my eyes and look at his worried face. I couldn't say a word, I looked around again, but the ghost was no longer there. My anxiety was faded as soon as Bale's fingers touched my shoulder.

'Wh–What…' I whispered while Bale helped me get back on my feet, holding me.

'The ambulance is here,' he replied, taking me out of the penthouse. 'We don't belong here anymore. Come on, let's go.'

☆

I felt drained as I breathed in the cold, fresh night air. My head was dizzy, and my eyes were half-closed, allowing hot tears to flow down my pale cheeks . I clenched my fists and tried to forget the nightmare, but an image of the ghost carved into my mind was only more upsetting. What was happening to me? Why had I seen all this? Was I going crazy, or was it a hallucination? Should I go to see a psychiatrist or a doctor?

I was so mired in chaotic thoughts that I didn't even notice Bale frowning and looking in my direction. As he pursed his lips , he took a deep breath.

'Are you all right?' he asked quietly, turning a

corner while gently touching the steering wheel. I just nodded, refusing to tell him what I'd seen. I didn't want him to think I was crazy. I had to figure it out on my own before I could tell others.

The car passed through the gates of the residence, and I shivered from the night chill. I got out of the Maserati and looked up at the beautiful house, seeing it for the second time.

'I thought you were taking me home,' I said quietly as I stepped forward.

'I didn't think you'd would want to be in an empty house alone right now,' Bale said quietly. 'Besides, this is your home now.'

Silently nodding, I didn't even argue with the residence owner, and stepped inside. My mother met me with arms stretched out but anxiously, seeing my tired and slightly sad face. I interrupted her even before she said anything, suggesting that I will talk about the evening tomorrow, maybe, if I feel like it. With a gentle hug, the woman sent me to my room upstairs and said good night . I only glanced briefly at Bale, climbing the stairs and once again experiencing a warm wave running through my veins. Why did this man have such a strange effect on me?

I was glad to touch the cool pillow with my cheek, looking out the open balcony, where the faint night breeze was blowing, swaying transparent curtains. My new room was spacious, embraced by delicate tones and very cosy. In general, I didn't mind staying here for a while. Something about it was familiar.

My eyes closed slowly, and I got lost in a deep sleep, forgetting today's nightmare.

THE DEVIL'S SIGNATURE: THE ABIDING PACT

☆

Turning away from the morning sun rays that tickled my nose and streaked my pillow, I was startled by the gentle knocking on the door. I sighed, then let the guest in and sat back down on the bed.

A skinny grey-haired woman in an apron, a blue dress, and narrow glasses entered the room with small steps, holding a tray in her hand and smiling at me kindly. Even though she was elderly, the woman was still stunning and elegant.

'Miss Mortis' the tender voice of a stranger drifted through my ears in a pleasant wave, 'I brought you breakfast. Mr Deemer said you were quite stressed last night, and I thought you were hungry.'

'Um, thank you.' I stared at an elderly woman, taking a tray with a colourful breakfast plate and a cup of hot tea. Just what the doctor ordered, I thought. 'I'm sorry, you are…'

'Oh, silly me!' The woman banged herself on the forehead, laughing. 'It's Rose! I look after the house, and Mr Deemer too. You can call me Rosie, miss!'

'I see.' I smiled, biting into the warm toast and looking around my room again, as I had no strength to explore the place at night. 'How long have you been working here, Rosie?'

'Oh, as long as I can remember!' The housekeeper waved her hand, carefully folding my dress from yesterday and hanging it on a chair by the dressing table. 'Mr Deemer took me in as a girl!'

'Eh?' I stared at a woman in a puzzled way. She flinched and covered her mouth with her hand, knowing she'd said the wrong thing. I just blinked a couple of times, trying to figure out what the woman had meant. Exactly how old was this man, because he looked damn great?!

'Oh, I completely forgot about the laundry!' Rosie changed the subject, stepping out of the room and leaving me alone. I shrugged and decided that maybe she was talking about Bale's father. I took a sip of tea and sighed. Yesterday's fatigue disappeared in an instant. My body was full of energy , and I was soon on my way to the bathroom.

After refreshing myself in the shower and looking through my suitcase, which had been brought by Alastor, I changed into a light summer jumpsuit. I put on sandals, and left the room, looking around the corridor.

Slowly walking down the spacious hall, I occasionally looked around the corners and into the next room, trying not to get lost and memorising what I saw on my way. I had already found a couple of extra bedrooms, a break room, and even a library on the second floor. That's what attracted me the most.

With that room, my curiosity overtook me, and I stepped inside, looking at the high ceilings, the endless collections of books, and a load of antique scrolls, encyclopaedias and magazines. It took my breath away, and, delighted, I walked my fingers across the dark wooden desk that stood by the wide bay window. Looking at the beautiful land behind the mansion, I glanced again at the desk. I bent over, touching a black feather in the inkwell. It tickled my fingers, and I was mesmerised by the gorgeous velvety black colour. It seemed real to the touch, but I had never seen a bird with that colour. The feather was long and large, slightly shiny . The black was deeper than the night sky .

I took a fleeting glance through several scrolls on the table, with no idea what was written in them, and was amazed at the antiquity of these objects. What language was this? I raised my eyebrows, seeing an old brown leather diary lying before me. A broken bookmark separated the pages in the middle, and I opened the book carefully, looking at the beautiful handwriting. It was a list of names and dates. As I flipped through the pages, I noticed a few names that had been crossed out. I put the diary aside, looking around in awe.

A shelf with similar journals caught my attention. Curious, I approached it, taking out another diary and flipping through the same lists. Weird; what kind of data was that? The dates written in the journal went back to thousands of years ago. Mr Deemer was fascinating to me now.

Thinking that there must be nothing else unusual in this library, I turned to the door, but I immediately realised that I was wrong.

My eyes stopped on the far side of the room, at a fireplace, a couple of soft armchairs and a small marble coffee table. Moving on, I stepped near the fireplace, looking directly at the portrait on a wall in front of me, or rather – a collection of portraits. The whole wall was hung with images of a man who looked so much like Bale. Each of them differed only in their attire from different eras, various hairstyles and facial expressions.

The oil paints were shining in the morning sun and

looking at the portraits at first glance, I was amazed at the resemblance to Bale. Were these his pictures? Or were they his male relatives, as people often looked similar to their predecessors? The only portrait that stood out was the one depicting a beautiful woman with long black curls, bright brown eyes and subtle feminine features. Strangely, she was very much like Bale – sister or mother, maybe? I didn't know much about Bale's family.

It was the expressions on their faces that caught my attention—the oldest of the portraits emitted energy, determination, and a cheerful spirit. But the further I walked to the other end of the wall, the sadder the person seemed. Deep brown eyes expressed fatigue, pain and incredible wisdom. That's the look I noticed in Bale's eyes.

'Odd,' I said, sighing. Perhaps all these portraits were depicting Bale over the centuries? My fiancé did seem to be a vampire…

Shaking my head to get rid of ridiculous thoughts, I left the library. I walked down the hall, continuing my lonely tour of Mr Deemer's residence.

There was a wide double door in front of me, slightly open and inviting. Without even trying to force myself to stop, I slowly pushed the door forwards and looked inside, glancing at the spacious bedroom. Lifting my eyebrows up in amazement, I was once again convinced that the owner of this house had great taste.

'No, I don't need his petty support; he wants to sell me the shares just because he's on the verge of bankruptcy,' I heard a voice say on the other side of the room by the balcony, making me shudder and hide behind the door.

I had little interest in Bale's phone conversation because his work issues didn't concern me. I was only curious to observe him while he didn't suspect he was being watched.

Looking out the door again, I froze in shock, looking at Mr Deemer's broad swarthy back. Bale wasn't wearing anything above his waist, only his black tailored trousers. He stood at the open balcony door and fastened his smartwatch on his wrist with one hand, holding his phone between his shoulder and ear. Though I thought Bale was an extraordinary person, he never gave the impression of a man who could have a tattoo all over his back. That's what surprised me the most. He just didn't seem like a type.

The pattern was very unusual; I'd never seen anything like it before. At the centre of the back, in a large circle, there was a symbol of the measuring scales against the background of several star rays and the sun. The geometric pattern of the scale merged with the image of an hourglass, which resembled an inverted sign of eternity, continuing down his spine and beyond the belt of his black trousers. At the top of the scale was another circle, smaller, with a symbol I did not know. It looked like an inverted triangle with an 'X' inside, the ends of which went over the edges. At the tip of the triangle, there was some kind of a twist. These scales and the symbol were joined by two 'horns' that reached the neck.

I was ready to admit that the tattoo on Mr Deemer's back gave him a rather seductive look, especially with his loose wet wavy hair, which barely touched his shoulders.

Fascinated by the beautiful view in front of me, I did not immediately notice that the phone conversation had ended. My naughty inner self was already mentally undressing this man in the darkest fantasies.

'How long are you going to stand outside the door?' Bale's hoarse voice made me flinch and instantly blush, trying to find the words of justification. A slight smile on the man's lips made me look away and put my head down guiltily as I went inside.

'I'm sorry, I...' I looked at him again. My mind was trying to find the words while I took my eyes off his perfectly ripped abs and muscular chest. Fuck, he was gorgeous! 'Just looking around.'

'Do you like what you see?' He squinted cunningly , coming closer, making me stare at him resentfully for being so suggestive. 'The house. I mean the house, sweetheart.'

'Ah!' My face was painted red again, and I told myself off for assuming the double meaning in all the phrases that followed from him. 'Yes, yes. Very beautiful.'

'I'm glad,' Bale answered, putting on a crisp white shirt and buttoning it up. I admitted that white looked great on his tanned skin.

'Um...' with my hands behind my back, I bit my lip and asked, 'What does your tattoo mean?'

'Do all the tattoos have to mean something?' Bale smiled, coming up to me and making my whole gut tense. Once again, that strange feeling of fear and attraction consumed me. It was like he was squeezing me with his energy.

'No,' I answered immediately, looking him in the eye and expecting another flirtatious act from him, 'but yours seems to have been done for a reason. There's a deep meaning in it that I just don't understand.'

'Well, I'll tell you about it sometime, then,' Bale whispered, leaning forward, and my palm itched in the desire to slap him so that he wouldn't get cocky. The silence hung, and I looked into Mr Deemer's eyes with disbelief, trying to understand what he would do next. Was this man flirting, teasing? He seemed to have decided to do something unpredictable… would he kiss me without warning? And as if following my thoughts, Bale looked down at my lips and squinted. The corners of his mouth rose in a smile, and I was soon covered with cold sweat, thinking of every possible way to punish the bastard. My gaze fell on a gold chain with a pentagram pendant around his neck, which shone in the sun's rays. I slowly moved my gaze to his eyes and made a note of his glistening earing in the shape of a star on his left ear. Ah, I forgot about that! Maybe, I was wrong in my assumptions about his style. I started noticing such little details as pierced ears with silver jewellery, shaved line on his eyebrow and even his taste in shoes. He wasn't typical CEO – more of a rebellious type.

His face slowly approached, and I closed my eyes, holding my breath. Though my pride ordered me to move aside, to not give this impostor an excuse to play with me, another part of my soul – playful and curious – wanted to know what would happen next.

THE DEVIL'S SIGNATURE: THE ABIDING PACT

'Step aside.'

'Huh?' I instantly opened my eyes. My body was covered with goosebumps from a dark whisper in my ear.

'You're blocking the door.' Suddenly he pulled away, giving me a serious look.

My mind exploded. *What a jerk!* Playing, teasing and then pretending nothing happened?! Although... nothing had happened. I didn't understand who I was angry with – him for his stupid pranks or myself for the hopes and desires I held but didn't understand.

'I'm sorry.' All I could do was squeeze out and let Bale out of the room, noticing a slight hint of pine following him. I swear I thought he would kiss me!

'Don't worry,' my fiancé said last. 'I won't touch you until you ask me to.'

'What?!' I was amazed again. No, that must have been a joke! 'Bale, wait!'

'Yes?' He kept walking while I chased him down the hall.

'What, are you reading minds now?' I raised my eyebrow, laughing and joking, trying to defuse the situation.

'Who knows?' The man shrugged his shoulders and headed down the stairs. I shook my head and glared at him with a displeased look. What a child! 'By the way, I'll be out of town for a few days.'

'Where are you going? ' I said, surprised, standing on the stairs.

'I have to go somewhere for business. Alastor will remain with you. Ask him for anything you need,' said Bale, opening the front door. 'Don't you miss me!'

'I would never!' I snorted, crossing my arms on my chest and hearing Bale Deemer laugh. In a way, I was sad. I was beginning to like that cunning man. He was pretty fun, and our banter was promising to become enjoyable. I really wanted to know more about him, and now I wouldn't be seeing him for a while.

Well, as far as I was concerned, Alastor had a credit card with my unlimited bank account, and I was certainly missing a couple of new outfits. As I reached into my pocket for the phone, I smiled.

'Lizzie? Are you busy?' Skipping up the stairs, I said, 'Would you like to go shopping and spend an immense amount of money?'

THE DEVIL'S SIGNATURE: THE ABIDING PACT

CHAPTER FIVE

Manoeuvring between passers-by, Lizzie and I had an absolute blast discussing my new exciting life while stopping at the expensive boutiques on Oxford Street at the same time.

Lizzie mentioned a recent newspaper article about London's wealthy bachelor and his mysterious bride, who was on the front page of the publication. I walked the streets proudly, satisfied with myself. I refused to be modest and spoiled myself with shopping . I was sure that everyone dreamed of being able to buy a lot of outfits and trinkets at least once without checking the price tag, and walking the streets with an infinite number of bags from branded stores. That's precisely what I decided to do, although Alastor was the one to follow us through the streets with bags and boxes, patiently waiting for us to be finished.

My limitless card was on the verge of explosion as I was waving it in front of the cashiers. If I decided to get all the benefits out of this marriage, I would do it properly. If I was ever on the verge of poverty, I could always sell a couple of pairs of Jimmy Choo's and live for another month.

My entertainment with Lizzie did not go unnoticed because, after a couple of hours of excessive shopping, I received a text message on my smartphone from my lovely groom-to-be.

'*I see you've taken my words literally, as my phone is tearing apart from the bank notifications. Are you purchasing every boutique in London?*'

As I laughed and looked at the dress on me in the fitting room, I nodded approvingly and looked at the phone again, responding to Bale's cheeky hint.

'*Do you want to take your words back? I would love to move back to my house and forget I knew you.*'

After a short pause, all I got was, '*Enjoy your day out, sweetheart. My treat.*'

This condescending prick! I would not allow pride to take over and refuse expensive gifts and pampering. I deserved this magnificent black Gucci dress by sacrificing my time, myself, and my reputation. I'd be wearing it to our divorce party!

☆

Feeling sorry for poor Alastor, Lizzie and I agreed to stop for a coffee break and buy my bodyguard a cup of hot brew and a filling lunch. He didn't object, bowing gratefully and taking the giant cup of coffee offered with a spark in his eye.

'So what have you decided in the end?' Lizzie asked, enjoying a chocolate fudge cake and looking at me with interest.

'I'll give him a chance.' I shrugged my shoulders, looking at the fragrant foam of my cappuccino. 'It would be foolish to miss out on such an opportunity.

Besides, he doesn't seem so bad. He gets cocky sometimes, but I do trust him a bit. There's a reason my father was close to him, and I don't see any objections from my mother. We'll live, we'll see.'

'Right,' Lizzie nodded, lowering her gaze and clenching her lips. I had known her for many years and understood well that she was hiding something from me. My friend worried about me, and I was grateful for such care.

'What?' I asked quietly, quickly glancing at Alastor. He did not pay attention to us as he was looking at his smartphone.

'Remember I told you that my family could feel people's energy?' Lizzie whispered, leaning towards me.

'Yes,' I nodded. 'I thought you said something about the ancient ability to feel evil souls, negative vibes or something like that?'

'That's right.' Lizzie smiled as she tucked her dark hair behind her ear. 'So, I consulted with my grandmother recently. I told her that I had a very contradictory feeling when I first saw Bale. It was like he was so attractive and...'

'And pushed you away at the same time?' I laughed, knowing well what Lizzie was talking about. My Japanese friend just nodded. 'Yes, I had that feeling, too. He has an inexplicable charm, elegance and magnetism. Still, at the same time, he scares and repels like something very dangerous.'

'My grandmother said that I must be careful around him,' Lizzie explained. She took in my baffled look. 'He gave me a weird feeling when I touched his hand. She told me how such an effect on witches was caused by demons that were hiding in human form in ancient times!'

'Demons?!' I exclaimed, making Alastor choke on

a piece of pie out of surprise. Ignoring the dramatic reaction of my bodyguard, I stared at Lizzie with a sceptical look.

'Listen!' She crossed her arms on her chest and snorted. Her bracelets made a jingling sound. 'I know that you don't believe in all this; that you're not a person of faith, and all these stories are crazy talk to you! But don't forget that I respect my family and their beliefs! Both my mother and father come from very traditional old families in Japan and China! And given the fact that I possess abilities that are unusual to others, I too am confident that there is something unknown to us in this world!'

I laughed, waving my hand at her. 'Believe what you want; I'm not judging you! Just the fact that my future husband is a demon is nonsense!'

'Hm.' Lizzie rolled her eyes, displeased and looking at Alastor, who was staring at us. 'I don't like *this* one either…'

'Forgive me, Miss Maio,' said Al gallantly, 'if I have offended you in any way.'

'You haven't—' she shook her shoulders '—but your energy is too different from what I'm used to.'

'Are you saying he's a demon, too?' I laughed as I took a sip of my coffee and smiled at Alastor's pale face. He sat like a statue under Lizzie's eagle eyes. 'Oh, come on, leave him alone. He doesn't look like a horned monster devouring babies. Alastor seems to be the purest of Bale's friends.'

'Thank you, Sophie,' my bodyguard said, before taking a sip of coffee. I only smiled gently, watching Lizzie's strict gaze. 'And for your information,' he added, 'such an image of demons had been instilled only by the legends and rumours used by ancient cultures to frighten enemies. In fact, demons in many faiths are quite human in nature and appearance.'

'Wow!' I was genuinely shocked by these words from Alastor. Noticing our surprised glances, Al coughed and seemed to regret what he had said.

'I'm sorry to get into your conversation,' Al said briefly.

'No, no, go on!' I nodded, eager to discover what else he was hiding from me. 'Where did you get that information, Al? Are you a believer or a shaman, too?'

'As far as I know, I am no shaman,' said Al, with a weak smile, which was rare for him. He had stunning, sophisticated features, and a certain charm when he smiled. The elevated corners of his lips gave him beauty and grace, making his whole face beam. Alastor was very adorable when he wanted to. 'Just like your friend here, I come from a traditional Japanese family who truly believed in ancient legends and honoured the souls of ancestors and the wisdom of previous generations.'

'I didn't know you were from Japan,' I advised. 'You do have an accent, but I didn't want to be rude, asking.'

'Sure, ma'am—' Alastor shook his head '—I was born in a poor village near Mount Fuji. My mother was Korean, and she fled to Japan during war times and then met my father. As a child, I did my best to help my family survive another winter, digging fields and caring for cattle. When it became possible to join the Emperor's service, I immediately agreed.'

'You worked for Emperor Akihito?' Lizzie was surprised, and I thought, for a split second, that she suddenly had great respect for my bodyguard. Al never confirmed it, only to point out that he had been a member of a gang since a very young age, then joined the army and gained respect and promotion. His story also included his family, and also his deceased wife, that had left him as a result of her illness.

My opinion of Alastor had suddenly changed a lot. I now saw suffering and pain in his eyes. He shared that he had never married afterwards, having devoted himself entirely to the love of his life, who had left him so early. Al's romantic side kept me warm and comforted. It was an honour to have such a noble and kind man as my protector.

Lizzie was also silent, she lifted her gaze, and whispered gomen in Japanese, expressing her condolences and apologising for her rudeness. Alastor only answered her with a smile. Shaking her head, Lizzie pouted her lips. But, shortly after, she threatened Alastor with a finger, reminding him that she still did not like him and that she would surely know his dirty secrets in the future. Al smiled once again and nodded approvingly.

'I think the problem is that Al's always so quiet,' my friend stated, pretending as if he's not there, snorting; 'all so serious. It gives me the creeps!'

'So, maybe we should find him a date?' I laughed as I winked at Alastor, who was staring at me, puzzled. 'Don't worry, Al. Nothing serious, just a bit of distraction! It's OK to have fun, too.'

'Yes, yes… even necessary,' Lizzie frowned.

'So why don't you and Lizzie hook up?' I whispered playfully, making the poor man even paler, as he seemed afraid to say anything so as not to be rude.

'Are you crazy?' my friend exclaimed, banging her hand on the table and making the cups shake. 'He's twice as old as me! Besides, I'm not available! I wouldn't trade my Roberto for anyone!'

'Well, as you wish.' I shrugged my shoulders with a smile.

Roberto Diniz was a lovely young man. Lizzie had met him while studying at university. She had decided to follow in their footsteps and continue her family's real estate business, also helping at her grandmother's local antique shop. Roberto had decided to go further, having received a doctorate in archaeology and now travelled the world in search of world history and unsolved secrets. At the moment, he was working in his hometown in Brazil. His sister Julia, though, occasionally spent time with Liz.

Lizzie waited patiently for Roberto, and when he finally arrived, they were the sweetest and cutest couple you could find. I knew that Lizzie was very loyal to her partner, as she was terrified of losing him, which is why she still had not dared to tell him the truth about her abilities.

'Let him be, then,' Lizzie said. 'Let this frostbite serve your evil husband.'

'Judging by your logic, my husband is the devil himself!' Lizzie and I laughed loudly, and Alastor almost dropped the phone, getting paler and quietly cursing us for such dark humour. I assumed the poor man couldn't get used to his employer being so disrespectfully spoken about.

I suddenly felt a slight chill on my skin and turned my gaze towards my friend, who was waving her hand to the side and frowning, pushing away a woman I had never met before. She was trying to snatch a piece of cake from Lizzie. Staring in surprise at this unusual scene, I squeezed my lips.

'Go away, I say!' my girlfriend whispered with a sigh. 'You're interfering, honestly!'

'Is everything OK?' I asked quietly, and Lizzie shook her head.

'Another ghost got attached to me!' Having pushed the woman away, Lizzie turned her tired gaze on me while I saw the ghost off with interest. My friend's expression suddenly changed.

'Sophie,' she whispered, and I looked at Lizzie, 'can you see her? The ghost?'

'Um…' I looked down at my empty cup of coffee.

'Oh, shit!' Covering her mouth, Lizzie's exclaimed, 'Since when?!'

'Just recently,' I answered quietly. 'I see ghosts everywhere and sometimes even strange visions of the living. I saw the ghost of a man who died of a heart attack at a party with Bale yesterday. Earlier that day, I saw him on the street, and I had visions about his death in my head…'

'Sophie, this is not a joke!' The witch grabbed my hands, and I looked at her anxiously. Alastor glimpsed at us periodically, pretending not to listen to our conversation. He didn't try hard to be unnoticed. 'Isn't that weird? You've only had this once before!'

'I know,' I said, nodding, 'as a child when my father brought me to work with him.'

'You said that when you came out of the elevator with your father, you saw the ghost of a man hanging in the air,' Lizzie said, and I nodded.

It was true; I remembered that moment as if it had happened yesterday. Dad was talking to someone in the elevator, discussing the business plan. I was just looking down, studying the pattern on the floor and noticing Dad's shiny shoes reflecting in the elevator door and the slender silhouette of another young man beside him. I couldn't remember the man's face because I was in a lousy mood that day and paid little attention to my surroundings. It wasn't until I got out of the elevator that I instantly saw a figure hanging in front of me. I was scared at the time, but the ghost seemed to be scared of something itself, staring at someone behind my back and instantly disappearing.

'I don't know what is happening to me, Lizzie,' I whispered as I clenched my friend's hands. The girl looked at me understandingly and smiled.

'I'm sure you'll find the answer,' she said encouragingly. 'I've been getting used to it for a long time too.'

I looked at her and sighed. She was right. I remember when Lizzie was subjected to terrible bullying at school and how hard it was for her to accept her abilities. I was terrified when she was honest with me one day and told me she was ready to take her own life because of the pressure and constant bullying.

At the time, Lizzie told me how she ran away from home one night. She ran as fast as she could, with her bare feet on the ground, in an unknown direction, away from everyone. Ghosts had haunted her all her life, and the girl just wanted to escape this world. Once on the bridge by the Thames, Lizzie firmly squeezed the railing and stepped over the ledge to the other side. She could not swim and was sure she would not get out if she jumped.

The ten-year-old girl was building the courage to jump, cursing her abilities, and ready to give up. But then...

The little girl heard someone else's footsteps, and the person passing by ending up changing her life. That was the turning point for her.

Lizzie always spoke about the woman she met with warmth and gratitude in her voice. My friend could hardly remember what that woman looked like. She had silky dark skin and beautiful grey eyes. Her beauty seemed extra-terrestrial and so divine and magical. Something about this woman was so mysterious and attractive.

Lizzie smiled when she told me how this stranger

just stood near her, looking up at the starry sky and enjoying the night air. It seemed as if she didn't notice the little girl beside her, ready to disappear from this world.

Lizzie told me what happened then.

The woman told her, 'You know, in order to get respect from others, you have to learn to respect yourself first. To accept yourself for who you are. You have only one soul. You are it. This is yours. Respect, love and believe in it,'

'W-what?' gulped Lizzie, staring at the stranger.

'Learn to forgive. I was in your shoes. I wanted to run away. I wanted to get it over with. I did not understand what made me different. Why is the colour of my skin so important? Why am I being judged by others? Why do I experience all this suffering just because I am different? Why do my powers scare them? I was angry at society. I was angry at people. And it became a part of me – hatred, anger, resentment.'

Lizzie was silent, looking into the deep waters of the river and shedding tears. She was shaking, trembling.

'But then I realised it was not my responsibility to drag all that with me. I carried the weight of other people on my shoulders. Instead, I learned to love myself. Respect myself. I threw away all negative feelings and accepted myself as I was. And then a different, stronger force woke up in me. Power of forgiveness…' The woman looked at Lizzie with her grey eyes and smiled. The girl pressed her lips and frowned, trying to decide what to do next. The stranger sighed, took a step back and turned towards the road. Lizzie was staring at her incomprehensibly. Why wasn't this woman trying to save her? Not dragging her to the other side? 'Jump if you want. It's an easy solution to your problems.'

'Why... why didn't you "jump"?' Lizzie asked.

'Hm, among other reasons...' The woman raised her head to the sky. 'I decided to prove to my enemies that I am above them. I will not bend under pressure and will not give up so easily. Instead, I will live to anger them more.'

And Lizzie did not jump. She returned home that night. She slept for days. She suffered from bullying for a while but soon changed her approach to people. And then... she met me at the age of ten.

'Don't worry,' she said now, and I drifted back from my memories. 'We'll have fun and get distracted with you this weekend!' she said.'

'Yes,' I smiled and nodded.

Suddenly, my friend came up with an idea. 'Listen, let's take him with us this weekend?'

I thought about it for a second and nodded again approvingly.

'I'm sorry. What are you talking about?' asked Al politely, and Lizzie and I winked at each other.

'Well, you're gonna watch after me anyway—' I shrugged my shoulders and smiled '—so you're going to hang out with us!'

'Hang out?'

'Sophie and I are going to a nightclub this Saturday,' said Lizzie cheerfully. 'You know, a couple of cocktails, dancing in the club and all that! To have fun and live while we're young! We shall take you with us!'

'Forgive me, Sophie, but...' Unwilling to listen to another tirade about the duty to his master, responsibility, and other boring stuff, I interrupted Alastor's speech with my firm decision to go. He did not argue with me and simply nodded silently, knowing that he probably had no choice.

As soon as we drove Lizzie home and waved to her tiredly, I sat in the car seat and took a deep breath, satisfied with today's shopping with my friend. For the first time in the last few weeks, I was able to relax and forget about all my issues, instead enjoying pure fun.

I devoted myself to body rest and meditation for the next couple of days. My head was full of thoughts about the upcoming wedding in two weeks, as the event organisers were frequent visitors in the estate. Inspired florists, restaurant owners with exquisite menu offerings and many other strangers who followed Bale's instructions were my regular guests lately. That's why it took me about two hours to scroll through the wedding dress catalogue with my assistant and choose the right design.

The upcoming event was the least interesting for me. I was never the kind of girl who dreamed of a lush white dress and a loud party. For me, the wedding process seemed like a dull and utterly unnecessary event for the sake of a simple contract signature.

'Wow, look at that beauty!' my mother exclaimed, browsing the magazines with different wedding dresses when it was just the two of us.

'It's a waste of valuable time for me,' I sighed, leaning on the back of the sofa and looking at the white ceiling with the beautiful crystal chandelier, 'and money. All that for one day.'

'Your father would have been so happy to see you on your wedding day,' Astrid said with a hint of sadness as she flipped through the catalogue pages. I glanced at her for a moment and bit my lip. My mother's face always changed when she talked about my father. I still saw her crazy love for him.

My memories were overflowing with stories from my parents about how they met. It was 'forbidden' love between people from different families. My mother was from an influential, prosperous family in the United States with Scandinavian roots. My father was a simple street musician and inventor who travelled the world. That's how he met my mother in California, instantly falling in love with her. And even though her family was against it, she did marry him. However, she paid for this decision by losing her family, when they broke off all ties with her.

Jeremy and Astrid moved to London, to his little apartment. Dad so badly wanted to make Mom happy that he did his best to start his own company.

'How did he meet Bale?' I asked quietly, not missing my mother's surprised look and her uncertainty at my question. She seemed to be trying to decide if she could give details while hiding some so as not to reveal other people's secrets.

'Bale was a very clever young man; he showed incredible intelligence.' Mom smiled, putting the catalogue aside. 'Jeremy had just opened his company then; it was a small branch, and he often travelled for inspiration. One day he went to Tokyo because Japan was famous for its advanced technology and novelties in nanotechnology development. I remember him being inspired by a little robot that played a miniature violin. That's where he met Bale in an old Buddhist temple.'

'In the temple?' I raised my eyebrow in surprise.

'Yes,' nodded Astrid. 'Bale was looking for inspiration at the time as well. He studied Buddhism and meditation and sought inner peace. When he met your father, he became interested in his work and ideas, deciding to start his own firm and join your father in partnership.'

'Where did he get the money to take that step? Is he from a wealthy family?' I asked, frowning and trying to figure out what drove young Bale to such a decision.

'I'm not sure.' My mother shrugged as she looked away and pressed her lips. She was lying, and I saw it. It was useless to ask further, for any explanation would be a lie rather than the truth. 'I knew nothing about Bale's family. I think he's an orphan who got on his feet himself.'

'OK,' I only sighed without listening. I felt angry that even my own mother refused to tell me the truth about my future husband. Even though I was calm because she wouldn't let me marry someone who would hurt me, I wasn't happy to be deceived.

'He was a charming young man.' Mum smiled as she got up from her chair and fixed her silk skirt. 'Very clever for his age, educated, extraordinary. He was often fiery, emotional and explosive. But, over the years, he changed.'

'He looks very tired, as if he's lived forever—' I noticed my mother smiling nervously and looking away '—but he has a spark of invincible wisdom in his eyes.'

'That's right,' Astrid nodded as she headed for the door, 'there's a lot to learn from him.'

'So, what did he teach you?' My tone seemed to have un-intentional note of resentment and disappointment . Astrid stopped for a second without turning around and sighed.

'To appreciate myself,' she replied quietly before leaving the room.

My interest in Bale was growing. I'd heard a few different opinions about him now, but none of them was negative. It surprised me, and it also alarmed me. A man who showed such a dangerous aura couldn't be so noble and good. He was clearly hiding something, and I had to know the truth.

My curiosity was growing too, as Rosie spoke softly about Bale's personality, brewing me a cup of coffee the next morning. She shared some stories with me about how kind and gentle her master was. The maid insisted he was the only one she could talk to openly, telling him all her fears and secrets. Bale always shared his advice and was a reliable support, never treating Rosie like a servant. She was a close friend to him, part of the family. Sometimes she could also comfort him, covering him with a blanket when he fell asleep in the library working on his documents or feeding him when he would forget about dinner.

As I contemplated my future husband, I thoughtfully looked at the transparent drop of rain that was slowly trickling down my windowpane, which was trying to keep up with the speed of the car on the way to the café the following day.

As we drove through the deserted streets, Alastor and I travelled silently until I asked him to politely stop by the small bakery, which was still closed. The owner of the place had already accepted the delivery of new goods, and he often shared hot croissants with me.

With a smile, taking a paper bag of delicacies, I winced at the pouring rain, rushing back to the car. One more step, and I felt like I bumped into someone's shoulder. Turning aside in surprise, I looked into the shiny grey eyes of a strange woman standing in front of me with a frightened, miserable look.

'I'm sorry, are you all right?' I asked, watching the

woman raise her hand and reach to me. Believing that I had pushed her by accident, I gave my hand in return, but immediately froze as the cold sweat from stranger's fingers passed through my palm.

Dumbfounded, I pulled back in silent shock, staring at the ghost that was reaching out to me with a desire to touch. My heart stopped, and my legs suddenly went numb. I couldn't move with the fear. The woman came closer, looking at me, and I closed my eyes, clutching my bag of baked goods to my chest and wishing was a nightmare.

'Sophie!' Suddenly, there was a low voice, and I opened my eyes, raising my head and looking frightenedly into Alastor's eyes. The woman was not around anymore, and my bodyguard stood anxiously in front of me, grabbing me by the shoulders and shaking me lightly.

'Al…' I whispered, looking for the missing ghost.

'You all right?' continued the man, and I only nodded faintly, leading him to the car and rejoicing at the warmth of my seat. Alastor sat down at the wheel and looked at me again, ensuring I was OK.

'I'm sorry; I saw something.' I smiled nervously, raising my eyes to the point of encounter with the stranger and freezing again, for the woman was standing in the same place, with her cold eyes looking at me. As I turned my head to the side, I looked at Al, and for the first time, I was afraid of his gaze. I was sure it was the ghost of the woman he was looking at, frowning and seemingly sending threatening thoughts in her direction. For a second, I thought he saw her too or was I crazy? 'Al?'

'The window is completely fogged.' He smiled as he leaned towards me and wiped the window with his palm. My doubt suddenly went away. No, he couldn't see. I guess he just noticed the window was all foggy from my erratic breathing.

As I climbed into my seat and waited for him to move away from me, I took a fleeting glance at his profile in front of me. He was indeed a very handsome man. I focused my attention on his earring. The shiny ruby, hanging in a drop, was shimmering with scarlet colours, and the gold was glistening in the rays of sun that were breaking through the clouds.

'How did you get that?' I asked, paying attention to the deep scar on my bodyguard's neck that went down from his ear to his neck. A straight line was hiding under the collar of his shirt.

'This?' He finally moved away, immediately putting his hand on the scar and blushing. 'It's a long-ago combat wound.'

'It must have hurt,' I said, buckling up when he started the car.

'It's not a pleasant feeling to be stabbed in the neck,' my bodyguard said with a grin. I was amazed that he was still alive after such an attack! Sometimes I forgot what a dangerous job my new friend had.

'You were protecting Bale?' I asked him carefully, unaware I was touching on a taboo topic.

'No, I was attacked by old enemies from a gang,' Al replied gently.

I nodded and looked forwards at the streets of London and the bright sun, which peeked from the clouds and foreshadowed a new day. I knew he used to be a criminal gang member, as per his story, and he had a specific tattoo sleeve on his arm and half of his chest that was showing from underneath his shirt. Very common for yakuza, as Lizzie told me once.

'How long have you known Bale?' I asked again, believing it was Al who could reveal the true nature of my fiancé to me.

'Sometimes I feel like I've known him for

hundreds of years,' Al said, laughing, and I smiled. 'I met him in Japan. When my wife Asami died, my five-year-old daughter was also sick after a while.'

'Daughter?' I was shocked to say.

'Hai.' Al nodded as he turned a corner. 'Master Bale gave me the indispensable help that allowed my daughter to survive. I swore to serve him for the rest of my life. I want to repay him for his kindness.'

'That's very noble, Al.' I smiled again, looking at my protector and realising how beautiful this man was. 'And your daughter...?'

'She survived,' Al replied gently, 'but I haven't seen her since my contract started.'

'What?' I looked at the man with surprise and misunderstanding.

'That was the agreement,' said Al. 'My daughter lives, and I enter the service, forgetting all ties with family and relatives. It's been decades, now.'

'This's brutal!' I exclaimed, glad to finally find what I was looking for. No matter what everyone said, Bale wasn't perfect at all, and his selfishness and cruelty had finally shown themselves!

'It's a deal, Sophie,' Al smiled, 'and it's right. My job is dangerous, and if I had stayed close to my baby, I would have exposed her to enemy attacks. What matters to me is that she survived, found happiness, and achieved what she wanted. The rest, it doesn't matter.'

'But...' I said it hoarsely, frowning and sulking, 'you'll see her again, won't you?'

'Who knows,' said Al in a distant voice, and I knew he didn't want to talk about it anymore. The subject was hurting him, and it was time for me to stop. 'Perhaps a miracle would happen, and I would meet her. Not in this life, but in another.'

'What's her name?' I asked him softly.

'Hanako,' said Al quietly, 'like blossoming flowers.'

'It's a beautiful name,' I said softly. 'I'd like to see her one day.'

'I don't even have a picture of her,' Al replied sadly, stopping the car outside the café and looking at the steering wheel thoughtfully. 'All I have left of her is this earring. It was Asami's gift to her.'

Al's long fingers touched the ruby in his ear, caressing the stone that brought back memories.

I pursed my lips and tried to hold back tears in my eyes; for such fate was unfair. Al deserved to be happy like no one else. And I hated myself for being helpless and unable to support him. Could I repay Al for his protection and friendship? Maybe I could talk Bale into letting Al go see his family?

☆

Having treated Al to a cup of hot coffee and smiling at his ritual of reading the newspaper in the corner of our café, I sighed. I continued my morning routine before the café opened. Alastor had already managed to chase away a couple of curious journalists from our premises as they were hunting for some new information about Bale Deemer's new bride.

Martin tiredly walked downstairs with an exhausted look, proving that he'd once again stayed up all night playing online games.

Our routine followed its usual course. During the lunch break, I stared at my notebook, drawing a sketch of a stranger and sighed. Despite the odd morning, the day seemed quite ordinary and uninteresting. Shortly after taking a sip of cappuccino, I raised my hand, crossing out my drawing in an inexplicable gust once more.

'Not happy with the result of your work?' When I turned I was surprised to see Mike standing near me with a friendly smile. After greeting him I asked Martin to make a cup of fresh coffee, remembering to check with Al if he wanted anything else. After receiving a polite 'no', I made room for Mike to sit beside me, putting my notebook in a pocket. 'How are you?'

'As always.' I shrugged. 'I enjoy my rich lifestyle and rare unusual events around me.'

'Unusual events?' Mike asked cautiously, glancing at Alastor in the corner.

'Um,' I sighed a tired sigh. 'Never mind, it's nothing.'

'Have you settled in your new home?' Michael asked carefully, trying not to give away his worry, though not very well. His kind face always showed even the smallest white lie.

'Yes, quite settled,' I replied, watching Martin fuss about. 'A beautiful house, gorgeous garden, a kind maid. I can't complain.'

'OK,' Mike nodded, 'well...'

'You wanna know if I kicked my fiancé out yet, don't you?' I raised my eyebrow, and Michael only pressed his lips together. 'No, no need for that. Bale constantly disappear. Always busy, busy—' I sighed '—and now he's away for work.'

'He's not hurting you, right?' Mike continued, and I smirked.

'You serious? Me?' I lifted my head up proudly, rolled my eyes and waved my hand. 'Come on! You know me. I'm a tough cookie! That arrogant man can't break me that easily! Even though he does scare me sometimes...'

'Scare you?!' Michael was ruffled, almost spilling his own coffee. I stared at him in surprise and amusement, baffled by his dramatic reaction.

'Sometimes it seems like he's reading my mind,' I explained, noticing Mike's serious look and starting to feel uncomfortable in his presence. Honestly, Mike puzzled me more than Bale sometimes.

'Then don't think about anything in front of him,' Michael answered quietly, taking a sip of coffee. I raised my eyebrow and snorted. ' Don't think,' that's easy to say! Besides, I didn't really think that Bale was getting inside my head in search of my secret thoughts! What nonsense!

'Mike, you should go out more. You've been odd lately,' I smiled. I stood up and headed towards the window. Michael suddenly jumped out of his chair and grabbed my hand, turning me around and looking at me anxiously, blushing a little.

'I…' he swallowed, frowning and trying to pick up words, 'I'm worried about you.'

'Why?' I asked, straight to the point, without flinching. For some reason, anger started to grow in me. That wasn't fair. I had felt longing feelings for this man for so many years and suffered the unrequited love. Still, he gently rejected me, talking about the fact that he sees me only as a friend and that he doesn't plan to start a relationship. He wished to follow the call of his heart and stay loyal to God. I accepted that side of him. And now… he stirred my fading feelings again and reminded me of them every time.

'I don't want you to get hurt,' Mike answered, and I plucked my wrist out of his palm. 'Sophie…'

'Don't worry,' I replied, biting my lip and frowning, 'I have a great bodyguard, and he won't allow me to get hurt. And you'd better think about your future rather than my problems.'

'Do you like him, then?' Mike asked with no

shame in his eyes, and I was appalled by such a question. How dare he even ask me that?

'Well, that is none of your business, if I'm honest,' I replied angrily and looked away. To be fair, I wasn't sure how to answer that. I wasn't in love, but I certainly felt attracted to Bale for some reason. I mean, he was good-looking, with a confident attitude, wealthy and very intelligent. The whole mystery around him also attracted me even more.

'Sophie, I care about you and—'

'I'll take care of myself, Michael.' I looked at my friend, letting him know that I no longer wanted to talk about this. He seemed to be confused about his own feelings, too. 'I'm not your concern. You made it clear to me that there is a line between us that we have no right to cross. And I respect your decision. So be kind, respect mine, too.'

'I'm sorry,' the blond man said, nodding.

I calmed my nerves and smiled, trying to ward off angry thoughts. As I stepped forward, I hugged Michael, feeling him shuddering and immediately letting him go.

'Thank you for worrying—' I kept smiling '—but I'm fine, really. If anything happens, I'll let you know.'

'OK,' Mike softened his gaze and reluctantly let go of my fingers. I was disillusioned by his gaze and felt the weight in my chest. The embarrassment never left me, and I needed a distraction.

My working day was over, and I gladly sat down in the car with Alastor, eager to get to my room and lie down on the bed to get a good night's sleep. My dear mother had gone out again, and I could enjoy some solitude and silence.

Unfortunately, my trip home was delayed by the

endless traffic. I sighed an irritable sigh as I dreamed of taking off and just rushing into the sky with my non-existent wings, away from this gloomy environment. After spending a meaningless half an hour in barely moving traffic, I looked at the upside-down bus and a couple of crashed cars nearby on the other side. An ambulance, firefighters, and police were surrounding the scene, and I felt guilty for being angry for nothing. After all, these people were less fortunate than me. Some of them probably wouldn't come home. The trollies with wounded bodies covered by the sheets quickly disappeared inside the ambulance. My body was shivering, and my head was killing me. What a nightmare…

My sweet dreams were interrupted by a series of notifications on my phone, and I slowly pulled my hand out from under the blanket. When I looked at my watch, I wasn't happy. It was very early, and I refused to get up at 6:00 am on a Saturday morning. Grunting, I looked at the screen of my bright smartphone and was surprised at the news feed. It was filled with endless alerts. Opening the first article, I briefly read about yesterday's accident. The collision between two cars and a bus had terrible consequences, with twelve people killed and about twenty injured. The accident was caused by a crack in the ground that had unexpectedly appeared. The victims' names and photographs followed the article to allow everyone to express their condolences to the bereaved families. I quickly ran my finger across the screen and immediately froze. My gaze stopped at the third photo, and I stared into the young man's blue eyes.

As I jumped out of bed, I ran up to my bag. I pulled out my notebook, flipped through the pages and looked at the crossed-out portrait of a young boy I had quickly sketched on paper the day before. Bringing the phone near my laptop, I sat down on the bed and gulped. There couldn't be any mistake... it was that boy. I'd never seen him, but there he was, looking right at me. Swiping my finger on the screen a second time, I flinched and threw my phone away. I recognised the faces. The other seven were exact copies of my portraits in the studio from earlier. It couldn't be true. I was going crazy.

Tying my wet hair into a ponytail after a quick shower and putting on a sweatshirt, I literally flew out of the house. I sat hopped on my bike without thinking twice and started to pedal. I had to make sure. I had to know!

Manoeuvring between cars and breaking a couple of highway codes, I was looking forward to my home, impatient and in a hurry. An hour's ride turned out to be quick, so I threw my bike aside, jumped off it and opened the front door with shaking hands, forgetting to lock it behind me. My feet carried me into my studio, my heart beating a double beat, and my head dizzy. I panicked.

Starting to dig through the dusty portraits randomly, I finally found some of the ones I needed. Having laid out seven bright pictures of strangers on the floor in front of me, crossed out by a red stripe, I took my phone out of my pocket and opened a page of the news feed, flipping through the pictures of the victims. It was as if by magic, one by one, each of them completely coincided with my portraits, causing me to gulp in horror and fear.

Once I sat down on the floor, I ran my hands through my hair and tried to bury myself in it. So, what was happening to me? What kind of witchcraft is this?! How to explain such coincidences and what to do with them? Why did I see those who were about to die in my imagination? Why did I see ghosts?!

My thoughts were interrupted by a faint rustle, and I turned my head back in a sharp movement.

'Mom?' I got up off the floor, breathing heavily and headed for the door. I didn't see anyone in the living room, all alone in an empty house. Only now did I think about how Alastor probably went ballistic over my absence. I'd have to apologise to him.

When I noticed the front door open, I got mad at myself for not being careful and locked it. Turning back to the living room, I met the gaze of a stranger who looked ready to attack me. His eyes were black as pitch, his skin had a blue rotting hue, and a strong stench of death followed him. Immediately bouncing aside, I stumbled away.

The intruder followed me, climbing the stairs to the second floor and dodging a steel statuette that had previously stood on a chest of drawers in the hall before I threw it in his direction. Locking the door to the bedroom, I panicked and tried to put my thoughts together.

'Think, Sophie, think!' I whispered, looking around the room and trying to think of something to protect myself with while the stranger tried to break my door. I grabbed a chair by my desk and flipped it over, kicking it a couple of times on the leg, before pulling it. The wood cracked and broke.

The door began to open, and I gathered my strength, ready to meet the offender and stab him in the chest with my DIY weapon. It wasn't the first time I'd defended myself, and this time was no exception. My phone rang in my pocket. I pulled it out, and, seeing Al's name, I immediately answered, holding the wooden stake in front of me.

Al began to say something about being unable to reach me and so on.

THE DEVIL'S SIGNATURE: THE ABIDING PACT

'Al!' I panicked and exclaimed. 'Help me, Al!'

Trying to find the right words and explain briefly that I was at my house, locked in a room and about to be attacked, I rejoiced when Al told me that he was near my house, knowing that I would most likely go here if I wanted to be alone.

'Sophie!' Alastor's voice rang out behind me, and I turned around nervously, looking out the window and seeing my bodyguard outside. In a panic, I turned to the door that was on the verge of breaking.

'Al!' I shouted as I looked out the open window and begged for help. 'He's upstairs!'

'Jump down!' Al ordered strictly, frowning and stretching his arms as if convincing me he'd catch me. I wanted to challenge that offer, but the sound of door splintering made me change my mind. As I stepped on the windowsill, I lunged forward, but my assailant grabbed me by the hood of my sweatshirt and pulled me back. He squeezed my forearm and tried to grab me, but with an accurate stab of my weapon into his ribs, I jumped forwards without thinking twice, falling into Alastor's arms.

As I hugged his neck tightly and tried to get my breath back, I felt his strong hands on me, comforting and reassuring me that I was safe.

'It's all right, it's all right,' he continued, carefully putting me on my feet and examining my face to ensure I wasn't hurt. All I did was nod, confirming that I was safe, and then Al immediately gave me the car keys. 'Run to the car! Lock the door and wait for me!'

'What?' I couldn't understand his plan. 'W-where are you going?'

'I won't be long,' Alastor growled, and once again, just like that time in the car, I was afraid of his glare. His bright grey eyes seemed to have darkened, and the whole essence of Al expressed danger, rage, and bloodthirst. He took out the gun from the back of his jacket and aimed straight. I did not want to be in his way, so I rushed to the car, following his order.

Trying to breathe and soothe my heart, I looked at the front door of my house, where Al had gone and had not returned yet. Police! I have to call the police! I grabbed the phone and unlocked it with trembling hands but immediately jumped as the front door opened and my abuser flew out of the house, followed by the furious Alastor. He did not let him get away, grabbing the man by his coat and sending a couple of stiff blows to the stranger's face. I felt cold sweat running down my spine while Al was beating the shit out of the stranger, throwing him around like a bag of dirt. Al's eyes showed a hunger for blood and violence. I'd never seen him like that. Clutching the man by the throat against the wall, Al whispered something in his ear and let go, allowing the man to cough while Al dialled the number. Calling for Bale's security, Alastor waited for the arrival of two black cars, which took only ten or so minutes to come and handed the intruder into the hands of those who arrived. They left as fast as they appeared.

☆

On the way to the estate, I wanted to ask Alastor what had happened, but I didn't. It seemed to me that when I asked for details, I was digging my own grave and was on the verge of getting involved in something very dangerous and unnecessary. The time would come, and I would know. The important thing was that I was safe, and Al's silence was proof of that. I should have apologised for not telling him I had left. But the man seemed to have guessed my feelings.

That's why he didn't say a word to me when we got home. He only asked Rosie to make me a cup of tea and sat down in the chair in front of me, answering someone's message. I noted once again that I should listen to Alastor and rely on his protection.

Panic finally subsided, and I took a sip of hot tea. I wondered what Bale would have said when he found out about this. I didn't think he'd be happy.

Anticipating another dispute with the estate owner, I briefly looked at the phone. A message from Lizzie appeared on the screen.

'Be ready by seven!' I read the message with a smiley face from my friend and looked at Alastor.

'Hey, Al,' I called my bodyguard quietly, giving him a cheeky look. 'Thank you.'

'You're welcome, Sophie.' He smiled softly, and a warm wave passed over my body. I was grateful to him for his understanding.

'Are you ready for tonight?' I asked a question, trying to forget today's unexpected adventure.

'Pardon me?' He raised an eyebrow.

'Lizzie and I are going out, remember?' I got up from the couch, headed for the door to go pick out my outfit. 'I would like your constant protection, Al. Please.'

'Of course, ma'am.' Al smiled again, and I nodded, rejoicing immensely.

THE DEVIL'S SIGNATURE: THE ABIDING PACT

CHAPTER SIX

    The bright lights, loud music, shaking floor, and mass of sweaty bodies dancing passionately with the rhythm made my heart rate increase. The atmosphere of the nightclub and the madness within completely devoured me and made my imagination flow with freedom and wildness.

    Lizzie pulled her black curls to one side and looked back, glancing around the nightclub, trying to find a small table for the three of us. Her crescent moon earrings glistened together with glittery black lipstick. Walking around in her short shiny dress that truly complimented her petite figure, my friend managed to spot a place.

    I strolled in my black cocktail dress with a deep neckline and an open back, happy with the newly bought outfit. I held my clutch tighter, hoping to not lose it as I had on my previous night out.

Alastor, serious as always, was looking at the surroundings in confusion, walking behind me while no doubt cursing Lizzie and me deep inside, for I was sure he was most concerned for my safety in this busy place. I was ready to admit that Al looked great in his grey jeans, white shirt and silver jacket. Seeing him without a suit was unusual, but it was lovely too. Assuring my bodyguard that everything was all right, I grabbed his hand and dragged him and Lizzie to the bar.

It was hard to get Al to relax. Lizzie and I enjoyed our third cocktail and danced to the music, laughing from the heart and letting go of our worries. Al stood near us with a poker face, and any human who approached us was considered a threat. Al was standing by us like a wall and chasing away uninvited guests.

'Relax, frostbite!' smirked Lizzie, shoving Alastor with her shoulder and handing him a bottle of beer. He just shook his head.

'Come on, Al!' I tried to shout out the music. 'Have some fun!'

'I don't drink at work, ma'am,' Al answered loudly, but Lizzie gave him the bottle and rolled her eyes, suggesting that he was 'always' at work. Our stubbornness did win, and my bodyguard took a sip, still glancing around. Lizzie got him arguing that she could handle alcohol better than he could. And if he refused and failed to stand up to his deeds, he was not worthy of defending an important persona like me. Lizzie was adamant that no alcohol would affect Al if he was a true professional in his field. Alastor seemed visibly offended by that statement. As it turned out, it was enough for Al to relax and give himself up entirely to the atmosphere of fun. He immediately emptied the bottle and ordered a couple more.

    The night was in full swing, and Lizzie and I had a complete banter, giving Alastor no rest and noticing few interested female glances on him. The scoundrel was really attractive, I had to admit it.

    'Hey, let's dance!' Lizzie pulled Alastor's hand, ignoring his protests. I only laughed merrily and watched as my friend showed off her dance manoeuvres around Al with pleasure while he stood there, blushing with embarrassment.

    'Come on, Al! Show your skills! Your fighting moves are well flexible, so you must be good at dancing!' I pushed him.

    'Yeah, show me what you got, frostbite! Or does age forbid you, old man?' Lizzie laughed, and I pressed my lips, noticing an unfriendly spark in Alastor's eyes. I guessed my friend had found his weak spot.

    Probably, that is why always serious Al, having emptied the last bottle of beer, stepped towards Lizzie and stood before her as if daring her to a duel.

    The music took on a different rhythm, and Lizzie and I flinched when Alastor raised his hand fast and slowed down as if running his fingers through his hair. Making a smooth movement from shoulder to waist and below, he crouched and rose again, turning around and giving himself entirely to the music. Lizzie and I looked shocked and could not even find the words to describe our surprise.

    Who'd have thought that humble Al would have danced as well as the boys from K-pop boy bands? Every movement he made worked with the rhythm, and people slowly began to part, amazed by the abilities of my bodyguard.

    Lizzie and I threw ourselves onto the dance

floor. We ultimately gave in, staying near Alastor, who had gladly accepted my friend's challenge and arranged a competition with her. Now, watching them with amusement while they continued their dance battle, I allowed the music to consume me and let myself free.

I was so immersed in this wild night that I didn't immediately notice someone slowly approaching me with a confident step. The black lacquered shoes reflected the light and a dark suit glittered in the laser beams. The fire was burning in the man's brown eyes, and the smug grin on his lips seemed predatory and evil.

Inside a busy circle of people on the dance floor, I ignored the dizziness and lightness in my body. My intoxicated mind wanted freedom of action and endless fun.

'Can't I leave you without adventures even for a couple of days?' There was a low voice in my ear, tickling my skin and covering my body with pleasant chills. Pulling aside sharply and turning around, I stared into dark-brown eyes.

'Bale!' I exclaimed, expecting him to be here least of all.

'You seem to have broken Al.' My fiancé raised his eyebrow as he looked up at the merry Alastor and glanced back at me. I had already forgotten the effect of his presence. I was now completely shrouded in the mystical aura of Mr Deemer.

'Not everyone is snobby like you,' I snorted as I continued dancing, 'some people like fun. You were not invited here.'

'Hm,' Bale's laughter touched his lips as he examined me head to toe and looked into my eyes again, with a lustful grin and glistening eyes. 'I invented fun, sweetheart.'

'Yeah, right, whatever.' I shrugged my shoulders and turned away, refusing to fall for this insolent man's tricks. The music was replaced by another familiar tune. My body suddenly spun, and Bale turned me towards him with one movement, pressing me against his body and making my cheeks blush. The rhythm of the music intensified, and I felt Bale's increasingly hot hands on my hips, pushing them aside and making me move under his command. My body followed Bale's every move as if under the spell of those gentle hands. He kept me close to himself, even though I held my palms firmly on his chest, trying to keep my distance. I could feel his knee between my thighs as I bent backwards and up again, and I flushed from such familiarity. How dare he tease me so?!

I was also annoyed by the fact that Bale hadn't blinked once, continuing to look me in the eye and grin. He knew exactly what he was doing. Those hands were so slow…

Sharply turning me around, he put one hand on my thigh and the other on my waist, tickling my neck with his nose. I was about to explode when he inhaled the scent of my perfume. A hot wave passed through my body, making the butterflies inside my stomach flutter and making my head spin harder. Everything inside me tightened. I still didn't know if it was Bale that was affecting me like that or if the alcohol was playing in my blood. All I knew was that my body was succumbing to those controlling movements. I didn't want to step aside by following the urge and responding to Bale's call without resisting.

Turning my head in his direction and feeling his stubble on my cheek, I intuitively raised my hand.

I threw it behind his neck, pressing it harder and opening my lips. My mind screamed and prayed to stop, claiming I had only given in to the moment. Still, my body refused to retreat and miss the opportunity.

I'd never been so attracted to anyone. Something about this man was magical, inhuman. His eternally hot hands were burning my skin, and it seemed to me that I was inside the heart of a bright fire that enveloped me, lighting me up.

My fiancé seemed to have gotten carried away with his game, as his hands allowed themselves to be superfluous, clutching my thighs tighter and making me hold my breath. I was surprised at his self-control when I pressed my lower back against his lower abdomen, only to find him entirely in control of himself. I was sure I had heard a soft animal growl coming off his lips when I pressed my thin hands closer to him and threw my delicate fingers into his dark hair, shattering a neat ponytail at the back of his head. I inhaled his unusual scent of pine and… smoke. He smelled of fire. It seemed like it was burning inside him, as if his blood was hot lava, flowing through his veins.

The music was coming to an end, and I prayed for a continuation. Those slow hands suddenly let me go, and I didn't come to my senses immediately, looking at Bale with some misunderstanding and disappointment.

'I'm tired. It's time to go home.' He smiled and looked at Alastor, the bodyguard flinching when he noticed his master.

☆

Breathing in some fresh air while standing

outside, I was glad I hadn't done anything I'd regret and didn't give in to hidden desires. My head seemed to have vented, and my body was now taken only by anger and resentment as I felt defeated in this game. Belial Deemer was manipulative by nature; he knew the power of his looks and energy. And it pissed me off.

'Since Al is completely wasted, I'll drive,' Bale answered, taking the keys from Alastor who was standing on the sidewalk with a guilty look.

After the four of us rushed into the car, with Al stumbling and trying his best to stay dignified, we drove away from the nightclub.

'I'm hungry!' mumbled Lizzie, looking at the street lights. 'Let's grab a bite to eat, huh?'

'Mm, good idea!' I smiled when I looked at the indifferent Bale. 'Hey! Can you make a stop somewhere? I'm hungry.'

'I'm not Al to take orders from you,' Bale answered while driving.

'Please…' I squeezed my lips and rolled my eyes.

'I'm amazed that you managed to break my bodyguard,' Bale said, pulling around a corner where we could find a good place with fast food.

'I'm sorry, sir,' Alastor replied, holding back the hiccups. 'I tried to argue with them, but the witch pissed me off—'

'Eh?!' Lizzie exclaimed with a dramatic voice, catching a displeased look from Alastor. 'You haven't been forcibly dragged, frostbite!'

'Lies!' Al raised his finger, throwing his head back and trying to cope with dizziness.

'Lizzie, to be honest, you were the one who took him to the dance floor.' I laughed as I heard my friend swear.

'I'm glad he tagged along,' Bale replied quietly, changing his expression from sweet to serious. 'I hope you won't do anything stupid anymore and run away from home without an escort.'

'Al, you traitor! You gave me away?!' I exclaimed, looking at my bodyguard angrily. He shrugged his shoulders and nodded positively, without even saying a word. I squinted and pressed my lips. I couldn't trust anyone in this world!

'What are you talking about?' asked Lizzie, moving closer and looking at Bale and me. I opened the food bag when I took the order from the drive-through window. I had to share my experience from this morning with Lizzie and receive a few swear words back from my friend for not telling her about it earlier.

Having calmed her and explained that I didn't want to worry her and that I had gotten used to it a long time ago, we moved on to the subject of the accident and my portraits.

'Sophie, this is no longer a coincidence!' she gasped.

'I don't know what to do,' I sighed. 'I feel like death is haunting me everywhere! I think I'm going crazy.'

'How long have you been followed and attacked?' Lizzie asked while chewing her vegetarian burger. I thought about it, and scratched the back of my head.

'I don't know… I think I was first kidnapped when my father died,' I answered. The silence hung; Bale continued to drive as if ignoring my words. 'Hey, do my abilities scare you?'

'Why would they?' I was puzzled by his words.

'Who knows, maybe I'm a witch or

something,' I snorted, receiving a reproachful look in return.

'You're not a witch, trust me.' Bale laughed, and Alastor snickered for the first time. I think he grunted as well. 'I would know.'

'Ha-ha!' I waved my hand, biting a piece of my kebab. 'How would you know?! Maybe I'm hiding my dark nature deep inside! Or do you not believe in such things?'

'Eat and don't be silly,' Bale replied calmly, making me pout and pay attention to my kebab again.

'Lizzie is a witch. You believe her,' I mumbled as I looked out the window.

'Because only a real witch could make my extremely professional bodyguard so drunk,' Bale sighed tiredly, making Alastor grunt again. Lizzie laughed, and I pouted once again, accepting my failure in this argument.

After sending Al off to his bedroom and changing into comfortable pyjamas, I refused to go to bed, as the remains of alcohol in my blood still filled me with energy and desire for fresh air. Passing by the library, I couldn't help but notice a familiar silhouette at the table.

'May I come in?' I asked quietly, drawing Bale's attention while he put stacks of papers on his desk. With an affirmative nod, he took a sip of coffee and continued to read the documents, fixing glasses I was seeing for the first time . This man's serious business appearance was genuinely amusing. 'Is that from work?'

'Yeah.' He flipped through the pages then signed something. I looked at him silently and raised my eyebrows.

'Don't you get tired? Do you take any

breaks?' I laughed as I examined the room and appreciated the antiquity of some things once again.

'It's a job I can't quit,' Bale replied quietly. 'No one else is going to do it.'

'No job would offer irreplaceable position.' I rolled my eyes, and Bale smiled. I couldn't find anything else to say. It wasn't that I had nothing to speak to him about; quite the opposite. It was just that I didn't think this was the right time to discuss my concerns. I needed a reason.

'Thank you for taking Alastor out,' Bale said without raising his eyes, and there was my reason. 'It was time for him to have some fun.'

'You're welcome,' I answered with a light smile. 'He is a good man.'

'Mm.'

'He has great respect for you,' I started, 'even though you don't let him see his family.'

Here it was, silence. I patiently endured Bale's stern look when he raised his eyes at me. I bit my lip. I think he knew exactly what I was leading to.

'Alastor is a very devoted and good friend,' said my fiancé, as he stood up and walked towards me, hiding his hands in his pockets. 'He is the only one I am willing to entrust my life to. But the contract between us is indestructible and binding.'

'Is that why he can't see Hanako?' I raised my eyebrow when Bale stood right in front of me, looking at me with a threat in his glare and showing that I was asking for a fight. Even though this man scared me sometimes, my anger prevailed over my fear.

'Hanako is dead,' he replied quietly, and it was as if an electric shock passed through my body. No, it couldn't be. I was sure Al's daughter was alive. Isn't that why they had an agreement?! 'I helped him, just like I promised. Hanako survived the illness, grew up, got married and had a family. However, after a while, she left this world.'

'Oh, my God...' I whispered, and Bale flinched with disgust at the phrase, 'Al...'

'Al knows,' said Mr Deemer, and I stared at Bale again in surprise. 'He doesn't know the details of her life, but he knows the most important things.'

'But... but he said he believed that one day he would see her!' I said with sadness in my voice, looking incomprehensibly at my interlocutor.

'Who knows,' Bale sighed. 'Maybe in the afterlife.'

My mood was completely ruined, and I didn't even know what to say. Poor Alastor had lost everything he had.

'Do you have any plans for tomorrow?' he asked.

'Huh?' I took my mind off the topic.

'The wedding is in two weeks. In the meantime, I'd like to introduce you to my company and also spend some time with you.' Bale headed back to his desk. 'I'm asking you out on a date.'

'The last date ended with a tragedy,' I mumbled, recalling the terrible moment of those events.

'Shit happens.' Bale shrugged his shoulders, and I snorted, amazed at his calmness. *What a heartless prick!*

'And where are we going?' I crossed my arms on my chest and trampled my foot.

'It's a surprise.' Bale smiled, and I looked suspiciously at him. 'Dress comfortably. You're going for a long walk. A very long... walk.'

☆

The self-righteous peacock didn't lie. We had to walk really, really... really far. To my surprise, Al got a day off thanks to Bale being my chaperone, and it should have convinced me I was safe. Poor Alastor suffered from a hangover and buried his nose in his pillow, trying to get some sleep.

Rosie woke me up early, apologising and explaining that Bale was waiting for me downstairs and I had to get ready as soon as possible. Outraged that I had been woken up at 6:00 a.m., I headed into the shower room, angry.

After getting dressed and tying the shoelaces on my sneakers, I looked at my reflection in the mirror and ensured that I looked pretty decent. My wet hair was starting to fluff and freckles were shining under my light make-up. My lace T-shirt was hanging from one shoulder, my light jeans were tight around my slender legs, and a beige jacket over my shoulders should have covered me from the morning chill.

Coming down the stairs, I was surprised to see my fiancé standing at the door, looking thoughtfully into his smartphone. I was ready to admit that the casual style really suited him, even though it wasn't usual to my eye. The grey jeans with a black T-shirt and a brown leather belt were accentuated with boots of the same colour. A light black jacket was stretched over the top. Half of his dark hair was tied back in a small ponytail, while a few bottom strands were left loose.

'You're not wearing a suit?' I laughed as I approached him. Bale hid his phone in his pocket and nodded approvingly while examining me. The man didn't honour me with a reply. Bale opened the door for me, and we got into the car, heading in an unknown direction.

As it turned out, my fiancé decided to show me a place I'd never been to before. As I walked around Borough Market, I felt an indescribable rapture and hunger as I watched a variety of fresh foods. The vendors roasted juicy meat in front of their sleepy customers and filled their display shelves with freshly baked Yorkshire puddings, baked potatoes, bright fruits and vegetables, shimmering fish in the sun, and all sorts of things that made me drool.

Delighted with the treats that Bale paid generously for, I stuffed my stomach with everything that was offered. It was indescribably delicious!

'Damn, I've never been here before! Been living here all my life, but never got to visit this place!' I was trying to talk with stuffed cheeks. 'I seem to be always so busy that I never get to go anywhere like this.'

'It's great, isn't it?' Bale smiled, and I chuckled, staring at him again. He seemed to genuinely love this place – what a surprise. 'I've always been amazed at how evolved people's imagination is. The human race is so diverse and creative. Food, in my opinion, is great evidence of human genius.'

'Mr Deemer, you're an odd man.' I smiled as I chewed up a piece of BBQ meat while holding a box of goodies in my hand.

'Can't I enjoy the food?' I was surprised to see Bale offended.

'Enjoy as much as you want,' I laughed, 'but I am surprised by your love for humanity.'

'Because humans are great,' he finished as he kept going. All I did was smile and follow him. *Whatever you say, Mr Alien.* I didn't argue with his conclusions. I had my own opinions on people and wasn't much impressed by my kind.

An invigorating stomach-filled street market stroll was continued with the journey through central London on foot. Soon we pulled up to an alley and walked into a quieter London neighbourhood filled with colourful flowers, rocky paths and the cosy streets of Warren Mews.

Enjoying a hot cup of coffee and keeping my hands warm with the paper cup, I would periodically look at my companion while we chattered about all things possible. I was once again convinced of his wisdom and intelligence. He really knew what he was talking about.

Bale Deemer had many interests – from history, and knowing incredible facts, to cultural studies and psychology. He answered any of my questions broadly and openly, sincerely. He was well-outspoken and very educated as well. I was inadvertently interested in his style of conversation. His aristocracy and manners were sometimes mixed with his sarcastic personality and occasional playful charm.

'How do you know so much?' I was surprised, looking at my fiancé from the bottom up as he was so tall.

'I've had a lot of time.' He shrugged, looking ahead and his glance became thoughtful. 'I often spend my time alone, and my curiosity had never faded. I read a lot. I explore. Observe.'

'It's amazing. You're like a walking encyclopaedia!' I laughed, and Bale smiled softly, making my heart beat faster and my cheeks burn for a second. Charmingly cunning, this man was…

'How old are you?' I asked. He clenched his jaw and looked away. 'Oh, what? Is it a secret?'

'How old do you think I am?' he asked.

'Hm, you look about thirty… four?' I thought

and he smiled gently. I didn't understand what was the big deal.

'Are you from a wealthy family? You seem very sophisticated,' I squinted, trying to find out the truth. Bale had only sighed and looked away.

'I'm not from a wealthy family,' he replied, 'I made my own fortune. However, you could say that I am of blue blood.'

'Oh, royalty! And here I thought your snobby personality was just a pretentious act!' I snorted and caught a disgruntled look. 'So what happened? Mom said you were an orphan. Is that why you're not telling me your age? You don't know?'

'Do you have no manners at all?' Bale raised his eyebrow, and I chuckled.

'I need to know who I'm marrying,' I said and turned away, bored, looking at the colourful flower beds. I heard a laugh from his side. Somehow that chuckle of his made my heart warm again.

'I left home,' my companion answered briefly, and I stared at him in surprise. 'I didn't get along with my father, and I eventually left my home nest. We still don't talk.'

'What about your mother?' I asked, softer.

'I never had one.' Bale sighed, and I looked at him incomprehensibly. He didn't seem to have planned to tell me anymore. I thought I'd find out about it later.

Who are you, Bale Deemer? Suddenly I thought I couldn't take my eyes off him anymore. He found a place deep in my heart, and I was ready to curse him for it. I guess now I knew what my mother, Alastor and even Rosie meant. Bale really was an extraordinary person. He seemed like a strict, serious, intelligent man with a bit of sass and free will, but sometimes he expressed utterly different traits. He also presented to me as being so humane, traumatised, and soft, all at the same time, as if contradicting himself. And I couldn't help but feel I had known him much longer than I thought. My whole body was relaxing near him, my mind gave free rein to my feelings, and a few days of acquaintance seemed an eternity... He frightened me. Frightened me with his mysteriousness and inaccessibility, but still, he seemed familiar.

Our date ended at Bloomsbury Bar, where I sipped delicious cocktails and enjoyed a cosy, intimate setting.

'Did you have a good time?' Bale asked softly, playing with a straw in a glass. Gentle music was playing through the speakers and I shifted in my chair, giving myself up to comfort.

'Yes, thank you,' I nodded and lowered my eyes in embarrassment. What was wrong with me?! Why did my cheeks burn every time I looked at him?

'I'm glad,' he replied as he leaned over the back of the chair and looked out the window by our table, glancing at the nightlights outside. I was surprised to see that time flew so fast with him. I was enchanted by how bright his dark-brown eyes shone in the lantern's light, shimmering with an amber hue as if a fire was playing in them. His beautiful cheekbones were tense, and his neat beard stubble outlined his strong chin.

'Sometimes you have a sorrowful look on your face,' I dared to say, making Bale turn to me. 'Is something bothering you?'

'Everyone is bothered by something,' he replied quietly, smiling sadly. 'I'm just tired.'

'If you work without a break, it'll only get worse.' I rolled my eyes.

Bale just smiled and sighed. What was bothering him? What was he thinking? I was sure he was hiding so much from me, which saddened me. Somehow, I felt selfish for thinking I was the only one with the baggage and troubles in my life. I never really thought that Bale might have a past of his own. Only now did I fully realise, that while I lost my father... Bale lost his friend, his mentor.

☆

The trip home was quiet, the silence between us was a little awkward, and I failed to understand why we'd suddenly become so distant. I didn't think I said anything that would hurt him.

Parking the car at the estate, Bale stared ahead and got lost in deep thought.

'Are you all right?' I asked, tilting my head and trying to look him in the eye.

'You don't have to do this if you don't want to,' he said without turning to me. I blinked. 'Marrying me, I mean.'

'Why would you say that?' I smiled as I turned to him and tried to defuse the situation.

'You don't have to,' he replied, 'and I won't insist. Forget the contract and live as you wish. The debt is paid, and I will not ask for money back.'

'Your impermanence scares me!' I laughed, immediately silent, catching Bale's serious look. What made him change so dramatically?

When he got out of the car, he walked in my direction and opened the door, waiting for me to get out.

'If I let you get close to me further than this, it might hurt you,' Bale said in a sad voice, closing the door behind me.

'Are you implying that I can learn all the dirty secrets you and my mother are trying to "protect" me from?' I made an annoyed snort.

'Perhaps,' he nodded. I flinched at the fact that he didn't deny it.

'I don't approve of your decision—' I frowned, looking straight into Bale's eyes '—but I have no right to pull anything out of you. I hope the time will come for you both to reveal your secrets, knowing that I am not a little girl and quite capable of withstanding the pressure of your dark mystery.'

The pain secretly grew in me, and my heart wanted to scream. I was still in the dark because of these two, which annoyed me. I wanted to believe that I could decide for myself and make my own choices rather than blindly following others' advice.

'I don't want to be a burden to you,' said Bale, 'and I don't want to take away your freedom. I stick to certain rules. You won't get what you're looking for from me. My presence in your destiny has already affected your future, and I don't want to make it worse for you.'

'I don't know what you mean,' I said coldly. 'You suggested this marriage. Why did you change your mind now?'

'I haven't changed my mind,' the man replied quietly. 'I'm only giving you a chance to change yours before I let you come closer to me.'

'What's wrong with that?' I smiled.

'If you get close to the fire,' Bale whispered to me, 'you can get burned.'

'Oh, stop being so cringy! I agreed to this marriage for my own benefit, you know that.'

'I see the way you look at me,' Bale smirked, and I blushed, hating him for being so straightforward, 'and I just want you to be careful.'

'Go to hell!' I snorted. When I took a step forward, I bumped into Bale as he blocked my way.

'I'm already there,' he said, inches away from my face. His voice low and raspy.

'Step away, please. I'm tired,' I cut off, pushing him away with my hand, but he stood firm on his feet, looking down at me thoughtfully from above. 'Bale! I'm not playing these games! Please, step back.'

The estate owner was silent, standing in front of me and still looking into my eyes. It pissed me off even more. *Twatwaffle*! He's teasing and playing with me again! He knew perfectly well that I was embarrassed and that my heart was tumbling in my chest. And for that, I hated him. He read me like a book. He knew what I was thinking and what I wanted. And even so, he stood there with a grin and just tortured me. His eyes expressed uncertainty, and doubt as if he was struggling with himself deep in his heart. What was troubling him so much? Why did he keep me at a distance and not let me get to know him? Why was he afraid to admit that he was attracted to me?

I was eager to avenge him for such audacity, so I grabbed him by the collar of his shirt and pulled him fast, landing a kiss on his lips and feeling a gentle stream of heat on my skin. I was ready to fall through the ground, but it was too late to back down. With my lips moving, I finally got Bale to react, forcing him to open his mouth and respond to my kiss by holding me down and taking the lead. With my hands down on his shoulders and my arms around Bale's neck, I was about to melt, seized by the strong and warm hands of this condescending man that was prepared to suck my soul out with a deep and passionate kiss. His tongue twirled with mine, and I felt my lips getting numb when a sharp tooth bit my lower lip. *Damn, he's so freaking good at this!*

A gentle moan involuntarily escaped from my lips. I panted, inhaling a dizzying scent of pine and smoke that was enveloping him as Bale pulled away from me for just a second before drawing to my side again. He grabbed my hips, lifting me up so that I could wrap my legs around his waist. He sat me on the car's hood, running his hand under my T-shirt and squeezing my waist.

Oh, my God, is this really happening?! My cheeks were burning as if they were scorched. My heart was bursting out of my chest, but my body responded to every touch of this man. His heavy breathing aroused my mind, while Bale's gentle touch burned my skin. I shifted my core closer to him, trying to numb that tight nudging sweet pain down below, hoping to feel his arousal.

I was sure I could now reveal his secret desires by putting my hands under his shirt and feeling a muscular torso with my palms. The butterflies were stuck in my abdomen again, and I sighed a faint sigh, wanting more. I wished to devour him. This man kissed me like no one ever had before, and my deep fantasies were bursting out. Bale took off my jacket, and—

'Sir, there's a conference call waiting for you,' Al's deep voice sounded, and I flinched. Bale refused to tear himself away from my lips, throwing my leather jacket at my bodyguard and waving his hand at him, ordering him to go. Intensifying the kiss, Bale grabbed my face with his broad palms, ignoring the disturbance. 'You're ten minutes late already.'

Finally, Bale moved away and looked at Alastor with a murderous glare. The latter seemed utterly indifferent to what was happening.

'Fuck... Fine!' Belial answered in a husky voice, looking at me briefly as I put my head down and was ready to bury myself in the ground so as not to feel so embarrassed. My cheeks were burning. As well as my whole body. 'Pardon me, I have to go.'

'Uhuh,' I mumbled, nodding and quickly running inside while Bale was fixing his tie. Unphased and with no expression on his face.

I couldn't blame myself for starting to like him. It would be foolish to deny it because he was attractive, smart, and charming. A whole package, I'd say. I was puzzled by the thought of why he gave away an aura of danger sometimes. So, what was hidden in that man that attracted and repelled me simultaneously?

As I pressed my back against my bedroom door, I slid to the floor and buried my face in my knees, trying to calm my heart. My mind repeatedly reminded me of the blissful kiss, and I was ready to burst into a million pieces just to stop thinking about it. My lips were still pulsing from the passionate moment.

'What's wrong with you, Sophie?!' I exclaimed, banging my hand on my forehead.

☆

'You've fallen in love,' Lizzie said monotonically. I dropped a cookie out of my hands and stared at her with a dazed look. Mike choked on his tea and then looked at Lizzie. Paying no attention to fussy Martin behind the counter, I sighed angrily and swiped the crumbs off the table.

'What do you mean?'

'Oh, don't deny it!' The black-haired girl waved her hand. 'Your voice changes when you talk about him, your eyes shine, and your cheeks blush! You have a crush on him, hun.'

'I barely know him, Lizzie, don't be stupid!' I answered strictly, hiding my eyes. Mike nodded positively without interrupting us both.

'So what?' my friend asked. 'You've learned enough about him from other people. Some couples have lived together for years but don't know anything about each other in the end! It's not about time. It's about the impression he made on you in those fleeting moments you had. Besides, he's a spectacular guy, I'd say. I'd be more surprised if you didn't feel attracted to him.'

'And why is he considered attractive by everyone?' Michael sighed with a shake of his head. 'He sounds pretty repulsive to me.'

'Yeah!' I said, and the blond man smiled, rejoicing.

'You wouldn't understand, Mike,' Lizzie waved. 'His energy is repulsive, but his face… has a share of devilish charm in it.'

'Nonsense.' I clenched my hands on my chest and looked at my friend with a touch of resentfulness.

'Why aren't you glad?' Lizzie laughed. 'You're getting married anyway! Well, that's good! She's fallen in love with her own future husband!'

'I'm not in love!' I stood up and banged my hand on the table, moving away and taking care of my clients.

No, I refused to believe it! I couldn't fall in love with him. And denial is a river in Egypt. I mean… I could fall for Bale, but I shouldn't have! I swore that I wouldn't give in to his tricks and lose the game! My purpose was to use him, just like he used me. To fulfil the terms of our contract, to profit and to get rid of the insolent man! That was all!

But instead… my heart seems to have already made a choice. It would be foolish of me to argue with the obvious.

I was falling in love with Bale Deemer.

THE DEVIL'S SIGNATURE: THE ABIDING PACT

CHAPTER SEVEN

As I walked through the majestic halls of the luxurious office building of the Infernum Enterprise, I tried to hide my amazement. The high ceilings, the open plan and the Art Nouveau design gave the hall a real sense of a different world. The glass building was close to the famous Shard skyscraper. Even now, walking on the black marble floor towards Belial Deemer's main office, I could observe an extraordinary architectural marvel. It looked like a giant crystal.

I was met by the company employees' serious looks, noticing their expensive suits and designer dresses while they politely greeted me. Alastor, who accompanied me to my destination, slowly told me about the company, its many departments, and other essential details I had to be aware of.

I learned that Bale had several thousand people under his command, from the smartest engineers in the Department of Technological Development that strolled in designer clothes with their fancy phones and gadgets, to lawyers and accountants in their suits and ties. The central departments included Design, Engineering, Information Technology and Computer Programming, Marketing, Finance and Accounting, Human Resources, Advocacy and many other departments unknown to me.

Going up in the glass elevator to the 40th floor of the building, which seemed to be the top floor, Alastor and I came out into a spacious long hall, both sides of which had open views of the city behind the vast windows. There were a couple of couches and a coffee table in the hall's centre. All this was surrounded by thick vegetation and a small waterfall by the wall. There was absolute silence in the hall, and a smiling secretary in a black dress with wavy red hair gently greeted us and pointed to a double door with behind her back, allowing me and Al to pass.

My bodyguard touched the gold door handle and opened it, revealing a spacious office furnished with exquisite design. The bright floor reflected the sun's rays, which burst into the room through tall windows with an open balcony. A fluffy charcoal-coloured rug spread out in the middle of the office's dark walls, and tall shelving units with many books and magazines surrounded the place. Large marble pots with green topiary trees were placed around the perimeter, surrounding a black leather couch and a pair of armchairs with a wooden coffee table in the centre. There was a glass desk on the other side of the room, where my fiancé sat reviewing documents and checking data on his computer. Modern lighting, with an abstractly decorated ceiling, illuminated the office, and quiet ambience music played in the speakers.

'Thank you, Al,' Bale answered calmly, inviting me to find a comfortable place to sit down. As I slowly got to the couch, I gazed at Al as he bowed and left.

'It's beautiful here,' I said quietly.

'Rebecca, can you get some coffee, please?' Bale pressed the phone button and got an obedient answer from his secretary outside. Soon I was enjoying a hot latte, waiting for Bale to be finished. 'Sorry, I've got a lot to do.'

'It's OK.' I shook my head, showing that I wasn't offended. I avoided looking at this man as events a couple of days ago were spinning in my memory. I was embarrassed by his reaction because Bale didn't seem to have thought about it since, and was acting as usual. He was profoundly serious and distant, making it awkward.

'Are you hungry?' he asked while sitting in front of me and putting some papers on the table. 'I can order lunch.'

'No, thank you,' I answered quietly, clenching my lips and feeling goosebumps over my body. Fuck, he's doing it again! This weird effect of his voice! When would I finally stop reacting to it that way?! The realisation that I was also beginning to experience deep feelings for this insolent man increased my tremor and heartbeat.

Bale didn't insist, immediately changing the subject to my responsibilities and the company itself. The long and tedious explanations about the characteristics of Infernum Enterprises, my personal duties and other nonsense tired me noticeably. The company owner told me how I should understand the content of primary documents, study the marketing structure and get acquainted with the main features of departments and new projects. He also ordered that Alastor would be responsible for my training and assistance.

'Why do I have to try so hard?' I asked tiredly after hours of reading documents and learning complex terminology. 'I'm not going to run your company. Isn't this marriage temporary?'

'Are you so determined that this is just a short-term measure?' Bale raised his eyebrow, and I looked at him in surprise. I did not understand the meaning of his question.

'I...'

'I wouldn't have taught you all this if I didn't expect to see you near me in the future,' my fiancé answered calmly, causing the blush on my cheeks to appear and making me look down. Was he serious? Bale really wanted to extend this marriage and make it completely authentic. 'Your father's helped me a lot, and I'm sure he'd like you to inherit his company. Besides, I need someone to look after the corporation if I'm gone.'

'But... I thought it was just a deal,' I said quietly, sipping a new cup of coffee.

'If that's what you want, I won't hold you back,' said Bale, 'you're free to do whatever you want. But as a precaution, I still want to make sure you know my work as closely as possible if you suddenly change your mind and want to stay a little longer. Or if you just want to be my business partner after the divorce.'

'Why did you change your mind?' I frowned, angry for a reason I didn't know myself. I found his tone offensive and his words insincere. I was uncomfortable with Bale speaking as if this marriage was more of a convenience than a welcome union, even though it was initially a treaty.

'Because I want to see you by my side,' said the man, making me flinch. It was not an answer, more an excuse.

'Why?' I kept insisting.

'What do you want me to say?' He smiled as if he were reading my mind and seeing perfectly well what I was expecting from him. The embarrassment overcame me again, and I put the mug aside, looking into his eyes and keeping silent. 'Do you want me to say that I like you? That I'm in love with you and I don't want you to go?'

'Perhaps,' I answered briefly, overcoming modesty and fear. There was silence, and I began to regret raising the subject. To be honest, it was foolish of me to expect a clear answer from this man, of whom I knew little.

'Why? Do you want to admit that you care about me?' Bale laughed, and I just squinted, biting my lip and keeping quiet. The grin changed to a serious look, and the man stood up from the couch, hiding his hands in his pockets and staring down at me with a disgruntled look. 'Sophie, as I said before, I like you. You're a beautiful girl, intelligent and strong in character. You're attractive, and you deserve more than you have. You have a hidden power in you that you don't even know you have. However, I can't say that I feel anything more for you, and I wouldn't want you to be offended and take it as an insult.'

'Hm.' I smiled disappointedly, wishing to leave this office.

'And no matter how trivial it sounds, it's not your fault,' Bale continued. 'It's just that I pushed love away a long time ago. I don't accept love as a feeling. For me, it's a weakness, a burden, and another opportunity to put myself in danger.'

I clenched my palms and sighed. Strangely, his words sounded as if he genuinely believed what he was saying. These were the thoughts of a man who had once been hurt. It seemed like he couldn't trust anyone, expecting betrayal from everywhere. That fact made me interested in him even more. So, what happened in his past? Who hurt him so severely that he shunned that feeling? Was his father the cause?

'I don't want to live near a man from whom I can't get love in return,' I smiled sadly as I got up from the couch.

'I can't answer you with the same feelings,' Bale said quietly, 'but I can provide you with care, safety, and a good time. And I'm willing to do that until you decide to leave.'

'Isn't that a burden for you?' I raised my voice, turning to him and looking at his guilty eyes. 'Why are you doing this? Why me, Bale? What are you and my mother hiding from me, huh?'

'I promised your father I would take care of you,' the man answered, silencing me. 'I will keep that promise because Jeremy did the impossible for me, and I owe him my life.'

'What did he do for you?! Did he help you start a company? To hell with it!' I snorted, grabbing my bag and heading for the door.

'He died because of me,' the man responded quietly, making me stop and freeze. Did I mishear? Did I understand his words correctly?

'What?' I slowly turned around to my interlocutor.

'The night he died, he was attacked because of me,' Bale continued. 'He had information that would help me change the flow of my life and justify my reputation. He paid for it with his life. I never found out what he wanted to tell me.'

My heart went down to my feet, and I felt my legs weaken. I couldn't believe what I'd heard. All this time, I'd been trying to figure out what my father had done and why was he the victim of someone else's attack. But in the end, the culprit was… Bale. I was only his object of redemption to my father, no more.

The person I was angry with most was my mother, who knew about everything. And despite all that, she pushed me into this marriage and let me get into other people's issues and problems. It wasn't fair.

That kiss… no more than a gust of a moment, an answer to my inner call and a simple attempt to please me. No hidden meaning into which I'd been twisting myself.

Anger was slowly building up in me, and my mind was already thinking of a plan for revenge on everyone who'd played with me. I believed in the fairy tale, hoped for an easy fate and gave in to the impulse. Stupid!

I wanted to hurt this man. To hurt him more, even though I knew well that he had already gone through hell. But I wanted him to burn in the flames of shame, disappointment, and hatred. I refused to be a puppet in the hands of others and wanted to take control. My rage stirred the blood inside me, and I was ready to continue this cruel game.

'The deal,' I suddenly answered, paying attention to Bale, 'is that I will stay by your side for as long as I see fit. I'll look into your company and face the press as your wife. I don't want your care, just financial help. I won't expect anything from you I'm not meant to get.'

'OK,' Bale answered before I opened the

door and left him alone in the office, walking to the elevator and holding back my tears.

It was a tiring month; a stupid waste of time and patience. I was eager to play by my own rules. I'd make that stubborn fool fall to his knees in front of me, begging me to stay. He would burn with excruciating love for me. Bale would desire me and dream of me. And that's when I'd trample him to ashes. It would be my payment for empty hopes, the loss of my father, and deception. It may have been a wrong choice, and I made a cruel decision, but… it was too late to retreat. The evil inside me had woken up.

☆

Looking at my reflection, I lowered my gaze to the lush hem of my wedding dress. I decided to take my game to a different level, so I changed my dress design at the last minute. A week before the wedding, I used all my artistic skills to sew my own wedding gown. Standing in front of the mirror of one of the wedding venues in the South-East of England, with beautiful gardens and a view of an ocean, I stared at the black velvet on my wedding dress. It was a result of hard work and a few sleepless nights, but I was proud of my gown.

I collected a few black feathers from Bale's library that were scattered on the floor and under the furniture. I never understood where they came from, but they were the perfect décor for my craft. These feathers were covering my breasts and part of my back, hiding only those parts of my body that were bound to be hidden. The feathery bodice dissolved into a lush black velvet in a luxurious floating skirt with black lace and dark pearls. My outfit was as black as my soul inside.

My hair fell freely on my shoulders with chestnut curls tickling my neck. My face showed a smile, and my eyes… they were cold, indifferent, and expressed a detached look.

'You're beautiful, dear.' Astrid smiled as she fixed my dress and held back tears in her eyes. She didn't dispute my choice of attire. I quietly thanked her and asked her to leave me alone for a moment so that I could gather my thoughts and finally go outside to meet my future.

Looking at myself in the mirror for the last time, I said a goodbye to the Sophie I once knew. I followed my decision and refused to back down. I wanted vengeance.

Turning away from the mirror, I slowly plunged into the darkest part of my soul. My insides, for a reason unknown to me, thirsted for violence, and cruelty. I wanted to grab my black shoe with its golden heel and stick it into Bale Deemer's heart. My reflection slowly acquired a wild grin, bright eyes dimmed, and it seemed to me that a different person was standing in the mirror for a second. I wanted to destroy everything around me, create chaos, and make everything burn with a bright fire. My desire seemed so strong that the mirror suddenly cracked, and I shuddered, instantly coming to my senses.

'Hey,' Mike looked out the door, blushing and opening his mouth, gawking at me. Smiling in embarrassment, he came closer and examined me head to toe. 'You look magnificent.'

'Thank you,' I answered, raising the corners of my mouth in a fake smile.

'Unusual choice of colour. Are you all right?' he asked me anxiously, touching my chin and raising my head so that I could look him in the eye. I just nodded and sighed. 'You don't have to do this if you don't want to.'

'I want to,' I answered immediately, with my eyes down. Michael looked at me silently and seemed to be thinking about something. Maybe he wished he'd stopped me earlier, or perhaps he'd let it all happen from the beginning. Maybe he also wished he had been on the other side of the altar where the man I hated was waiting for me, the one my heart was still reaching for, contradicting my mind. 'It's time…'

'Yes,' Mike answered, hugging me tightly and trying to comfort me with his warmth.

Tense, I frowned and squeezed my lips, trying not to let the old feelings reappear and give in to the moment. Mike took a deep breath, inhaling the fragrance of my perfume and shuddering slightly, slowly pulling away from me and stopping an inch away from my face. I noticed his blushing cheeks, blurred gaze and inner struggle with himself.

'I don't know what it is, but there's something inside you that I can't resist. Your aura has visibly changed, and I can no longer fight it.'

'Mike,' I said softly, trying to take a step back, but he held my shoulders firmly and leaned forward, rushing towards my lips and making my heart beat stronger. Panicking and desperately trying to decide what to do next, I was ready to give up and close my eyes. Still, a sharp memory of the dark-brown eyes staring at me made me turn my head to the side, not letting Michael kiss me. Embarrassed and guilty, he looked at me and pulled away, muttering his apology. I only smiled slightly and sent him away, making an excuse that he was just swept away by my dress and didn't know what he was doing. Closing the door behind him, I lowered my head, soothing my heart and putting my thoughts in order.

'Come on, Sophie, pull yourself together!' I barked at myself, slamming my palms on my cheeks, standing up, opening the doors, and taking a step forward. It was time...

As I squeezed a bouquet of blood-red roses in my hands, I held my head high. My steps were smooth, confident, and slow. The closer I got to the altar, the louder my heart was beating. My eyes were locked on Bale and his smirk as he saw me. His eyes were those of a predator. He observed me with his brown eyes, looking me up and down and squinting. He noticed my sudden change in the outfit, but his look seemed to show that he approved of it. Hell, it seemed to me that he was proud of it for a moment! What a prick...

He reached his hand to me, and I took it with displeasure.

'Love the dress, sweetheart,' he whispered when we turned our backs to everyone. I gulped. He glanced at the black feathers on my dress that covered my breasts. 'Where'd you find those?'

'Your library was full of these,' I snapped. 'Any problem with it?'

'Oh, if only you knew what they are,' he whispered back, snickering. I frowned and didn't honour him with a reply.

Looking at the horizon behind the priest's back, saying our vows as he spoke of a marriage blessed in heaven before God, I noticed a slight dissatisfaction in Bale's eyes at the edge of my eye and only smirked, amazed at his impatience. If this man was so sceptical of religious traditions, why would he insist on this show in front of so many paparazzi and unknown guests?

Having listened patiently to the whole tirade, I finally leaned over the contract and put a neat signature under my name. It was Bale's turn, and with a beautiful hand movement, he put his signature, attracting my attention. The smooth autograph depicted the graceful letter 'L,' followed by an 'i,' 'o,' and 'r.' As I raised my eyebrow, I whispered the name 'Lior' with my lips for the first time. I wonder if that was his second name? As soon as Bale's hand lifted off the contract, I suddenly froze, noticing the signature shine with golden light. Looking at the priest, who wasn't expressing any emotion and looking at the guests, I thought I had imagined it.

The union was made, the contract was signed, and now I was Sophie Angela Mortis-Deemer.

Closing my eyes, I felt a dry kiss on my lips. I immediately pulled away after Bale had done his duty and now looked into the cameras held by journalists and bloggers. 'I hate you', I suddenly thought, and I noticed my husband's fleeting gaze on me. I looked away, clenching my lips.

It was done. I was married and had become a legal co-owner of Infernum Enterprise. Now I was the subject of constant public interest, and my every move could be reflected in the press. Brilliant...

Dearest mother began embracing Bale and me, allowing other guests to come to us with congratulations. Acting with insincere joy, I politely accepted kind words and wishes. With embarrassment in my eyes, I shook Michael's hand and noticed his angry look directed at Bale. My husband didn't back down either, smiling while squeezing Mike's hand painfully.

Mara also attended our wedding for a reason unknown to me. The woman was standing in the distance by the bar, talking to Rosie about something. To my surprise, they both seemed like good friends. Fleeting jealousy suddenly seized me, and I looked at the other half of the guests, whom I didn't know.

Lizzie threw herself in my direction, circling beside me and enthusiastically telling Roberto about my dress. At the same time, he politely greeted me and congratulated me.

The feast was in full swing, and I slowly gave in to the cheerful atmosphere. Tired of waving my hand at the guests passing by, I slowly moved my gaze to the next visitor, flinching and opening my mouth.

'Congratulations, Sophie,' said the green-eyed man in a deep voice that I already knew. The same tall brown-haired man with a scar on his face had come to our café before.

'Raf, good to see you,' Bale smiled, shaking the man's hand and hugging him, tapping his back. I was surprised to see both of them so friendly, seeing the stranger's keen gaze when he looked at me from head to toe. 'Sophie, I'd like you to meet my brother, Raphael.'

'Brother?' I was surprised. Here's some news for you.

'We rarely see each other because he lives far away from here, but sometimes this long-lost relative does visit his little brother.' Bale laughed. I noticed sincere joy in his eyes for the first time. It was fascinating.

'Let me apologise for my manners last time,' Raphael said gallantly, looking at me with his emeralds, 'I take those around my brother very seriously. And when I heard that he was about to get married, I just had to check on his chosen one.'

'It's OK,' I said uncertainly, accepting his apologies and watching both brothers discussing something amusing. It took me a long time to look into Bale's eyes and see the joy and love I had never seen before. So he could still smile like that... It was a shame he only felt that way about his brother. Raphael's fleeting gaze made me shudder and become wary again. Something about this guy was odd. At first, he radiated an aura of arrogance and overrated self-esteem. He was most likely a skilful ladies' man by the looks of it. Although it was probably the result of our first encounter, now he seemed the absolute opposite. At least everything was falling into place now.

The evening was in full swing. Guests were gathered at the feast, and music played. Downing my glass of wine, I sighed tiredly and flinched when Bale stood up from his chair next to me and placed his hand in front of me. I stared at him with a question in my eyes.

'Would you honour me with a first dance?' He smiled, and I gulped, hating his pretentious act. Placing my hand into his palm, I followed my husband onto the dance floor. I was sure he knew I was a skilled dancer, as I'd practised with my father just for fun. The music changed, and I felt his firm grip on my waist. My cheeks flushed, but I continued to stare at him.

He made a step to the side, and I followed. He moved to another side, and I repeated. He gently lowered his hand, sliding from my waist to my arm and allowing me to spin around my axis, then placed his palm on my waist again. Tango. So stereotypical. He was testing me. I smirked inside. I joined the game and stepped towards him, allowing my body to touch his as my dress followed us in the passionate dance. I felt my cheeks flush once again as he tickled the back of my neck with his fingers and placed his palm on my back, bending me backwards and staring into my eyes. He was trying to fluster me. However, I was competitive enough to get back up, squeezing his hand and lifting my leg while slowly rubbing it at him. I opened my lips and allowed my face to get close to his, for him to feel my breath, my heat. I felt his shiver. And I smirked. We got lost in this endless play, dizzy and eager for each other's touch. Circling around the hall as if it were just the two of us, I was sure this man was the Devil in disguise. And I wanted to submit to his power, his fire. His moves got desperate, his hands squeezed me tighter, and his face flushed with desire, wild passion, and dominance.

'I would ravish you right here in front of everyone,' he whispered in my ear, and I felt his grip tighten. And oh God, I wanted to allow him any bold fantasy. Just for a moment. For a split second, his lips were less than an inch from mine. 'I'd keep the dress on, love.'

And as quick as this dance got to a heated level, the moment fled with the music. And I was left to my own desire once more.

The sun hid behind the horizon, and I left my seat discreetly. I took off my heels and walked on the wet grass, raising the hem of my dress and stepping onto a small stone bridge by the pond near our event. I sighed, looked up into the sky, and got lost in thoughts as I walked across the bridge. I wasn't a believer, but somewhere deep in my heart, I hoped my dad would see me and enjoy my wedding. Who knew, maybe Heaven did exist, and he smiled at me from there, hiding behind cotton clouds.

'Are you looking for angels?' There was a light chuckle behind my back, startling me and making me trip, almost falling into a pond. A firm hand held me by my forearm and pulled me back, allowing me to stand firmly on my feet.

'R-Raphael!' I exhaled, thanking him for the help and gently taking a step back.

'I'm sorry, I didn't mean to scare you,' he laughed, and his beautiful face suddenly acquired a different, unfamiliar shade. For the first time, I found this man charming, and his features were similar to those of Bale, his skin was darker though. 'So, what are you doing here alone, running away from your wedding and looking for answers in the clouds? Asking angels to grant wishes?'

'Hm,' I laughed, 'unfortunately, I don't believe in angels.'

'Really?' Raphael was surprised and looked up at the sky, thoughtful.

'Do you believe in these things?' I was amazed, slowly glancing at him. The man didn't answer, looking at me with a smile and mysteriously shrugging his shoulders. 'You should meet my friend Michael. You'd get along.'

'Is that the one who spends a lot of time in the church?' Raf laughed, and I nodded approvingly. 'We know each other.'

'Eh?' I opened my mouth and raised my eyebrows.

'I often visit God and have seen your friend more than once,' Raf replied. 'A lovely young man.'

'Amazing,' I said. 'Is Bale visiting with you too?'

'Oh, no,' Raf waved, smiling, 'my brother has a special kind of resentment for God, and he ignores his existence in pure principle.'

'Why is he so offended?' I asked quietly.

Raf suddenly got a serious look and pressed his lips. I understood that I'd asked something I shouldn't have.

'Everyone has their reasons,' Raf answered wisely and smiled again, 'but Bale sins by vengeful personality and rarely forgives.'

'Lucky me…' That made Raphael smirk. It seemed that this man was not as bad as I thought. When I got to know him better, I thought he was pretty pleasant.

'Are you trying to steal my wife?' There was a familiar voice behind our backs, and Raphael and I turned around, looking at tired Bale walking in our direction.

'It's a sin not to steal such beauty,' Raf said, smiling, and making me blush.

'It's true,' my husband gently agreed, and my heart missed a beat for a second. Damn it! Calm down, Sophie! 'Would you leave us alone, please?'

'Don't burn her with your flame,' Raf replied, winking at his brother and patting him on the shoulder as he moved away. Bale's eyebrow raised, and he glanced at his brother as if he were sending him a mental stream of curses in response.

'How are you?'

'Very tired,' I sighed as I looked up at the horizon and groaned from the evening chill. A warm jacket fell on my shoulders, and I looked at Bale, surprised, while he was not even looking at me, continuing to stand aside. 'Thank you.'

'Do you hate me?' he suddenly asked, taking me by surprise and giving me the creeps. The heat from his jacket was burning my body, and a slight scent of his cologne mixed with the usual aroma of pine made my head dizzy. I didn't answer. 'I'm used to it, don't worry.'

'Sometimes, I get the feeling that you're

not who you say you are,' I said quietly as I looked at my bare feet.

'Maybe you're right,' he said, and I frowned. 'I'd hate for you to know my secrets.'

'Are you afraid I'd tell someone?' I laughed.

'No, I'm afraid I'd scare you away and that you'd hate me more.' He looked at me, and I gazed into his brown eyes. What did he mean by that? What were these terrible secrets lurking in his heart that could frighten me?

'Are you a vampire?' I blurted out, genuinely surprising Bale and making him laugh.

'Well, that's unexpected!' He kept laughing. 'You don't honestly believe in vampires, do you?'

'Don't you?' I was surprised, relieved and calmed down. Well, one thing I found out for sure is that Bale wasn't planning on drinking all my blood and turning into a bat.

'Don't be silly—' my husband shook his head '—there are no vampires. Of course, some individuals are fond of drinking human blood, but they do not sleep in the coffin or fry in the sun.'

'Then what's so terrible about you?' I raised my eyebrow. 'Do you have a weird fetish? A hidden basement where you torture your victims? Are you a serial killer?'

'Hm. Basement, you say? Your creative mind amazes me.' Bale shook his head and waved his hand. 'Not exactly.'

'Then what?' I asked impatiently, standing in front of him and looking straight into his eyes. Mr Deemer's face got a serious shade, and he smiled with sadness in his eyes.

'It's much more terrifying than that…'

I never got the answer. Interrupted by jolly Lizzie and Roberto, Bale and I returned to the feast, forgetting our conversation. In fact, pretending to have forgotten.

I never dared to go back to this topic, even when we were on the first-class flight to Venice on our honeymoon. My intuition was eager to ensure I didn't ask for additional information from Bale. Something told me I'd rather not know his secret. It wasn't about the danger. It was about the burden. His secret seemed too heavy. Maybe that's why he was so desperate to keep me from himself. Was that the reason my mother kept silent? Did she know that I couldn't bear the truth and it would hurt me? I never understood what was expected of me…

CHAPTER EIGHT

Venice was considered to be one of the most romantic cities, and it really was. The emotional atmosphere here was enchanting and mesmerising. There was peace and quiet in the streets, disturbed only by the screams of lonely seagulls, the rustling waves, the sound of the bells of St. Mark's Cathedral and the melodic singing of gondoliers.

Locals started their morning with a cup of aromatic espresso. Its scent hovered in the air almost around the clock, as every meal at any restaurant or café traditionally ended with a refreshing drink.

Here I was, sitting on the veranda of our cosy hotel room, enjoying an evening cup of coffee. My honeymoon with Bale was quite short, taking only a few days, as my busy husband had to return to work and leave London soon for another business trip. That's why I was content with my last night in Venice while my husband thoughtfully read through documents and signed contracts in the next room. That's how these few days passed. We only went out a couple of times for lunch and walked around the city almost in silence, and in the evenings, I was alone while Bale dived into work.

When we arrived, I was perplexed because our room had only a king-size bed. Still, I soon realised that only one of us was going to sleep because Bale didn't even touch the pillow, sometimes falling asleep in a chair at the table. On the one hand, I felt sorry for him, but on the other... it annoyed me. Even though I knew his intentions and unwillingness to love me, my pride was hurt.

I considered myself quite an attractive young lady and did not want to accept the indifferent attitude of my husband. No one forced him to declare his love to me... at least not now. A well-spent passionate night could relax both of us, especially if I was meant to be married to an insolent bastard for a long time. My youth was fragrant, and I demanded attention!

My mother went to the United States, claiming she had to make a final payment agreement for my father's company, so I had as much fun as possible.

Having worked out a seduction plan for my husband, I made sure to borrow his shirt for the night, as it barely covered my bottom, as was required for my devious plan.

'You're not going to bed?' I asked uninterested, passing Bale and pouring myself a glass of water by the dresser.

'I have a lot of work to do,' he replied without taking his eyes off the papers. I snorted, downing the contents of my glass and putting it loudly on the dresser, getting his attention to myself. Bale looked up, gazing at me from head to toe without changing his face and again paying attention to the documents.

Stubborn bastard, I thought, with my lips pressed and walking back to the bedroom.

'Do you ever sleep?' I asked with a sneer. I finally got the reaction as my husband took off his glasses and rubbed his nose, raising his gaze at me and tiredly leaning on the back of the chair. His lips curled in a smile, and I frowned.

'Do you want me to go to bed with you?' He raised his eyebrow, and I proudly perked my nose up.

'Not at all.'

'Oh, I think that's exactly what you want. Are you trying to seduce me?' The smile touched his lips again. All I did was blush and snort a little, turning away. 'I thought I told you I wouldn't touch you unless you begged, dear.'

'Ha! Is that why you threw yourself at me that night and were prepared to take me right by the car?' I snapped. He tried to blame me for being insolent. Bale got up and slowly walked towards me, making me tense.

'You kissed me first. I only did what you wanted me to do,' he replied, looking at me provocatively, buttoning up my shirt. I frowned again and held back the urge to slap him. He was playing with me again, but I wouldn't give in this time!

'Burn in Hell!' I sizzled and got even angrier when Bale smiled again, tilting his head and biting his lip. He was playing with me! I slammed the door in front of his nose and jumped on the bed, burying myself under the blanket and cursing my husband.

Even though I had hoped deep in my heart that he would come in, I was deeply disappointed the next morning when I woke up alone.

No, that's absurd! He knew that despite the deal, we were both drawn to each other, but he refused on principle to even touch me. And that was after two months of getting to know each other, a very passionate kiss, a wedding and a definite hint of his interest in me! He tried to break me, but how wrong he was! I was not going to give in to his pressure and was ready to continue the war.

☆

'Maybe he's gay?' whispered Lizzie, making Michael laugh as he sat next to us. He immediately shut up, seeing my murderous look. 'What?! He doesn't sleep with you, gets married for his own good, takes care of his looks... it all hints at that.'

'That's such a poor stereotype, Lizzie! He kissed me!' I whispered, interrupting my friend and making Mike embarrassed.

'Hm, only when you first threw yourself at him!' Lizzie took a glimpse at him. 'He's covering his tracks! He's trying to prove otherwise!'

'You kissed him? Like... really kissed him?' Mike seemed to turn pale. I ignored his anxiety. 'Did anything happen after? Are you OK?'

'What are you talking about?' I curved my eyebrow and looked at Lizzie.

'You didn't get sick, or hurt?' the blond man went on, and I smiled.

'Mike, are you serious right now?' I snorted.

'I'm telling you, he's not interested in you,' Lizzie shrugged.

'Don't be silly,' I rolled my eyes, 'I could have sworn that if it hadn't been for Al at that moment, he would have undressed me right there! The way he kissed me... no one's kissed me that way before. It was so damn good!'

Michael choked on coffee and blushed. I

looked at him reproachfully and shook my head. So childish, honestly!

'I don't know, I don't know...' Lizzie snorted.

No, I refused to believe what she said. I knew that Bale was very interested in women, otherwise that bitch Mara wouldn't be hanging around him in that penthouse. It hurt me even more because I knew for a fact that he'd had several sexual relationships. However, he refused to sleep with me! It was an insult to me. It also prevented me from fulfilling my plan to make him fall in love with me and break his heart.

☆

Thoughtfully looking at my husband sitting across from me at the dinner table, I was slowly trying to finish my steak. My head refused to think of anything else. I demanded an explanation.

'Al,' I reluctantly called my bodyguard who was standing at the door.

'Yes, ma'am?' He came forward, looking at me. I stared at the plate and sighed.

'How many women has Bale had before me?' I asked straight, forcing my husband to look up at me and get distracted from the newspaper. Alastor looked at me in surprise.

'A lot, ma'am,' Al answered honestly, making me smile and Bale frown, looking reproachfully at the indifferent Al.

Hm, a lot, then. He chose me as his wife, expressing his gratitude to my father. However, he wouldn't come close to me. I'd heard that sometimes men deliberately hid their hidden interests behind fleeting nights with women so as not to reveal their actual preferences. Perhaps that was the terrible secret he was hiding from me? He wasn't a vampire. He's not a fetishist...

Gay, I thought, and Bale suddenly choked on a glass of water. Looking at me with an insulted look, he threw the paper aside.

'I'm not gay!' he responded loudly, causing a tight smile to show up on Al's lips.

'I didn't say...'

'But you thought about it!' He stood up from the table. I couldn't even find a word in return, believing sincerely that he'd read my mind. 'It's written on your face! Enough with your assumptions! Woman, what's your problem?!'

'You're my problem!' I burst out, looking at the plate again. Bale's eyes closed when he started rubbing his temples and waving his hand towards Al, asking him to leave the dining room. The bodyguard stepped out, but I could hear him behind the door.

'Sophie, what do you want from me?' I was tired of him asking.

'Nothing,' I shrugged, lying.

'Why do you want me to climb up your skirt so bad?!'

'It's not what I want!' I was embarrassed, standing up from the table and throwing the napkin to the side. 'I just don't understand why you're not even trying. I understand what you said then, and I know you're not interested in a relationship, so be it! I just don't understand your inconsistency!'

'Sophie...'

'You know very well how I feel about you! It's the result of your wicked games and your manipulation! First, you let me hope that there might be something more than an empty contract between us. But then you ruin all hope with your detachment and your drama. I'm like a toy in your hands that gives in to your mood and impulses.' As I walked past Bale, I punched him on the shoulder and looked at him fiercely. 'You forget that even though you avoid serious feelings, it doesn't mean that others don't feel them! You're talking about care and protection, but you're holding me in a bind, giving me conflicting feelings and doubts. Either set clear boundaries and do not play with me, or tear up this crappy contract and let me go! I'm not a little girl; I'm sure I'll survive the truth, and I'll make a decision that I think is right for me!'

'Sophie!' He grabbed my hand before I left the room. Al opened the door and quietly waited for my further actions. Clenching my fists and stopping, I looked down and waited patiently for Bale's excuses. Despite my anger and hatred for this man, I still wanted to hear his reasons. It was as if a spark of hope was still bothering me. And it made me angry, for the very contradiction tormented me. It made me regret my decision to play with fire, but it still made me fall deeper and deeper into this abyss.

I was in love with him. Hardly, irrevocably. But the lack of returned feelings, that I got used to, burned me from the inside. First, it was Michael. Now it's him. Bale wouldn't push me away ultimately, but he wouldn't let me in. It was this competition between the two sides that weighed me down. For the first time, I was grateful to Michael for rejecting me clearly, because I didn't have any doubts about being rejected by him. Bale was different...

'Sorry,' Bale said quietly, 'you're right.'
'What?' I flinched.
'You're right.' He repeated it when I turned to him. 'I shouldn't play with you. I promised your father not to tell you the truth about what surrounds you. And so far, both I, your mother, and even your

father have successfully kept you from what was happening. However, I can see that you won't rest until you get some answers. I knew this day would come sooner or later.'

'What are you talking about?' I frowned, feeling that I had touched the forbidden subject and would soon regret it.

'I'll tell you what you're so eager to know,' Bale answered, and I noticed how Alastor looked up at his master and flinched. 'And I'm sure I'll regret it, for the information you will hear will be a heavy burden on you. It will completely change your view of life, your opinion of yourself, and your nature.'

'What are you talking about?'

'What if I told you that the world around you is only a fragment of reality?' Belial's eyes were squinting.

'You scare me…' I whispered, trying to get my hand out of his firm palm. Bale leaned forwards and whispered in my ear, giving me the creeps.

'You don't know what fear is. And I'll show it to you.'

I froze at his deep, almost inhuman voice. Bale rushed to the door with the last glimpse at my frightened eyes, 'Before we can talk, I have to stop by the sponsors' meeting. You're coming with me.'

'Yes,' I nodded, not even daring to argue with him at the moment. Bale's personality seemed to have changed completely. It was the first time he'd shown the frightening look that made the blood freeze in my veins. His voice was firm and persistent. My gut did not even dare to contradict him. By obediently following him, I prepared myself mentally for the worst. The truth was close, but I suddenly wanted to run away, and forget about trying to solve all the mysteries. What did I sign up for?

☆

Waiting for my unknown fate in complete silence, gripped by fear and uncertainty, I sat on a leather sofa in the middle of an empty apartment in the Shard building in central London. Several floors below, Bale Deemer was finishing his conference. Alastor stood silently at the door, allowing me to gather my thoughts, which was not comforting. I didn't even dare ask him what was expected of me.

I shuddered at the knock on the door, and I glanced sharply at Al as he turned to the entrance and opened it. I saw him fall to the floor after a loud shot, grabbing his chest and bleeding out. Fear and shock completely enveloped me, and I jumped off the couch.

'Al!!' I screamed, immediately rushing to the bodyguard. Three strangers broke into the apartment, one of whom took a couple more shots before Al stopped moving. In disbelief, I covered my mouth with my hand and held back my tears, rushing away to another room. The uninvited guests followed me, spreading out into the rooms. I crawled behind the sofa in the bedroom as one of the men searched under the bed and ran back into the living room, rushing to the open front door. Realising that I had left my phone, my shoes, and all the hope for salvation behind, I glimpsed at Alastor's lifeless body in the puddle of blood and rushed away in fear.

The group of intruders noticed my escape and ran after me, chasing me down long corridors until I ran to the fire escape and set off the fire alarm on the way, forcing the guards and others present to start evacuating, buying myself some time.

As I went downstairs, I noticed two men coming up, which seemed to be in the same group as my pursuers. Their eyes were black, and their blue shade skin resembled the man who had attacked me at home. Pointing at me and speeding up the pace, they made me rush back upstairs, looking for a way out. To my great regret, I was surrounded, as two more men were already waiting for me from above.

Giving myself up to panic and fright, I squeezed into a corner and grabbed the fire extinguisher that was hanging near me. I was not gonna give myself alive, that's for sure! Reflecting the attack of one of the intruders, I kicked him in the face with the extinguisher, throwing him aside. Taking my chance and running past the wounded man, I opened the fire door. I found myself again in one of the corridors that led to a vast hall with a crystal chandelier. Coming down the stairs of the spacious lobby, I stopped to see one of the criminals' weapons raised in front of me.

'Don't move!' he screamed when I took a step back and looked up, noticing the other three coming down to grab me, surrounding me in the middle of the hall. Squeezing the railing, I was ready to throw myself forward. Anywhere but standing still!

However, right before me, someone pushed my assailant aside, taking the gun and shooting him in the head. A black smoke-like consistency left the attacker's body and disappeared. Alastor stood before me alive and unharmed, only in a bloodstained shirt.

'Al!' I exclaimed in shock. 'But how? I saw it—'

'Sophie, look out!' Alastor interrupted me by pulling me towards him and shooting a man running behind my back. Looking at Al as if he was a ghost, I froze in mute shock. It was my mistake because while my bodyguard was fighting off a group of assailants, I was grabbed from behind and dragged without the possibility to get up. Feeling pain in my head from being pulled by my hair, I resisted by scratching my abuser's hands and bruising him.

'Al! AL!!!' I shouted in panic, drawing my friend's attention to myself, pushing the bandits away and rushing to me. Still, I knew he wouldn't make it because a gun had already been put to my head, and my heart stopped.

Suddenly there was a blow, and I felt incredibly relieved when my hair was let go. Crawling forwards in a hurry, I turned around and met Bale, who grabbed one of the men's throats and twisted that man's neck right in front of me.

'Get up!' he growled, helping me get back on my feet and pushing me forward. I didn't know what was going on anymore. The hall's door suddenly swung open, and Bale and I turned around. There was another shot, and I saw my husband falling to the floor with a bullet in his head. When I looked back, I was confused. I didn't even digest the fact that he was... dead. Bale was dead.

Run... where? What to do?!

Panic. Fear. Despair.

'*You bastard, I'll burn you alive!*' Bale's deep baritone was heard, with notes of growl. Staring at the silhouette of my husband, I lost any ability to speak when Bale stood up with his head down. Slowly, confidently, unharmed. It wasn't the fact that he was alive that surprised me. It was something else. Bale Deemer's wavy hair hung on his face, and a pair of long sharp horns shone on his head in the light of a dim chandelier. As I opened my mouth, I took a step back as he slowly raised his head, taking off his jacket. My body was suddenly seized by an indescribable horror. The usual brown eyes I had been dreaming of every night lately had acquired a golden hue. In these eyes, the fire was burning, shining with an amber shade. I knew these eyes...

The bullet mark on Bale's forehead disappeared like it had never happened. Bale straightened his back in a bright haze resembling a blue flame, and I was covered in a cold sweat as two lush black wings spread out of the blue fire behind his back, tearing his shirt apart. The beastly, murderous look was locked on my abuser, and I couldn't even move. This indescribable spectacle was truly terrible and beautiful.

A desperate attacker tried to throw himself at Bale. Still, Mr Deemer stopped him with one movement of his hand, grabbing the man by his face and making his body catch fire with a bright flame. Another stranger tried to grab a weapon from the floor. Bale only raised his hand, and the villain got thrown into the air as if at the command of a single movement of the beast. The stranger flew to the side, breaking his spine from the collision with the railing near the stairs.

Seeing Al fighting the group, I threw myself in horror at another door that led to the stairs of the observation deck of the 'Shard' building. Soaked in water from the sprinklers, I trembled with fear and cold, in shock, rushing to rescue, though I knew deep inside that there was no way out. As I heard the footsteps behind me, I stormed into the site, shaking from the strong wind outdoors.

Hiding behind one of the columns underneath the glass, beyond which I could see the whole city, I tried to cope with the fear of heights and turned my head away.

The intruder broke in and desperately started looking for me while I slowly sneaked behind the columns. When he noticed me, he fired a shot, making one of the glass sides near me crack.

Desperate to survive the night, I swore to never do anything reckless again and to never accept arranged marriage proposals. Bale Deemer wasn't human, and I regretted being so eager to learn his secret. Now I had no way back. I was terrified. I was a part of something unexpected.

'*Found you!*' The mentioned beast grinned angrily, grabbing my pursuer and throwing him aside with one easy movement towards the cracked glass, causing it to break into pieces. Bale raised his hand and forced my abuser up into the air. Turning his clawed hand and making the man scream in pain, grabbing his chest and begging for mercy, for the man's heart was shrinking, and his body was covered in bright fire. Bale lowered his hand, and the man fell, screaming with nausea, tripping over the shards, and losing his balance. He flew down, and I was left alone, gasping on the roof with my nightmare.

With trembling feet, I tried to stand still, looking at Bale. He was silent in front of me. The rain started, washing away my tears. The velvety feathers of his black wings moved in the wind, his eyes shining in the light of the city's nightlights, his look expressing regret, anger, and anxiety. He knew. He felt that I was afraid of him.

'*Sophie*,' he said softly, raising his hand, but I immediately took a step back.

'Stay back!' I screamed, panicking and ready to burst into tears. What the hell was going on?! It couldn't be true. Such things didn't exist! 'Stay back…'

'*Sophie, I…*'

'What are you?!' I exclaimed, shaking my head in denial. I was still hoping to wake up looking through those golden eyes. Tears flowed treacherously down my cheeks, and I sobbed with my hands covering my mouth.

'*The Devil,*' Bale answered briefly with his hand down. I couldn't understand him, so I stared at him and smiled nervously. *I'm sorry, what?* Did I mishear? '*I'm the Devil, Sophie. Satan, Lucifer, Samael, Shaitan, the evil of this world. Call it what you want.*'

'What?' I whispered, putting my hands down and taking another step back.

'I told you it was better for you to not know.' He smiled sadly and spoke in his usual voice, making a step forward. 'I won't hurt you...'

'Stay back!' I stopped him, putting my hand forwards and taking a step back again, forgetting where I was. I immediately realised my mistake. As I stepped on the shards of broken glass with my bare feet, I felt weightless, and my heart suddenly stopped when my body dived down from the building.

I never realised how tall the Shard was.

In despair, as I stretched my hand forwards and allowed the scream to escape from my lungs, I rushed to the ground, feeling dizzy and fearing the inevitable death. People say that all your life flashes before you when you die, but all I thought about was not wanting to die. Not now.

No, I'm not ready!

The glimmering lights of the skyscraper and windows blended together, and I stared upward, noticing the worried look of a dark angel that had stretched his arms forwards in an attempt to grab me while flying down. Trusting my instinct, I pulled my hands towards him, allowing my monster to reach me with his strong hands, soaring up, waving his stunning wings the colour of the night sky.

Clutching his neck to feel safe, I looked

silently over his tattooed back, feeling the feathers tickle my fingers. The lights of the night city swallowed us both, and the dark sky covered us with its starry canvas and grey, puffy clouds as my Devil parried amidst them, slowly sinking to the outlines of Hyde Park.

Bale stepped aside silently, leaving me on the ground on my shaking legs, allowing me to get my space. Staring at him with a frightened look, full of misunderstanding, distrust, and despair, I shuddered as he sat down on the grass and lowered his wings, looking away, letting me gather my thoughts.

I was scared. Terribly scared. I wanted to escape that nightmare, so I rushed away, running into an empty road and catching a taxi passing by. Locking the door and clasping into the seat, naming the address, I looked out the window in fear, wiping my tears and seeing the dark silhouette of the winged creature that had soared into the night sky and disappeared into the darkness.

THE DEVIL'S SIGNATURE: THE ABIDING PACT

CHAPTER NINE

Freezing and soaked to the bone, I trembled at the entrance of Maio Manor, standing at the doorstep. A beautiful house in traditional Japanese style stretched before me, bringing the atmosphere of antiquity, calmness, and peacefulness.

Yawning, Lizzie opened the door abruptly, staring at me with fright and surprise. She looked at me from head to toe and threw herself at me, anxiously looking around, hoping to see my abuser.

'Sophie! Look at you!!' the girl exclaimed, pulling me forwards into the house. 'You're all soaked! What's happened?'

'Who's there?' The voice of Lizzie's grandmother was heard from upstairs.

'It's OK, oba-san, it's Sophie!' my friend answered.

'T-Taxi…' I uttered with a hoarse, barely audible voice, sobbing with the last of my strength. Realising that I had never paid for the taxi, for I had no money.

Lizzie grabbed her bag from the chest of drawers at the entrance. She dug up her purse, ran out of the house and gave the driver the long-awaited cash.

As she walked me inside, Lizzie locked the door, making the little wind chimes ring, and took me further into her room, immediately towelling me in and wiping my wet hair.

'You look terrible, Sophie,' whispered Lizzie, sitting on her knees in front of me and stroking my lap in comfort, looking into my tearful eyes and frightened face. 'What has happened?'

'The Devil...' I whispered with my lips alone.

'What?' Lizzie shuddered and frowned.

'Lizzie...' my voice suddenly shook, and tears flowed down my cheeks again. 'He... he is the Devil...'

'Sophie,' my friend sighed, hugging me and stroking my head, 'did he hurt you? Did he hurt you?'

'No.' I shook my head, clutching my friend's shirt and refusing to let it out of my hands. I needed warmth and comfort. I didn't even know what to think. 'He... he is a real... Devil.'

'Sophie, what do you mean?' Lizzie looked me in the eye again.

'It is true, Lizzie.' Tears were overflowing, and I cried out loud, praying that it would all be a nightmare. 'Everything you have said is true! Demons, spirits, and this... this monster!'

Realising that it was pointless to try and drag some useful information out of me, Lizzie changed me into dry clothes. She covered me with a blanket and brought me some hot camomile tea, sitting next to me and waiting until my hysteria had subsided and I could gather my thoughts.

When I told my friend about the terrible night, I saw her eyes getting wider and more serious. She believed me instantly, and it made me even more scared. Telling her how I had seen Alastor's lifeless body in front of me, which was almost untouched in the end, only confirmed Lizzie's theory that he was not human. Neither was Bale...

'Sophie, calm down,' whispered Lizzie, 'the demons won't get you here. Our family is known for its witchcraft abilities, and when I tell you that I know a couple of spells, I mean it. My grandmother's powerful spell protects this house from all evil spirits and demons from day one. They won't even step in here...'

'And him?' I looked at Lizzie frightenedly. 'He is the Devil, Lizzie. He has everything under his power...'

'I don't know about that, Sophie,' my friend answered quietly. 'Let's hope he doesn't come here either.'

There was silence, and Lizzie and I stared at the floor, wondering what we should do next. It was naive to think that I could hide or run away. If Bale was who I thought he was, he would find me everywhere. I had endless questions in my head, even though some of the things were now clear. I understood why I had such conflicting feelings about this... man.

'Do you want my phone? Do you want to call your mom?' asked Lizzie softly, and I flinched. Mentioning my mother only made me angry, and I squeezed a cup of tea.

'No,' I said coldly, frowning, 'I'm sure she knew! All this time, she knew. Now I know what secrets they've been hiding from me, and I won't forgive her for that!'

'Do you think she has the answers?' my friend asked.

'I am sure of it,' I nodded, 'and I intend to ask her

as soon as she returns.'

'I think it's the right thing to do,' Lizzie agreed and put me to bed, shrinking by my side and hugging me. Looking at the white ceiling and the dim light from the moving flame of the candle, I sighed and touched a golden ring on my ring finger. My body shuddered, and my heart trembled for a second.

'Lizzie…' I quietly called her.

'Hm?' she responded.

'I… am the Devil's wife.' I felt my lips shaking. With horror, I understood the meaning of what I'd just said. As strange as it sounded, unrealistically, it was true.

'Sounds scary and… cool, to be honest!' Lizzie laughed, trying to cheer me up. All I did was smile a little and close my eyes. Cool… you can't tell otherwise. 'Hey, wanna see a trick?'

'Sure,' I sighed and looked at my friend, who sat before me and took a candle in her hands.

'My grandma told me that there is a reason why witches are considered to be Devil worshippers,' Lizzie said. 'Our power is drawn from the negative energy of this world, as it is stronger and so powerful. However, it doesn't mean it will harm anyone. Truth is, we have nothing to do with the Devil. The pentagram is a sign of the balance of nature, the five elements. And spells are just magick that allows us to gain power from the Universe. That's magick with a 'k', that differs from all the fictional term. It's a real type, the ritualisation of one's spiritual intentions.'

'You said once that humans could be capable of doing magick a lot more.' I smiled, looking at how my friend lifted her hand and softly touched the candle flame. Moving her fingers, Lizzie made the flame follow her hand, transferring to her palm and illuminating a brighter and warmer light. I awed in silence and gulped, looking at my friend.

'Humans still don't know what purpose a big part of our DNA serves. We normally use only about two per cent of our body and mind power, however, those who can handle magick have opened the door to their soul, mind and body altogether, allowing a stronger power to awaken. Intelligence is partly inherited, so the ability to awaken magick skills are the same.'

'I never knew you were so skilled,' I whispered, looking at the flame dancing in my friend's palm, then slowly moving up and down, following the movement of her hand.

'I have so much to learn—' Lizzie smiled '—but my grandma and my mum are showing me a few tricks. There is so much for me to know. I wish I had a longer lifetime!'

'I wish you could use your magick to solve my problems,' I laughed, and Lizzie made the flame disappear, looking at me with sadness.

'Sophie, I feel any supernatural power around me. I felt it in Bale, and I feel it... in you.' I twitched and frowned. 'I can't explain it, but something inside you is so powerful and strong, and it's trying to get out. I see that! But... I can't promise you it will resolve your problems. Maybe, this is the purpose that you were looking for. Maybe this power within you will lead you to something great?'

'Or something destructive,' I answered quietly, and Lizzie sighed, nodding.

'Maybe,' she said after a while, 'but I will always be beside you, OK? You came into my life for a reason, hun, and I am sure our friendship and meeting have a greater meaning. Don't take it all upon yourself, Sophie.'

'Thanks.' I smiled gently and hugged my friend.

I couldn't sleep that night. As soon as I closed my

eyes, those amber irises crashed into my memory, looking through my soul, making me choke and drown in emptiness. Fear enveloped me again, and any rustle outside the window made me shiver.

As I turned a gold ring on my finger, I suddenly thought about everything that had happened. I was trying to figure out the point of all this farce. Why did Bale have to sign this contract with me? And then it hit me.

'Lizzie!' I exclaimed when my friend and I sat in the living room and finished breakfast. Her mother had long since gone to work, as had her father. And her grandmother went to her little antique shop. We were alone again with my friend, and the house was now at our disposal.

'What?' She dropped her chopsticks out of her hands, staring at me in fright.

'Deal!' I answered. 'My marriage to Bale is a deal, isn't it?!'

'Um,' my friend nodded and suddenly froze as if she understood what I was saying. 'Oh, shit, Sophie!'

'I made a deal with the Devil...' I whispered, widening my gaze and looking at an empty plate. 'I sold my soul to the Devil, Lizzie. What will become of me now?'

'Sophie, I was thinking about it last night, and what's weird is... Bale didn't make you do anything, did he? He was very thoughtful and gallant, and now he's left you alone, not rushing after you.'

'So what?' I looked at my friend, confused.

'Don't you think that's weird? Maybe it's got a hidden meaning? Why would the Devil want to marry you? And why isn't he following you? If he wanted to kill you, he'd have been here long ago.'

'Perhaps,' I sighed as I tried to think of Lizzie's

words.

'I know I'm talking about something you don't want to hear, but Sophie…' Lizzie stopped briefly, 'I think you should ask him.'

'I do not want to see him, Lizzie—' I shook my head, hugging myself and pushing away evil thoughts '—his image is still in my head.'

'I understand,' my friend nodded.

There was a knock on the door, and Lizzie and I looked at each other. I shuddered and reluctantly got on my feet, following Lizzie into the hallway where she opened the door. I stared frightenedly at Alastor, standing on the threshold, and I took a step backwards.

'Hello, Sophie.' Al bowed politely and looked into Lizzie's face . 'I have brought your things.'

'Ah…' I couldn't even find the words, watching Al stretch out my bag. Afraid to step forward, I waited until Al tried to get in. With an understanding smile, he took a step forward. The threshold was suddenly electrocuted, pushing Al aside, and leaving a slight burn on his face that almost immediately disappeared. With my hand over my mouth, I was about to scream. Mixed feelings suddenly overwhelmed me.

'Ouch!' mumbled Al, looking at Lizzie with displeasure. Once again, I saw how his grey eyes become almost black, shining. 'A protection spell?'

'You won't even step foot in this house, you monster!' Lizzie whispered proudly, standing before Alastor. My bodyguard sighed and tilted his head to the side, which caused his neck to crack a bone, and he tiredly ran his hand through his hair.

'Sophie,' Al suddenly said seriously, looking at me with his dark eyes, 'I only came to bring your stuff.'

'Who are you?' I spoke coldly. Al shut up and looked at me thoughtfully. He seemed to be trying to decide if he should have been the one to tell me part of the story. But deep down inside, I still preferred it to be Al. My heart forced me to trust him.

'I am a demon, Sophie,' Al answered honestly, and I felt my throat dry. Seeing my confusion, Al smiled a little and bowed again. 'I will not hurt you, my lady. And I never tried. I sincerely want to protect you.'

'Lizzie, can you let him in?' I asked uncertainly, and my friend looked at me, surprised. 'I want to talk to him.'

'I cannot lift the spell just for him,' replied Lizzie. 'If I do, any demon can sneak in.'

'Then let's talk outside,' I whispered and took up the courage to step forwards as I approached Al and came to the door.

☆

Sitting by a small pond at the main gate of the manor, I let Al approach and sit by my side, offering my bag. Cautiously taking it from his hands, I looked at Lizzie, who had sat by me as my guard.

'What do you want to know?' Al asked quietly, and I pressed my lips.

'Everything, I guess,' I answered a couple of seconds later, 'but I don't even know where to start.'

'I'll tell you something that can help you understand "why", Sophie,' Al nodded, 'but you'll have to ask for the rest...'

'From Bale?' I looked at the bodyguard, and he pursed his lips, making me look away and frown.

'Sophie, what I'm about to tell you will seem unrealistic, strange and hard to believe. The reason why all this has been hidden from you is that this information is too heavy and incredible for human perception. By telling you the truth, Master was afraid that this knowledge would be an unbearable weight for you, as it would completely change your understanding of the world. We hoped that we could solve your security problem before we had to reveal our identities. However...'

'Things didn't go according to plan,' I whispered, raising my eyes to Alastor. He only smiled and looked up at the bright sky.

'This world is much more than humankind knows. The boundless universe is divided into many worlds. We are aware of three. The one you live in is known to you as planet Earth in the Milky Way galaxy. The other two are beyond your reach,' began Alastor. 'But you know them well. You call them Heaven and Hell. We call them Caelum and Infernum. They're not located where humans assume – up or down. They are, instead, parallel worlds of another dimension withing the same galaxy.'

'So, Heaven and Hell do exist?' Lizzie was surprised.

'Heaven and Hell are very vague concepts, limited by the explanations of known religions and beliefs. For us, these are just two different limitless realms created by opposite energies. The positive energy of the universe became the base of Caelum. It was the first world known to supernatural beings, created by the immense energy of the cosmos. And Jehovah's power controls that energy. You know him as God.'

'God?' I whispered, suddenly realising that by thinking of Bale as the Devil, I hadn't even contemplated it as confirmation of the presence of God.

'God himself no longer remembers how long he's owned this world. He only controlled the flow of Caelum's energy by dividing it and giving it to different creatures such as seraphim, angels, cherubs and later humans. His ability to create was the exact opposite of that of an equal creature,' Alastor continued, sighing, 'and you know that creature as Death. No one knows who appeared in the universe first.'

I continued to look at my bodyguard with interest.

'Now, all this is just what we know, not particularly the full truth. God and Death always go side by side, balancing this and other worlds. Over time, the positive energy of the universe has accumulated so much that its flow has changed. At its peak, that energy split and created the opposite of itself. Negative energy. It was faster and stronger. In the end, its flow created another dimension, known as Infernum – Hell. And although God could travel both worlds, his creatures didn't possess the same ability.'

'So, angels can't go to Hell?' Lizzie asked.

'They couldn't until God created the third world.' Al shook his head. 'In that realm – yours, which we call Statera – both energies collided and continued their eternal flow as if in a cycle. Positive energy came from Heaven, negative energy came from Hell, flowed through your world like a filter and returned to its rightful place.'

'Like the eternal engine of the universe,' Lizzie nodded, and Al smiled. I had forgotten all my problems for a moment, for his story was painfully interesting.

'God had a weakness for inventions and new creatures and often brought something new into your world. That's how living creatures came into being. Soon, God presented something else to his angels. This creature was so similar to them but so different. And thus, humans were those creatures . The humans in Heaven absorbed positive energy. Still, for an unknown reason, they could share this energy in the same way as the universe: inside themselves. In the end, emotions were born. And that was the main difference between people, angels, and other divine beings.'

'Wait.' I took a clear look at Al. 'Humans? But… I thought it was only Adam and Eve in Heaven?'

Al shook his head. 'People's records and beliefs are inaccurate, endless translations of texts, retold stories and the flow of time affected the truth. Your faith is based on inaccurate sources, though there is no religion as such. Our realms cannot be called a religion. These are worlds, parallel universes, and the truth about them soon split into several theories that formed the basis of the different beliefs of your world. Some people call divine beings angels. Some call them aliens or pagan Gods. But the truth is everyone is right, and wrong in their own way.'

'A bold statement in our world.' Lizzie raised her eyebrow.

'It's a very sensitive subject in your world,' nodded Al, 'but our truth doesn't change from that. Even though God created Earth, he did not invent the Universe, and there are other Gods like him in those many galaxies and star systems. We don't know much about them either. So, the negative energy and emotions have touched celestial beings as well. And the first to experience it was an angel known as Lior.'

'Lior?' I frowned, and suddenly the signature crashed into my memory. 'Bale?!'

'That's right.' Al smiled.

'Why Lior? 'Lizzie asked. 'Wasn't the Devil's name Lucifer?'

'Again, this is a mistaken belief.' Al gazed at the koi fish slipping into the pond. 'Lucifer's name comes from the concept of "light bringer" in ancient cultures. In other faiths, he was named Samael, Satan, Loki,

Anubis, Aidoneous and so on. Lior, on the other hand, is the actual name of the famous angel. This name was given to him by God himself. Lior was a very kind, gentle, friendly angel. His curiosity and interest in his father's work, and his new inventions and creations always differed from others. Lior's energy was very bright, like a star, from the first seconds of his creation. That's why God gave him that name. "Or" means light. Lior means "my light", as Jehovah called him.

'Lior...' I whispered with only my lips, and suddenly I felt warm. I couldn't understand why the name affected me, but it really did bring light into me while pronouncing it. After mentioning the name, I felt the fear of amber eyes suddenly replaced by calmness and memories of brown irises.

'After events known as an exile from Heaven,' Al interrupted my thoughts, 'of which the truth is never known to anyone, Lior was forced to leave Caelum and find his home in Infernum, where he took control of the negative energy of the universe. And having lost his luminous essence, Lior gave up his birth name, becoming Belial or Veliar, as people sometimes call him. And that's where the name Bale came from, which is how you know him now.'

'But since he was such a wonderful angel, why did he...?' I tried to think about it.

'Why did you see him so gruesome?' Al smiled. I nodded with my eyes down. 'Negative energy, as I said, is stronger and faster than positive energy. That's why it's easier for people to give in to bad thoughts and emotions than to make themselves smile. Eventually, his essence absorbed too much of this energy, destroying his true self. The human population has increased. The Master has absorbed more negative energy since.' Alastor looked into the sky. 'The tranquillity of the soul was replaced by a bright fire in his eyes, his beautiful appearance was complemented by dark nature, and his white wings absorbed the blackness of human souls. And though Master still resembles his former self, his long-lasting soul is forever covered with the marks of human anger, hatred, fear and other negative emotions that he has to take upon daily.'

'Is that why he became known as true evil?' I gasped with a frown. Al shook his head and looked at his cell phone.

'Your vision of the Devil is wrong. Satan was never the root of evil and trouble in your world. It's not stated anywhere, just a rumour. All the negative events one encounters are the result of one's own choice,' Al answered. 'By banishing Lior from Heaven, God gave him a punishment to work to the end of times. The Devil's task is to give the man a choice. The Devil never pushes man to the wrong path. He tests him and allows making the right move. And when a person sins, then after his death his soul goes to Infernum, where the Devil's judgment passes it, and he decides where this soul will go next.'

'Hell?' Lizzie was surprised. 'Do all souls go to Hell?'

'It is commonly said that the road to Heaven is through Hell,' Al smiled. 'Master is the judge of human souls. Thus, his last name Deemer appeared – a translation of the word "judge" from the ancient language. He weighs the path of man's life and, depending on what energy outweighs it, sends them either to Heaven or leaves them in Hell. But, I wouldn't want to go into details because I think the best thing is for you to find out the rest from the Master.'

'Then what can you tell us about demons?' I

asked, worrying about the fact that I had to talk to my husband.

'Over time, Master decided he wanted to give people the opportunity to do better. Despite his reputation, the Devil has always loved people and admired them as beings. That's why he spent centuries in your world getting to know humans, to understand them, and be like you even a little bit.'

'Portraits!!' I suddenly exclaimed, recalling my discovery in Bale's library.

'Yes, my lady, you're absolutely right.' Al nodded. 'They depict Master in different centuries of your world. This is his personal collection of memories. He can be quite sentimental.'

'Then... what kind of journals did I see in his library?' I couldn't understand.

'As I said, Mr Deemer allows people to have opportunities. Sometimes that opportunity is unattainable.'

'Deals?' Lizzie smiled. Al nodded, and I suddenly understood the chain of events. Of course, how could I not? Everything had its price.

'Master is offering a deal. The fulfilment of wishes in return for the soul,' Al answered thoughtfully. 'When a person dies, his soul is brought before the court. Instead of going to Heaven or serving his sentence, the soul enters into eternal service to the Devil as a demon. These demons respond to the torment of the human soul, offering a deal instead of my Master to increase productivity of Hell. Consider this business to the benefit of both sides.'

'Al, so you...' I whispered, suddenly looking at my bodyguard and realising a terrible secret.

'I was born in the Kamakura period in Japan. It was a difficult time. There was a war between Minamoto and the other clans. The emperor needed protection, and that's why the samurai classes dominated. Even though I lived in a small village with my wife, I promised to do my duty and fought honestly for the honour of my emperor.' Alastor was suddenly silent for a moment and closed his eyes as if recalling the events of old times. 'There was an epidemic of diseases because of the war. My dear wife could not survive and left me too early. And even though I tried my best to protect my baby from all diseases...'

'You made a deal with the Devil to save her?' I finished instead of my bodyguard. Al smiled gently and looked at me with kindness in his eyes. His look was full of pain and happiness at the same time.

'My soul must have despaired too much,' Al answered quietly, 'for the Devil himself appeared before me at that moment, not one of his servants. I was terribly scared, but I didn't hesitate for even a second. I begged him for help... He did not even say a word but just gave me a smile. It was so odd, so unexpected. It was like my fear was taken away with one brush of his hand. I suddenly felt like everything was going to be OK. My heart told me that I did the right thing. By shaking my saviour's hand, I was eager to honour him, not God. He was the star I had been praying to all along. He was the first to hear me, and I was ready to follow him to the end of the world, that's how much I trusted his words .'

'But your daughter has passed, hasn't she?' I gulped with a frown.

'Yes,' said Al with sadness in his eyes, 'she died. She was eighty-five when she left this world.'

'What?' I froze, and my heart skipped a beat. Alastor looked at me and laughed.

'Sophie, Bale kept his word and saved her,' said Al. 'She recovered, got back on her feet, got married and even had children. She lived a beautiful life, even though I wasn't there because I died shortly after she recovered.'

'But, I thought he...' I shook my head and refused to believe what I heard.

'As I said, my lady, our Master's reputation is built on wrong facts. I signed the contract; my wish was granted. Soon I entered into his service, giving up my human name, and received the name Alastor.'

'A human name?' asked Lizzie curiously. 'What kind of name?'

'I can't say it.' Al smiled. 'I have no right. When I became a demon, I gave up my human past.'

I still had a lot of questions, but Al insisted I talk to Bale. My bodyguard didn't want to burden me with more information, giving me time to think about what I already knew. I had a long time to think about what I heard and what else I wanted to know.

Politely bowing again, he promised to return soon after reporting to Bale. Though Al could not enter Lizzie's house, he made it clear to me that he was prepared to stay outside in the car as long as was needed to ensure I was safe.

Feeling Lizzie's warm hand on my shoulder, I smiled sadly as I looked at my friend, and we turned to the house. I urgently needed to rest and relax a little, but my plans had been hindered by unwelcome guests. Two of them, to be exact.

'Lizzie...' I whispered as my friend looked aside and frowned as she came closer to me. Two strangers were standing on the doorstep of the house. One thing I knew at once was that they weren't human. A dark-haired man with a thin face was surrounded by a smoky haze, an effect I only saw in evil spirits, like those who'd attacked me last night. The woman standing beside him also had no clear gaze, looking aimlessly into the distance and whispering some absurdity in a low voice.

'Possessed souls!' Lizzie whispered and grabbed the bag on her shoulder, pulling two Japanese tessen fans made out of steel and opening them in her palms. I only managed to open my mouth, but Lizzie refused to stand still and ran at the uninvited guests. The man grabbed her shoulder, but the witch skilfully folded the fan, hitting the intruder's elbow and making his hands open, letting Lizzie grab him by the side, bending down and sticking her steel fan into his neck.

Whispering a spell unknown to me, my friend made her tessen shine brightly. The wounded evil spirit made a nauseating scream and vanished into thin air.

I didn't even have time to think about what was happening as the possessed woman threw herself at me with a frightening look. However, my reflexes didn't let me down, and I still managed to duck by grabbing her hair and pulling back, turning her hand out. However, my assailant turned out to be agile, grabbing me by the wrist and pulling me towards her, squeezing me by the throat.

'Sophie!' Lizzie's worried voice was heard, and my friend swung a steel fan, throwing it forwards and sticking the sharp blades of the accessory right down the throat of the possessed woman. Lizzie whispered a spell again, and the woman's spirit immediately vanished.

My feet were shaking, and I sat on the grass in fear, rubbing my sore wrist and staring at my friend in shock.

'Do you always carry a weapon with you?' Breathing heavily, I put my hand through my ruffled hair.

Lizzie shrugged. 'When you are a witch, the

invasion of evil spirits becomes commonplace. I prefer to always be prepared.'

'Excellent skills.' I shook my head, in disbelief at what had happened to me recently.

'My grandmother knows a couple of useful samurai tricks,' Lizzie said proudly and helped me up by escorting me inside the manor. 'They were possessed by evil spirits; looks like they are the ones to attack you constantly. You are a part of something big, honey. Come, you must rest.'

When I took my phone out of my bag, I looked at a recent message from my mother, who asked me where I was. Apparently, the news had reached her, and now I had to find out the truth from the one who kept the most from me. After replying to her, I got myself together and tried to think about what I wanted to know in the first place.

Astrid did not take long, as the taxi soon arrived at Lizzie's house. I clenched my fists, opened the estate door and waited inside, walking from side to side to restrain my anger. Looking at my mother's anxious face, I pressed my lips when she stepped on the stairs. Don't blow up, Sophie, don't blow up. Lizzie passed by with a tray of tea and looked at the guest as I took a deep breath and waited for my mother to step forwards to enter the house and give me a hug as usual. Another second, another step and the door electrocuted, pushing Astrid back and burning her face, making her green eyes as dark as night.

The tray of tea fell to the floor, my heart stopped, and Astrid looked at me with an incomprehensible gaze, grabbing her cheeks and letting the burn instantly disappear from her face...

THE DEVIL'S SIGNATURE: THE ABIDING PACT

CHAPTER TEN

My body refused to listen to me. Even though I tried to step forward, my legs completely disobeyed me and made me stand still like a statue. I had goosebumps, my head got dizzy, and my heart was beating in a mad rhythm.

I remained standing in the middle of the hallway at Maio Manor, looking into my mother's eyes who was standing at the doorstep and staring at me incomprehensibly . I could see the fear in her eyes; Astrid didn't realise what was keeping her from moving further.

'You know…' I said quietly, feeling my eyes

stinging from the coming tears. It was hard for me to find the words because I realised that my whole life was a complete and utter lie. A cruel, cold deception from people close to me that hoped to hide the truth about my origins, my family, and the world in particular. Lizzie stood behind me, silently looking at my mother in disbelief. At this moment my tears failed to flow down my cheeks. No, I had no intention of crying . My body was slowly filling with anger, resentment, hatred and the feeling of betrayal. Pathetic. My whole life was just pathetic.

'Sophie,' said Astrid gently, raising her hand and trying to reach out to me, but I only smiled and squinted, biting my lip so as not to explode and shout out loud. 'Honey, what happened?'

'Remember I told you that Lizzie belongs to a family of very powerful witches, dear Mother?' I asked sarcastically, finally taking a step forward. My mother's look changed. She had become more serious. 'It is incredible how her grandmother's spell works so perfectly against all the darkness in this world. Especially against demons…'

'Sophie…' my mother said quietly, lowering her hand and looking at me guiltily.

'You know, I can understand why my husband thought he could hide the fact that he is the Devil in the flesh !' My voice rose, and I clenched my fists in an attempt to hold myself back. 'But my mind refuses to understand how my mother could think that she could hide from the fact that she is a demon!'

'Sophie, listen,' Astrid said, sighing. She looked around, trying to think of a way to get close to me, but the spell's barrier kept her from entering. Once again, questions appeared in my head; I had an unbearable need to know the answers. Still, I knew that at this moment, right now, I wanted to run away from everything, be alone with myself, and just forget about the last couple of days. My emotions outweighed my sober thinking. The panic attack was rising.

'I don't want to hear your explanations now,' I answered quietly, glancing down and looking at the floor, wanting to fall through the ground. 'I need time. I must decide for myself what I want and will do next. These two days were a real Hell for me... Although—' I smiled bitterly '—how should I know? I haven't been in that Hell yet, unlike you.'

'Sophie, you have to listen to me!' my mother insisted, but I raised my head sharply and looked at her with a hateful glance.

'Really?' I raised my voice. 'Now you want to talk?! Well, what a shocker! Haven't you been saying daily that you have nothing to hide? That all your secrets are just for my protection, and they also concern other people? What made you change your mind now?!'

'Sophie...'

'Get out of here!' I couldn't help but shout. My mother kept silent and stared at me with a guilty look, sighing and surrendering. She knew me too well and understood that I was not ready to forgive her. I had to cool down. By nodding, Astrid took a step back and slowly turned around, walking away. I only watched her, silently letting my tears drop and thinking that my ordinary life was now lost forever. I had memories of my happy childhood, of my father's kindness... of his kindness to me. I remembered how my mother smiled and how I dreamed of being like her all my life. My body sank into nostalgia for her embrace, tender voice, and quiet lullabies. My high school years were full of joy and fun, and blissful years at university and unforgettable time with friends now seemed fake.

It all mixed in my head and slowly sank into darkness, deeper and deeper, lost in the endless stream of lies and pretences that now filled my life. Sophie, who once looked at me in the reflection in the mirror, broke into pieces. It was a collapse of my own self. A demon child, the Devil's wife – who was I really? Sophie Mortis-Deemer, who was she?

Closing my eyes for a second to calm my soul and try to forget all that for a moment, I heard footsteps outside and opened my eyes, looking into Michael's troubled face. Surprised by his appearance, I watched him climb the stairs and walk up to the door with my breath held back.

The waiting tormented me from the inside, and I prayed that he would not be thrown aside. Not him... anyone, but him. Lizzie came up to me and squeezed my wrist as if trying to give me the support I needed. With her heart sinking, we waited for Michael. A step and...

'My God, you scared me!' Grabbing me in his arms, Mike breathed a sigh of relief. Tears swept through my eyes, and inexplicable joy filled me. I still had a part of my old life... There was still someone by my side who could remind me of my former joy. 'Lizzie, thank you for calling! I suspected something was wrong when Sophie didn't show up at the café the second day.'

'Of course.' Lizzie smiled gently and began to pick up the shards of broken cups on the floor. I stared at Michael in silence and tried to remember every feature of his face. He was real. He was close to me and kept my mind in order, keeping my soul from succumbing to chaos.

'What happened?' my friend asked me, squeezing my shoulders and looking into my eyes. 'Lizzie said something happened between you and Bale?'

THE DEVIL'S SIGNATURE: THE ABIDING PACT

'Michael,' I whispered quietly, smiling, 'Tell me, aren't you a believer?'

'Uh, yeah...' he frowned.

'Do you believe in the Devil?' I asked him directly and kept looking at him, seeing how his eyes changed. My heart flinched for a second. Something made me think he knew exactly what I was talking about.

'Sophie...'

'You knew,' I whispered as I opened my eyes wide and shivered. No, no! This can't be happening. Not Mike! Anyone but him! 'Michael, you knew!'

'I knew who he was,' my friend answered honestly, with his hands down and nodding, 'for a long time. He often showed up near my church, and sometimes I felt his unusual energy. He did not hide his origins much, to be honest. I swore to God to watch over the Devil so he wouldn't do anything foolish or stupid. I was always ready to try and stop him.'

'But...' I gulped, 'you said you didn't know each other, right?'

'Yes, we did,' said Michael. 'I'm sorry I lied. I couldn't tell you the truth because by mentioning our acquaintance, I should have told you who he really was, Sophie. And this, you know...'

'Sounds unreal,' I finished for him, and Mike kept quiet. Excuses... I'd heard excuses lately, and nothing more.

'He is the Devil, Sophie, and the last thing I wanted was to see you by his side,' said Michael, 'but I also knew very well that there is no better protection for you, given the danger you have been exposed to several times! I've been watching him for a long time, and seeing that he's genuinely protecting you, I only dared to watch, ready to intervene if needed.'

'He's the Devil, Mike.' I smiled tiredly and sadly.

'How will you stop the Devil? Do you throw a glass of holy water at him?'

'It doesn't work, by the way...' Michael answered quietly, making me and Lizzie glimpse at each other. 'These are outdated beliefs that have simply become a tradition. No cross, holy water, or prayer can stop the Devil or demons.'

'How do you kill them, then?' I turned pale.

'Only divine power can destroy what God created,' Michael responded gently, but I never understood the meaning of his words. I didn't ask either, as fatigue and lack of sleep finally wrapped around my body.

'I must rest.' I left them both and went to Lizzie's room with the desire to be lost in dreams.

'She's having a hard time,' I heard Lizzie tell Mike, 'and I hope it's the only thing you've kept from her, because she can't stand more lies. Sophie is already on the verge.'

☆

Almost unconscious from the strong concussion, I opened my eyes and stared at the ground underneath me. I didn't fall, hovering in the air, scratched by broken shards of the windshield. It seemed as if I was just hanging in weightlessness.

Slowly turning my head, I looked back and noticed my saviour pressed against the steering wheel with his head, bloody from many scratches, immediately healing before my eyes as if they were never there. His outstretched arm pointed towards me until his fingers twitched and his wrist moved, allowing my body to lie softly on the ground.

Getting out of a damaged car, the young man ran up to me, and I looked into his bright amber eyes. For the first time, I thought about how beautiful they were. It was as if the sun was living in these eyes, warming with its fire. He smelled of pine. Like a forest.

'Who are you?' I whispered, but the stranger lifted me up and hid me behind his back when he saw the headlights of the approaching cars. I looked down at my protector's hands and couldn't resist touching the blue flame on his skin. To my surprise, I did not feel a burn but only a tickling warmth as the flame gently touched my fingers.

'Hide,' the young man wheezed, and I fled behind the wrecked vehicle, watching our pursuers run out of the cars. Some strangers attacked my protector, but he refused to give up. He continued to fight back with ease. However, it seemed to me that he was weakened for a reason I didn't know. The flame of his shining veins became brighter, and his eyes started to show a crimson hue.

My heart told me he was suffering. It was as if the pain was filling him from the inside, and he was trying to contain it. Feeling an inexplicable rush of energy, I looked at my hands and was struck by how brightly my skin shone. The white light was radiating energy, getting brighter every second. My body seemed to know what to do.

Getting on my feet, I came out of hiding and rushed forward, screaming desperately.

'NO!' a young man tried to catch me, but I slipped out of his hands and threw myself at one of our abusers, making my light flash, pushing him aside and letting his body shatter into bright shards, evaporating.

Amazed by what was happening, I looked at my hands again and suddenly believed I could do anything. I could protect myself and keep my promise to my father. I'll get out of here. I will live and make my dad proud!

Having dealt with another offender as well, I rushed to the young man. He fell on his knees in front of me and I grabbed his neck. He gave me a firm hug, covering me from the attacker. What I wanted to do most was to protect the two of us, to get through it all. I could do it. I had to!

With a slight push, the ground shuddered. A bright flash spread and all the remaining violators were thrown aside, their bodies exploding into millions of pieces. I felt dizzy as I slid down and fell to the ground, held by strong, warm hands that gently laid my head down. I opened my eyes and smiled weakly. He was still here.

'I did it…' I whispered, looking at my saviour's dazed and troubled face.

'How did you…?'

'You still haven't told me who you are.' My eyes were slowly closing, and I almost gave in to my consciousness. 'I… Sophie.'

'Lior, my name is Lior,' I heard and smiled again, feeling incredible warmth coming from that name.

'Lior…' I whispered. 'What a beautiful name. And you are… beautiful.'

'Sophie, wake up!' He rubbed my cheeks, but my tiredness took over.

'Like an angel…' I smiled last, looking into the beautiful amber eyes before closing mine.

☆

I shuddered and sat on the bed abruptly, staring into the darkness and breathing as if I had woken up from a nightmare. It's been so long since I'd had this dream! Rarely had I remembered the accident, but… it was the first time I had complete memory since I woke up in the hospital.

Looking out the window, I noticed the first glimpses of the sun and jumped out of bed. Something was giving me an uncontrollable desire to be home right away. Trying not to wake Lizzie, I put on my T-shirt and jeans. Mike brought my bike yesterday, and I was ready to ride it!

I fixed Lizzie's flip-flops on my feet, dashed out of the house and grabbed the bike, which was near the entrance. Going out the gate, I noticed Alastor's car nearby. My bodyguard looked at me and nodded politely. I just turned to the road, sat down on my bike, and rushed forward.

When I found myself at the entrance of my house, I hurriedly dug the keys out of my bag and went in, embracing the morning darkness. Turning on the light and hearing Alastor's car parked outside, I closed the door. I rushed into the studio, removing the sheet from the vast canvas and looking into the bright amber eyes that sparkled with gold and looked right at me. As I lifted the brush from the table, I lowered it into a glass of water, stirred the colour palette, and gave in to my impulse.

My hand was moving by itself, floating on autopilot on the canvas and pouring colours over the dark background of the painting. I lost track of time and forgot where I was. Now my thoughts have only been immersed in the palette of paints. Drizzle, another one. Moving up, then down. And so on, until my fingers let the brush out by dropping it on the floor. My feet took a step back, and I stained my forehead with my hands, removing my hair and smearing paint on my face.

With my lungs full of air, I felt relief for the first time. I tried to finish this portrait for years, but I couldn't. And now…

Now I was looked at by a lonely, handsome young

man in a dark shirt, sitting on a cold marble throne surrounded by blue flames, which was reflected in the blackness of his wavy hair. And only golden amber eyes filled the portrait with life, pain, despair and boundless desire for peace.

'It will be the pearl of my collection,' said a voice behind me, making me wince. I didn't turn around as I knew the owner of this baritone. As I continued to look at the finished work in front of me, I frowned and wrapped my arms around myself.

'I didn't invite you in,' my voice seemed to be breaking. Fear still gripped me when I realised I was in the same room as the King of Darkness himself.

'I didn't get in through the door,' Bale answered honestly, and I closed my eyes, understanding the horror of his words. Of course, he didn't need an invitation. This man could have shown up anywhere and anytime. 'I have the power of teleportation. And telekinesis…'

'So I was right when I thought you could read my mind,' I laughed bitterly. There was silence, but I stayed put, not wanting to turn around because fear kept me from moving.

'I also possess boundless energy, superhuman physical strength and the forces of nature,' the man continued, 'I am immortal, not subject to old age, hunger and fatigue. I am free to change the features of my appearance to seem younger or older or shapeshift to whatever my heart desires. This quality helps me to remain unnoticed by humans all these years.'

'Why are you telling me all this?' I asked, opening my eyes and sighing.

'I'm telling you the truth about myself,' the man answered, and I felt him approaching. Goosebumps ran over my skin, and suddenly I felt cold as if I'd been immersed in icy water. Horror and fear penetrated deeply into my soul.

'Are you going to kill me?' I asked quietly.

'I never wanted to,' Bale answered again, and I gulped. 'I promised your father I'd protect you.'

'It was you, wasn't it?' I asked, putting my hands down and looking at my palms. 'You saved me that night when he died.'

'You yourself,' said my husband, 'and you have a power that grows within you which is unknown to me. And over the years, this power tries to break free, allowing you to see what others can't. To experience things that others don't even think about.'

'Is that why you weren't surprised by the news that I see people die?'

'Yes, I knew you had this ability,' Bale replied, 'but I don't know why or where it leads to.'

I flinched. 'Is that why you decided to marry me? To keep that power under your control?'

'A little bit,' the man confessed, and I frowned. 'I was really interested in your strength. But I'm not trying to keep it under control. I just want to know what kind of power it is. I've never seen anything like it in millions of years, and it's hard to surprise me.'

'It's crazy...' Covering my face with sweaty palms, I sighed. Even this conversation seemed absurd. Millions of years? The Devil? Souls? Heaven and Hell? What have I gotten myself into? Do I really hear all this?

'I know it's too much information,' Bale said, and I turned towards him sharply.

'Don't you dare read my mind!' I whispered and suddenly kept silent when I saw my husband for the first time in a couple of days. Strangely, he had changed a lot.

As he leaned against the wall, he hid his hands in his pockets, tilting his head to the side and looking at me with a tired look. His white T-shirt and ragged jeans surprised me a lot as I was rarely presented with his informal style. When I noticed the light glow, I looked at the blue flame that slid over his skin and made his veins glow blue. It was the same effect I had seen in my memories. Bale's appearance wasn't healthy.

'What's wrong with you?' I dared to ask.

'I have endless negative energy, and being in the human world for this long is unhealthy for me. I have to return to Infernum regularly to release this energy, allowing me to come back here.' Bale ran his hand through his hair, and I noticed the ruby on his ring shining brighter than usual. 'I hadn't been there in almost a month, so after recent events, I took advantage of my powers and only increased the flow of that energy, and it's bursting out. Keeping it under control is getting harder.'

'What happens if that energy breaks out?' I frowned.

'Something like a possession. I completely lose control and give in to destructive instincts.' I shuddered. 'The last time it happened, Pompeii was destroyed.'

'Why aren't you going back to Hell?' I felt cold sweat over my body, and I stared at him, scared.

'Because I can't go back until I'm sure you're OK and until I find those who attacked you a couple of days ago,' he answered. I looked down. 'I'll be back as soon as I feel I'm not coping anymore. This ring helps me keep my energy in control.'

I looked at the shining red ruby on my husband's finger. Wiping my dirty hands with a tissue, I walked past Bale, wanting to get out of the studio, but he grabbed my hand tightly, forcing me to turn around. I was immediately tense and frightened, looking at him with a bit of rage. Bale's eyes weren't dark-brown but reflected a light golden sparkle. He was on the verge.

'You asked for answers,' he replied quietly, glancing down from my eyes, slowly looking at the hand he held and touching my wedding ring with his finger. 'I will give them to you.'

'I'm scared.' Bale looked at me, but I couldn't take his glance and turned away. 'You scare me. Your nature terrifies me, and I'm petrified to be by your side. I'm not ready to hear the answers…'

'Come home,' he replied quietly, letting go of my hand.

'I'm home,' I replied coldly as I moved away and felt a gentle breeze as I looked at the empty space in the studio. He disappeared as invisibly as he had appeared. It scared me even more, making me believe in the reality of what was happening.

I had to gather my thoughts and figure out what I wanted to do next. To do that, I had to get my life back on track somehow. Maybe I needed to go to the family café to get myself busy in a lively atmosphere and immerse myself in the daily energy of a familiar routine.

I'd think about it later… I needed some air.

THE DEVIL'S SIGNATURE: THE ABIDING PACT

CHAPTER ELEVEN

Watching frothy milk in the metal jug, I automatically moved my hand up and down, allowing the coffee machine to heat the contents in my hand. Filling an espresso mug with hot, airy milk, I gave the customer his latte with a smile and looked at my watch. Closing time was approaching, and I had to get home soon. Suddenly my heart was dull and bitter. I needed to immerse myself in the darkness again, thinking about my experiences and problems.

Martin was humming something under his nose as he walked past me, and I just stood there looking at the empty tray.

'You're distressed, child,' a quiet woman's voice sounded, bringing me out of prostration and making me pay attention to a familiar face.

'Thana...' I said, raising the corners of my mouth and looking down.

The woman smiled sweetly and touched my palm, giving me a warm feeling and a sense of inexplicable calmness. This woman always amazed me with her aura. The heart calmed down next to her, thoughts faded away, and the soul was hovering in peace and tranquillity, as if in a long-awaited dream after severe fatigue . Her smile gave me confidence that everything would be all right, that all worries were behind me.

'Any obstacles can be overcome,' said Thana and her bright eyes shone. 'The important thing is to believe in yourself. Solve problems by trusting your intuition, not someone else's advice.'

'Thank you,' I replied, wondering how much her words had cheered me up. Strangely, even though this woman didn't know what I was going through at all, she could tell by looking at me that I needed support. Her words were so needed as if I had been waiting for them at that moment .

Thana smiled again and blew a kiss, thanking Martin for the jasmine tea and leaving our café empty.

I decided to walk the woman to the door and waved as she stepped to the other side of the road. In a blink, the approaching car lost control as it headed straight towards Thana. I couldn't even breathe, pulling out my hand, as the woman was suddenly pushed away by a stranger, saving her from an unpleasant outcome.

The cowardly driver instantly fled, and I ran up to the woman, helping the stranger that had saved her to put Thana back on her feet.

'Thana! Are you OK?' I asked, worried, and looked at the young man as he lifted my client's bag from the ground.

'It's hard to kill me, sweetheart!' Thana laughed, and I sighed lightly, laughing. 'Thank you, handsome, for your courage!'

'The important thing is that you are OK,' replied a young man with sparkly blue eyes and beautiful wavy brown hair that touched his shoulders. He seemed very friendly and shy, as he occasionally hid a glance from Thana and me.

'God bless you,' Thana smiled and once again confirmed for me that she was OK. The young man nodded at us and hurried away, blushing a little.

It was time to close the café, and I walked to the door tiredly in a desire to lock it. Martin washed the last of the mugs and rushed back upstairs, looking forward to a gaming night with his friends, while I changed the sign to 'Closed'.

'Sophie!' An agitated voice surprised me, and a delicate hand appeared between the door and the joint, not letting me lock up the café. Astrid stood on the doorstep, staring at me and trying to decide if I was ready to meet her. 'Please, can we talk?'

Silently letting the woman in, I closed the door and walked smoothly towards the coffee machine, brewing two cups of fresh coffee. Sitting in front of my mother at the table, I stared at the mug and frowned.

'Sophie,' Astrid replied quietly, looking at me and suddenly going silent. She didn't even seem to know where to start. I wasn't even sure what information I was looking for. 'I'll tell you everything I know.'

'You're a demon, right?' I asked her directly without raising my eyes.

'Yes,' Astrid answered briefly.

'Alastor said that when you serve the Devil, he gives you a new name.'

My mother nodded. 'It's true; I was given the name Astarta.'

'It's very clever to name your café after yourself,' I laughed sarcastically, glancing away and avoiding looking at this woman with all my might. 'Then why do you call yourself Astrid?'

'It's my human name,' the woman answered, and I looked at her with surprise.

She understood that I knew the rules of the contract and didn't know why she had the right to use her human name. 'My contract with Belial terminated long ago. I don't serve him anymore. I'm relieved of my duty.'

'How?' I asked, looking into her eyes. Mom smiled softly and took a sip of coffee.

'I will tell you my story, Sophie,' she said with a sigh, 'the story of me meeting your father and Bale. But first, there's something else I have to tell you. Sophie, your father, he was special.' Astrid's eyes shone brighter as if she remembered something delightful.

'Did he know who you are?' I asked her cautiously.

Astrid nodded 'He knew. Sophie, Jeremy is your father's human name.'

'You gotta be kidding me…' I whispered, feeling the creeps all over my body. I couldn't accept the fact that my father wasn't who I thought he was either… He was my last joyful memory, and I wasn't ready to know it was a lie as well.

Astrid smiled. 'Your father's real name is Jeremiah. Here…'

My mother gave me a ragged, crushed sheet. When I unwrapped it, I looked at an ancient image, similar to an icon, on which there was a graceful angel with white wings, holding a crescent moon in his hands studded with bright stars. His silhouette was in the middle of the clouds, and below was a small signature.

'Jeremiah, ruler of the moon and the stars,' I read, looking up at my mother in disbelief. Did I understand her correctly?

'Sophie—' Astrid smiled '—your father was an angel.'

My heart stopped for a split second. Staring at the image, I tried to determine how I felt. My soul had no anger, disappointment, happiness or other emotions. There seemed to be an emptiness inside me...

The memories of warm summer evenings came back. My father and I were sitting in the garden of our house, watching the night sky and looking at the stars, dreaming of visiting the moon and discussing our dreams and desires. I felt tears streaming down my cheeks. The realisation that I had just received proof of the angels' existence suddenly became a chain of thoughts about my origins. A share of my hope still kept me afloat because I thought that, as the daughter of a demon, I still had a human part in myself. But now... could I call myself human?

I sobbed loud. I couldn't stand it. I hid my face in my palms, crying out loud and finally letting all the accumulated feelings escape. Like a child, I dreamed of turning back time, of being the Sophie I could no longer be. Having completely lost myself, my reality, I sunk into oblivion, sadness and darkness inside me. I broke down and cursed the day I'd met Bale. Our meeting didn't bring anything good into my life. It just ruined it.

My mother's warm hands squeezed me, allowing me to cry and express all my feelings. Silently waiting for my tears to dry, Astrid pressed me to her chest and stroked my head, smiling weakly.

'I will tell you the truth, Sophie,' whispered Astrid, 'because now you're ready to hear it. The truth will be hard, but I know you can handle it. You have a long way to go to accept your new self and discover your new world, and I will help you. Listen to me, Sophie, OK?'

With a slight nod, I let my mother pull away from me and wipe my tears with her thin, beautiful fingers, fixing my ruffled hair and serving a cup of hot coffee.

'Everything happened so long time ago,' Astrid sighed, 'but I remember those events as if they had happened yesterday... A new century was taking place in medieval Sweden. After some significant events in the world, many in the country were dissatisfied with how the king ruled the Kalmar Union, an alliance between Denmark, Norway and Sweden. There was a rebellion that led to a change of government. Eventually, the Kalmar War between Denmark and Sweden began in 1611. King Christian IV convened an army, and all men were obliged to give their lives for victory.'

I watched in silence as my mother stirred the coffee with a teaspoon and occasionally looked at the image of the angel in front of me. Everything seemed unrealistic and strange, but I kept listening, trying to remember every word.

'I worked as a kitchen maid in a rich man's house, earned barely anything, but I had enough to live,' continued my mother. 'I made friends with my master's daughter, Molly, and we were besties. I shared joy and sadness with her and always told her my innermost secrets. I shared the news of my new love interest with her as well. It was a handsome young man. Oscar, his name was...'

'Did you love him?' I chuckled as I raised my eyebrow.

'I was twenty-five at the time, a bit younger than you,' my mother sighed. 'In those years, I should have been married long ago, but I waited for a special person to marry. When I met Oscar, I realised that he was the man I had been looking for. We dreamed of living together, having our own house, family and other trivial things. But, my heart was broken when he was called to war. I prayed to all the gods that he would come back to me. My love was pure, and innocent then. I couldn't see life without him.'

'Wow,' I smiled.

'I stumbled upon a fortune-teller on the outskirts of the city and wished to know from her what fate awaited my lover... I still remember her beautiful teal eyes—' Astrid was silent for a moment then smiled sadly '—and she told me of his approaching death. I was so desperate that I wished to find a way to get him back with all my heart.'

I frowned. 'Were your requests heard?'

The woman smiled. 'Yes, a handsome young man appeared before me on my doorstep in the early morning. His appearance was striking, his narrow almond-shaped grey eyes were unusual for our city. Even today, he still gives away this mysterious vibe of a polite gentleman.'

'Wait,' I interrupted my mother and looked at her in surprise, 'it was Al?!'

'Alastor was the demon who offered me the deal,' Astrid said, and I was speechless. Was that really possible? How closely connected were they all? 'He promised me that Oscar would return safe and sound as I had wished. And in return, after my death, I would have to join the Devil's service. I was so desperate that I signed without hesitation, waiting by the window every day until, finally, one day, my beloved returned. My dreams came true, we were together again, and I forgot about my deal, completely giving in to love.'

'So, what happened?' I knew from my mother's tone that the sad part of the story followed next.

'Love filled my head, and I did not immediately notice that Oscar appeared more often in the house of my employer, justifying that he had waited for me.' Astrid looked down. I realised what the catch was. Knowing my mother's naive personality, I realised she had been betrayed. 'So, one night, I caught them both together when I looked into Molly's room. My life crashed in an instant. I swore to get even with them, to tell her father about their connection and get revenge. But… on the way down, I felt a kick in the back and I fell down the stairs, breaking my neck. And before I died, I saw Molly laughing in my face.'

There was silence, and I looked at my mother with pity, imagining how terrible she must have felt. I got up and made some more coffee to give her a moment. I brought her a hot brew and sat at the table again, waiting for her to continue.

'When I opened my eyes,' Astrid said, 'I was in a different place. I was standing in front of a wide, tall marble gate in the dark desert. It seemed like… everything was covered in sand, but then I realised that my feet were walking in the ashes . I could see a calm, clear river in front of me, shining blue, and the demon Charon was waiting for me on the shore to take me across the Styx to Infernum. Approaching Pandemonium, I froze in silent shock, watching the beautiful city that shone with colourful gleam. The northern lights were shining over my head, and I felt happy for the first time in ages – my soul felt at peace in this place. Infernum was almost the same as a human realm. There were gourmet restaurants, inns, taverns and libraries, and busy streets and markets. In the middle of the city was a beautiful marble castle, with high towers and columns wrapped in blue flames. It was the house of the King of Darkness himself.'

'Is it nice?' I laughed, not surprised at the luxury of my husband's home residence.

'It's a fabulous place.' Astrid smiled. 'I never thought I'd get to see such a wonderful world. For me, even Heaven couldn't have been more beautiful. Infernum has a certain vibe. It's like a city of dreams and fantasy.'

'I always thought that Hell was baking,' I said, surprised at my mother's words.

The woman shook her head. 'Not at all. It used to be at first before the Devil we know did some renovations. And it's not as full of light as this world, or Heaven, but it's not in the darkness. It's a beautiful city, immersed in a dark starry night. The eternal flame is only present on the city's outskirts, where Infernum's prison, Tartarus, is located. That's where the souls are serving their sentence.'

'Are they being tortured?' I asked quietly, imagining the eternal torment of poor people who are mocked by the Devil himself.

Astrid waved her hand. 'Absolutely not!' she said, laughing. 'It's barbaric! Scary tales made up by people to frighten the innocent. Punishment exists, it is true. But souls serve a punishment in relation to their actions. For the most part, these souls are only locked up in a prison cell without being able to go free, spending centuries alone with themselves. It is a kind of torture, of course, but no one burns them alive. It's a kind of opportunity to think about your evil deeds and repent. After their repentance, their souls are released and given peace by escorting them to Heaven.'

'Are they all eventually released?' I was surprised.

Astrid shook her head. 'Not all of them. It depends on the level of their atrocities. The most inveterate violators stay there for eternity, forcing them to go through their own fears until their spiritual energy runs out and breaks into millions of pieces, completely evaporating. But such cases are rare. These foul criminals include serial killers, tyrants, child molesters and other filth. They are in a special ward of the prison.'

'Tell me more about that place,' I asked curiously.

'Infernum is like a magical world!' Astrid exclaimed. 'When you end up in the Gehenna desert under the starry sky, you walk through the marble gates of Hell to the river Styx that shines with its glistening blue waters. Charon takes you into his boat, and you slowly drift through the dark caves of Hell Mountains covered with ash. The river flows through them with splashing waterfalls, and then those magical waters push you into the Tunnel of Tartarus Hills – the darkest of those caves glimmering with crystals and diamonds.'

'That sounds fantastic,' I sighed, imagining being there.

'As soon as you are embraced by that darkness, you feel incredible peace and serenity. And then—' Astrid closed her eyes as if remembering the journey to Hell '—the river's waters start to shine brighter and finally reflect a distant glistening of lights. As you come out of the tunnel, you are blinded by the beauty of the shiny skyscrapers and enormous buildings of the megapolis embraced by the evening light. The city is mixed with modern and old architecture. The starry sky envelopes the city while every building glitters with thousands of lights of any known colour. The famous Hell gems reflect the stars' shine, which makes the city so bedazzling. Those gems are so beautiful, Sophie!'

'The buildings are made of them?' I asked, surprised, trying to imagine it all.

'Yes, from those jewels and all the glass, making them look like crystals poking out of a geode. It's endless and fascinating. When you step on the ground, it brightens with colours with your every step, as if you walk on the illuminated carpet.'

'Wow...' I whispered.

'The city is full of life! Demons and celestials are all around you as if it's a separate world. Well... it is!' laughed my mother while I was in disbelief that such a place could exist. 'It has its own magic, Sophie! Entertainment includes restaurants with magical foods, theatres, beautiful hotels and inns, and apartments out of this world!'

'But why?'

'Well, while the soul awaits its judgement, it has the pleasure to spend some time in Hell while waiting. There is a whole business there, sweetie. Not only Bale's marble castle is present in there.'

'What do you mean?' I asked, interested, forgetting about the coffee.

'Well, I was brought to the courthouse for a hearing. While I waited my turn, I could stay in one of the inns. I enjoyed gourmet restaurants, studied the city, and met other souls and demons, half-demons, and legendary creatures I'd heard about in fairy tales. It all turned out to be real, and I learned how big the universe is. I realised that the celestial energy of many realms had created a huge variety of creatures I had never met before.' My mother smiled again. 'Only now do I finally know that many folklore stories, legends, and other tales are half true, and there really are creatures in the world that many believe in. And each creature has its own history of origin and essence of existence. That's how I learned that souls who are not qualified for punishment or peace in Heaven, because their actions are equalised, are appointed to the position of Angels of Death.'

'The Angels of Death?' I asked.

'They also serve a higher power, not the Devil,' Astrid explained, 'but Death.'

'It's all so confusing...' I mumbled.

'Believe me, honey, there are more celestial and supernatural beings around you than you think. I can't name all of them because it's not my secret to share, and they're free to tell you the truth about themselves when they see fit. The Angels of Death take the souls of the dead and bring them to Hell for judgment. Normal people will not see them because they are considered ghosts, but if the Angel of Death wants, they can appear before the living.'

'So what happened to you when you went back to court?' I asked, looking at my mother.

'I got a new name, a new job. I had to work for Belial and offer deals on his behalf because I was desperate for love and wanted revenge for my pain. That's how I met him, in court. At the time, he did not travel much around the world, often staying at Infernum. Now his duty in court is mostly performed by his deputy, the demon Ifrit. She takes her work very seriously.' My mother rolled her eyes. 'I became Astarta and started making deals with people, passing contracts to Azazel, Bale's secretary. He gives them to the Devil for his signature.'

'So that's what those contracts were on his desk...' I said thoughtfully, recalling my findings in Mr Deemer's library. 'And those journals, then...'

'Lists of those who made a deal with him. The ones who became demons have been crossed off the list.'

'But, how did you get out of the deal?' I asked, confused.

'A hundred years ago, as I walked the streets of Pandemonium long after the death of my former lover Oscar and his girlfriend, I was on a way to the castle. Belial, by the way, personally sentenced those two, allowing me to observe, imposing a cruel punishment on them, and making me realise that I must appreciate myself more. Belial was going through some existential crisis and left for the human world in search of inner peace. And that day, I saw Hell's sky shine with a bright light. Soon, a white-winged angel descended on the city of Hell, baffling everyone present with his appearance. Angels could visit Hell, but it was rare, as they personally visited only on significant occasions. It was mainly about severe world events, like wars or mass epidemics. In such cases, there were agreements on the organisation and distribution of souls. Now, that angel was...'

'Dad...' I whispered.

'Jeremiah was desperate to find Belial, wanting to talk to him about something urgent. Fate brought him right before me that day, and we immediately felt that spark between us. His blue eyes pierced my dark heart,' Mother told me with a loving sigh. 'Belial was in hiding, and Jeremiah asked for help finding him. I couldn't refuse, wanting to stay near this beautiful angel just a little longer. It was as if something inside me was pushing me to get closer to him. Soon, we found Bale after a long search, and your father told him something that changed the course of events.'

'What did he say?' I asked, eager to hear more.

'Sophie, you know the legend of the forbidden fruit, right?' Astrid asked.

I nodded. 'The Devil seduced Eve, and she ate an

apple...'

'Well, first of all, it wasn't an apple; it was a piece of fruit from the Tree of Knowledge that looked more like a mango.'

'And secondly?'

'It's a false legend...' My mother said, and I opened my mouth but couldn't find the words. 'Jeremiah found out the truth from someone who knew Eve and Angel Lior very close. That's the man who told your father the secret. And that man was Adam...'

'I'm starting to think I'm going crazy.' I sighed as I tried to deal with the headache that was beginning to break out. My mind was boiling, and I refused to believe what I'd heard. My mother smiled sadly and took a sip of coffee.

'Jeremy said that Adam has changed a lot since returning to Heaven. Before his exile, he was very open, funny and simple-minded. But, after his death and his return to Caelum, he became agitated, quiet and lonely. Adam rarely talked to angels or other souls, and preferred solitude. Sometimes he could only talk to your father, and he was the one who once told the truth about what had happened.'

'And what's the truth?' I wondered.

'According to him, Eve wasn't seduced. Neither did she pluck the fruit herself nor ate it. Adam mentioned some kind of a bowl with an unfamiliar drink that Eve once gave him. She told him that by drinking from it, they could gain power that would bring them closer to God. Your father never found out why she had decided so or from where she had received this information. As a result, Adam and Eve were banished from Heaven, and the blame for the temptation fell on the Devil that had been exiled.' My mother sighed as she leaned on the back of her chair.

'But his innocence has not been proven in Adam's words either,' I frowned.

'This event occurred shortly after Bale was locked inside the Heavenly castle by God, as a result of punishment for... something,' Astrid answered. 'I'm not too familiar with the story. This fact is confirmed by Adam himself. He saw Eve shortly after. It proved that the Devil could not have been near Eve because he was in a different place then...'

'No way.' I shook my head as what I heard sounded absurd. 'But... then who pushed Eve to sin?!'

'No one knows.' She shrugged her shoulders. 'Adam said that only Eve knew the whole truth. Adam went to Heaven first, waiting for Eve to arrive there soon. But...'

'She never came back?' I whispered in surprise.

'No one knows what happened to her soul,' Astrid replied quietly, and I gulped. How so? According to Al, all souls go back to either Heaven or...

'Is she in Hell?!'

Astrid shook her head. 'I didn't see her there. I'm afraid whoever's trying to hide the truth by framing Bale and driving Eve and Adam out has gotten rid of the poor thing in the same way as with your father.'

'What do you mean?' I gulped.

'Your father's soul didn't return to Heaven, Sophie,' my mother explained, saddening me, and I lowered my eyes. 'It just vanished. It was as if his energy ceased to exist. However, only pure supreme beings like the Devil, angels or God can destroy the soul. His soul evaporated, and the only reason his body stayed was due to a spell I will tell you about. Someone tried to get rid of Bale, then Adam and Eve. When they found out that Eve owned the truth, they got rid of her and let Adam return just because he did not know anything and was not a threat in the end.'

'But Dad found out that Bale had been framed and decided to find out the truth. That's what Bale meant when he said he was responsible.' I finished for my mother. 'He ended up dead because apparently...'

'He found out something,' Mum answered, and we shut up for a second. Now I understood well the cause of my father's death. The question that tormented me for a long time finally got an answer! My heart was beating faster, and I felt a rush of energy.

I looked at my mother, as something struck me. 'Father told me something before he died. He said I was the key to the light.'

'Maybe he thought you were going to reveal the truth?' Mom asked, and I shook my head. I'd been in the dark about demons and angels and whatnot, so what could I know? How could I have revealed the truth? 'Did he tell you something, Sophie?'

'No.' I shook my head again.

'Um...' Mother said. 'I don't understand.'

'So that's why I'm being hunted...' I said slowly, as realisation hit me. 'The enemy thinks I'm a threat.'

'Bale, knowing that he is the reason for everything,' said Astrid, 'feels he must protect you. Jeremy gave his life for the truth. Believe me, Sophie, Bale never tried to hurt you.'

'But, how did you get out of your contract?' I remembered.

'After searching for Bale, Jeremy and I became so close that we couldn't imagine separation. We had so much in common! It seemed like we'd known each other our whole lives... It was inexplicable, and I never thought I'd find my love after my human life. But it was difficult. Any bond between demons and angels, like with humans, is a taboo.'

'Why?' I asked with curiosity.

'Our energy is different,' my mother explained. 'Demons exist through negative energy, angels through positive energy. In humans, it is mixed together and is always uneven. Celestials and demons have only one kind of energy, and when confronted with the opposite, they can destroy the weaker being.'

'Right, so that is why people cannot be compatible with supernatural beings either, as the pure energy of the celestial or divine being can simply destroy the human?' I guessed and my mother nodded once again.

'Half-Demons that I met in hell are a bit different, though,' she said. 'When I became a demon, I soon learned that there are souls that refuse to follow the deal with the Devil and periodically rebel against their master, wanting to return to the human world and live forever without duty. They often become evil spirits. For such rebels, there are Hell Hunters. They are the demons who work for Bale and occasionally appear beside you. These are demons of special rank that hunt rebellious runaway violators and evil spirits that affect the balance of this world.'

'Evil spirits?' I was surprised.

'Yes, these are souls that are forced to serve their sentence and, as a result, run away from Infernum, or desperate souls that refuse to accept that they are dead or have been stuck here for too long. They possess humans or those who recently died, hoping for life to continue,' Astrid explained.

'Ew,' I shivered from such a thought.

'Such evil souls attacked you as a child when you were saved by your father. I think they were controlled by our enemy. It gets very gruesome.' Astrid sighed and took a sip of coffee. 'In the end, it often results in women being raped by the possessed, and the they die soon after pregnancy as the foetus would have a supernatural force that kills the mother.

The child in their bodies may still survive thanks to the energy, and such children become half-demons and are taken to Infernum by Hell Hunters. They are born demons, not made. They are provided with a residence in Hell without danger to the human world. Often such half-demons become Hell Hunters thanks to their strength and stamina.'

'Then, how did you and Dad...' I frowned, but Astrid only smiled and sighed.

'Your father tried to return to Heaven to speak to God and tell him about his doubts regarding the night of exile, but he could not go through the pearly gate. Something was holding him back, and we soon realised that the mysterious traitor was also trying to get rid of Jeremy.' Astrid changed her tone. 'We found Bale soon after, and your father told him what he knew. Bale never liked to owe people, so he asked Jeremy what he wanted in return for the information.'

'I suspect he asked for your freedom.'

My mother nodded. 'I got myself out of the Devil's contract and became a free demon by getting my human name back. However, being in the human realm, we put ourselves in danger. Our energy is stronger than normal, and if we cannot go back to our world for a bit – Heaven or Hell – then we could lose control of our power and damage this world. And even though I was free to return to Infernum, the road to Caelum was closed for your father.' Astrid sighed and ran her hand through her hair tiredly. 'We had to find a way to contain Jeremy's energy. As a friend, Bale told us about a witch he knew called Lilith who lived in New Orleans. That's where we went...'

'Lilith?' I was surprised. 'Isn't she, according to legends...'

'Adam's first wife?' Mom laughed. 'Yes and no. She was his partner once, as I am aware. I won't

THE DEVIL'S SIGNATURE: THE ABIDING PACT

disclose her past as she's my friend, but you can always ask Bale.'

'That's the last thing I'm interested in,' I fussed, cross-handed on my chest, expressing my displeasure that I would still have to talk to Mr Deemer.

'Lilith is a powerful witch. She helped us with a deterrent spell that allowed us to be in the human world without having to return to our realms. The spell is still in effect today—' Astrid smiled, looking at her wedding ring '—and thanks to it, our power has slowly fallen asleep deep inside us, making us human-like.'

'Have you practically become human?' I was surprised.

'Yes,' my mother nodded, 'and though we didn't get old and we still could see souls and all… your father eventually lost the ability to acquire wings. I have lost the ability to control souls with my mind like I used to. And one day, the spell allowed us to experience something only living beings could.'

'Hm?' I raised my eyebrow and stood up, taking my mother's empty cup.

'We had you.' Mama smiled widely, and I felt a familiar warmth that ran all over my body. 'It was the greatest gift for us. And even though we never knew what kind of power you had, we raised you in the human tradition for your own safety.'

'I see dead people, Mother,' I answered monotonously as I cleaned the dishes, 'and have a dark power inside me that keeps showing up in my dreams. But this has never happened before. This has recently appeared.'

'I think you're being influenced by Bale's energy,' Astrid nodded in understanding, 'and it's starting to awaken your power.'

'But, what kind of power is that, Mom?' I raised

my voice. 'I'm not an angel, I'm not a demon, and I'm clearly not human…'

'I don't know, honey,' Astrid confessed honestly, and I pressed my lips. 'It comes from your dad. I saw it only once. That's for you to find out. I'm not sure if there's anyone else in the world like you.'

'It's all so confusing.' I grabbed my head and sighed as I looked out the coffee shop window. 'So… are you dead?'

'In a way,' she replied. 'When the soul becomes a demon, it acquires a physical body. We can feel emotions, we can feel pain. However, we are not considered to be alive, like humans. Because we can't reproduce, or get old, or die of natural causes. And even though for some this might seem tempting, after few decades you realise that it is tiring to be in eternal service without the ability to let your soul rest. We have no contact with our families unless they pass, and even after that we are not allowed to follow them to heaven. It's like being stuck in a routine that you can't get out of. Forever.'

'It does sound very sad,' I nodded.

'Imagine how Bale feels,' Mum said and I gulped, 'his soul is one of the most ancient one. And while demons can occasionally get out of contract at some point by earning their release after many centuries or special deeds, the Devil can not leave his job.'

'I feel like I'm in a dream, and everything around me is just a haze.' I whispered.

'You need to rest.' Mum stood up from her seat, hugging and stroking me on the head for comfort. 'Sophie, it doesn't matter who we are. What matters is that you will always be my daughter. How you live and who you think you are is your choice. I will support you in any way, so don't worry about it so much.'

'I have more questions than ever.' I hid my nose in my mother's lush blonde hair and hugged her back.

'Remember one thing, Sophie,' my mother answered calmly, 'there are many mysteries and secrets in the world. And although we seek to know the truth, we must not forget that we do not always get the answers to those questions. I can't promise you that you'll find out your father's secret or that you'll be able to wake your power. Maybe it'll remain a mystery to you forever, and you'll have to accept it... And in the end, you'll just be the human who'll live the life the way you wanted.'

'Yes...' I nodded and let my mother out of my arms. With a gentle smile, she ran her palm over my cheek and headed for the door, grabbing her bag.

'Rest,' she said finally, unlocking the door, 'and think about everything and decide what you want to do next. If you decide to return to our house and go on with your life as it was, I understand. Bale and everything about him is just a temporary part of your future. You don't have to change your life, knowing the truth. Bale wasn't kidding when he said your contract was a temporary measure.'

'OK,' I answered quietly and waved to my mother.

She was absolutely right. Whatever I decided to do would not mean that I would find the truth. Maybe I'd still be the Sophie I didn't want to forget?

THE DEVIL'S SIGNATURE: THE ABIDING PACT

CHAPTER TWELVE

Wiping off the dust from an old living room dresser, I stopped for a second and looked at the picture in front of me. Glancing at the happy faces of my parents standing and hugging a younger me with all their love, I gently smiled and sighed. Those memories would always be the sweetest for me, no matter what would happen in the future.

As I organised the paint tubs in my studio and cleaned up, I felt pretty proud of myself and headed for the door, taking a brief look at the portrait in the corner. As I frowned, I took a few steps forwards and stood in front of my best artwork. Golden eyes stared into my soul with longing, and the blue flame seemed real and warm. Damn, he was handsome.

I lived in my house all alone for almost a week. Returning to the café, I did my job, talked to Michael and Lizzie, and once again immersed myself in the home atmosphere, thinking of a plan of action.

My anger was slowly subsiding, changed by curiosity and interest. I fought with myself internally, not letting emotions take over my mind. I thought that everyone went through something that was pulling them down and was hard to deal with. But it was time to stop worrying about what I couldn't change. I wasn't human. My origins would always be crucial to my future, no matter how hard I tried to escape. So it was time to accept myself and move on. To learn about the new me.

Aware that Alastor was sitting outside in the car, I sighed tiredly and headed for the front door to invite the poor man for a coffee. He had been watching me for a week, like a shadow, without invading my space and just being around as a protector. I couldn't challenge the fact that despite his demon nature, Al was someone I could trust completely. He seemed more human than other people. He was loyal, understanding, and kind.

When I opened the door, I noticed the man standing next to his car, looking at his smartphone screen. I was about to invite him, but the phone rang, and Al answered the call.

'How bad?' He frowned, and I noticed the worry in his eyes. 'Don't do anything! I'll get there as soon as possible. Hold him back!'

As soon as he got in the car, Al noticed me, and for a moment, he stopped, trying to decide whether to leave me or stay. Seeing my questioning glance, Al started the engine and lowered the window, looking into my eyes.

'Sophie, I'll send a replacement right away, but I have to go!' he answered while sending a message to someone asking them to come here right away.

'What's wrong?' I frowned, but my bodyguard just smiled a little and pressed the gas while turning the car around. Something was telling me it was about Bale. Mentions about his uncontrollable energy suddenly popped into my head, and it didn't take long before I grabbed my bike and left, chasing the car. Despite the anxiety and instinct that told me about the danger, I couldn't cope with the curiosity and headed towards the Devil's estate.

As I approached the main gate, I noticed Al's parked car and walked in, not knowing what to expect. I decided to ring the doorbell first, and waited patiently for the door to open. As I heard the footsteps, I met Rosie. She looked anxious . The housekeeper hadn't expected me at the door.

'Oh, Sophie,' she mumbled. She shuddered at the loud noise upstairs and gulped nervously. 'This is not a good time for you to be here. It's safer for you—'

'I must come in,' I answered insistently, letting Rosie understand I was not leaving. The maid closed the door behind me and guided me with her gaze as I went upstairs, hearing someone scream louder and louder. My heart was thumping, and my legs were shaking.

I walked into the long hallway near my bedroom, passing a couple of other rooms, and slowly headed to the library. The noise was coming from there. The door was open, and I flinched. As I took another step forward, a man flew out of the room. I assumed that poor fellow was one of Bale's Hell employees. With his back against the wall, the man slid down and rubbed the back of his head, looking forward in fright. When he noticed me, he staggered up and moved away, leaving me confused.

As I approached the door, I pulled my hand to open it wider, but I ran into Alastor. He jumped out of the room and stared at me in surprise.

'Sophie!' he whispered, looking back and pushing me aside. 'What are you doing here? It's dangerous here right now!'

'What's going on?' I frowned, trying to look over Al's shoulder and noticing Bale in the room . Pushing the disgruntled Al away, I stared silently at the object of my curiosity.

I froze in silent shock, watching angry Bale scatter his people around the room, thundering about. I tried to make sense of it, but Bale's inhuman voice only made me fearful and confused. It sounded like his voice was getting lower and almost growling. He was gleaming with his amber eyes and grabbing one of his employees by the collar.

'I'll burn your soul if I have to!' Bale growled, squeezing his employee's jacket harder. The silvery horns reflected the bright sunlight, and the black wings swept around. Like an angry beast with clawed hands, the Devil roared, and his white canines were ready to tear anyone apart. Only now did I notice his veins shining brightly under his tanned skin as if a blue flame was wandering through his body. A bright-blue line was reaching his neck.

'I'm sorry, sir, it's n-not my fault!' the unfortunate victim said, stuttering. 'I r-really tried, my lord!'

'Get out of here!' Bale threw the young man and furiously shoved a pile of papers from his desk, banging his palm on the wooden surface and leaving a crack in the furniture. It was the first time I'd seen him so wild, uncontrollable and angry. Now he looked more like the Devil to me.

Bale shouted, again and again, turning around abruptly, and staring at me for a second. I gulped, seeing the hatred in his eyes and feeling the danger approaching. Bale's eyebrows frowned, and he took a step forward, speeding up the pace. His pupils dilated, and he rushed in my direction like a tiger. Al clenched my shoulders firmly, pushing me aside and throwing himself forward, holding back his master.

'Sir, don't!' Barely coping with the angry Bale who seemed to be trying to throw himself at me, Alastor turned his head in my direction and gave me an anxious look. 'Sophie, run!!'

Obedient, I took a step back, seeing poor Al thrown out of the room . I felt I was being chased. I turned around and looked at the approaching Devil with horror, as he looked like he was hunting me down. Destroying everything in his path, leaving cracks in the walls and crumbling furniture, he tried to take off with his wings, but the narrow corridor did not allow him such freedom. Coming down the stairs and skipping a couple of steps, I stumbled past a horrified Rosie, who opened the front door. As I approached my goal, I hoped to be able to get out of the house, but the door slammed in front of my nose when Bale teleported and stood up before me.

I immediately got up, and jumped away from him, not letting him touch me and hoping to hide in the kitchen, grabbing the first thing I could find. Clutching a knife in the palm of my hand, I pointed it towards the Devil, knowing it wouldn't help much.

'You...' he growled as he approached.

'Stay back!' I screamed as I heard the footsteps from above and noticed Alastor and Rosie. My mother also entered the house, frightened as she looked at what was happening. Bale swung back again, and the dinner table moved, pressing Al against the wall. My mother tried to rush to my aid, but Rosie held her back, explaining that Astrid couldn't handle the Devil.

'Bale, please!' my mother begged. Still, the fallen angel only accelerated his move until I took a chance and threw a knife at him, making the blade stick right into the shoulder of the angry Devil. He stopped, and in a calm motion he pulled out the cold weapon and threw it aside, raising his golden eyes at me and making my heart beat faster from fear. Instantly he appeared before me, grabbed me by the throat and pressed me against the wall. Desperately gulping the air, I squeezed his shining wrist with my hands, feeling tears slide down my cheeks in terror.

'Let go!' I wheezed, feeling Bale's fingers squeeze.

'I hate you the most!' he whispered, frowning. 'In every way possible, you showed discontent when I refused to tell you the truth. You were pulling it out of me, letting yourself be disrespectful to me. And when you got what you wanted, you blamed me for your fear?! You're nothing but a vile, proud, weak human who thinks the world is spinning around her!'

'Please, let go...' I answered quietly, feeling myself suffocating from a lack of oxygen, and my head started to spin.

'I didn't touch you, and I didn't even give you a reason!' He raised his voice, and I noticed a grudge in his eyes. 'But like all others, you gave in to prejudices and believed the rumours rather than draw your own conclusions! You're all like that, people. Blaming others for your failures and wrong decisions, justifying your insolence and impudence with pure motives!'

'Bale...' I almost whispered as I kept fighting, 'you're hurting me... please. B– Lior!'

It was my instinct to call his true name.

I felt my husband's hand flinch, and his grip loosened. Instantly coming to his senses and letting me go, Bale took a step back and stared frightenedly at me as I knelt, coughing. A second later, his wings were gone. Mama ran up to me, stroking my back, and Rosie held out a glass of water.

Looking into Bale's amber eyes, I was relieved when a dark-brown tint returned.

'Bastard, what are you doing?!' My mother threw herself at him, losing her fear and slapping the man. Bale didn't react by letting my mother blow off steam. He didn't seem to believe what he had just done. My mother completely lost control, pushing the Devil aside and standing like a shield in front of me.

'Sir, you must go…' Alastor said to him as he approached Bale.

The Devil only glanced at me and turned around, stepping away. I was suddenly shrouded in unbearable resentment and anger.

'Hey!' I shouted, but Bale didn't even budge. I got up on my shaky legs and followed him, ignoring my mother's worried requests to leave him alone. I couldn't let that insolent man walk away without explaining himself. 'Bale! BALE!'

'Sophie, please…' Al shook his head when I got upstairs and stood on the library's doorstep while Bale was collecting some documents.

'Don't you dare ignore me, you jerk!' I shouted angrily and didn't give up. I demanded an explanation and an apology. 'You throw yourself at me with a death threat, and then pretend to repent? To hell with your repentance!!'

'Ma'am…'

'Bale, you bloody winged pillock, I'm talking to you!' I threw a pillow at my husband that I grabbed off the couch. He didn't turn around to me, approaching the mirror on the wall. Feeling a growing rage, I still gave in to my emotions. 'Look at me when I'm talking to you, LIOR!'

There was silence, and I immediately regretted not

holding back. When I noticed the man standing still, I glanced at Alastor, who was staring at me with a shocked look. I knew by his expression that I had crossed a line . The air got hot in the room, and my gaze fell on a metal statue on the coffee table that began to melt. The flames in the fireplace broke out, and I gulped as Bale turned towards me. Giving me an angry, hurt, and painful look, the Devil closed his eyes, took a deep breath, and tilted his head to the side, letting his neck joints crack. His eyes shone with a golden spark.

Trying to cope with the fear, I prepared mentally for another shitastrophy, but it did not happen. Instead of an angry burst, Bale just turned to the mirror, which shone with an azure flame, and moved forward, stepping into a blurred reflection of himself that was replaced by a bright light. Fascinated, I watched the Devil disappear inside the mirror portal. I gave in to the weakness in my legs and fell to my knees, relieved and glad that this horror had ended.

My skin was cold, and I was shaking. I pulled a blanket from the sofa over me. Taking a sip of hot tea that Rosie brought me after the chaos settled down, I silently looked at my mother's disgruntled face. I sighed.

'We're leaving,' Astrid responded thoughtfully, surprising me with her decision. Noticing my confusion and anger, my mother frowned. 'Now, I'm not sure that you're safe here.'

'Oh, really,' I laughed without even arguing that I was never safe here. My life, as I understood it, had never been safe.

'Ma'am, forgive him—' Rosie looked at me beggingly '—I know he scared you. But I can assure you that he didn't mean to hurt you. Master has been unable to control his impulses recently as negative energy has prevailed. It's like an obsession he can't control. A disease.'

'Why didn't he go to Infernum earlier?' I asked calmly, looking into the dark liquid in my cup.

'He was desperate to find out who was behind all these crimes,' Al answered tiredly, sitting beside me. 'He didn't want to leave it for a day, holding himself back until the last and searching for the traitor day and night. He didn't want you to get attacked again.'

I turned to the old woman. 'How did you meet Bale, Rosie?' I wanted to hear others' stories about my husband, trying to make clear conclusions before I decided to leave this house and never come back. I wanted to forget this man and everything about him. I wasn't ready to live with someone who could strangle me in my sleep.

She gave me a gentle smile. 'I'm glad you asked,' she replied. 'I was born in London. I became an orphan at an early age. Lack of care forced me to rely only on myself, and I survived as much as possible. I wasn't even registered at birth because my father left my mother before I was born, never to know about me. My mother suffered from postpartum depression, and took her own life shortly afterwards.'

I took a sip of tea and frowned, imagining the horror of a little girl left alone in this world.

'Running away from the orphanage regularly, I wandered the city's outskirts, spending my days in the streets. I preferred to sleep in a cold corner of the alley rather than in an orphanage bed. I was dreading the days I'd be placed back in a foster home where I wouldn't last long. I'd never had any luck with foster families. Once, the husband of a good woman who took me in turned out to be a child molester, chaining me to the bed and letting go of all his twisted fantasies... I was only eight,' Rosie continued, stroking her apron, and I gulped with my eyes down. 'So I'd often steal from people on the street, pulling wallets and valuables out of their pockets and purses to survive. And one day, I noticed a beautiful gold ring with a ruby on a man's finger. I grabbed him by the hand and pulled the jewel off. Even though the man could easily catch me by the collar of my torn jacket, he just looked at me as he continued to walk...'

'It was Bale, wasn't it?' I laughed.

'Soon after, that same night, I bumped into him again when I was wandering the streets. But something had changed. His amber eyes paralysed me, so I continued to stand and look into the eyes of my beautiful nightmare. For a second, I was relieved because I was hoping he would just kill me, and I would finally find peace because I didn't dare to take my own life.' Rosie smiled. 'And this strange young man just walked up to me, took the ring from my pocket, and sat in front of me, looking into my eyes. I don't know what he saw then... maybe it was my despair. But, patting me on the head, the man put his hand down and spread his velvety black wings in front of me, simultaneously terrifying and striking. His feathers merged with the darkness of the night, and his eyes shone with a golden spark. I immediately realised that the Devil himself was in front of me, and that he'd come for my soul.'

Rosie stopped for a second and looked into my eyes, trying to realise something for herself.

'For the first time, I felt calm and satisfied,' she continued. 'I just stood there waiting for my fate. But... with a smile, the King of Darkness stretched out his hand and called for me. He asked if I could keep a big house clean and tidy if he took me with him. My soul reached out to him because I felt my happiness was next to this man, not on the streets. And I went with him...'

Al spoke then. 'The master brought her here in the middle of the night, asking me to feed her and give her a room. He told Rosie that her job was to keep her new home clean and to wait for her master with a delicious meal on the table and a sincere smile. I told Rosie about Infernum and life behind the scenes.'

'And since then, I've done all I can to support him,' Rosie said. 'He was my father, then my first love , and now... he's my beloved son. And I didn't regret following him that night for a second, even having seen every aspect of his personality. I was never afraid of him because my heart trusted him completely. I thought he understood my pain, my loneliness. Maybe that's why he took me in... apart for other reasons.'

'You sound as if you admire him!' I said, looking at the woman tiredly.

'I do!' Rosie answered. 'I prayed to God every day, but only the Devil heard me... For him, I would climb the mountain and not let anyone hurt him! There is no deal between us, and he does not treat me like a servant. I'm part of his little family, which he cherishes. And there is no better reward for me.'

My heart suddenly felt a little lighter. Looking at Rosie's elegant way of cleaning cups from the table, I was once again convinced that I couldn't base my decision about the future on one opinion only.

'What are you gonna do, Sophie?' Mom asked quietly, looking at me. When I bit my lip, I thought carefully about everything. My heart was still in doubt.

'I'll tell you later,' I answered as I got up from the sofa and headed for the door. 'Al, when will he be back?'

'Given his condition, about a week or two from now,' my bodyguard answered. Nodding, I opened the door silently.

☆

Sitting at the shabby table by the window, I briefly examined the city library. Soon after the events with Bale and everything around me, I rushed to study the books I thought could help me understand. Flipping through pages with religious content, mythology and folklore, I read articles about the Devil, angels and God, the differences between faiths and their similarities. I tried to find information about demons, angels and witches. I read about shamans, skinwalkers , fae and other supernatural stuff. As I accumulated knowledge on the subject I was interested in, I reflected on every word, weighing up the truth and fiction.

While studying images, maps and symbols, I learned patterns drawn in the pictures with the Devil. The same symbols I saw on Bale's back, on his tattoo. I even rejoiced at the find, studying the meaning of symbols I'd once seen. I could understand the horns, as they seemed to express Bale's true nature. The shape of the hourglass must be hinting at his immortality.

'Immortal...' I thought and gulped. It was difficult to comprehend.

The scales spoke of his work as a Judge of the World. The shape of the star and sun seemed to reveal his celestial beginnings as the bearer of light. The 'V' symbol was explained in the book as a sign of male and female nature – the balance of this world.

How interesting.

I was amazed by the deep meaning of his tattoo.

Suddenly the thoughts of Belial's broad back crashed into my memory, and his muscles and strong arms seemed to wrap me within. I shook my head and rolled my eyes ; I was covered with goosebumps. No, Sophie! You're not going to think about it! When I looked again at the book and ran my eyes through the pages, I thought of the golden eyes that penetrated my soul. And the soft, kind smile on the Devil's lips. My thoughts immediately brought back the memories of that fiery, passionate kiss.

'Shit!' I jumped up, drawing the audience's attention and immediately blushing. Grabbing the books and returning them to the library receptionist, I said goodbye and caught her reproachful look before leaving. Apparently, the fifth day of research on the supernatural had an adverse effect on me...

Escorted by Alastor, I decided to pay a visit to the corporate building, trying to gain some information from people working for Infernum Enterprise. Obviously, mostly everyone spoke warmly about their magnificent employer, which didn't surprise me. Bale seemed like a strict, fair but understanding boss. That annoyed me. It seemed as if I was trying my best to find anything wrong with him. Anything that would give me a reason to run away. Except for him being a Devil in the flesh, obviously...

But the more I sat in the chair of his main office, the more I looked at the bookshelves with his favourite manuscripts and books, the more I studied his contracts and looked at his beautiful handwriting, the more I found myself drawn to the Devil.

It was time to talk to the only person who could distract me.

'Lizzie, are you free tomorrow?' I said when I heard 'Hello' on the other side of the phone. When I got a definite answer, I asked my friend to meet me at my café. Lizzie was the only one who could help me sort myself out…

THE DEVIL'S SIGNATURE: THE ABIDING PACT

CHAPTER THIRTEEN

'So, what did you decide?' Lizzie asked with interest when Martin brought us two cups of tea with a few slices of cake. With a smile and a nod of gratitude, I turned to my friend and drew attention to Lizzie. I took a day off because I wanted to concentrate on myself and my drama rather than work. Since my mother was busy meeting a friend, I decided to look after the café, though not as a waitress.

'I'm not sure,' I sighed, sobbing. There was a mess in my head, and I couldn't handle the chaos of my thoughts alone.

'All right, let's think.' The witch cut a piece of chocolate cake, shoving it inside her cheek, rushing to chew. 'Do you want to continue this marriage? Is your goal still the same? To benefit financially and earn yourself a freedom while getting protection from Bale?'

I nodded. 'I'm still up to it, but I'm not sure if it's the right thing to do? Given my origins…'

'Sophie, nobody said that you have to follow the path of your supernatural origins,' my friend told me. 'You have every right to continue your life as a human being. I, too, do not want to become a full-blown witch and cast spells left, right and centre! I have chosen the path of a simple Lizzie, who is sometimes fascinated by the history of magick and spells in her spare time. Sophie, do you remember how much I struggled with myself?'

'Yes.' I held her gaze.

'Hun, I was ready to end my life just to avoid hearing another word from the bullies about me being weird and freaky. I saw dead people everywhere. I couldn't make out the difference between living and dead! I was scared to even open my mouth just to ensure people didn't think I'd gone crazy talking to myself! You know how lonely and destructive that was?' Lizzie started to get upset, and I gulped. I knew exactly how hard it was on her. 'Dammit, Sophie, I don't know what exactly stopped me from jumping into the river from that bloody bridge, but I sure don't regret it! Some force made me step back. This force made me rethink my life, to understand that maybe… just maybe, there is something there for me that I am meant to do with those skills. But at no point did I stop being my usual self! I continued to be a normal human, worrying about my future, studies, job, and relationships. I never agreed to lock myself in the room with a crystal ball and read fortunes! It's your choice, Sophie.'

'I feel that if I do not choose a new path, my

father's death will have been in vain...' I answered quietly, and Lizzie smiled softly.

'I understand,' she said quietly. 'Then let's think about something else. How does it make you feel to think about Bale? How worried are you about his true identity?'

'Lizzie, he is the Devil,' I whispered, 'naturally, I am terrified!'

'And?' The witch raised her eyebrow. I looked at her, confused, and she just smiled. 'Sophie, you are not entirely human yourself. Your union doesn't seem so unacceptable! Besides, you told me that common knowledge about the Devil is wrong. Haven't you made sure that his story goes much deeper?'

'Yes, but...'

'And tell me the truth, girl—' Lizzie waved her hand and squinted cunningly '—you fancy him.'

'Lizzie, I liked him,' I corrected my friend, displeased, 'until I found out—'

'Yes, but does the fact that he's a fallen angel, Lord of Hell and a guy with a grudge at his daddy change the fact that he's still the same Bale you met? Did he change his personality, his behaviour?' Lizzie wondered, noticing my stubborn look. 'Except for his tantrum a few days ago! You asked for it... '

'Eh?!' I resented my girlfriend. 'Since when are you on his side?!'

'I am not on his side!' She sighed. 'It's just that I can understand his anger. He couldn't help it, and that's his mistake, but he warned you several times and knew well what you would do if you knew the truth. And you didn't listen to Al when he asked you to stay home! I understand you too, trust me because I still can't believe the whole story! And that's with my family history!'

'Do you think I should continue this farce?' I

leaned on the back of my chair, crossed my arms on my chest, pressed my lips, and realised I had no choice.

'Is that a farce?' Lizzie asked quietly, and I looked up at her. A friend smiled and looked into the cup of tea, smoothly running her finger along the saucer's edge. 'Sophie, however you deny it, you did have strong feelings for him. I'm not saying it's love... But maybe it's the beginning of something more? You're thinking about him, and it's a fact. Right now, all you're repulsed by is knowing who he is. But the rest of it hasn't changed. You're still attracted to him, his care and kindness keep you warm, and you're interested in him. And now, if I'm not mistaken, he'll be even more interesting for you. Just imagine what stories he can tell you!'

I only sighed and did not dispute Lizzie's words. She was right, I was still attracted to Bale. And now I knew that it was not just his devilish charm that had an effect on me, but his sincere openness and willingness to support me. And even though Bale was only acting out of a sense of duty to my father and me, rather than with love, he was still sincere.

'Sophie, listen—' my friend smiled, and I looked at her thoughtfully '—you shouldn't be worried about who he is. You didn't care much about the fact that I was a witch, did you? So, what's the reason for your fear now? Are you that desperate to live a simple human life?'

'I don't know,' I whispered softly, frowning.

'Are you scared to open a new door for yourself?' Lizzie kept smiling. 'Do you think that if you decide to learn more about yourself, you will not be able to return to your previous life?'

'Perhaps.'

'Sophie, nobody likes change. It's frightening,

away from comfort,' Lizzie replied, taking my hand and holding it tightly as a sign of support. 'But change is always for the better. Didn't you want to achieve something in your life? Perhaps, this is your chance? If you continue to fight yourself, you will fall into a great abyss that will only destroy you. Accept your new life and benefit from it! Discover the secrets that surround you, and learn the truth. Who knows, perhaps this is your destiny? As it is with our friendship?'

'What does this have to do with our friendship?' I laughed, looking at my friend with gratitude.

'Well, maybe the day we met at school, you sat by my side in the cafeteria purely intuitively?' Lizzie raised her eyebrow, making me think. 'There were a lot of kids around you, but you sat near me. A girl, all alone, who was avoided by everyone because of the grim aura around me. Something made you look me in the eye and be the support I needed. Perhaps it was your inhuman nature that made you feel comfortable next to the one that was like you?'

I remembered the day I met Lizzie. She was right: I had many friends at school, but when I saw that silent, lonely girl in the corner of the cafeteria, I felt an inexplicable bond with her. Something was calling me to get closer to her, and my heart told me she would be more important to me than any other person. Her indifferent, cold look seemed so sincere to me that I immediately smiled at her and reached out to introduce myself. I wanted to protect her from those who always teased her and called her a 'witch' by watching out for the poor girl. But I wasn't attracted to her by pity. I was captivated by interest. I wanted to know more about her. I felt like we were alike...

'You have made me stronger, Sophie,' Lizzie replied, 'because of you, I began to smile again. I stopped running away from myself and accepted my gift and developed it. You didn't even withdraw when I was able to prove my abilities to you. You just got closer to me.'

'I thought you would hex me if I ran away,' I mumbled as a joke, and Lizzie laughed. 'But perhaps you are right. I have always reached for something greater without noticing it myself.'

'I am not saying that unconditional love will break out between you two and that you will live happily ever after—' Lizzie stood up from the table and grabbed her tote bag with a cauldron image on it '— but perhaps a union could be forged between you, much stronger than love? You know, he is the Devil, but despite my first reaction, I don't feel bad energy thinking about him now. This aura is negative, it's a fact, but it's not bad. Maybe he deserves a chance. Otherwise, why did your father try so hard to justify the Devil? Think about it, Sophie... Maybe the whole world is wrong about him. Then what's it like to live all these centuries alone when the world turned against you? Sophie, hun, you're alike... more than you think.'

'Hm?' I looked at my friend as if I didn't understand the last phrase.

'You both feel uncomfortable in this world, needing help but not daring to ask for it because of your ego. You are drawn to each other not only by strength but also by the same fate. You both want justice to find answers to eternal questions about your past.' After patting me on the shoulder, Lizzie waved goodbye, saying, before she left, 'Think about it... He was God's favourite, Sophie. There must have been a reason.'

I looked down and sighed. Her words echoed in my head, and my heart was surprisingly calm. For the first time in years, I was thinking clearly.

After putting the mugs in the dishwasher, I said a short goodbye to Martin and headed for the exit, facing a broad male chest. I stepped back and smiled faintly when I saw the bright emerald eyes.

'Sophie, I was hoping to see you.' Raphael smiled gently and tilted his head in a charming gesture.

'Hello,' I answered quietly, without hiding my surprise. 'You've been looking for me? What for?'

'Bale told me that you have some exciting knowledge,' he said with a wink, and I looked back, taking him outside. Strolling near the man who was almost twice as tall as me, I sighed a tired sigh.

'I'm still trying to digest the new information,' I mumbled when Raphael and I turned the corner. Alastor parked nearby, giving us a chance to talk.

'Hm-m,' Raf extended, 'I understand. It's not easy to get used to the idea of you being the Devil's wife.'

'Yes.' I confirmed and smiled a little. 'Well, are you really his brother?'

'Yes, the oldest one,' chuckled Raf.

'And you…' I started by trying to remember mythology and biblical stories. Raphael looked around, making sure we were alone in the narrow alley. He pulled back his shoulder, and two enormous white-grey wings opened behind his back. Brown-tipped feathers were shaking in the light wind. Shining bright, Raf smiled broadly, reaching out his hand to me.

'Do not fear me. I'm Archangel Raphael,' he replied as I stared at the wings behind his back, getting used to the new image of my brother-in-law.

'Holy fuck…'

'Don't blaspheme,' Raf smirked, instantly making his wings disappear, and I covered my mouth with a hand, gulping. I didn't seem to be able to get used to the wings. Raphael smiled gently and touched my hair as a sign of comfort. 'Relax, Sophie, we're not as scary as we seem.'

'But, I thought that after the exile, you angels don't talk to Bale...' I looked at the man incomprehensibly, and he shrugged his shoulders.

'Well, he's my little brother,' said Raf. 'I can't leave him just because he made a mistake. Bale is much more vulnerable than he looks. As one of his older brothers, it's my role to keep an eye on him. Speaking of which, when is my brother coming back from Infernum?'

'Um... likely tomorrow...' I tried to come around.

'Are you busy? Do you want to get some coffee?' Raf asked with a charming smile, and I nodded, following him to the nearest coffee shop and accepting a treat.

Raphael seemed to be a very gallant kind man who was sincerely concerned about his brother and wished him the best. Raphael gave out a warm and soothing aura that made me feel so harmoniously close to him.

'Look, I know exactly what it's like for you—' he smiled again, taking a sip of coffee '—it's not easy to process this information; to get used to the new world around you. '

'I just don't know who I am anymore.' I sighed as I looked into my friend's eyes . 'I don't know what to do, or where to go.'

'Do you know what kind of power you have?' he asked curiously.

'No bloody idea,' I sighed, 'and I'm not sure if I want to know, to be honest.'

'It's your choice, Sophie.' The archangel nodded, and I put my eyes down. 'Don't worry about anything else, darling. Doubt is a part of human nature. Don't jump to conclusions. Let your inner fears calm down, and think clearly. Weigh the pros and cons and stop looking at the world like others do.'

'What are you talking about?' I looked at him, puzzled.

'Sophie, our Father created people out of curiosity. He wanted to see what would come out of his experiment: a creature whose existence would not be based on obedience, fear of the Creator or an inner desire to please him. People have that freedom that angels can only dream of. You are full of emotions, and colours – enjoy them. Try everything you can without fear of consequences. Your life is so short, and you often waste it without absorbing all the wonders of the world. Enjoy your full life, Sophie. And it doesn't matter if you're human or something else. Because angels will never have that opportunity. We are chained to our Father, and, through Bale's experience, we all know what is at stake if we disobey. That is our nature, and that is how we were created.'

'Does that not upset you?' I asked.

Raf smiled. 'Sophie, angels avoid emotions. We try not to be influenced by feelings. We only do what is right and what our Creator demands. We are soldiers of Heaven, and it is our duty to lead the people to light. Only my brother is the exception from the rules, for he is subject to emotions and feelings through the difference in his creation. And believe me, he's not so bad, Sophie. Bale has one weakness that makes him obedient.'

'Which one?'

'Love,' Raf replied quietly, looking at me. 'He loses control and becomes vulnerable by giving in to love.'

'But, I thought angels couldn't love…'

'But he's not an ordinary angel, is he?' The man

winked, and I thought about what he'd said. 'This vulnerability isn't as bad as it looks. Maybe it's what holds that monster inside him, cools his rage and makes Bale's negative emotions disappear.'

'You're worried about him, aren't you?' I smiled, and Raf gave me a soft look.

Raf sighed. 'He's my brother, Sophie; he deserves a second chance that he's never been given. I believe in redemption and want to keep him safe from pain and disappointment. I have looked after him since the beginning of time, and I consider it my duty to continue doing so.'

'That's very noble of you,' I said, laughing, and Raf smiled.

'I'm glad you came into his life. He changes; I can see that. He's become kinder, softer. Those are good qualities, Sophie. If you decide to accept him, I'll only be glad. I think the time of the frightening angry Devil has come to an end. We need more good in this life. '

'Thank you for supporting me, Raf,' I said softly, and the man gave me a blissful smile.

'You're part of my family now, darling,' he replied, 'and I'm always happy to hear your concerns. Healing is my special power.'

'Thank you,' I nodded when Raf and I left the café. On my way to the car, I received a strong hug as a gift and felt a little relief, 'you're an angel.'

'In the flesh,' Raf laughed, and I smiled joyfully. 'And Sophie, if you learn something about your power or something new about yourself, don't hold it inside you. Share with me, and I may be able to give you some good advice and help you manage your doubts. Don't give into fear.'

'OK.' I nodded and Raf said something about his meeting with a friend, but I didn't listen because my head was full of thoughts about celestial beings.

'Raphael!'

'What?' he answered with a smile, turning around and looking at me with his radiant eyes the colour of spring grass . Amazed once again by his charm, I clenched my fists and sighed.

'Does God... does he really hear prayers?' I asked. Raf smiled and nodded.

'He does, Sophie, every single one of them!' he replied. 'But he's not answering them for one simple reason.'

'Huh?' I was surprised.

'People are in control of their own destiny,' he explained quietly with a smile, 'and you don't need his help. You're afraid of change and have forgotten how wonderful it is to give yourself up to the unknown! Whether it's life, death or something else. There is nothing to be afraid of, for the soul is eternal, and it will find its way out!'

Watching the angel disappear around the corner, I felt an inexplicable burst of energy and inspiration from Raphael's words. Was it the effect of his divine power, or strong words? It wasn't important. Now, I was just smiling, standing alone in an alley and looking at the sky. The faint and wispy clouds were slowly floating along the blue canvas. The wind made me take a deep breath and cheer up. My decision was almost made, and there was only one person I needed to talk to in order to end my doubts.

'Al!' I shouted and soon heard the engine start. The car immediately approached me, and Alastor looked at me from behind the window. As I got into the car, I looked at the puzzled bodyguard. 'Can we make another stop, please?'

☆

It was a late in the evening, and the car slowed down by the sidewalk in front of the tall, magnificent church. Asking Alastor to stay in the car, I walked to the entrance of God's house, waiting to push the door forwards and dive into a serene quiet atmosphere of prayers.

Loud voices not too far away got my attention and I glanced into the corner of the main entrance. I looked at the priest involved in a heated argument with someone else. To my surprise I saw that he was speaking to the same young man who had saved Thana from imminent death.

'Eric! I will not repeat it again!' the priest growled. 'You are an embarrassment!'

'Forgive me, Father,' the young man lowered his gaze, pressing his lips.

'It is all your mother's influence, I am sure!' the man waved his hands. 'She is not disciplining you at all! You will humiliate me in the eyes of God! Your sinful soul cannot be cleansed at all! Your dirty, disgusting desires oppress me! What will the community think!'

'I only expressed my thoughts! It's just art, Father!' the young man tried to justify himself. There was both immense frustration and guilt written on his face.

'Filthy drawings of naked men are not art! Your notebooks are full of it! Shame, Eric!' the priest snorted. 'I hope it's just a phase as you disgust me! A man cannot lust another man!'

'I'm sorry, Father.' The young man put his head down, and I pressed my lips because I felt a terrible injustice to this young man. Nowadays, people's interests and sexuality should not be judged, but it was not the case.

'From tomorrow, you will join our parish! I will

make this wicked devilish desire leave your mind.'

'Why can't you just—'

'You live under our roof, son! We provide for you, we raise you, we are responsible for you!' whispered the priest angrily. 'You are seventeen years old and should start acting like an adult! Enough with your perverted fantasies! This phase of yours is absolute filth, Eric. Do not dare to disobey me in the presence of the Lord!'

'Yes, Father,' the young man barely answered, and I stepped to the door. No matter how much I wanted to interfere, it wasn't my business, and I could only make it worse for Eric. I had to deal with my problems before I could help someone else. However, to think that the Devil would be blamed for such an unfortunate fate of the boy...

How was it Bale's fault?

I opened the door to the church and took a deep breath.

The warm, dim light from the candles immediately enveloped my body, inviting me inside.

Passing by lonely empty benches, I was heading towards the altar, behind which I could see a golden cross shining in the light from the candles. My gaze ran through the colourful walls and ceilings, which depicted beautiful white-winged angels, cupids and saints. I was immediately engulfed in an atmosphere of grace and peace.

'Sophie?' a surprised voice sounded behind my back, and I slowly turned around, looking into the eyes of an old friend. 'What are you doing here?'

'Michael.' I smiled softly, looking into his blue, radiant eyes and came closer to him, noticing the white collar of his black shirt. He was a transitioning deacon as far as I knew. 'I came to tell you the truth about me...'

As I watched Michael's changing expression, I continued my story, hoping my truth would not push my friend away. Every word was hard to say, especially when Mike's look expressed uncertainty, doubt, and something else I couldn't recognise.

After telling him what I'd heard, I pressed my lips in silence and waited for him to digest it all.

'Now I know what kind of power it was that attracted me to you,' Michael answered quietly, making my cheeks blush. 'If I hadn't promised my service to God, I swear, Sophie, I wouldn't have let you out of my hands.'

'Um...' I looked down and tried to deal with the embarrassment.

'A heavy burden fell on your shoulders.' Mike peeked at me, and I bit my lip. 'What will you do?'

'I wanted to consult with you.' I smiled . 'Tell me, do you think it's a sin to agree to be the Devil's wife?'

'I... I don't know, to be honest, Sophie.' Mike got confused, and I noticed a note of disappointment in his voice. 'Are you sure you want to do this?'

'I've decided that what I want to know the most is who I am. I also want to finish my father's task and help Bale, if he truly was framed,' I answered, and Mike looked sadly into my eyes.

'But, what if your father was wrong?' Michael asked, and I looked at him in surprise. 'What if the Devil did what he is blamed for? Do you still want to try?'

'I only want to know the truth,' I answered, with a weak smile . 'Mike, I'm tired of deception. There are so many secrets and lies around me that I'm lost in their continuous stream. I feel like I can't get a breath of fresh air until I get out of this abyss. That's why I came here and told you the truth about me... I value our friendship and don't want to keep anything from you.'

Noticing Michael's changed expression, full of pain and uncertainty, I suddenly felt the weight on my heart. Did I burden him with this information? Did I make it worse? Would he want to continue communicating? I didn't want to lose him... Maybe I should have left him alone for a while, to let him process all the information.

'Sophie!' suddenly he called to me when I turned my back, ready to leave. 'Wait... I... have to tell you something.'

With a gulp, I prepared for the worst, but the creaking of the main doors and someone else's footsteps distracted me, forcing me to turn my head and face those brown eyes of my nightmare with fright.

He was here.

Smoothly, slowly, the Devil approached me, walking on the stone-cold floor of the church and making the flame of candles burn brighter, a golden hue reflected in his eyes. I could feel a slight hint of pine in the air. It was his scent.

Bale was approaching me. Shivers ran through my body, and my heart stopped as if waiting for the unknown.

'This is God's house. You don't belong here,' Michael said sternly, standing in front of me and making Bale stop. The Devil was still looking at me . Holding his hands in his pockets, Belial smiled.

'Get out of my way. I didn't come for you,' he replied in his deep voice that echoed through the church walls. I trembled and my blood boiled .

'You don't belong here,' Mike said again, stepping towards Belial. The cold gaze of the Devil's eyes bore into my friend.

'Get out of the way,' Bale almost growled, his

eyes sparkling. 'I am stronger than you and your prayers.'

'But not stronger than God,' Mike insisted, and Bale frowned, ready to object.

'It's OK!' I blurted out. Michael shuddered and Bale slowly turned his gaze on me. Standing at the altar, I nodded uncertainly, and then Michael reluctantly took a step back and walked to me.

'Sophie...' He took my hand, and I just smiled, looking into his radiant eyes.

'Really, I'm fine,' I answered and let the man step aside, hiding behind the columns of church walls, leaving me alone with Bale. I knew my friend was only there for protection, but I was grateful to him for letting me handle things myself, trusting my gut and my heart.

It was time to face my fears.

Letting Bale get closer, I held back my fear by looking him in the eyes. He examined me from head to toe in silence, raising his eyes again.

'I want to apologise for not keeping my cool last time,' he began, looking away and ironically smirking at the images of the angels on the ceiling. 'I didn't mean to scare you. And I will not let that happen again.'

'Um,' I just said, letting the man speak.

'I thought long and hard about everything while I was back in Infernum. I was trying to understand why I was attracted to you. I've known about your origins for a long time, but it didn't bother me much,' Bale replied with his eyes down. 'Sophie, my soul is millions of years old, and I've seen a lot, including the history of humanity and the birth of this world. Damn it, I was there for first breath of the very first human. My old soul is tired, and I still do not understand why I am drawn to you – an arrogant, stubborn young girl who dares to look directly into the eyes of the Devil. I have met many in my way, and you are not unique in any way, apart from your strength.'

How rude.

There was silence, and I relaxed a little, observing complete serenity in Bale's eyes. Something told me that I was absolutely safe for the moment. All I could see in front of me now was a sad, tired man trying to make sense of himself.

'My interest in you grew the night you shielded me from attackers possessed by evil spirits when your father died. A little, frightened girl who blocked their way to save a stranger she had just met. Your courage and perseverance gave me hope that I had long lost. Surprised by your power, I wanted to know more about you, to see if there is something in the world that could break you.' Bale frowned. 'It seemed to me that by finding your weakness, I could find an excuse for myself because I had given up a long time ago and didn't want to seek the truth anymore. I accepted that I was the cause of all this world's troubles. I let people blame me for something I wasn't guilty of. It was easier that way than trying to prove otherwise. At first, I watched you from afar, seeing you grow up. You never changed, always stubborn and persistent and confident. And soon… I couldn't cope, so I took a step closer, forcing your power to wake up unwillingly. And that's when you changed…'

I lowered my gaze and gulped, frowning. Memories of my inexplicable abilities were really depressing because I was so scared for the first time.

'You weren't just scared,' he said, reading my thoughts, and I looked at Bale with displeasure, but he ignored my anger. 'You were lost. At first, I was suddenly happy that you weren't someone special. You gave in to the same feelings and emotions as humans do. Then I decided to repay your father's favour by agreeing to pay off his company's debts and giving you safety until I find his killer. But... when you first looked me right in the eye after that accident, your gaze filled with confidence, a desire to continue to fight and move on, I realised how wrong I was about you. And my hope woke up in me again, mixed with a new feeling I had long forgotten.'

Looking into my eyes, Bale sighed. I started to feel uncomfortable but kept looking at him, trying not to think about how embarrassed I felt, so I wouldn't reveal my chaotic thoughts.

'I saw a brave girl who had grown into a strong woman, ready to go all the way to reach her goal. Sophie, I can't give you love, as I told you before,' Bale said quietly. 'Not because I don't want to, but because I can't. This feeling is painful for me. I gave it up a long time ago. Perhaps one day I will tell you why. But as I said, I'm willing to provide safety, care, and everything you need. In return, I ask you for one thing...'

'What do you want?' I whispered.

'Trust.'

Looking at Belial's begging glance, I felt a light breeze from the open window of the church, calming the rhythm of my heart. The words of this man were sincere and honest. I had no doubt that he was telling the truth.

'If I say no, what will happen to me?' I asked, remembering the deal. 'I signed a contract with the Devil. Did I sell my soul to you?'

'The only reason I had to call a priest to sign our contract was because,' said Bale, 'I decided to marry you. As a son of God, an Archangel, I cannot approve this contract without God's blessing despite my current status. It wasn't a contract for a deal, Sophie.

You didn't sell me your soul. You just gave it as a sign of trust, a bond.'

Bale took a step back, pulled his hands out of his pockets and took a deep breath. The flame of the candles swayed, and a bright azure glow appeared behind the man's back, whose eyes had found an amber hue, while two sharp horns shone behind his wavy black hair. Spreading his wings as black as night, Bale did something that made my heart miss a beat.

Down on one knee, the Devil appeared before me in his pure form, with his head down. With silver horns and a bow in front of the altar of an empty church surrounded by beautiful angels. The light of his blue flame was reflected on the golden cross behind me, and what I saw was contrary to all the rules of this world. The feathers of his black wings were swaying.

'I gave you my soul as proof of my loyalty to you,' Bale answered quietly without raising his head. 'My signature is evidence of that; this contract is unbreakable, indestructible, even by God himself. Only you and I can end this union. I can feel you in every corner of the world, and you can call me to your side anytime. United, even after Death, for eternity.'

I didn't know if Michael had seen the magic, but I was sure he wouldn't have been able to say anything because even I was speechless. Tears suddenly appeared in my eyes. My whole body was full of overwhelming feelings and emotions . What I saw seemed unreal, strange, but, at the same time... incredible. It appeared that for the first time since we'd met, I saw the true beauty of the angel Lior, kneeling down and offering his soul to me as a gift.

The Devil bowed down before me, and I couldn't help but kneel before him and silently wrap my arms around his neck, hugging him tightly and feeling a sigh of relief that sounded from the lungs of my fallen angel.

'Let's go home,' I said quietly, hiding my nose in his neck and feeling his firm arms hugging me back, squeezing as hard as he could and not letting me breathe. For a moment, I wondered if God had seen his son. Was he proud of him?

Somehow I thought it was brighter and warmer in church...

Somehow I thought it was lighter and warmer in church...

CHAPTER FOURTEEN

Lonely rain drops danced chaotically on the glass surface of my car window. I was tiredly looking in one direction and waiting for us to arrive at the estate. Quiet music on the radio, Alastor's smooth driving, and the sound of the pouring rain made my eyelids heavy. Giving in to the charms of the sandman, I relaxed my body, letting my head fall to the side and touch the Devil's strong, warm shoulder beside me.

My deep sleep was occasionally punctuated by moments where I woke briefly, noticing the night-time glare of bright streets, the shine from the headlights of passing cars and neon signs from various boutiques and restaurants.

After a long drive, I felt a light breeze and heard the door open on my side. My eyelids refused to open, my body shrouded in cosiness and warmth. Feeling weightless, I inhaled the familiar light fragrance of pine and smoke. Once on the fresh crispy sheets, I was sweetly wrapped up under a blanket and got lost in my own fantasies of a dreamy world.

I was enveloped by the darkness around me. Turning my head, I felt a cold chill on my body and gulped, hugging myself. I didn't know where I was, but it was terribly lonely and scary. Making a step forward, I heard an echo of my own steps and sighed.

A mirror appeared in front of me, and I curiously looked at my reflection. I felt a terrifying horror enveloping me as I saw myself. My chestnut hair turned black, my eyes were staring with a cold evil look, and their colour slowly changed from bright blue to an almost ink-black shade. My reflection smirked and showed a killer grin, lifting its hand and reaching to me. I stepped back, but my reflection stepped out of the mirror, following me.

Shaking from the cold, I reluctantly opened my eyes and looked towards the open balcony door. The night breeze of the coming winter let itself in, and I slowly got up from bed with a desire to close the door. With a fleeting glance at the bright stars, I tried to remember what horrible dream I had. A slight rustle from outside caught my attention, and, having pulled a fluffy throw from the armchair, I put it over my shoulders, stepping barefoot on the wooden floor of the balcony. Looking at the beautiful estate with a flower garden, tall maple trees with autumn yellow foliage and a cosy marble garden pavilion, I noticed Bale walking on the grass, which was wet from the night dew, raising his eyes to the night sky.

THE DEVIL'S SIGNATURE: THE ABIDING PACT

I sighed, leaned against the balcony railing, and wrapped myself in the throw. *I wonder what it's like to have such an ancient soul?* To see the birth of this world, to watch its development and history? It must be very tiring. I understood why Bale always seemed so calm, peaceful and silent. Well, almost always... Over the years, his rage and fire had gone out, and his soul was exhausted. People's general opinion of the Devil as the root of world evil, a rebel, and a lover of trickery and sin was very wrong.

However, humans also become calmer over the years due to their nature. They seek peace and quiet in their old age. As time passes, we all begin to appreciate the world around us in its natural, raw image. Simple human cravings and desires become so insignificant... we gain wisdom and plunge into our own solitude.

And Bale was no exception. His whole nature expressed the fatigue that consumed him. His body and soul were overflowing with the energy of the worlds he was responsible for. And maybe, in the beginning, he was an angry, resentful son of his father, eager for revenge, showing his displeasure and rebellion, running away from new responsibilities like a young teenager. But now I thought he accepted himself for what he was. He allowed himself to surrender to the appointed role of a Judge of the World, absorbing the energy of it, which was now overwhelming him because of the increased population of the world, the increase in negative human emotions and devastating energy. I wasn't surprised it was difficult for him to contain this power over time, requiring a frequent return to Infernum.

I suddenly thought about what Bale had said before. He signed an agreement with me, a pact, giving his soul to me as a sign of trust and gratitude.

His words that the pact couldn't be broken, even by God himself, still surprised me. Apparently, despite the higher powers, some things in this world were beyond God's control. Perhaps this was the world's balance, the natural force that made it possible for everything to exist.

My understanding of the world suddenly became more explicit, my interest in the new side of myself increased, and I was eager to learn more. What was waiting for me? What was waiting for Bale? What will happen to this world and to others in the future? Will this power be eternal, or will everything come to an end one day ? Will it all ceize to exist?

As Al said, perhaps even God will give himself to Death one day. Will someone else come to take his place? Will Death itself disappear? These questions were spinning in my head, but I understood that no one knew the answer to these questions, not even divine beings. Apparently, that's what my mother had in mind – there will probably remain unanswered questions in this world...

I smiled, thinking that many people don't even know about the reality. Some people may just live their days thinking about small, personal matters. They wake up every day without paying attention to whether the sun is shining brighter, whether the rain is getting colder... whether it ends today or tomorrow. People rush to work with their eyes glued to their smartphones, heads down. Do they even think about how nice it is to stop for a second and lift your head to the sky? To look at the clouds or lift your face in the pouring rain? People do not notice the shimmering colours of autumn and do not see how different each fallen leaf is from the others. Hurried city dwellers will not notice a green caterpillar on a bright flower as they pass by. We prefer to look at passers-by as if they are background objects, rather than glancing at smiling people, wondering what good things have happened in their lives. We mumble and get angry at those we don't even know, judging strangers, before we think about the hardships in their lives that we may not even know about. And in the end, we expect others to understand and accept us.

This is human nature.

'You're thinking too loud,' a quiet low voice rang out beside me, making me jump and stare at Bale, who'd appeared at my side. As I took a step back, I tried to calm my frightened heart as the man watched the stars in silence. 'You're right. People rarely think about the world around them, plunging into their own selfishness. In their old age, they regret missing what life had to offer. However, people are not as bad as they seem at first sight.'

Hiding his hands in his pockets in his usual gesture, Bale smiled gently and looked down at the night moth that touched the railing of my balcony. Unwilling to start a quarrel about the fact that I disapproved of Bale's ability to read my mind, I kept quiet and looked at the insect's white wings.

'Humans are amazing, in fact,' continued Bale. 'They are a perpetual mixture of emotions and feelings that we celestials have no control over. They have a wonderful ability to sincerely rejoice, to be sad, and to be angry. People are overflowing with self-sacrifice and selfishness at the same time. Man can forgive and love... We, celestial beings, don't know what it's like. Love is unattainable to us, unknown. We know only devotion to our beginning and father, against whom we dare not go, unlike people. Human is like a canvas – your emotions and feelings are different colours, unique in their meaning, different from each other.'

'According to the accepted beliefs, the angel Lucifer had some feelings,' I began with caution, 'rising up against God because of pride and jealousy towards people…'

'And I came to terms with that belief,' Bale smiled sadly, and I pressed my lips. I thought about what I wanted to ask him out of the many questions spinning through my head.

'What really happened?' I looked at him. Bale took a sigh, and the night moth rushed up. Its wings reflected in the chocolate-brown eyes of the Devil.

'I really did rebel against my father,' my husband replied, and I raised my eyebrows in surprise. 'Not because I was jealous of people… but because I loved them.'

'Out of love?' I asked, baffled. 'But you said you couldn't control—'

'Yes,' Bale interrupted me, and I went quiet. 'You know, I've always been different from my brothers. And there's a straightforward explanation for that.'

'Tell me,' I said quietly, drawing Mr Deemer's attention and noticing his doubts about whether I should know. 'Please…'

'When God created his angels, he tried to give them perfect features like his own. Obedience, loyalty, strength. These were the creatures until Caelum's energy reached the limit and bifurcated, generating a negative side. And then God decided to use that energy to see what would come from it. Father was always a fan of experimentation.' Bale sighed, and I smiled. 'And he used that energy when the time came for me to be created. And even though I wasn't much different from my brothers, I still showed different character traits due to the negative energy inside me.'

I was surprised. 'What was the difference?'

He smiled. 'The first difference was my curiosity. I was the only one who expressed interest in Father's innovations. I was excited when I watched him and the creation of your world. These emotions were positive, but they only originated from the negative energy inside me. This energy that he used was the first specimen of the negative power of the universe. Although it was limited at first, and my father only used a drop of the negative flow, the effect was substantial. Father was amazed at this quality. He was still wary, so he did not repeat his experiment again and did hide the remains of this original energy, which was the basis of my creation, forever. He decided to watch me and learn. He studied his unique child closer .'

'That's why you were his favourite,' I grinned, and Bale looked back at me sadly.

'As time passed, my father shared an idea with me that made me more curious,' he continued, 'and soon he showed me his new work. It was an amazing creature. So similar to us, but without the ability to fly or control a huge force. This creature seemed physically weaker, but... the eyes. They burned with a power that none of the angels had ever owned. These eyes were full of emotions, feelings unknown to me. My gut wanted to know more about them. And this creature became closer to me than any of my brothers...'

'Was it a human?' Bale nodded. 'Adam? It was Adam?!'

'Lilith was the first human created by God. However, she shared divine magickal powers, like him. She was his first experiment. She had the free will of a human but the powers of divine creatures. Father wanted to experiment further. So he created Adam, a simple weak human with no celestial powers.

I spent all my days with him. We talked day and night while I studied him and succumbed to his infectious change of feelings and emotions. This creature seemed so similar to me but was still different from everyone else. Lilith followed my father's every step; she wanted to learn more magick, to reach her ambitions. But Adam was a free spirit.' A weak smile touched the Devil's lips again. 'He will always remain my great... first friend. However, Father was still not happy. Something inside him seemed to be thirsty for more. He tormented himself for a long time, trying to understand what was missing. I was baffled, as were my brothers and sister...'

'Sister?!' I stuttered in surprise.

'Yes, according to legends, there are seven archangels in Heaven. In fact, there were only four. The eldest was Raphael, then Mechahel, and soon I showed up. Well, after my creation, my father shifted his interest back to a more feminine image and created my sister – Gabriel,' Bale answered, looking at my surprised face. 'However, the church was quite misogynistic through the centuries, and Gabriel was often presented as a man. She's a little annoyed by it.'

'Oh...'

'You see, humans indeed are created in his image. Latest image. God doesn't really have a physical body. He's the cosmic energy that can take any form it wants. The first few seraphim, like Metatron, were created the same way, frightening to the human eye. The can shapeshift, but it still doesn't change their terrifying looks. I possess the power of shapeshifting, thanks to the abilities he gifted me; however, I was made in a more humane form. For a long time, long before Heaven was his home, God would travel the universe in different shapes. At some point, he took a feminine androgynist form, and soon after preferred a male image. He can be white, black, young or old, human-like or in animal form.' Bale continued. 'And even though he created humans by assigning certain biological attributes to each, he gave them free will to be whatever they want to be. God never intended to create any borders in human development and evolution. Later humans created those borders, moral principles, and rules that limited their freedom and imagination. Heaven was free and accepting of all sorts of individuals. Nature evolves, and so should people.'

'I see.' I suddenly remembered Eric. I wonder, would he feel better hearing this? That God would never judge him.

'Well, my father thought that Adam's creation was quite successful. And one day, when I found myself in his workshop where he was working on his inventions, my life changed. I stood in front of a marble table, and there laid a creature superior in beauty to all the angels of Heaven. I looked into the eyes of my father, who was trying to understand what was missing in this perfect creature. When he asked for my advice, I replied that it was glorious. Her whole essence made my gut burn with a fire hotter than Hell. The pattern of her discoloured skin was perfection. So unique, so…' He went quiet for a second. 'My hand reached out to that blond hair, which became brighter than the sun from my touch. My inner power grew in me. This was the main distinguishing feature from my brothers, as none of the angels could control the natural elements or revive life like my father and, in the end, me. He asked what name I wanted to give this creature. It was different from Adam and Lilith. It was so fragile, so petite.'

'Eve…' I whispered, watching Bale's sad eyes. I couldn't believe it.

'Eve,' he confirmed, 'is the name I gave her. And my whole world turned upside down when she first opened her eyes and looked at me. Something inside me was trying to escape, and it was frightening. I didn't know that feeling, and for a long time, I tried to run away from it. I watched as she was promised to my best friend as his mate. I couldn't even take my eyes off her. I saw how alike they were; how compatible they seemed. But the unknown power inside me made me approach the human woman. I struggled with myself until one day she touched my hand. At that moment all my energy exploded inside me, taking control and making me dive into my desire.'

'You were in love with her...' I could barely hear myself say it, and I looked down, trying to get my thoughts together. What I heard tonight completely reversed my understanding of familiar legends. Now I knew why Bale was cold and distant. I understood his pain, his torture and his tragedy. My lonely Devil shunned the feeling that had burned him and destroyed him from within... love. *Love for Eve caused his new beginning.*

'The angels are not allowed to love.' Bale closed his eyes as he read my thoughts. 'It was against all the rules, and I broke them by betraying my friend and taking what wasn't mine. Eventually, on my way to my father to confess my sin and deciding to take all the blame to save Eve from his wrath, I only awoke God's rage and disappointment. By taking all of God's wrath upon myself, I begged that she would not suffer. This fragile, pure creature that I'd broken and tainted.'

'And then what?' I asked, on tenterhooks.

'My brothers were there to support me. Waiting for my fate, I couldn't see the one I longed for. I found out that she had devoured the forbidden fruit by wanting power comparable to God's. All the guilt fell on me, and then I saw Father questioning me about what I had done. I kept silent. I was confused. He was omniscient. He knew the truth, and yet he blamed me. I was broken, and I succumbed to a new feeling of anger for the first time. I was ready to explode and destroy everything because the one who could save me admitted my fault. She left me, and betrayed me, just like my Father. Left without a chance for redemption, I heard the most horrifying words in my life from him. He rejected me... by sending me to Infernum. Angry, I went against him, knowing I would lose. I was only desperate to put an end to it all. I swore to get even with him and that woman who broke me.'

'You were waiting for her, weren't you?' I asked bitterly, feeling incredibly eager to comfort this man. 'You waited for her soul in Hell?'

'And I punished her personally,' Bale replied quietly, making me flinch.

'What? So... have you seen her?' I couldn't believe my ears. 'But, how could you? My mum said that...'

'She stood before me, looking at me with her bright, beautiful eyes.' I noticed the muscles in Bale's arms getting tense, expressing his desire to contain his anger. 'I watched her kneel before me, silently, without saying a word. She admitted her guilt by agreeing to be punished.'

'And you... never asked her what happened?' I asked him impatiently.

'I did. She failed to confess,' Bale said quietly. 'I was overwhelmed with anger, and I didn't want to hear excuses. I just wanted to hurt her as much as she hurt me. Besides, if she wanted to tell the truth, she would have done so. Eventually, she took the hit, protecting the one who set me up. And that was enough for me to make a decision.'

'What happened to her?' I asked him carefully, hoping she didn't suffer.

'Her soul is imprisoned for life in the most remote cell of Tartarus, where she is in total darkness and silence, subject to her own solitude. It is a cell that no one can get to, as I have placed an eternal seal on it, held back by my own energy.' There was silence, and I was shocked, staring at Bale. How so? All this time, she was by his side? Eve knew the truth that could completely turn this world around.

'Why... why don't you keep asking her who's behind all this?!' I raised my voice by pushing Bale on his shoulder. 'That's the key to everything!'

'I asked—' Bale frowned '—but she still doesn't speak. And no torture can unleash her tongue.'

'No way...' I whispered and walked away from Bale. 'How so? It's...'

'It doesn't make any sense, does it?' Bale said. 'And yet, here it is. Even after she has nothing to lose, she keeps the truth to herself. Maybe it's revenge or something, I don't know... All we know is that your father found out the truth. And that's what caused his death.'

I tried to build a chain of events by trying to understand what I had just heard. Adam never found out what Eve was hiding. Whoever set Bale up let Adam return to Heaven, which means Adam was no threat to that criminal. That someone was sure Eve wouldn't reveal his identity, but why? If he wanted to, he'd have gotten rid of her, but he didn't do it, which means he was sure she wouldn't talk. Why not? What stopped Eve from confessing? Was she really an accomplice?

'What about Lilith?' I suddenly remembered looking at Bale. 'Isn't she Adam's first wife?'

'Lilith was created before Adam and Eve,' he replied. 'There were about a dozen humans in Heaven, and Lilith was one of them. But she was the only one with the power of magick. Father didn't gift other humans with it as he wished to have creatures that didn't rely on such powers. The poor woman was in love with Adam, even though he thought only of Eve. One day Lilith and Adam drank from Heaven's Springs, which had a slightly intoxicating effect on people, so they gave themselves up to simple human pleasures and passion.'

'What?' I laughed in disbelief.

Bale laughed. 'Eve wasn't too upset about it, because she truly loved Adam as part of the family rather than as her husband. But Lilith was unhappy when Adam blamed it all on the despair from losing Eve to me and a drunk mind. Shortly after people were banished, Lilith realised she loved the human world madly and wished for eternal life. I heard her prayer, and she eventually became the first person I signed a contract with.'

'But she's still alive, right?' I asked.

'Yes, she lives in New Orleans currently,' Bale said. 'Eternal life has allowed Lilith to increase her power, to make it stronger, and, in the end, she has become the first witch of this world. The poor woman struggled a lot through this life, from the horrid treatment of several cultures towards her race to the terrifying events of the seventeenth century during the witch hunt. She was on the run then, and since she was still learning magick, she wasn't as strong as she is now. She would quickly run out of strength after using spells, and this weakness allowed her pursuers to catch her. Lilith was tortured and burned alive several times before escaping and ending up on a slave ship to Jamestown, Virginia.'

'Oh my…' I gasped at such horrible news.

'I was unaware of her struggles for some time. The times were dark and terrible. I was absolutely swamped with contract requests. I can't believe she still didn't give up on life; however, she did ask me for help in ending it once, though. But, I couldn't help her as I am not allowed to break my own deal.'

'So, she's not a demon?' I confirmed.

'No, she's just immortal. At first, people were immortal by creation but soon lost this feature after an exile. She was the woman who stopped your friend from jumping off the bridge that night.'

'What?' I was shocked.

'Yeah, she saved Lizzie. But Lilith's immortality was my mistake. Now, I don't promise eternal life in return for the soul. I can't kill for a deal. Neither do I promise divine power or the return of the dead.'

'Can you?' I was surprised.

Bale nodded. 'If the soul has not disappeared as a whole, then, theoretically, yes, but Death does not approve of it because this process is messing with the universe's balance. In exchange for life, there's a great price to pay. The balance of life is disturbed if the price is not paid, leading to world disasters.'

'Oh.' I nodded in understanding and bit my lip. So even in the divine world, there were rules.

'You are freezing,' Bale said, suddenly taking a step in my direction and touching my shoulders with his hands. A warm stream ran through my body as if I'd taken a sip of a warm drink, giving me goosebumps and a pleasant feeling inside my stomach.

'Wow!' I exhaled intermittently, raising my eyes to Bale, smiling softly while letting go of my shoulders.

'It's only a small fraction of my power,' he replied, sighing and opening his palm, allowing a bright flame of fire to appear in his hand. 'I had plenty of time to develop my abilities, explore the world's energy, and become stronger.'

I smiled sadly. 'I can't even imagine what it must be like to live so many years.' Bale looked at me and smiled back.

'It's exhausting, but it's also motivating.' He looked up at the sky and closed his eyes as he breathed in the cold air. 'I was able to see all the secret corners of the world, learn most languages, try rare dishes, and just watch humanity change.'

'Now I understand how wrong people's opinion of you is.' I pulled the throw tighter on myself. 'I, too, succumbed to the general belief of the Devil as a known seducer of souls, a ruthless and insidious creature.'

'Hm—' Bale smiled '—they're not entirely wrong. There was a time when I wasn't much different from that image. However, it quickly became boring. As time passes, you learn to appreciate peace and wisdom rather than a loud lifestyle and a dubious reputation.'

'I wish I could see you that way.' I laughed, not even trying to imagine my husband so rebellious.

'Hm—' he squinted mysteriously '—perhaps one day, you'll get a chance.'

'Oh, yes, I remember!' Suddenly, it hit me. 'Your portraits! I saw a woman…'

'Oh, don't remind me.' Bale rolled his eyes, and I raised my eyebrows. The man sighed and shook his head as he saw my disgruntled look. 'As you know, I can take any shape and image I want. Times were wild. I was trying to occupy myself with something when I was bored. Men, women… I didn't care then.

Still don't, really. I explored all kinds of pleasure.'

'Is that you?!' I exclaimed, remembering a beautiful girl in the portrait.

'I wanted to get Marie Antoinette's attention.'

'The Queen of France?' I was no longer surprised at the mention of Bale's acquaintance with historical figures.

'In secret, I learned that she preferred women...'

'You filthy lecher.' I shook my head and sighed. Bale just smiled.

'I almost managed to get her, even though I knew the consequences of that connection. However, I only wanted to have some fun. That time I didn't think much about what was happening to humans after a sexual connection with divine beings.'

'So, what stopped you?'

'She was executed.' Bale shrugged his shoulders, and I covered my mouth with my hand. *Oh, what a pity...*

'Since then, I've vowed never to take that form, even though I once broke that vow.' He gulped and twitched as if trying to shake off an unpleasant feeling. 'Men are just magnetically attracted to my feminine nature, I barely escaped the clinging hands of the city perverts.'

'Ha-ha,' I laughed. My opinion of Bale had changed a lot, but I still felt like there were a few things I didn't know about him. 'I heard you had a murderous reputation in the past.'

'Yes, I did...' He looked away with sadness in his eyes.

I was silent for a moment, trying to figure out what I wanted to know. 'I still don't know what I'm going to do next. I'm not sure if I want to be near you or if I want to go back to my human life. I'm still afraid of who you are. Everything seems so unreal and...

weird.'

'I understand.'

'However, I wish I had a choice.' I looked at my husband with confidence, and bit my lip again. 'I want to know what you were like.'

'I'm afraid it wasn't a pleasant sight.' Belial shook his head and stepped aside, but I grabbed his hand and held his palm tightly.

'Please, Bale,' I said quietly, 'I must know! I have a right to know this…'

Silently looking at me for a moment, with doubt and confusion, the fallen angel nodded affirmatively and slowly raised his hand, touching my forehead with his thumb.

'I'll show you…' he whispered, sending a gentle stream of energy into my head and letting my mind fade, sinking into a bright stream of other people's memories.

My soul seemed to fly through the world's darkness, slowly warming my body until it finally found itself amidst the bright, hot flames of Hell, which seemed endless.

Panicking, I shuddered from heartbreaking screams around me. The voices were begging for mercy . A burst of vicious laughter echoed through nothingness, and I froze, looking into familiar eyes. Their golden hue became bright red. Snow-white beast canines and clawed fingers clutched the poor soul of the sinner, and bare, black, leathery bat wings reflected the bright light of the flame. This unknown Devil scared me, frightened me, and pushed me away. His silver horns seemed twice the size of those I'd seen before, and their sharp ends were marked with blood, curling.

My consciousness suddenly moved further into the thick chaos and panic, desperate people fled the city, when an erupted volcano covered everything, absorbing Pompeii with lava and taking every living soul with it.

In the distance, quietly watching this disaster, the Devil stood on the hill, grinning and waiting for survivors to turn to him for help. It was that wild, beastly Devil that had once attacked me.

Over and over again I was thrown in time, forcing me to watch the cruel games of the fallen angel that took out all his anger on the human race. I saw oceans swallowing cities under his supervision, wars breaking out, and desperate people falling to their knees before him, offering souls in return. And only the cunning, contented, and proud look of the Devil was the answer to them.

'You promised me fame!' There was a disgruntled voice of a man when I was thrown forwards again. It was a room, an office maybe. The interior was ancient and old-fasioned. Belial looked at the unwelcomed guest with a calm look. The man threw the papers off Bale's desk. 'What is it?! Why do they talk such dirt about me in the city?'

'Isn't that true?' Bale grinned, bored, looking at the man.

'It's not what I asked!' The man was outraged. 'You promised me fame. You broke the deal!'

'Oh, no,' the Devil whispered, grinning, 'I promised you fame, and you got it. But you didn't specify what fame. Now, leave my office, and I will see your rotten soul in Hell.'

'I will not serve a liar like you!' a man snorted, and Bale slowly rose from his chair, his eyes gleaming with a stern look at a frightened man.

'Don't play with me, human,' the Devil whispered. 'I kept the deal and gave you what you wanted. Next time, specify your requests. And if you dare to avoid the deal, I will lock you forever in the eternal flames of Tartarus. Now, get out of my sight!'

Suddenly, I was shaken, and my consciousness returned, forcing me to take a step back and sigh, silently looking at calm Belial waiting for me to come around. With my head down, I pressed my lips and clenched my fists, trying to forget the terrifying look of the Devil with blood-red eyes. That horror... that monster... was Bale, too. That's the part of him that was so deep inside that he kept hiding.

'What made you change?' I asked quietly, overcoming my fear and looking at him again.

'My anger slowly faded away and gave way to loneliness. There were few pure souls on my path that brought back memories of my former love for humanity, and I gave in to indifference for a while. But then I met someone, and my life changed.'

'Who was it?' I was curious.

'I can't say now.' Bale gave me a gentle look. 'It was a long time ago, in the fifth century in Constantinople. I'll tell you about it some other time.'

'What else can you do besides read minds and control energy?' I asked him, leaning against my balcony railing and trying to change the subject.

He shrugged. 'Many things... telekinesis, immortality, and other powers. Do you want to see it?'

'Sure.'

'Come, I'll show you something.' Belial extended his hand, looking at me with his chocolate-brown eyes. Watching his palm for a moment, I reached out my hand to him in return, letting the Devil lead me.

Stepping down the hall stairs, I slipped into my pumps, grabbed a warm shawl from a hanger, and followed Bale outside, heading for the garden and standing under the starry sky. As I wrapped myself tighter in the shawl, I shivered. I could see my breath, feeling the cold air enveloping my body.

Bale stood in front of me, gently touching my shoulders again and sending another wave of heat through my veins, making my cheeks burn, either from a hot stream inside me or from embarrassment. Looking into his dark eyes, I suddenly froze when I noticed them slowly acquiring a golden hue, shining brighter and brighter with an amber palette. It was the first time I had seen the process so close-up, and my body was still as I was utterly fascinated by the beauty of those eyes. It was as if the sun was shining inside them, bringing light.

Bale stepped back a little, put his hands down and turned his palms up. Looking straight into my eyes, he took a deep breath and moved his fingertips in an almost imperceptible movement. My lungs were filled with fresh air thanks to the breeze gently touching my cheeks, dancing with the strands of my hair. And then, I held my breath.

As if by magic, a dark, sleeping garden suddenly began to come to life… Red and yellow roses opened their petals, and peonies bloomed under the moonlight. Chrysanthemums, tulips, hydrangeas and gerberas – all the colours of the possible palette appeared before me like a floral carpet in the middle of the garden. As I looked to the edges of the estate's hills, my heart beat louder. Like fragile snowflakes, the blossoming wild cherry flowers fell to the ground in a beautiful wicked dance with the wind.

'Bale…' I whispered, hardly believing my eyes and covering my lips with cold hands, as if afraid to take an extra breath so as to not break the spell of this unusual sorcery.

The horizon behind Bale's tall figure slowly began to take on a golden hue – the sun was about to appear.

The sky was covered with strokes of orange and red, like fire. The dawn foreshadowed a new day. Bale's palms rose higher and suddenly clenched into fists. He opened his hands again, creating something I hadn't even dreamt of. As soon as his palms opened, shining with bright azure flames, the sky suddenly spilt a beautiful green, white and blue light, shimmering with emerald shades and merging with the bright colours of dawn. Aurora... so bright that tears appeared in my eyes. The flower pollen slowly soared upwards, reflecting the heavenly glow like fireflies.

Surrounded by all this magickal, beautiful scenery, I looked into the Devil's eyes when the first sun rays appeared behind him, gradually mixing with the divine polar lights. *'Light-bearer,'* I suddenly thought, remembering Alastor's words. Suddenly, I understood the meaning of my dark angel's name. Lior was the angel that brought light into this world. And despite his dark nature, his soul now shone as bright as Aurora. I refused to believe that a creature capable of creating such beauty was a monster.

The Devil created the Garden of Eden on Earth, in the middle of which I was standing now. And for me, this power was a sign of how much God loved his son... Such a gift was deserved only by the beloved child. Bale's anger and resentment towards his father kept him from seeing the truth. Devil or angel – he was beautiful both in body and soul.

My heart suddenly bounced, and tears flowed down my cheeks. I didn't know what kind of storm had suddenly broken out inside me. Why did my feelings suddenly rush outside? Why did my heart hurt, and my soul move forward, forcing my legs to step towards my husband? Was it a reaction to a celestial in front of me? What was this inexplicable pull that prevented me from stopping until I found myself in front of Belial and squeezed him in my arms as if I was possessed?

Breathing rapidly and letting tears pour down my cheeks, I squeezed Bale's neck harder as if trying to dissolve inside him. Silently hugging me back, he closed his eyes and let me come to my senses.

What the hell is this? Why am I acting like this? Why can't I stop? What was this overabundance of emotions that I'd been feeling? Everything inside me was burning, my heart was beating, and my head was humming.

'Sophie,' Belial's quiet voice sounded, gently pulling me away. 'You're... glowing!'

'Huh?' I looked at him incomprehensibly, wiping my tears and suddenly flinching. My palms reflected a bright white light and my whole body shone. Like a light bulb, I was glowing. 'What is that?'

'Your inner power must be reacting to my energy.' Bale laughed as he reached for my palm with his hand, touching a bright light. 'It's ironic.'

'Why?' I asked when the tears dried up, and my face showed all baffling emotions .

'Your father was an angel in love with the moon and stars,' answered Bale, 'and his daughter now shines like them.'

Looking at my palms, I gulped and pressed my lips. I was a little scared to see myself like that but still fascinated. Watching the glow slowly disappear, I took a deep breath and squeezed my palms. Something inside me burst out when I was near Bale. But, why, I didn't know...

Looking into the amber eyes of my fallen angel, when they slowly found a dark-brown hue I put my head down and tried to hide my embarrassed look from this man that looked at me so intensely. Though my hidden desires pushed me towards him, my mind still reminded me of who was standing before me, and it was frightening.

'You're afraid of me,' Bale said quietly, lifting my chin and making me look at him again. I hugged myself, then pressed my lips . 'You know I don't want to hurt you, Sophie.'

'I know...' I looked away.

'I still have so much to tell you, but I don't want to burden you all at once.' The Devil smiled sadly. 'Don't worry, I won't put you in danger. That's why I always asked Alastor to be near you.'

'So he could protect me from my enemies?' I asked.

'And from me, if necessary,' Belial answered quietly. I stared into his brown eyes, realising the meaning of his words and nodding approvingly.

'I am not giving up my promise, Sophie,' my husband said seriously, 'and if you decide to go your own way, I will not stop you. This marriage is truly temporary because I don't want to keep you at my side by force.'

'Then, what do I do until I decide to leave?' I asked, unsure.

'You're free to do anything.' He smiled, and I noticed him come even closer, clutching my palm in his . 'And if you want to push me away, I won't insist.'

A storm was raging inside me, and I froze on the spot, trying to put my thoughts in order and calm my heart. I think Bale noticed my panic and my doubts, understanding and moving away, leaving me alone.

He turned his back on me, walking towards the house. I looked down at the green grass, feeling incomprehensible frustration and dissatisfaction. I was still not sure what I was feeling. My body and mind struggled with each other. Fear and desire blended together. My soul seemed to be struggling with common sense.

But then why, I still...

'I wanted a kiss,' I whispered to myself, feeling my cheeks burn. Why? Why did I want it so much? I was afraid of him, I stayed away. But... I was ready to let him do it.

'What?' The man went still with his head turned in my direction. 'What did you say?'

'I...' With my head up for a second, I blushed, and that's when my thoughts started sobering up. The butterflies went quiet inside me. 'Nothing.'

'Sophie,' Bale's eyes sparkled, 'what did you just say?'

'Never mind.' I turned my eyes away and already scolded myself for such carelessness, knowing that I scorched the fire in the Devil's soul.

The man crossed the distance between us in a fraction of a second. He suddenly pressed me to a tall apple tree, hovering over me from above and putting his hands on the sides, not letting me move.

'Bale!' I said cautiously, trying to push him back, but he stood firm on his feet.

'Say it again,' he whispered, frowning. Did he try to find out whether he imagined it or not?

'Please...' I didn't have the strength to fight him, so I put my hands down and turned my head to the side. 'Step aside, Bale.'

'Sophie,' his voice sounded quieter, calmer than it was a second ago. He touched my cheek with his hot palm and turned my face towards him, 'Is that what you want?'

'What?' I sighed. 'What do I want?'

'You want me?' His eyes looked down on my lips . Even if I said no, he couldn't stop. I knew it. His limit had been reached, and it was my fault for teasing him. 'To kiss you?'

'I...' Looking at him, gazing into these waiting eyes full of hope, I tried to follow my common sense. *Why is he looking at me like that?* Why hasn't he done it already, like before? Why was he waiting for my answer? He... said that love is foreign to him. He knew our physical connection couldn't cross certain boundaries for my safety. However, did I want him?

Hell, yes, I did. I wanted him badly. Everything in me begged me to lose myself in these gentle strong arms, to give myself up to the Devil's flame and burn in it, right down to the ground.

'I guess...' I whispered. That was enough. Before I'd even finished, he was devouring my lips, making me gasp in surprise. He pressed me so hard against the tree with his body that I felt like I was about to dissolve into it. His palms held my face, his fingers tangled in my messy hair, and his breathing was fast.

But despite this impatience, this passion and impudence, he was gentle. In a way that I could never have imagined he'd be. It seemed to me that Belial was trying to vaporise his breath in me. Like a young boy, he explored every corner of my mouth without missing an inch. I was dizzy. The lack of air got me clinging my fingers to his forearms in a fit of panic. My body was begging for a breath of oxygen, and I moaned for help.

Giving me a second to breathe, the fallen angel's lips slid from my lips to my neck. The tingling feeling and the newly arrived butterflies accelerated every beat of my heart when his tongue left a wet path on my throat. My hands squeezed his collar, pulling him closer to me, and my head leaned back.

'B-Bale.' I could hardly hear myself whisper. 'Wait... no...'

'Don't torment me,' he said, growling, biting my

neck slightly with his canines. 'I can't stop now.'

'Please…' I was losing it, his hands roaming on my waist, lifting my T-shirt and burning my skin with his every touch. My mind was contradicting my body. Words tried pushing him away, but hands clenched him until my knuckles went white. 'You can't.'

With a silent growl, he tensed up, moving an inch away from me and putting his palms back on the tree trunk. His head was down, and I could see him trying to get a hold of himself to cool his heat. I looked at him, embarrassed, trying to understand why I wanted to feel his lips, his hands and his whole essence on me so much. His eyes were bright amber, wild, devouring. My head was dizzy from the circling scent of pine and smoke. As if I was standing beside a campfire in the middle of the deep forest.

Oh, fuck, I was going crazy. My head was spinning. The awkwardness started to grow, and I wanted to forget it all and disappear. With shaking hands, I touched his face, making Bale lift his head and look at me with a blurred, lustrous, and begging look, like a beast that was dying of thirst. His eyes shone in the light of the stars, and they were beautiful. How strange, those very eyes could be so angry and cold. But now, they have warmed even the farthest corner of my soul.

'Why me?' I whispered, still feeling my cheeks burning. My gaze fell on his lips again, and I fought my desire. My body language said it all.

'I don't know, Sophie,' he answered irritably, clenching his cheekbones. My insides tightened. The only thing I could think of was that he… loved me. But was that possible? Did he know how to love?

When I decided that words were unnecessary, I pulled him towards me. The man gulped, waiting for my actions.

My soft lips fell on his, giving him a light, sweet kiss like the touch of a butterfly that tickled the skin with its velvety wings.

Bale's heart was rejoicing. I could hear a growing rhythm in his chest. I refused to tear my lips away from him, and he only pressed me harder against him, opening my lips and kissing me deeper.

It was a limit of our bond, and we dared not want more. Taboo was a wall that held us back. However, for a fraction of a second, I wanted to dissolve into it, forgetting that the one who burned me with such a passionate kiss was the Devil himself…

THE DEVIL'S SIGNATURE: THE ABIDING PACT

THE DEVIL'S SIGNATURE: THE ABIDING PACT

CHAPTER FIFTEEN

Slowly opening my eyes and staring at the white ceiling, I rubbed my face and felt a nagging pain in my back. I'd fallen asleep uncomfortably. Trying to move, I suddenly realised that my head was definitely not on the pillow...

When I turned, I flinched. My gaze fell on Bale's peaceful sleeping face while he put his head on the back of the couch he was sitting on as I laid down by his side, resting my cheeks on his lap. As I looked around the room, I sat down and turned back.

The memory was slowly returning, and I rolled my eyes. Yes, of course, we did! After yesterday's madness, Bale and I returned to the house, thinking that going to bed was no longer a good idea, as the morning had greeted us with a bright sun. And we would certainly end up doing something... forbidden. That's why we'd settled in the living room, ordering Chinese and watching a couple of movies.

Apparently, fatigue still defeated me, and I fell

asleep soon after, as the movie was finished and I didn't remember the end of it . Bale, as I understood, decided not to bother me and let me rest for a while.

Looking at the watch on Belial's wrist, I realised that the day was already in full swing as the time was approaching two o'clock in the afternoon. As I turned my head towards the sleeping Devil, I smiled fleetingly. I had never seen him asleep. For all I knew, he didn't need sleep or food. However, something in this image was very humane and sweet now.

'Oh, are you awake, madam?' Rosie's quiet voice sounded when she brought a tray with breakfast to the lounge.

'Rosie, good afternoon,' I nodded, gratefully taking a treat, biting off a piece of toast, and looking at the table full of leftovers with Chinese food. 'I'm sorry we made a mess.'

'Oh, come on!' The woman waved her hand, picking up the boxes from the table. 'This is your home; you're free to do whatever you want! And I'm glad to see Master resting rather than working all night! I can't even remember the last time he let himself fall asleep.'

'Sleep is a luxury, Rosie,' the Devil's hoarse voice sounded as he stretched out and opened his eyes lazily, leaning forwards and biting my toast.

'I thought you don't sleep at all,' I said, surprised, grabbing a cup of coffee.

'Basically, yes,' Bale answered, getting up from the couch and leaning his neck to the side, letting it make a cracking sound. 'But I can still enjoy the simple human needs if I want.'

'What are your plans for today, sir?' Rosie smiled as she watched the Devil in a wrinkled shirt, barefoot, with messy hair falling on his shoulders. He was heading for the door and I observed him with amusement.

'Shower first,' Belial said wisely.

'The weather's good today,' continued the woman, 'why don't you two take a walk? A weekend like no other?'

Bale yawned and looked at me as if he was silently asking if I wanted to get out of the house. Thinking for a second, I shrugged my shoulders and nodded. Well, why shouldn't we?

Walking along the stone paths of the narrow streets, I looked curiously at Bale, who seemed to know exactly where he was going. Trying not to ask questions, I let him lead me, trusting his refined tastes and love for the beautiful secret places of London. I had long noticed Belial's obsession with remote spots, which easily penetrated into the soul and left a warm and iridescent feeling after a visit.

I wasn't wrong about him this time either. Involuntarily smiling brightly, I squeezed his forearm more tightly. We found ourselves in the heart of the Neal's Yard district, London's secret landmark. Surrounded by a few shops, cafés, and buildings that were painted in bright, unique colours. A courtyard of meetings, conversations and music, like a magical world in the middle of a metropolis.

Having wholly freed myself from worries, I was immersed in fun and excitement. Running into cosy shops and dragging the King of Hell with me, I was inspired by the palette of this place. My artistic nature simply burned inside me. It was terrific in here! I didn't want to go home at all. Even the cold weather that foretold the approach of winter couldn't stop me. It seems that I smiled and laughed sincerely for the first time in years. Full of joy, I also infected Bale with my happiness as he opened himself up to me a little, telling me stories of his travels around the world, interesting facts and details about what he had seen.

Listening to his story about his adventures in the Dark Ages over a cup of coffee, I plunged into this warmth between us. Part of me got sad because my whole life was not enough to listen to his stories.

For the first time, I thought I wanted to be near him all eternity, even though I couldn't. One day my life would end, and Bale would continue his journey around the world in eternal solitude. But even if it was a short period of our friendship, I wanted every drop of warmth and happiness from this relationship.

'Where did you get this?' I asked curiously, looking at the silver bracelet on Bale's wrist.

Glancing at the jewellery, the man smiled and took a cunning look at me as if trying to figure out if I should know the secret behind this bracelet.

'It was a gift from one of the most beautiful women who once lived in this world,' Bale shared, and I felt a stab of jealousy in my heart. I knew well that he had lived many years, and I may not have been the Devil's first wife, but... the thought of his previous amorous adventures still hurt a little.

'Ex-girlfriend or wife?' I asked, looking at the bracelet.

'I wasn't married before,' Bale responded thoughtfully, making my pride glow with happiness, 'and it was hard to call her a girlfriend. I would say... the object of my interest and an excellent friend.'

'I'm intrigued!' Smiling, I took a sip of coffee.

'She was a famous person,' Bale continued his mystery, 'a strong, wilful, proud woman. She was worshipped by nations and followed by the most respected war leaders. I met her on my way to the Egyptian capital on one of my travels.'

'No...' I whispered with my mouth open. 'No, you didn't! Are you serious?! Cleopatra?!'

Bale laughed. 'She wanted power badly, and I was there in time to offer her a deal.'

'Are you kidding?' I whispered, looking back. 'Cleopatra herself was your mistress?!'

'Not exactly a mistress.' Bale corrected me. 'At the time I had no physical relations with human women because I mostly spent time at Infernum. She attracted me with her temperament, and I gladly made a deal with her, giving her the power she desired. She was a tough character, but I liked that woman. Despite the love of Caesar and Mark Antony, she always returned to my secret chambers in her beautiful palace, trying to get more than a deal from me. I, frankly, didn't mind. We became friends. Really close ones. She gave me a bracelet as a sign of our special bond.'

'So, after the infamous suicide, she started serving you?' I was surprised, refusing to believe that Cleopatra herself was now a demon serving the Devil.

'Souls that take their own lives don't go to Hell. They get stuck here forever until their energy runs out, and it might take centuries if not more. However, it wasn't suicide,' Bale said quietly, and I stared at him silently. Nothing could surprise me anymore.

'Oh?'

'After Mark Antony's death, captured by Octavius, she still continued her secret meetings with me. In the end, I surrendered and let myself share a bed with her .' I blinked, trying to understand where he was going with it. 'It was our mistake.'

'What do you mean?' I asked, completely forgetting about the taboo.

'Sophie—' Bale sighed as he looked me in the eyes '—there's a reason I only share my bed with demons. For the same reason any divine creature is not allowed to have a connection with humans.'

'Ah, yes...'

'It's fatal for a human,' he replied, and I kept silent, recalling my mother's story. 'Her body couldn't stand the energy I shared in the process, and eventually, her heart stopped almost instantly. In the end, I had to portray her death as a suicide. One of my demons entered her chambers as an ordinary peasant with a pot of herbs, without the guards suspecting him. There was hidden a snake hidden in a pot, and it left a bite on Cleopatra's hand.'

'And you weren't noticed?' I was surprised.

'Well, I might have taken a little advantage of my ability to change my appearance...' Bale looked up, and I raised my eyebrow. I didn't particularly understand what he meant by that. 'Only maids were allowed into her room...'

'Eh?!' I exclaimed, immediately looking back to make sure I didn't attract people's attention. 'Really?'

'I must say, I came out as a pretty decent girl for the first time...' My husband laughed. 'I have improved my female image since.'

'And... then what?' I asked, intrigued.

'Now she's offering deals on my behalf.' Bale smiled. 'We're still good friends, even though occasionally in the past we have given in to our desires out of boredom. She's doing a pretty good job. Cleo mostly appears before powerful men like politicians, businessmen and other rich humans whose greed and lust succumb to her beauty.'

'I see. Bale, tell me, what future do you see for us?' I asked seriously, looking into the mug and thinking that my vision of the future with him should be clear.

'What are you talking about?' He didn't

understand my question and the sudden change in the subject.

'As your wife, what can I expect from the future with you?' I looked at my husband and pressed my lips.

'I told you, Sophie,' Bale said quietly, looking out the window, 'you're free to do whatever you want. Once I've found those who present danger, I won't hold you back unless you want to stay.'

'And what if I want to?' I asked. Bale frowned as if I had hurt him with my words.

'Then... stay,' he replied as he bent in front of me and looked me in the eye.

'And then what?' I asked again. 'Bale, whoever my parents are, we still don't know who I am. And we may never know. I'm not sure if I'm human, at least in part, because I'm subject to ageing, hunger, and fatigue. I'm likely to grow old and meet Death at some point.'

'Let it be.' Bale shrugged his shoulders. 'What's bothering you?'

'Despite the special circumstances of our marriage, I still want to have a family, to enjoy the little things in my personal life,' I continued. 'Can I get it with you, Bale?

'I can't give you a family, Sophie,' he answered as he kept looking at me.

'Can't, or don't want to?' I asked.

'I can't,' he said again. 'It's not that it's impossible. Theoretically, there's a chance. Demons can't have children because they're dead. However, angels and celestial beings have the energy of life, so they are quite able to continue their kind, as my father did once. It's rare, but it does happen. That's where cupids come from. But... You're right. We don't know if you're at least a little bit human. And if you are, then I'm not gonna let what happened to Cleo happen to you, too.'

'So, you won't let me get as close as I wish?' I smiled bitterly , and Bale pulled away with his hands crossed on his chest. 'Bottom line, you leave me no choice. Either I stay by your side, sacrificing dreams of a happy family, children, love and simple physical connection. Or I leave you and get to experience those desires.'

'I'm sorry, I can only offer you safety and wealth. Our physical connection can be limited by certain foreplay and boundaries, but can never go further than that. Not without risking your life,' he answered quietly.

I sighed. I wasn't mad at him but rather at myself. Why did I think I could find simple human happiness in my situation? My husband wasn't human, and I didn't know who I was. It's stupid to dream about things that aren't meant to happen.

'Why did you offer marriage, Bale?' I frowned, biting my lip. He looked at me and glanced at the coffee mug with his fingers touching the edge of the pottery. 'Now I know it has nothing to do with my dad's company, I'd inherit the money anyway and your excuse about sponsors and shares was a lie. Marriage means something to you.'

'I need to know where you are so I can easily find you in danger. The contract with me gives you not only material support but also safety. Thanks to this contract, part of my soul belongs to you, and in the end, you are protected by strong energy that repels the enemy. Think of it as your own shield against low-level demons and evil spirits. It's like an invisible cover for your energy,' Bale responded. 'Everyone's energy has a certain scent; my shield hides yours. It's a safety measure, even though you're partly inhuman.'

'So, I'm immortal?' I whispered.

'No, as far as I know, you're not. This shield will protect you from most creatures except high-ranking spirits, demons and those who possess celestial power, like angels. An angel can destroy anyone, but God.'

'So, they can kill demons?' I asked.

'Yes. Demons have several ranks, those that are stronger are hard to kill. Those in special ranks, like Alastor, are almost impossible to kill unless you're an angel. This is due to a power they're gifted by me.'

I raised my eyebrows. 'How do you choose?'

'Again, it's intuitive. I can feel the soul, the power in it. There are weak and insignificant ones, and others are bursting with power. It's a bit like comparing human physical stamina and willpower. Some can run a marathon, and others can barely lift a finger. It's down to nature.'

'So, you give more power to those who are stronger by nature?'

'I give them demon powers, that only accelerate their inner potential.' Belial smiled. 'Most demons can also be killed by special weapons forged from Hell's fire. Hell Hunters mostly use them, as well as demons of the highest rank.'

'Are there a lot of them?' I was fascinated by the whole structure of Hell City.

'Seven for now,' he answered and I didn't hide my surprise. 'They are gifted with additional power from me, including control of a certain element of nature, supernatural strength and others.'

'Is Al one of them?' I asked.

'Yes, he can control electric currents and create lightning. Azazel is gifted with the power of water control, the other two control fire and earth. I still haven't found a demon worthy of the air element.'

'Wow,' I gasped.

'Asmodeus, the general of my demon army, has unlimited strength, like me.' Bale took a sip of coffee. 'And then your mother.'

'W-What?' I whispered. My mother? She was the highest rank of demons?

'I gave her the power of soul control. Her energy was beyond the peak since she arrived at Infernum, but it seemed to be locked deep inside her as if something was restraining it. However, after I gifted her with my power, she became one of the most feared demons in Hell. A Soul Crusher, she was called. But the power was gone after Lilith's spell.'

'No way.' I couldn't find the words to comment.

'You have a strong bloodline, Sophie. Your father also belonged to the highest rank of angels, equal to me and my siblings. He wasn't an Archangel, and to be honest I never understood what exactly he was, but he was extremely powerful.'

'And how do you kill an angel?' I was wondering, noticing Bale's surprised look. 'It's not like I was planning anything…'

'Hm…' Belial smiled, seeing my sincere curiosity. 'Angels can be killed by those equal to or above their level.'

'So… can you kill an angel?' I followed a logical chain.

Bale shrugged his shoulders. 'I haven't tried it, but I suppose so.'

'Right,' I mumbled, sighing.

Strolling through the evening streets of London, heading for the car, Bale and I barely exchanged a word. My head was full of thoughts about my future and what was right for me to do next. He seemed to just let me figure it out myself, knowing my thoughts perfectly and trying not to get into my personal chaos.

'Is there anything else you're interested in?' He tried to cheer me up as we walked around Piccadilly Circus.

'I have many questions, but I'm not sure where to begin.'

'Hm.' My husband, hugging me with one arm, drew me closer to him, keeping me warm.

'He's one: are all angels as hot as you?'

'You flatter me.' Bale smirked.

'Temperature-wise, Bale—' I rolled my eyes '— I'm talking about body temperature!'

The cheeky man laughed. 'No, not all of them. It's my special ability. I can control the forces of nature, including water. And most of the human body is made up of water, like blood. I can warm it up with a simple thought. My body, however, got used to the special heat of the Hellfire, and in the end, I literally absorbed it into myself.'

'I thought Infernum wasn't a place filled with eternal flames...' I remembered what my mother had said.

'Not now, but when I got there first, Infernum was a newly born world, and just like this planet, fire and lava have been raging in that world for a long time. Soon that negative energy settled and subsided, allowing me to build a city.'

'So there's literally fire flowing through your veins?'

'You could say so,' Bale agreed, and I smiled.

'Why is your flame blue?' I asked then, when we turned onto another street full of people.

'Blue flame is the hottest,' Bale explained, and I nodded. Belial was a living firecracker, as I understood it.

'Hey!' He frowned, shoving me on the shoulder and looking at me with displeasure.

'My thoughts are my own business!' I snorted. 'If you break my personal boundaries, don't complain about what you hear!'

'No respect for the elders...' Belial shook his head, and I smiled again at my thoughts. *Not just a firecracker, but a very ancient one...*

'Rude,' the fallen angel answered, putting his hands in his pockets, and I cheered up.

'Hey, Mr D, brother!' called a hoarse voice nearby, drawing our attention. Approaching us with a lazy gait was a dark-skinned man with a broad smile and black wavy long hair, and the sight made a grin appear on Bale's face. I looked at him in surprise. He had a very mellow, chilled, and friendly aura around him. The man was quite handsome. His ruffled beard, ragged 'boho' trousers and colourful shirt stood out from pretty much everyone else. Despite the evening chill, the swarthy guy was walking around in his flip-flops.

'Jay, brother, what are the odds?' Bale laughed, hugging his friend and patting him on the back. 'Maggie let you go out? I don't see you often on these sinful grounds.'

'Oh, you know her.' The guy waved his hand, and several wooden bead bracelets made a rattling sound on his wrist. 'She is always so moody. She kicked me out again and told me not to come back until I matured and learned some responsibility. Just because I forgot about our one thousand nine hundred ninety-first wedding anniversary.'

'Did she, now?' Bale nodded, smiling, 'And you don't seem to be grieving.'

'Mr D, my friend, what's to grieve about?' Jay laughed. 'There's no angry wife, no father with his constant nagging. Freedom, that's all! Responsibility, they say... I've been walking this Earth with my bare feet for decades, helping people and teaching them life, taking responsibility for human sins! And what did I get in return? A wooden cross up my butt and an Easter bunny with a basket full of chocolate… They even got the dates wrong!'

'Hey, hey, come on!' Bale laughed again, patting his friend on the shoulder. 'You know well it was all a cover-up for major pagan extermination, don't take it personal. Where are you staying, anyway?'

'Moses, Muhammad and I recently got back from our trip to Europe. We're renting a room here in London. We've been hanging out all day, my brother! Who cares where you sleep? I'm a chippy; I can build my own bed if I need to!'

'It's true.' Bale laughed. 'Oh, yeah, sorry about the manners… This is Sophie, my wife.'

'Ooh! Mrs D, so it's not a rumour?' Jay reached his hand to me. I shook his hand and suddenly felt a huge release and boost of energy. 'The Devil settled down, finally!'

'Times change.' Bale smiled faintly. I looked silently at the friendly dialogue. If my knowledge of mythology and religion did not let me down, by building a logical chain and realising who was standing in front of me, I gasped.

I covered my mouth with my hands and stared at Bale in shock, then at Jay. As they both waved goodbye to each other, I continued to stand in the middle of the street like a statue, staring at a departed new acquaintance.

'Are you OK?'

'Bale, don't tell me that was…' I whispered, watching my husband smile. I wasn't exactly prepared for such surprises.

'Yes, this was my half-brother, Jesus, well, Yeshua, his true name is.' Bale took me by the hand

and led me to the car. 'He's a lover of freedom, peace and wine. His frivolous and kind nature often makes his wife Maggie, sorry, Magdalena kick him out from the Silver City until he gets some air and comes back.'

'I can't believe I just met him!' I whispered, shaking my head. 'This is mental!'

'Aw, the stories about him are a little different from the truth.'

'What do you mean?' I was surprised again.

'Tell me, do you really think Jesus is the result of immaculate conception?' Belial asked me when we got in the car, and he started the engine.

'Um... to be honest, I haven't given that any thought in my twenty-six years of agnostic life.' I shrugged when we turned the other way.

'I'll tell you a story that only some in our circle know,' said Bale. 'The famous Mary was a minor when she married Joseph. That's why legends call her a virgin. It's a mistranslation of the word from an ancient language, which actually meant "maiden", that is, a young girl. This marriage, like many others then, was not a marriage of love, but an arranged one. Young girls were mostly sold by their families. Joseph was not a bad man; he cared for Mary and sincerely respected her, but they had no children.'

'Didn't Joseph have other children as per some texts? What about those from another marriage, according to legends?' I asked.

'The kids were not really his, even though it wasn't announced,' Bale explained. 'And the reason for that was very simple.'

'OK...?' I raised an eyebrow, and Belial smiled.

'Joseph had little interest in women, so to speak.' He shrugged and my mouth opened. 'Mary, on the other hand, was in love.'

'With Joseph?'

'No, dear, not him.' Bale sighed. 'The man she loved was the one who changed Mary's life forever, letting her give birth to a world legend. That man broke his own rules that made me who I am.'

'God?!' I exclaimed.

'My father always watched his creatures with interest. When he met Mary while wandering the earth in search of inspiration, he could not believe how such a pure and innocent creature could live in this cruel world. Now, don't forget that times were different. The church wasn't born yet. The Roman Empire was in power , and the days of Israel and Judah kings were long gone. Many Jews were taken to Babylon for exile. Still, some returned and lived in the Roman province s, clinging to their religion and customs.'

We were approaching the house. When we stopped the car, Bale turned off the engine and sighed.

'When Jay introduced himself as a son of God, he got a bit misunderstood. All he wanted was to bring peace and allow people to believe in themselves and their inner power, advising that this was the original message of God. However, Jewish religious leaders found him a threat due to poor communication, gossip and exaggeration.'

'Right,' I nodded.

'Mary was a woman of Nazareth, and even though she was young, she was truly beautiful. She had dark skin as she spent all her days outside with her family tribe, nomads and travellers. During those times, women handled family finances as they were responsible for all trading and bargains. So even though today she would be considered a minor, in those days, she was a young adult woman ready for marriage. Because don't forget that life expectancy was much lower,' Bale explained. 'So, God was travelling, and they met. And as a very wise young woman, a herbalist and a kind, pure soul, she immediately attracted divine energy. As I mentioned before, God is cosmic energy, a celestial power, so it was more of a union between souls rather than the love between a man and a girl. They were obsessed with each other. You call it love at first sight. We think it's just a simple fate that bound them together and was impossible to break. This connection was so strong that God broke his basic rule by crossing all boundaries. He made the same mistake that I did. Seeing Mary die in his hands after the close encounter between the two, he gave her some of his energy so that she could continue to live until that energy dried up. And, as I said, divine beings can theoretically make life.'

'So, Mary got pregnant,' I whispered. 'It was not an immaculate conception, but a divine one…'

'Exactly.'

'Wow…'

'I met Yeshua in Hell after he died, and I liked him immediately. He's a cheerful little fellow, very different to my father. We became friends, so we meet periodically on Earth, travelling the world.'

'Amazing…' I thought, fascinated. Apparently, it was only part of the information I was about to learn today as Bale quickly changed the subject.

'I'm sorry, you've been through a lot.' Bale smiled weakly as he looked at me and shook his head.

'It's OK,' I replied. 'It's all so interesting, though I can't believe it.'

'Sophie, I never thanked you,' the man said quietly, touching my fingers.

'For what?' I felt his tension and the way my cheeks started to burn. I shuddered at such a gentle touch, lowered my eyes, and held my breath.

'For accepting me,' he replied. In silence for a

second, I looked up at him and smiled gently, with no reply. Looking into my husband's brown eyes, I tried to understand. What was I supposed to do, after all? Should I have stopped and prevented this man from getting deeper into my heart to avoid the pain of parting in the future? I accepted my feelings long ago, even though I tried to escape them for a some time. However, my heart has already made a decision, though not in my favour.

'I think... I'm in love with you,' I said weakly, hiding my gaze and feeling Bale's hand flinch. I overcame my embarrassment and yet dared to look at him. The ambiguous, guilty look of the fallen angel made my heart skip a beat. He could not answer back, and I knew it.

'Sorry, I can't...'

'It's fine!' I was smiling, trying to push away the sadness. I took my hand from his. With a bite on his lip, he frowned angrily, knowing he'd hurt me, though not on purpose. When he unbuckled his seat belt, he suddenly reached sharply for me, an inch away from my face, and I secretly wished I could touch him. And maybe my wish would have come true but... Bale pulled away and opened my door.

'I won't hurt you anymore.' He smiled sadly, and I nodded understandingly. He's right. It would only make our situation more complicated. As I got out of the car, I took a breath of fresh air and cheered up.

'Sophie!'

'Yeah?' I smiled, turning around while getting out of the car.

'Why don't you invite your friends to dinner next weekend?' Bale smiled softly. 'I think you need some friendly gathering .'

'You think so?' I laughed as I headed for the door. 'Well, then, that's what I'll do.'

'I'll cook,' replied the Devil, and I nodded.

Well, so be it. Maybe I was jumping to conclusions and worrying about something inevitable. Understanding everything step by step was worthwhile, slow and focused, rather than succumbing to chaos and panic. Anxiety won't help me either. By accepting Bale, I accepted the possibility that our relationship would never give me what I wanted.

Walking to the door, I smiled at him and headed towards my room, hiding tears in my eyes.

THE DEVIL'S SIGNATURE: THE ABIDING PACT

THE DEVIL'S SIGNATURE: THE ABIDING PACT

CHAPTER SIXTEEN

A chilly morning met me with bright sunlight and blue skies. I wrapped myself in a scarf and took a sip of hot tea in a paper cup , and smiled at Alastor approaching me with a bag of croissants in hand. Passing the treat to me, he politely opened the car door and let me in. I gazed at newly placed colourful Christmas decorations that had been hung up in London. I was always amused by our tradition of preparing for the holiday from early November. However, despite my scepticism, I still felt a share of pre-Christmas spirit.

The car moved, and we headed towards Infernum Enterprise, arriving at the office before most of the employees.

Sitting on the soft velvety couch in my husband's office, Alastor and I began to study the documents and papers, as he brought me up to speed with company updates. I was reading every line with patience and concentration, asking Al many questions.

I didn't even notice how much I was immersed in the company's business, as time was approaching noon, and I was noticeably hungry.

'Lunch?' Bale, smiling, walked into the office with a bag of sandwiches.

'I would say you're a mind-reader,' I said with a smile, 'but I won't proclaim the obvious.'

The Devil laughed. 'Actually, I just guessed.'

I gladly took a treat out of his hands.

'So, what's this project you're working on?' I asked while chewing, gratefully accepting a cup of coffee from Rebecca, the secretary.

'I plan on creating an interface where everyone around the world can store their personal information in one place,' explained my husband, 'something like a government social media with data on taxes, documents, social security and so on.'

'Wow.' I was surprised. 'It sounds interesting, but it's not safe.'

'Naturally, security will come first, with a lot of safety codes, programming and all,' agreed Bale, 'I plan to resort to voice recognition or fingerprint, or perhaps facial information. With this application, they can easily keep personal information with their passport number, social security number, tax information and even medical information without needing to store paperwork, risking losing it. Files will be available only to them, and even state organizations will not be able to request this information without the client's consent. So no controversy there.'

'Why are you so interested in this?' I couldn't understand because I didn't see any use for that app for a Devil.

'Hm, good question.' Bale took a sneaky glance at me while taking a sip of coffee. 'With the increasing population in this world, it becomes quite difficult for my employees in Hell to find a piece of specific information on someone in a short time. We need better control of the souls so we can keep track of their lives and have quick access to their information for trials in Hell.'

'Don't they all get into Infernum right after they die?' I asked.

'Yes, but it takes time for us to examine their lives, especially those who made a deal with me. We need to decide which area to send them into. My demons are divided into corporate levels and departments, making it easier for me to make future deals. Departments include Family Affairs, Personal Affairs, Love and Relationship Affairs, Abundance and Wealth, Revenge, and others. For example, Cleo was chosen to make deals with authorities. As a former Queen and great leader, she has the grip and the ability to persuade those individuals. She works for the department of Power and Politics.'

'Al, what department are you in?' I asked with interest, looking at the bodyguard. A little embarrassed, he coughed up and looked at Bale.

'I'm in charge of both Family Affairs and Love and Relationship Affairs,' replied the demon, 'I offer deals to those who are willing to sell their soul for the sake of their family or loved ones.'

'Like my mother...' I smiled and sighed. Al nodded, confirming my guess. 'Wow, in charge, you say!'

'Yes, Al is a demon of the highest rank, after all. He's also very unbiased and fair,' Bale replied.

'So, what's stopping you?' I went back to Bale.

'It wouldn't be a problem to get into the client's memories thanks to my power, but it's lengthy and tiring. However, as I enter the borders of any program and code, allowing technology to work even outside of this world, thanks to my control of electric waves.' Bale sat down in his chair and looked out the window. 'All I need is for a human to interact with the app once. As the human body produces electricity, and with just one use of the app their energetic waves would transfer to our electronic Hell data, providing us with all the information needed – memories, desires, hidden thoughts. So the app is just a cover-up. I couldn't care less about their immigration status or medical history.'

'So that's how you texted me while you were at Infernum! Your power!' I suddenly exclaimed, and Bale smiled, nodding.

'However, I need a skilful computer genius who can create this interface knowing my requirements and, in principle, understanding the meaning of this project.'

'So, you need someone who knows who you are?' I asked.

'This person should be my key contact between the worlds. Working personally for me and managing the project, the role will be to keep the IT department here under control while having contact with Infernum to send information in time to Azazel, who manages the distribution of demons in my world.' Bale sighed.

I nodded understandably. The case needed someone with whom Bale could trust his secret completely, knowing that the information would not spread. I knew that person had to endure a big burden of information, much like the knowledge that had been revealed to me some time ago. 'I am looking for such a person, and, until now, luck is not on my side. Ironically computer nerds don't have much of a desire for deals with the Devil, so I have no demons with the ability.'

'What's my role?' I asked him confidently, looking at a pile of documents.

'I want you to be in control in my absence,' Bale explained, getting up from the chair and heading to the couch I was sitting on. 'You don't have to worry about all the details because the management already has everything under control and will report back to you regularly, but I need you to be able to make your own decisions. I understand that you need time to learn everything, so Al is here to guide and help. You have the right to sign any documents. Even Hell contracts if needed, but I would countersign them later. Our bond gives you the same authority. Just make sure to use my special quill.'

'OK,' I gulped, feeling like a sack of responsibility had fallen on my shoulders. Bale smiled faintly and softened his look.

'That's great,' he said with a sigh, 'now, I have another assignment for you.'

'Oh my God.' I noticed him flinch. 'I'm sorry... Oh, my Devil!'

'In a week, there will be a WTN award event held in Paris – The World Technology Network – and our company has been nominated in the Environment category,' he explained, taking out his smartphone and checking the time.

'The environment?' I asked him again by taking an incomprehensible look at him.

'One of the main applications developed by the company helps the user to live a greener lifestyle,' said Alastor, drawing my attention to him. 'This application helps to recognise any product in the industry by scanning it, showing the user a few possible recycling options. It also allows the user to control their energy costs, receive recycling bonuses or perform small tasks to improve the environment, ultimately returning these bonuses to the user as coupons for shopping, entertainment or anything else.'

'I never thought you'd be interested in saving this planet.' I raised an eyebrow. He looked at me in surprise.

'This world is a pearl of the universe, I've watched its creation for a long time, and I've spent a lot of energy helping my father create living things,' Bale replied, disgruntledly looking at me. 'My argument with him does not concern this world, and I've always tried to make an effort to extend the life of this planet, as it deserves it.'

'OK, I'm sorry.' I said and smiled. Bale was serious about this case. I realised once again that the Devil wasn't who I thought he was. Despite his stern looks, daunting gaze, and constant pressure, Belial still sought justice and respect for the world. Such a tree hugger...

'So, what's my mission?' I asked, remembering him mentioning the event.

'You're coming to Paris with me as my companion,' Bale answered as he dialled the number. 'Alastor is also coming with us, and he needs a companion for the event. Could you ask your witch to come with us?'

'Lizzie?' I was surprised.

'She knows our true nature and your situation. It's easier. Besides, I'm sure you'll feel more comfortable having a friend near you,' my husband explained, and I smiled quite a bit, nodding. Oh, I could imagine Lizzie's face when I invited her to the event.

'Alastor will take you both to someone who can help you with your attire,' Bale said, starting a chat with someone on the phone. 'Paimon, got a minute to talk?'

I looked at my husband curiously when he stepped towards the desk and started writing something in his planner.

'Clear your schedule for tomorrow. I'll send you a VIP customer. Alastor will explain later, I'll pass a note. Yes, thank you.' Watching Belial make notes in his planner, I looked at Alastor with interest, and he noticed my perplexed stare. With a smile, he leaned in my direction.

'Paimon is the demon in charge of ceremonies and events at Infernum. In your world, he owns a boutique of fine tailor-made clothes. He's a big fan of beautiful gowns, costumes and masquerades. He's passionate about teaching people good self-esteem and confidence.'

I raised my eyebrows, nodding. There were many more uninvited guests from Infernum in this world than I thought. 'And why are they all gathered in London?'

'The army follows the King,' Bale answered my question, looking down at me. As I closed my mouth, I nodded and sighed with understanding. So, where the Devil is, there's a pack. It made sense. 'Don't worry, my demons are everywhere. It's just that there are more of them in London at the moment as I'm here. Sixty years ago, Eastern Europe was overflowing with my demons, and there was a real mess, believe me.'

'It must be great to see the whole world,' I sighed dreamily as I got up from the sofa and grabbed my bag in the plan to leave this office, as my head had started to hurt noticeably.

'The world is changing forever,' Bale said, 'and eternal life is not enough to see everything. Are you ready?'

'Where are we going?' I was surprised to see Bale

handing out a piece of paper to Alastor.

'We need to buy groceries for our dinner.' Bale winked, and I perked up, motivating myself for the weekend ahead.

Just then, the door to the office opened, and a familiar guest appeared before me. She glared at me from head to toe, with judgement on her face. The woman, standing in front of me in a black velvet blouse and tight leather jeans, was still as beautiful as I had seen her before. She looked at Bale, smiling smugly.

'How's married life?' Mara walked past me and I caught a hint of coffee and cinnamon from her. Approaching Bale's office desk, the intruder put a thin long finger on the edge of the furniture, picked an invisible lint with her black nail and bit her bright-red lip while looking at my husband. Her dark curls fell from her shoulder.

'Happy and blessed, Mara .' Bale sighed a tired sigh as he took a stack of papers from his ex-mistress. 'You didn't have to come. You could have given the contracts to Azazel.'

'He's always busy.' Mara shrugged her shoulders as she walked past Bale and gave me a defiant look. 'And he's no fun at all. Not like you. I missed you.'

'I'm a busy person too, Mara.' Bale looked at me with a chuckle and rolled his eyes at the insolent demoness.

'I heard you trashed your house the other day.' The woman laughed and reached her tattooed arm towards him. 'Renovations or a lovers' quarrel?'

'Yes,' I answered instead, as I walked to Bale and wrapped his tie around my finger, 'he's so fiery, you know. He pissed me off, so we had an argument.'

'What a pity.' Mara raised her eyebrow, sparkling with a disgruntled look as I ran my palm over the

Devil's beard stubble. He seemed to be satisfied with this invisible battle for his attention more than anyone else.

'Oh, it's OK. Quarrels strengthen marriages,' I whispered, bravely approaching the woman and smiling at her as softly and persuasively as possible. 'Do you have any more business with Bale? We were kind of in a rush.'

'Hm.' Mara smiled and bit her lip, taking her gaze away and heading for the door. 'Perhaps not.'

'Have a nice day, sweetheart! Thanks for the hard work!' I waved my hand theatrically. Mara stopped for a second and looked at Bale, crossing her arms on her chest and sighing.

'OK, fine, you win,' she mumbled, and I looked at my smiling husband.

'What's she talking about?' I asked him straight.

'I made a bet with her that you wouldn't leave me if you knew the truth, and you could stand up to any demon in my service,' explained Bale, and I shut my mouth, not knowing whether to be proud or angry.

'I like her.' Mara smiled but still looked at me with a condescending glare. 'Perhaps there will finally be a woman by your side who will kick your arrogant ass.'

'How rude.' Bale grinned, and Mara just walked away, waving goodbye.

'You are good friends, I see,' I said monotonously.

'Mara isn't as terrible as she sounds. She tries to seem tough and cold, but there's actually a lot of good in her. She just doesn't like to show it. She believes it makes her seem weak.'

'How long have you known each other?'

'Not as long as it seems,' replied my husband.' She has been a demon for only fifty years.'

'Really?' I was surprised. 'What department is she in?'

'Friendships and Amity.'

'Wait.' I sat down on the couch and frowned. 'Are you saying this rude, arrogant woman sold her soul for a friend?'

Bale nodded. 'Mara was an orphan. She had a very close friend, almost a sister, who had been in danger and sold her soul to save that friend. Mara's life has always been pretty rough, and she never found a family that was ready to adopt her. Eventually, she succumbed to a negative influence and hit the rock bottom. Drugs, alcohol, prostitution. But eventually, when she met her friend again, she decided to pull herself together and start fresh. She worked three jobs, saved up money for college and dreamed of a career and family.'

'How did she die?' I asked sadly.

'Car Accident. The driver was drunk,' said Bale, picking up the documents from the desk, 'and eventually, she started working for me. Her audacity and ambition are contagious, and she's very persuasive. And sometimes we've helped each other to forget the loneliness, as you're aware.'

'I pity her…' I felt my attitude change towards this woman who seemed to be stronger than me.

'She won't let herself break, and never takes her fate for granted. It's rather sad, though. She's one of the high-ranked demons. Mara controls fire. But let's get back to you now… I hope you don't mind that I've invited Raphael for dinner?'

I smiled. 'I will be glad to see him. He's family.'

'Should we expect Mike?' asked Bale suddenly, surprising me with his question.

'Um,' I panicked. 'I invited him, yes. Why?'

'It's nothing.' Bale allowed me to go ahead when we left the office. I kept looking at him and trying to figure out what was bothering him so much.

'Are you jealous?' I raised my eyebrow with a smile on my face. He huffed. This reaction greatly amused me, as I least expected such behaviour from the King of Darkness. I knew that he didn't like Michael, and those feelings were mutual, to my surprise, but I expected a bit more mature attitude from Bale.

'Never,' the Devil answered briefly, and I only snorted as I went into the elevator with him and Alastor.

It was supposed to be a fun weekend, and I was excited about it. Finally, I could relax with my family and friends. I had high expectations for the upcoming dinner that Bale promised. Juicy barbecue, plenty of drinks, and fun were on my schedule.

As I got out of the elevator, I walked to the exit with a smile, following Bale and looking at the high ceilings of the building. Breathing in the fresh, crisp air, I touched a passing man with my hand by accident, instantly feeling an electrical wave, and sinking into a chaotic set of visions. A flash, a loud sound of a gunshot, and I returned to reality, looking at Bale's worried face while he shook me on my shoulder.

'Sophie?' he called me louder when I looked at him.

'I'm all right,' I said uncertainly, looking straight and trying to find the man who'd passed me, but he had already disappeared from my sight. 'Just another vision...'

'I'll have to contact Lilith,' Bale replied, dissatisfied. 'She's in London. Your mother brought her recently at my request. Perhaps she can explain what's happening to you.'

I remembered my mother's words that she had met up with some friend from America recently. Perhaps that's the friend she was talking about. As I frowned, I was suddenly immersed in my own thoughts about how much I had yet to learn. Especially about myself…

CHAPTER SEVENTEEN

I opened the patio door, allowing a cold breeze to enter, and shivered from the chill. Winter was approaching, but our warm house needed to be aired out as the heat in the kitchen was unbearable. Belial played with his sorcery behind the stove and occasionally shared a culinary masterpiece, waiting for my approval.

The doorbell rang and distracted me from my thoughts, and I glanced at Rosie rushing into the hall. I looked at my mother in the lounge with her glass of wine, chatting with Lizzie about Hell and its beauty. Smiling, I headed for the door to welcome our guests.

'I brought a cake!' With a radiant grin, Raphael appeared on our doorstep. I smiled and let him in.

'Thank you.' I politely accepted the box and walked the guest into the lounge.

'I hear my brother is cooking today?' Raf asked, and I just nodded, looking forward to a delicious dinner.

'Raphael, this is Lizzie, my friend. You probably saw her at the wedding,' I introduced my new relative to my friend. He shook her hand politely, and Lizzie smiled blushingly.

'Oh, what bright energy!' Lizzie's eyes gleamed, and she looked at me impatiently.

'Oh, so you're the famous witch friend,' Raf said, laughing, and I smiled. Lizzie held her head up and put her glass of wine aside.

'I have to see them!' she said with enthusiasm. 'Can I see, please?'

'Forgive me, Raphael.' I rolled my eyes, shaking my head and noticed the angel's puzzled glance. 'She buzzed my ears with the desire to see your wings, as Bale refused to show his.'

'Ah!' Raf laughed, shaking his shoulder lightly and making his wings instantly open behind his back, allowing Lizzie to swell and enthusiastically gasp, reaching out to the feathers and touching them with a tickling sensation . Raphael flinched, patiently waiting for the witch to take it all in and slowly observing her with interest.

'Beautiful!' Lizzie exclaimed, her eyes full of tears of happiness. Raf smiled at her, blushing, as she stepped aside, and I smirked. Apparently, even this angel had a weakness for Lizzie's mad energy. 'I can't believe you don't think these are beautiful, Sophie!'

'I never said that!' I protested as I looked at Bale entering the lounge. 'It's just that I'm not used to it yet, and I'm honestly tense about these extra inhuman body parts.'

'Don't make a mess with your feathers,' Mr Deemer mumbled, handing out a glass of wine to his brother and waving his hand as he blew away a feather that had flown by. Raphael, shaking his shoulder again, hid his wings and sat in the armchair, watching Lizzie with a smile.

'Does Mike know you're an angel?' I asked with interest, and Raf nodded.

'He had seen my real appearance a couple of times,' the angel smiled, and I sighed.

'I imagine his shock. It must have truly inspired that God-loving priest wannabe!' Lizzie laughed, and I noticed Bale and Raf share a glance as they kept smiling. It seemed to me, however, that there was a different meaning behind that look, though I didn't bother getting into it. Maybe later...

'Bale, aren't you drinking?' I was surprised to see a glass of water in my husband's hand.

'Oh, no!' Raf laughed before Bale could say a word. Noticing my surprised and interested look, the angel smiled and shook his head. 'Bale and alcohol are incompatible, dangerous even!'

'I find the taste of liquor disgusting,' Bale replied, frowning.

'Bullshit! You love it! It's because you drank too much in the Middle Ages, brother!' Raf laughed again. 'Bale was a great drinker, but during the Middle Ages, with its frequent festivities, Bale gave up drinking because alcohol became stronger over time and Bale's control over himself got weaker!'

I laughed in disbelief. 'Do you get drunk easily?' The Devil who couldn't drink! Now that was news!

Alastor smiled. 'No, it's not that, Sophie. It's just that Master is completely out of control when drunk and becomes the King of Darkness that people imagine him to be. He plunges into an atmosphere of uncontrollable mischief, filth and chaos without hiding his true appearance. Last time, around the fifties, when Master allowed himself a couple of extra glasses of whisky – rock 'n' roll became a thing thanks to his involvement.'

'What?' I was surprised to see Bale's dissatisfied look. He seemed to burn Alastor with his glare. 'You invented rock 'n' roll?!'

'I didn't invent it. I inspired one of the musicians.' Bale shrugged. 'While sharing a bottle of good bourbon with him, I inspired the idea of an electronic guitar. By the end of the evening, he even stopped paying attention to my horns.'

I smiled, trying to contain the laughter bubbling in me. Yes, I had a lot to learn about my husband.

'You see, Sophie, us celestials might be powerful and all, but each of us has a little weakness. Our Father has a sense of humour and thought it'd be hilarious to give each of us a little imperfection.' Raf rolled his eyes. 'So, my brother here has a weakness for alcohol, it completely knocks his roof out. Mechahel is terrified of cats.'

'What?!' Sophie snorted. 'Why?!'

'Oh he just hates their intence glare,' Bale laughed. 'He believed they literally stare into your soul. Even if you're a celestial. He hates their judgemental nature.'

'Gaby can't lie,' Raf continued. 'Can't do it to save her life, honestly. When she tries, she starts stuttering and crying. It's like a curse for her, bless her soul.'

'So, what's your weakness?' Lizzie asked, curious.

'Hm,' Bale smiled when Raf shut his mouth. 'Raf is allergic to peaches.'

'Sorry, what?' I raised my eyebrows.

'Ironic, considering his main power is healing,' Bale continued. 'And, peaches are known to be a symbol for healthy life and vitality.'

'Not funny,' Raf mumbled and I tried to hold my laugh.

The doorbell distracted me again, and I opened the

door, to find myself looking into the divine beautiful silver eyes of a dark-skinned woman, who smiled mysteriously at me. She was wearing a long turquoise dress with a slit on the side. She had a gothic corset for a belt, a few colourful crystal pendants around her neck and long golden earrings – one of a sun with a dreamcatcher and another a crescent moon with stars. Her hands and arms were tattooed with runes and unfamiliar symbols.

'You look so much like your father,' the guest said in a melodious voice, and I gulped, frowning. She touched a lock of her silky black hair, and I noticed a few rings on her fingers – one with green jasper, another with moonstone and those with other unknown stones. Her hair was unusually long, straight and shiny, a few of her strands were braided and tied with crystal charms. Her black nails were long and sharp, wrists were full of bracelets. My eyes moved to her anklets and leather sandals. She had a few faded scars, but it didn't make her less divine.

'Lilith!' Bale exclaimed behind me. 'Come in, join us.'

I watched as the witch walked across the hall of our house, almost floating, elegantly bowing to the Devil and smiling at my mother. I caught a hint of rosemary and mint trailing after her. Raphael nodded, Rosie smiled and Alastor tensed... blushing!

Lizzie's eyes instantly lit up as she'd asked me about this witch many times since I'd mentioned her. Lilith seemed very good-natured, and polite, and had gladly accepted the invitation to dinner.

The cheerful feast was in full swing as Bale confidently threw a juicy steak into the air, forcing it to linger in the hot flames of fire that flared up in the hand of my Devil. When he mentioned the barbecue, I didn't think he meant his personal fire-control abilities. It didn't affect the quality of the food, though, as the meat was very tender and delicious. Ticking another box on the Devil's good qualities list, I thought he would be the chef in our kitchen from now on. I was a terrible cook.

Watching Bale discuss something with Alastor about work and business, I glanced at Raphael and Lizzie, who were sitting opposite each other.

'So, you're practising spells?' asked the Archangel with interest when he looked at my friend. Lizzie distracted herself from her vegetarian lasagne, prepared especially for her, and stared at the angel. A little blush showed on her cheeks, and the woman nodded. Such modesty from my friend amused me. Since when was she so shy around men? 'I guess that's great. People must be jealous of you.'

'I try to hide my ability from people.' Lizzie looked down, picking her food in a distractive manner.

'Why is that?' Raphael asked, surprised.

'People are frightened by such powers,' Lizzie smiled sadly.

'So, what, you spend your whole life pretending to be a regular human?' Raf laughed, and I turned my gaze to Lizzie. He made her feel uncomfortable.

'Unfortunately, people are often afraid of what they don't understand,' I joined in. I looked into Raphael's green eyes. 'Lizzie is distinguished by her unwavering courage, kindness and confidence. However, it does not mean that she is not offended by people's reactions.'

Raf sighed. 'People are cruel. That is true.'

'Humans were created like that, unfortunately,' Lilith answered quietly and exchanged glances with Lizzie, who smiled slightly.

THE DEVIL'S SIGNATURE: THE ABIDING PACT

'I never thanked you for that advice,' said my friend and Lilith nodded in understanding, sipping her wine. 'You saved my life.'

'There are millions of years behind me. Belial and I have come a long way together, and we are both full of bitter experiences. I can feel a lost soul miles away,' the witch replied, playing with her crystal pendants.

'I talked to Lilith about your abilities,' Bale said, and I looked at the woman with hope.

'Unfortunately, I don't have an answer to your question—' the witch shook her head '—I only used a spell to contain your parents' powers. Your natural abilities passed down from your father and mother are unknown to me and beyond my control. I'm afraid you'll have to keep looking for the answer, Sophie.'

'Is it true that you are one of the first humans?' Lizzie asked with interest while I tried to accept the fact that I still didn't know the most important thing about myself.

The witch smiled 'Yes, I was a child of God, his disciple. I knew Eve and Adam.'

'Wow,' my friend exclaimed as I glanced at my husband, who visibly tensed at the mention of his long-time acquaintance. 'I would love to learn so much from you!'

'Come to my little shop sometime; Bale will tell you how to get there. I can share some useful spells and potions with you. You might even get a couple of interesting charms, like the one around your neck…'

'Huh?' Lizzie wondered and looked at her marble pendant. 'It… was a gift. '

'Mm,' Lilith nodded, and I shifted my gaze to Lizzie, who glanced fleetingly at the witch, then at Belial, and then looked away. Her behaviour seemed a little unusual to me. I suddenly thought that I'd never asked her about the accessory. 'The pendant was made by a good friend of mine, Antony. It was a special order for Death herself. The stone was sourced in the marble caves of Hell. Antony used a special casting spell for it, created by a witch I know. Death presented it as a gift for me, and then I passed it to that witch. Antony works in my store now.'

'Is he a sorcerer?' I asked with interest.

'No,' Lilith replied, 'he's an angel. We call him The Jeweller, as he's a master of his craft. He left Caelum a while ago.'

'Oh?' I raised my eyebrows.

'He was a good friend of your father's, as far as I know,' my mother said, and I flinched. 'He made amazing charms, protective pendants and so on. His magick abilities are limited, but strong.'

'How did he end up in this world?' I wondered.

'Asked permission from our daddy,' Bale answered. 'Said he wanted to protect humans with his skills. To everyone's surprise, God didn't even question his request and gave Antony open access to this world with permission to return to Caelum anytime he wanted. It didn't take long for him to meet me, and eventually Lilith as well, since we had been travelling together for some time.'

'So, I gave him a job,' the witch continued, 'working in his little workshop in my store and making beautiful jewellery and charms and amulets. If I'm not mistaken, your pendant was also made by him, Sophie.' I touched my crescent pendant with a star. 'It was your father's once.'

'Unfortunately, not many people believe in the power of protective charms now,' Raf added. 'Faith is not as strong these days. Maybe that's why people are so cruel lately, and gifted humans like Lizzie have a hard time in this world.'

'If I had such beautiful wings like yours—' Lizzie smiled as she tried to cheer herself up '—I would rush to the clouds, to freedom, where I wouldn't have to be someone I'm not. But, unfortunately, I am only human. You Archangels don't understand that; you are not troubled by prejudices and human judgement.'

'It is true.' Raphael nodded, looking into Lizzie's serious eyes and clenching his lips . He seemed to understand that he had reluctantly upset my friend. 'I am sorry to have offended you.'

'It's OK.' The girl smiled gently, and Raphael raised his eyebrows in surprise. When he glanced at the witch for a moment, he looked away and coughed, hiding his embarrassment. I smiled slightly, knowing that the charm of Lizzie's smile could warm even the most frozen heart.

Later, while cleaning the dishes from the table, I looked happily in the direction of the dining room, where my friends and family were enjoying the conversation and remaining wine. For a second, I even thought we were a normal family, with no painful pasts, traumas or complicated future. With a sad sigh, I wished this day would never end.

Whether it was my pleading or just a coincidence, the doorbell rang, making me take my mind off everything, and I headed to answer the door as Rosie had left to visit her friend.

'Hey, good evening, hosts!' Passing a couple of bottles of wine into my hands, my new acquaintance Jay and a few other men walked uninvited into the house, drawing the attention of those present.

'Jay!' Bale exclaimed. 'To what do I owe a pleasure?'

'There's a rumour going around that the Devil is having a party!' our guest answered in a husky voice, putting a stack of bottles and snacks on the table. 'We couldn't have missed the party of the King of Darkness himself! So I brought some brew of my own making!'

'A party?' I asked again, looking at Jay.

'I brought a couple of friends here!' Jay pointed at the guys behind me. 'This is Muhammad, this is Moses and his sister Miriam, and this is Eros, the cupid we met on our trip. He just tagged along.'

Looking over at Lizzie, I shrugged and promised the witch that I would introduce all the Biblical and other characters a little later to her. To my surprise, the guests did not end there, for soon the whole house was overflowing with supernatural creatures drinking wine, sharing snacks and increasing the music volume by the minute. The Devil's residence began to resemble a college student dormitory by the end of the evening. I wasn't sure how to react to such a change but was quite happy to join the fun. Showing me off to all the guests, Bale introduced me to various demons, cherubs, biblical celebrities, and other divine beings. It seemed like there were no humans in our house at all.

I laughed at angry Maggie, who had appeared in front of her husband and dragged him away from the house, scolding him for leaving home once again.

As I poured myself a glass of wine, I felt a slight nudge on my shoulder and turned around.

'Oh, I'm sorry!' A young man with pretty feminine features said excitedly. His blonde hair were brushed back, his lean figure seemed fragile, and his baggy clothes made this charming little man look even shorter than he actually was. 'You are Sophie, are you not? The Lord's wife? '

'Are you a demon?' I asked in surprise.

'Mika!' the boy answered shyly with a smile. 'I'm

new at this, so I'm adapting a little.'

I smiled. 'Hm, aren't you a bit young to be selling your soul to the Devil?'

'Yes, ha-ha,' the demon blushed, and I smiled again.

'Mika is Azazel's apprentice,' Alastor explained, appearing behind me, and the younger demon bowed hastily to my bodyguard. 'Assistant Secretary of Hell.'

'Important role.' I raised an eyebrow as the boy galloped away.

'He sold his soul for a very desperate wish,' Al smiled sadly, and I looked at him with interest. 'Mika was born a girl. But he never felt comfortable in his body. And, after a long time of depression, quarrels with misunderstanding parents, bullying and other unfortunate life events, he finally got what he wanted, thanks to Bale.'

'It must have been nice to be free for once.' I watched the clumsy boy try to squeeze through the crowd. 'How did he die?'

'In that car crash we witnessed,' Al sighed. 'He was one of the passengers in that bus that we saw the other day.'

'Oh,' I sighed. 'Terrible.'

'Yes.' Al nodded. 'The Master is a little concerned about that.' 'The balance of this world is shaken for some unknown reason, and we all feel it. Something terrible is approaching. There are too many accidents, too many illnesses, too many deaths in your world, and Master feels it with his own skin.'

'His energy is unbalanced, isn't it?' I asked worriedly.

'Sometimes,' Al agreed, and I pressed my lips together, 'but it's too early to do anything about it. We don't know the cause.'

'How come Mika bace Azazel's assistant?' I asked. 'He's new to this and the role seems important.'

'Master said that Mika's soul has a very strong energy. He has lots of potential, it's just hidden. Mika's very smart, organised and responsible, so Azazel recruited him as an assistant.'

'I see,' I replied.

Al bowed to me and walked away, leaving me to my thoughts.

Lizzie gave herself entirely into the atmosphere and was already finishing her third shot of tequila, forcing poor Alastor to accept the challenge. My dear mother had warmed up the dance floor, the centre of the lounge to be exact. Some of the guests had gone outside into the garden.

'I'm sorry, I think our family evening plans have been disrupted,' Bale said, handing me another glass of wine. All I did was shake my head and smile.

'It's OK, it's more fun.' I grinned at my husband.

'I'll try to chase them away,' he said, laughing, and I just waved my hand. 'It must be difficult for you to accept all this. You've had a lot on your plate.'

'I haven't figured out what I feel yet...' I answered honestly. 'Give me time.'

'Of course,' Bale nodded, and I felt someone push me from behind, moving away. The only reason I didn't fall was because Belial was standing on the stairs, one step down. Holding me firmly, the man stared at my astonished eyes, which were an inch away from his.

For a second, there was nothing in my head, the noise suddenly sank into a distant echo, and I was waiting to see Bale's brown eyes, which slowly began to move towards me. As I froze, I gulped and opened my lips, but...

'I think someone is juggling your vase, Bale,' a loud voice sounded behind him, and I pulled back immediately. Bale turned around and looked at his brother. Raf smiled, pointing to the group of brave demons who were throwing a porcelain vase up high like a hot potato. Bale murmured something about a gift from the Chinese emperor and immediately walked away, lifting his demons by the collars with both hands and throwing them out the window. 'You seem to have accepted your destiny.'

'Not quite,' I smiled, 'but I'm close to it. My understanding of the world was wrong, and I'm only happy to know the truth at last.'

'Hm, very positive,' Rafael confirmed. 'What about yourself? Have you figured out who you are?'

'Not yet,' I sighed, and Raf smiled.

'Don't worry, all in good time.' The man winked at me, patting me on the shoulder, and I noticed Michael entering the house. As I apologised, I left the angel and went to meet my baffled friend to invite him in. Explaining the situation and convincing Mike that this mess had not been planned, I offered him a drink, even though he refused politely.

'Can I talk to you for a second?' he asked, trying to shout through the music, and I nodded, leading Michael upstairs.

Closing the door to a small guest room, I sat down in front of Mike in a cosy chair by the fireplace. Looking at my friend with a smile, I patiently waited until he looked around and gathered the courage to talk to me.

'What's wrong?' I asked softly. 'You look like something's bothering you.'

'Um, I've wanted to talk to you about something for a long time.'

'Yes, of course.' I continued to look at the embarrassed Mike.

'I haven't been completely honest with you. I'm sorry about that,' he said. I comforted him with a gentle touch on his hand and shook my head.

'I understand the reason, so don't worry about it,' I replied. 'The truth is so hard to tell. I was angry, that's true. But now that I look at the situation from another perspective, I understand why it was hidden from me. And I'm not mad at you.'

'Thank you.' Michael smiled guiltily. I knew how difficult it was for him to lie. 'There's something else you should know. My feelings—'

'Sophie!' Lizzie broke into the room, laughing. The witch, whose cheeks were flushed from alcohol, was giggling, grabbing my hand and dragging me out. 'You must see it!'

'What's wrong?' I was pulled by my friend down the hall as I noticed Michael following us. Hearing an echo of the loud music from the lounge, and it seemed to be no other than 'Pour Some Sugar On Me' by Def Leppard, I stood on the stairs and looked down at the kitchen island, on either side of which stood Al and Bale, staring at each other with a challenging look.

'Bale accidentally took someone's glass and drank a nuclear blend of alcohol!' Lizzie kept laughing. 'There's no stopping him now!'

'Oh no...' I whispered, shocked to see my silver-horned husband with his amber eyes. Fortunately, he did not open his wings, as it would've pushed all the dishes off the wortops, but his gaze expressed a complete lack of control over himself. The beast's grin gave me the creeps.

The intoxicated Alastor seemed to have accepted the challenge and, having removed his jacket and unbuttoned his shirt, he rolled up his sleeves and kept his eyes on his Master.

'Now say it again, you wretched samurai!' murmured Bale, wobbly on his feet, while Moses placed a few paper cups with some alcoholic blend in front of them.

'I said you are an arrogant douchebag... sir,' Al answered loudly, and all the guests whistled in anticipation of the fight.

'I'll end you!' Bale hissed, and, on Moses's command, both men grabbed the first cup, draining it instantly. Slamming them on the countertop, Al and Bale banged on the bottom of the cup, forcing it to jump and land bottoms up. So, the game continued with the next cup and so on, slowly approaching the end of the countertop.

Covering my mouth with my cold palm, I couldn't believe my eyes. Ridiculous! Lizzie was laughing to her heart's content, dragging Mike with her through the kitchen. I kept standing on the stairs, looking at the mess.

Shouting his victorious roar, Bale jumped on top of the aisle and grabbed a bottle of bourbon from Moses's hands, draining it to the bottom and throwing it aside, causing the glass to smash into pieces. Happy guests raged and shouted, praising Bale, and a wave of spectators just motivated him, pouring oil on the fire.

Moses shook the bottle of champagne, and the cheerful Devil grabbed it in his clawed hands, pouring foamy liquid over his head, shaking his hair, and letting all the champagne spill over his torn shirt and tabletop while he sang to the music. A loud growl came out of his throat, and I finally laughed, still amazed at the new side of oh-so-serious Bale.

When my husband noticed me in the middle of the lounge as I tried to pass by the crowd, he jumped off the island and grabbed my hand, pulling me over and pressing into my lips with a sweet kiss that tasted of bourbon. Guests whistled, and I looked down in embarrassment as the Devil grinned, and hot steam came off his lips as if he was burning from within.

The night was coming to an end, and most of the guests had finally left. I never got a chance to continue the conversation with Michael, as fun and joy drew me in, allowing me to forget myself and just enjoy some good company. Eventually, Mike vanished from my sight, and I promised myself I'd listen to him the next time I saw him.

Alastor managed to catch up with his master at the threshold of the garden, bowing to him.

'Forgive me, sir,' said the drunken samurai, struggling to stand.

'For what?' Bale smiled. 'For calling me a douchebag?'

'No, sir—' the samurai shook his head, confident '—for calling you that in front of everyone else…'

Adorable.

Lizzie helped me clean up while my mother said goodbye to her last guests. As I watched the campfire fade away in the middle of our garden, I leaned against the open door and smiled as I noticed Belial's wide back while he was sitting on the grass. His fingers were gently touching the guitar strings while the Devil was coming up with a tune unknown to me. As I walked towards him, I thanked Lizzie for her help and gazed at Alastor's sleeping face on the sofa.

Sitting beside my husband, who was slowly sobering up, I caught his smile and silently put my head on my knees while watching him play the guitar. Changing the tune, he picked up the beat and looked away, paying attention to the horizon under a starry sky.

> 'Transparent, like a water drop,
> A tired soul with million scars.
> A heart that makes its quiet throb
> Is lost between the worlds and stars.
> Abandoned on this road of life
> In the pain of empty loneliness,
> That cuts inside with a cold steel knife,
> And rips away my holiness.'

> 'Roaming the deep dark circles of Hell,
> God, Lord Almighty, I bid my farewell,
> I'll take the blame, the hate, the regret
> And I'll make sure that all pay their debt.
> The choice is given for all to make
> This holy promise I will never break.
> I'll open my arms to those you reject
> And Devil's prayer will seal the signed pact.'

With a smile, I closed my eyes and let the light breeze play with my hair, listening to the hoarseness in Belial's baritone and warming myself up in the light of a bright fire. The sound of the guitar was flowing in a gentle wave outside the beautiful garden, and I was once again reminded about how calming the voice of the Devil could be.

> 'Pride and rage, with envy and lust,
> It's all far forgotten and turned into dust.
> Called evil, unfair, with so many names,
> A Dark Fallen Angel surrounded by flames.

> 'The light bearer broken, unable to feel
> Lost all hope for the damned soul to heal.

THE DEVIL'S SIGNATURE: THE ABIDING PACT

Soaring through the night sky with dark angel wings
Son of the morning, his ballad he sings.

'Roaming the deep dark circles of Hell,
God, Lord Almighty, I bid my farewell,
I'll take the blame, the hate, the regret
And I'll make sure that they all pay their debt.
The choice is given for all to make
This holy promise I will never break.
I'll open my arms to those you reject
And Devil's prayer will seal the signed pact.'

Walking upstairs, I stopped near my bedroom door and looked into my husband's brown eyes. He was standing near, escorting me. With a slight grin, I thanked him for a wonderful dinner and great fun.

'Rest,' he answered, touching my fingers with his hands. As I pressed my lips, I lowered my gaze and let him approach. Feeling the heat of his body, I got goosebumps and tried to distract myself from lustful thoughts and take Bale's flirty behaviour for the rest of the alcohol in his blood.

'Bale,' I whispered as I took a little step back, showing him I didn't need comfort. 'You shouldn't...'

'I can hear your thoughts,' he said with the Devil's smirk on his lips, and I flushed from his straightforwardness, which he rarely showed to me. 'I can feel you burning inside.'

'Stop it.' I frowned, feeling my heart beat faster every time Bale stepped in my direction. His hoarse voice dropped to a whisper, and he leaned towards my ear, causing chills in my body.

'Admit it...' He seemed to be playing with me, and I was starting to have conflicting feelings. I was angry at him for his impertinence, but I was also excited about this unusual intimacy.

'Bale!'

'Do you want me?' Such words made my cheeks burn, and my gaze instantly fell on his bottom lip, bitten by a white canine . Belial's eyes sparkled with an amber hue, and I gulped from how scary and, at the same time, attractive he was. Like a predator, he hypnotized me so that I could be completely absorbed.

'You said that we shouldn't,' I tried to bring my husband to his senses, but Belial's drunken mind seemed to refuse to cooperate.

'Is that what you want, Sophie?' he whispered, licking his lips, and I shuddered as the butterflies inside my stomach choked on their wings. This Bale was a stranger to me, but the intrigue and his unpredictable behaviour drove me to my limit.

However, I was beginning to get angry. Bale played openly with me, teasing me without realising that it offended me because he knew very well that our connection could not be led beyond the line. Pushed aside, I came across the chest of drawers by the wall, slowly pulling away from my vicious predator, who was approaching, forcing me to sit down on the furniture and climb on top of it, keeping a cold look.

'Get away from me.' The voice was annoyingly quiet and not believable, and I was displeased to look at my husband, who gazed at me as if I was his prey. Bale only smiled as he leaned forwards and stopped an inch from my lips, looking straight into my eyes and watching me blush. As I pressed my lips in a thin line, I unconsciously lowered my gaze to the Devil's lips, expecting him to break the distance and make his passionate attack again, but... he just looked at me silently, opening his mouth and standing still.

I glared at him, puzzled, not knowing if I was angry or not. I mean, he hadn't done anything yet.

'You have one minute to do what you want,' the man said, breaking the silence, 'and then I'll step away from you. Take your chance wisely.'

I gulped. Oh, yes, right! Like I'll be doing what he expects me to do right now! Oh, no way!

After a brief look at Bale again, I frowned disapprovingly, trying to see if he really decided to do what he said. Would he insist and just stand there? What kind of games is he playing?

As I watched Belial remain in the promised position, I shuddered, looking again at his lips and cursing myself for the growing feeling of desire and attraction. I wanted to kiss him, to touch him again… Even my pride began to give in, pushing me to a desperate act. The struggle with myself raised many doubts, but I still gave in to a fleeting desire and moved an inch forward…

'Time is up,' Bale sighed, pulling away from me and taking a step back. My face flushed as I angrily squeezed the edge of the furniture where I sat, ready to tear the Devil to shreds. Cunning fox! Scoundrel! You bastard!

'I hate it when you play with me!' I whispered as I jumped from the chest of drawers and threw a decorative statuette at my husband, who escaped the blow by moving his head to the side. With a laugh, he hid his hands in his pockets and examined me from head to toe.

'You never answered.' He raised his eyebrow. When I snorted, I took my eyes off him. The Devil refused to surrender and came close again, circling me like a wild cat, whispering into my ear, 'Say it, Sophie, what are your secret desires?'

'I'm not one of your victims, Bale.' I was angry,

though my thoughts were clearly screaming in my head that I wanted to nail him to the wall and take control. Over his mind, over his body and his soul.

'Do you want me?' he whispered in my ear, standing in front of me, and I finally gave up.

'Yes...' I answered honestly, looking into his eyes seriously. Bale didn't seem to expect such honesty from me, as his face had changed expression, and he looked at me baffled now. I couldn't tell if he was disappointed that his evil game was over or if he was surprised that I had admitted it so fast. 'But as you said, it's impossible.'

'Fuck it!' He couldn't help but bend forward, meeting my weak resistance and giving me a passionate kiss, grabbing my face with his hands and drawing me to him. Unwilling to repel, I only let myself enjoy the momentary weakness of the drunk Devil and the warm blue flame of his hands on my skin.

Feeling him press me against the wall, I intermittently exhaled, feeling his hot palms under my T-shirt. I squeezed his top harder and pulled him closer to me.

Completely surrendering to this passion, my husband grabbed my hips and sat me back on the chest of drawers. Long fingers instantly slid down my back, running to the hem of the skirt and lifting it up.

'B-Bale...' I muttered through a kiss, frightened, but the Devil only occupied my lips, raising his hand higher and touching the inside of my thigh through the thin fabric of my underwear.

My head was going round, and I no longer understood what was happening. The desire completely enveloped me, and at this moment, I didn't care what would happen further.

I felt his fingers sneak further, hiding behind the

fabric of my lingerie and brushing between my legs. The goosebumps ran through my body, and I intuitively spread my legs, allowing his fingers to slip inside. I lost track of time as I squeezed his waist with my legs.

With my intermittent breath, I hugged him by the neck, holding him tight. Belial brushed my neck with his tongue as I moaned , hiding my face behind his shoulder and clutching his ruffled hair with my palms. My body was moving towards his hand, faster, eagerly. I could feel his fingers twist inside me.

'B... Ah!' As I threw my head back, I moaned louder as a hot wave ran through my veins. I still couldn't believe what I'd let him do.

'I can still bring you pleasure, love,' he whispered in my ear, and I bit my lip as I moved my hips towards him to let him get deeper.

Completely losing control over my body, I stopped holding back the moans and bit my husband's shoulder when an enormous wave of satisfaction swept me, making my body shudder in his arms.

My hand immediately fell on his belt, and it was my fatal mistake.

Instantly pulling away, he looked at me guiltily and smiled bitterly, whispering, 'I'm sorry,' then walking away so as not to tease us both even more. As I frowned, I took a deep breath and shook my head to regain clarity.

I had to find out about my power. My attraction to him must have a reason. My heart sought to know the truth about myself, and I swore not to give up until I had an answer and understood who I was. My gut demanded it.

'What did you find out, Dad?' I whispered as I looked up to the sky outside the window. The bright full moon shone, surrounded by glistening stars, reflected in the silver of my pendant.

THE DEVIL'S SIGNATURE: THE ABIDING PACT

CHAPTER EIGHTEEN

Taking a sip of a fresh, cold drink with lime, grapes and apple flavour, I looked around the wide room of an unfamiliar boutique with high ceilings, Victorian furniture and luxurious gowns on the display window. Glancing at the rich, vintage décor, I bit my lip nervously. With a happy smile, Lizzie texted Roberto, rejoicing at his imminent return from Rio.

According to Alastor, the mysterious fashionista Paimon that Bale had spoken to was a master of his craft. He often invented fancy gowns for Internum's masquerades, events and celebrations. The very fact of the frequent festivals in the other world amused me.

'Al, sweetie, I missed you so much!' Walking around with an elegant, feline gait, a handsome, tall man with long silver braided hair falling to one side of his shoulder was slowly heading towards us. The hairstyle reminded me of Norse warriors and Vikings. It truly suited him. His tight black leather trousers, boots with low heels and bright peach silk shirt gave his slim figure a refined look, pleasing the eye. There was a wooden wolf pendant on his neck. Bright-blue eyes sparkled with happiness and joy. As the shopkeeper circled around Alastor, he bent down towards my confused bodyguard. He inhaled the scent of his aftershave, glancing at blushing Alastor.

'You've stopped visiting me!'

'I beg your pardon, Paimon, Master did not need your services for a while.' Alastor bowed modestly and politely. The blue-eyed demon rolled his eyes and waved his hand, dramatically pouting his lips. Despite feminine features, Paimon was well-built. His broad shoulders were complemented by a wide back and muscled arms. Demon's face was very sophisticated, with sharply defined cheekbones, thin lips and thick eyebrows that were a bit darker than his silver locks.

'Belial has long disappointed me with his neglect,' Paimon sighed, 'and for the last thousand years, he has become quite a boring lad! Now, all he needs are simple suits and monochrome shirts! Where is the glamour, the grandeur, the charm?! I missed those magnificent times when Infernum was a feast and an eternal ball!'

'Let me introduce you to Sophie,' Al said, changing the subject while Lizzie and I quietly laughed at my embarrassed bodyguard, who seemed to struggle to get away from Paimon's attention.

'Oh, yes.' The fashionista smiled as he leaned towards me and kissed the back of my hand. 'The sugarplum that tamed our Dark Lord.'

'Good afternoon.' I smiled.

'Oh, charming!' The demon giggled, and I looked

over at Lizzie.

'And this is Lizzie Main,' continued Alastor, while Paimon also paid attention to my friend.

'Friends of the King of Hell are my friends.' Paimon bowed to Lizzie in a dancing gesture and threw his hair off his shoulder in an elegant manner.

'So you're the one responsible for all of Hell's outfits?' I asked with interest. Paimon proudly snorted.

'I am, sweetie,' he replied, 'and my talents are endless! My creations are magnificent and perfect!'

'Almost...' Al whispered, rolling his eyes and noticing Paimon's look full of reproach.

'Oh, screw you, I had artist's block!' Paimon exclaimed, and Lizzie and I stared at him incomprehensibly. 'Those were Dark Ages, depressing ones! All souls were full of negativity and longing, and I was at my lowest! My muse had left me, and I had only given in to the impulse of my refined soul!'

'Paimon is responsible for the Master's terrifying outfit with the red cloak, scarlet leather suit and the tail sewn on the back,' Alastor explained to us, having seen our confusion, 'which is why the human world often portrays the Lord of darkness in such an... unusual attire.'

'Oh,' I exclaimed, trying to hold the laugh and imagining serious Bale in red leather pants with a tail and a red cape. It'd be hilarious!

'Mistakes happen!' Paimon justified himself, and I only smiled softly.

'Why did you leave Infernum?' asked Lizzie with curiosity, taking a glass of champagne from a shopkeeper's assistant who, according to Alastor, was also from Hell.

'Oh, I needed a change! I needed inspiration!'

THE DEVIL'S SIGNATURE: THE ABIDING PACT

Paimon stretched his hands out, placing his palm to his face in a dramatic gesture and sighing. 'And humans... they're full of colours and beautiful emotions! Their imagination is limitless, amazing, and so inspiring! They never cease to amaze me! The diversity, individuality! There's so much to see and learn.'

'Tell me, are you the reason behind the devil's goat face in most biblical images?' Lizzie laughed, and I couldn't help but giggle with her, noticing Alastor grinning.

'Oh, never!' exclaimed Paimon, insulted. 'It's only an unfortunate joke of our Master. He once appeared to drunken Elifas Levi for a deal in all his glory. King of Hell, with his horns and rugged look, remained in the memory of the drunken occultist rather vaguely, for after a vow of abstinence, the poor deacon snapped and let his carnal pleasures loose. As a result, Belial's deep voice, a prostitute near Elifas and the images of goats in his own journals lined up a special image in his imagination. Since then, Belial refused to offer deals personally, unless necessary... ruins the reputation.'

'Well, now it all makes sense. Poor Bale!' Lizzie laughed. I only sighed and once again was convinced that human knowledge of the Devil was very erroneous and overloaded with overexaggerating tails. In fact, it was much simpler than that, as it turned out to be the result of drunken imagination.

'I truly hope that you will fill Master's lonely days with colour,' said Paimon softly, looking at me and gently touching my hair with a kind smile on his lips. 'He deserves to be loved. We all do, sugarplum, but unfortunately, not all of us can afford that.'

'Do you have a lover, Paimon?' Lizzie asked, and I looked to the man with curiosity. For a second, I thought I saw a glimpse of sadness and grief in the demon's eyes.

'I'm in love with my art, sweetie,' replied Paimon. 'Unfortunately the love of my life left this world a long time ago. Fate wasn't so generous to him as he suffered a lot because of his love for me. Times were rough, and people were not so accepting then. Well, some people still struggle to understand the freedom of love. They are not as aggressive, but I can still catch some judgemental looks.'

'I'm sorry to hear that,' I replied. 'I understand how difficult it must be, and it saddens me that humanity still can't get past the hate for those who differ from each other.'

'Oh, do not worry, babe—' Paimon waved his hand '—I'm sure my sweetheart's soul is finally resting in Heaven. I miss him dearly, but I wouldn't wish for him to walk on this sinful ground a minute more. He suffered enough, and it would deeply hurt me if I saw his torment again. At least not until people stop being so judgemental and intolerant.'

I smiled. 'You are very kind.'

'Well, enough chit-chat, my dollies! Al, you sexy piece of matcha cake, did Master pass me anything?' Paimon turned to the demon and Al gave him the same piece of paper I saw at Bale's office. As he thoughtfully read my husband's message, the apprentice snapped his fingers and nodded his head. 'Bellissimo! Well, let's take your measurements, ladies!'

Enjoying a cheerful atmosphere, Paimon's friendliness and exquisite treats, Lizzie and I enjoyed our day in Paimon's boutique called 'The Devil's Charm'. The blue-eyed demon thoughtfully recorded my and Lizzie's measurements, drew samples and spoke aloud to himself, deciding in which direction he wanted to create.

I felt happy here. At ease.

After receiving instructions from Paimon to return to his shop a couple of days later, Lizzie and I went out for a cup of coffee before returning home. I had to get home soon to look through a few business papers with Al, and Lizzie was to hurry to her grandmother's shop.

The cheerful talk of the day slowly replaced my worries about the future and my possible breakup with Belial in search of my own happiness.

'So, what are you going to do?' asked Lizzie while Alastor stepped aside to answer the call. I only shrugged and sighed.

'You know well that I want to achieve something in this life,' I replied, 'because I still don't know what is ahead of me and how much time I have. I wouldn't want to regret anything in the future. I want children, a happy marriage, and other simple human joys. I can't let my feelings for Bale stop me.'

'Do you love him?' Lizzie smiled gently, and I embarrassedly turned my eyes down.

'I think it's love,' I honestly said, 'but I'm still not sure. I undoubtedly feel something for Bale, but my fear of him still pushes me away at times because every minute I'm near this man, I realise who he is. It's hard to accept, even though I'm trying.'

'Um, I know what you mean.' Lizzie nodded and took a sip of coffee. 'Especially when he also can't guarantee you any feelings in return. Anyone wants to feel loved and wanted. It is a simple human need.'

'Besides, to be fair, I'm now more concerned about the power I possess.' I passed my friend my phone that showed the latest news on the screen.

'What's that?' she asked me, puzzled.

'You see that man in the picture?' I pointed to the

murder victim on the screen. 'He was shot recently in an alley. And I saw him recently outside Dale's office building. When I touched his hand, I instantly saw him dead. I don't understand what that ability is, Lizzie. Why do I see people die?'

'It is strange,' whispered Lizzie, 'and I also spoke to my grandmother recently, and she mentioned that the number of souls that had left the world had increased recently. Catastrophes seem to occur more often in the world, and people die at higher volumes than usual.'

'Does it mean that something terrible is about to happen?' I asked, worried, noticing Alastor's serious look.

'The Master is trying to figure it out,' replied the demon. 'He also noticed that the balance of this world is broken. Many deaths occur outside the planned list, and this may be a sign that something unknown and terrible is approaching.'

Waving goodbye to my friend, I got into the car and closed my eyes, wishing for a fraction of a second to not think about my worries. Once again, I missed my old simple boring life, where my only concern was work. I didn't care much about love at the time because my unrequited feelings were directed at Michael, and they were not meant to be accepted. I suddenly wondered what Mike wanted to tell me. I wasn't able to get through to him on the phone for the past few days.

Asking Alastor to stop by my house, I walked into an empty room and looked around. The silence was tense, the rooms were cold and it made me sad. Once this house was overflowing with happiness and joy, and now it was just an empty shell without much meaning. When I let Alastor in, I made him a cup of coffee and asked him to wait for me until I could gather some of the necessary things.

Going upstairs, I went into the master bedroom and looked at my father's portrait. A radiant smile on a slender beautiful face, wavy brown hair and bright-blue eyes lifted my heart as I felt a warm wave over my skin.

When I climbed into the attic, I grabbed a couple of spare brushes and paints, so I could have some distraction at Bale's estate. Brushing off dust and sneezing, I headed for the stairs, but when I tripped, I bumped my head and rubbed a sore knee. At first I couldn't see why I'd fallen, but then I spotted an unfamiliar old wooden box. I lifted the object from the floor, and brought downstairs with me, into my room. Sitting on the bed, I looked at the trinket. Strange, I had never seen it before. The pattern of stars with the moon was carved into the lid of the jewellery box. There was no keyhole or lock.

Shaking the box, I heard a knock and rustle, making sure there was something inside. No matter how hard I tried, I couldn't open it as it seemed to be completely sealed. When I sighed, I decided to take the box to the estate, in case I thought of anything while there. The ringing of the doorbell distracted me, and I rushed down past an interested-looking Alastor as he put the cup of coffee aside and stood up.

'Good evening, Sophie!' A barely visible smile touched James Haniel's lips on the doorstep when I opened the door. The cold, grey eyes glanced at me, the sharpened cheekbones tensed, and the dark hair ruffled with the wind.

'James!' I was surprised to say hello.

'Sorry I came uninvited. I was hoping to see Astrid?' Michael's father said politely. I let him in and introduced Alastor. The men shook hands, and

James mentioned that he'd met my bodyguard before.

I smiled. 'He works for my husband.'

'Oh, sorry, I didn't even congratulate you!' James grinned, fixing his leather jacket. Advising that my mother is hardly ever in this house, I offered the detective a cup of coffee. Getting cosy on the couch, James told me he wanted to talk to Astrid about my father's case.

'Did you find something new?' I looked at him with hope, but the man just shook his head.

'No, sorry,' he replied disappointedly. 'The department has not received any new information for many years, and the superiors are officially closing the case. That's what I wanted to say.'

'Oh.' I looked down and pressed my lips. Well, I guess now Belial was my last hope. 'It's all right, I understand. You've dedicated your whole life to it, and I think it's time to turn the page.'

'I tried desperately, you know that, right, Sophie?' James looked at me guiltily, and I smiled, nodding.

'Of course,' I answered. 'Don't worry. Why don't you tell me where Michael is? I can't reach him…'

'Oh, that rascal,' James said, laughing, 'you know he's always gone for a few days at a time. He seemed to want to visit some abandoned church in the hope of restoring it, I don't know. We haven't talked much lately.'

'Yes, he's gone a bit quiet lately.'

'Michael has always been like that since he was a child.' James sighed. 'When Sarah, rest her soul in peace, decided to adopt after our failed attempts to have a child, I resisted the idea for a long time. When I met little Michael, something changed my mind… Something in his eyes was inexplicable, cold, scary. I was amazed at how such a small child could have such an adult and serious look. He did not speak much, did not require attention and did not play with other children.'

I looked at the man in surprise and leaned near Alastor, who was staring thoughtfully at the floor without disturbing our conversation.

'Strangely, he is the exact opposite now,' I said.

'Yes, when Sarah saw him, she immediately decided that he would be taken home.' James laughed. 'Even his manner of speech was not childlike. His thoughts were very logical, and clever. However, his love for God was already present because when asked about his future, he answered firmly that he would serve God and help people. That's what caught me in him – this aspiration, firmness in his personality. He took every misfortune in the world very close to his heart and often blamed impure power in everything.'

I shuddered and remembered Michael's meeting with Belial, remembering their hated looks at each other and their inexplicable coldness.

'Does he have a grudge against the Devil?' I wondered, noticing James's incomprehensible look and trying to figure out what he knew of my scepticism. 'Not that I believe it, but he did… show it.'

'Hm, yes. As you know, Sarah left us because of her illness. She held on for a long time but still, sadly, lost the battle. But, for some reason, Michael was convinced that she had died of the Devil's will.'

'I don't understand…' I shook my head. 'Doesn't he say it's God's will?'

James nodded. 'Yes, but Michael was very attached to Sarah, and when she left, he was convinced that he had seen the Devil by her side. Since then, he thought Sarah might still be alive for a while if it was not for Lucifer's dark powers.'

I shuddered at the sudden ringing of the detective's

phone and flinched when I looked at Alastor. He looked straight at me with a serious look. As James answered the call, I frowned and stared at my bodyguard. Something inside me suggested that he knew exactly what had happened. That's what I needed to find out.

James was walking around the room, passing by my studio and glancing there, suddenly stopping. Lowering his phone, James slowly walked into my studio, attracting my attention. Following the man, I patiently looked at him while he stood surrounded by my portraits, crossed out by a red stripe.

'James? Is everything OK?' I asked when a man slowly turned to me and looked at my face with a suspicious look. I felt the chill, gulped and raised my eyebrows.

'Sophie, what are these portraits?' asked James hoarsely.

'Um...' I panicked.' Just portraits of people.'

'These people...' James pointed to a group of portraits of the bus crash victims. 'I recognise them. Each of them was seen in the morgue during the investigation. And this one... he died in a fire. And this woman, she... she was a murder victim. How...?'

'Well—' I tried to make up an excuse on the move, as I knew well about this detective's observant abilities '—I saw their pictures in the papers, so... got inspired, and wanted to honour them.'

'Right,' he mumbled, looking at a couple of my new portraits that hadn't yet been crossed out by the red line. 'OK, I have to go.'

'Is everything OK?' I asked worriedly when I noticed the detective pressing his finger at the camera app on the phone. Trying to not sound too alarmed , I stood firm.

'Yes, yes,' he said thoughtfully, 'just a lot to do. It

was good to see you, Sophie.'

He knew... Guess I was a suspect now.

After closing the door behind the man, I begged all known godly creatures for him to not start sniffing around. I knew that many of the painted victims were not in the papers, and I could only hope that he would not notice it. The thought of having to move my studio to the estate suddenly hit me.

'Al,' I called my bodyguard, 'what happened to Michael's mother?'

'I'm sorry, ma'am, I can't tell you all the information because of confidentiality,' Al answered, looking at me guiltily.

'Does Bale have anything to do with this?' I asked strictly, frowning.

'Yes, ma'am.' The bodyguard nodded, and I promised myself to ask my husband about everything. He wouldn't dare withhold this information from me!

Asking Alastor to help me load my things into the car, I closed the door of my house and pressed an old jewellery box against my chest, looking at the empty windows, and breathing in the fresh evening air. My heart was pounding rapidly, and a feeling of something bad did not leave me. I always listened to my intuition, and now it was telling me that I had to prepare mentally for the events that would turn my life upside down once again.

THE DEVIL'S SIGNATURE: THE ABIDING PACT

CHAPTER NINETEEN

A vast hall with bright, crystal chandeliers, luxurious decor and many important guests plunged into noise and music presented itself before me. Glistening expensive jewellery blending with the radiant smiles of all those present . Magnificent outfits, celebrities, and a variety of cultures – all of it overwhelmed Lizzie and me when we entered the main hall. A short flight to Paris few hours ago and the delight of the forthcoming event made us squeal, and we restrained our emotions with the last of our strength.

Escorted by Alastor in his silver suit, Lizzie fixed a curl of her wavy hair and put a hand down on her obi belt. She was wearing a long silk white dress with a lilac ribbon at the waist and a pattern of a wild cherry blossom all over the dress. Paimon was convinced that the details of Lizzie's birth culture complemented her appearance the most.

She looked gorgeous.

Squeezing Belial's hand while he stood there in a black suit and silky blue shirt, I took a deep breath and then a step forward, fixing the hem of my extraordinary dress. The black velvety fabric tightly enveloped my figure, delicately drooping from my chest to my waist and below, freely falling down to my feet in layers, and shimmering from black to bright azure at the hem, reminiscent of the flame of my Devil, creating the illusion of the blue fire around me. Belial was not only pleased with Paimon's work but he was truly impressed with the abilities of his designer. Noticing Bale's frequent gaze – he seemed to cope with the secret desire to hide me from unnecessary eyes – I proudly lifted my head and followed him inside the hall.

Paparazzi, journalists and guests surrounded us, and I gave in to the incredible atmosphere of the event, enjoying new acquaintances and getting used to a new lifestyle. Fine dining, live band, the glitter of silverware and jewellery – all this made me dizzy and excited.

The Devil's warm hand gently lowered on my waist as I looked into his brown eyes while he pressed me against him in a slow dance. Feeling his heart beating, I let him guide me, following his every step. As I circled the hall, I dreamed of staying alone with Belial to see if his heart trembled for even one second, being so close to me. Did he wish to touch me, to give in to his impulse, as I did? However, the firm and calm look of dark-brown eyes brought me back to reality, and I was once again convinced that we were destined to go in different directions in the future. Perhaps it was my last dance with the Devil. Something told me that our separation was forthcoming. And my intuition never failed me.

The evening ended as quickly as it had begun. The

feeling of restlessness never left me, and insomnia was my uninvited guest that night. Sighing tiredly and leaning against the railing of the balcony in my private hotel room, I stared at the bright moon that illuminated the sky. The cool air and the smell of approaching winter filled my lungs, and I shivered from the cold. Pulling the sleeves of my sweater up around my fingers, I turned back and took another look at Paimon's creation. The dress was truly beautiful, and I really wanted to wear it again someday.

There was a slight rustle behind me, and I turned my head towards the intruder.

'You'll freeze.' Bale grinned, hovering in the air and landing softly on the railing of my balcony, spreading his gorgeous black wings.

I gulped, lowering my gaze, and he immediately cocked his shoulder, making the feathers glow with a blue flame and the wings disappear. Crouching on the railing, my husband invited me closer to him. Burying my nose in his chest and letting the man hold me, I breathed in the scent of pine and closed my eyes. He was warm. His heart was beating a steady rhythm in his chest, and I hugged him back tightly, sighing.

'What's bothering you?' he asked. 'Your thoughts are erratic.'

'I don't know,' I answered, opening my eyes. 'Something makes me unsettled. There's something dark and unknown inside me. Sometimes I don't recognise myself in the mirror, and it scares me.'

'Maybe it's just my negative energy affecting you,' Bale said, and I nodded. Yeah... maybe.

'Am I the only one who thinks we're breaking up soon?' I asked him bravely. There was silence, and I frowned, biting my lip.

'I still haven't found your kidnappers,' Bale

answered reassuringly. 'Until I'm sure you're safe, I won't let you leave my side.'

'Then I hope you'll never find them,' I whispered, and I heard a chuckle in response.

'Sophie, you have a beautiful future ahead of you. I want you to experience human joys – family, physical love, and old age. It's so much better than wandering this world forever. It's great and interesting in the beginning, but the soul gets tired with time,' Bale replied, and I closed my eyes. I understood his concern.

'What if I made a deal in exchange for a wish, and I became a demon in the future?' I pulled away from him and looked into his brown eyes. Bale smiled and ran his hand through my hair.

'I'll grant any wish you want for free.' He winked. 'The perk of being married to me.'

'You're an idiot!' I snorted and smiled back. I knew he wouldn't go for it. I wasn't sure I wanted him to, either. I dreamed of family and children. I was trying to prepare myself for the fact that this relationship wouldn't last forever, hard as that was to contemplate.

☆

Looking out the window of the aeroplane, I was preoccupied with my own thoughts, only vaguely taking in Lizzie's conversation with my husband.

'I can't believe you don't own a private jet!' My friend was shocked, drinking a cup of coffee and sitting across from Belial at the next table of our little rental jet.

'I have no reason to own an aeroplane.' Belial raised his eyebrow. 'I have wings and the ability to teleport. This little thing is only necessary for your transportation.'

'I was hoping you'd show off your pilot skills!' snorted Lizzie and Bale smiled.

'I have Alastor for this.' He nodded at my bodyguard, who was now in control of the transport. 'It's cheaper for me to rent a plane than spend money on unnecessary stuff I won't use.'

'Hm, fair enough.' Lizzie shrugged her shoulders as we flew over the fields of Somerset. The colourful fields and hills were drowning in the sunshine, the cattle walking by the small farms, and the grey ruins of an old church on top of Burrow Mump Hill. With my eyes closed, I sighed and immediately clung to my own seat when the plane suddenly shook. Feeling the loud roaring of the engine and the squeaking in the pilot's room, I glanced worriedly at Alastor as he held the control of the plane and pulled it to himself, reporting interference on the radio.

'What's going on?' My voice was quiet as I felt the shake again. Belilal jumped from his seat, ordering Lizzie and me to buckle up and headed for Alastor.

'Turbulence?' Bale asked seriously, but Al just shook his head.

'The engine is failing, sir,' Al explained, switching the buttons, and Lizzie and I looked over at each other, full of fear and panic. 'The steering wheel is out of control. I'm trying to reduce the thrust, but it's not working! Loss of hydraulics; there's some kind of interference that prevents me from activating emergency mode.'

'Have you reported?' Bale frowned, and Alastor grabbed the radio.

'Mayday Mayday, Bristol Tower, Nextant 500Tx, rudder height out of control, loss of hydraulics. Parking over a field three miles from Somerset, emergency landing request.'

'Mayday Nextant 500Tx, an emergency call accepted, wind 270 degrees 15 knots, send 7700 if you can,' was heard on the radio in response.

'Sir!' Alastor exclaimed. 'I'll try to glide if possible for an emergency landing. Maintain the optimal speed for a potentially safe landing!'

'I knew something was wrong...' whispered Bale as he entered the main compartment.

'What are you talking about?' I asked when the plane started shaking harder, and Alastor announced the emergency again on the radio, jamming the engine and dropping fuel to avoid further fire as the plane started to smoke.

'From the very beginning of the flight, I felt the energy of something unusual,' Belial growled discontentedly, looking at the seats, windows and walls of the plane.

'Dropping the fuel, sir!' Alastor shouted.

'Don't bother. It's not a technical failure!' Bale answered, standing in the middle of the plane and closing his eyes, frowning. 'I'm trying to figure out where the energy is coming from.'

Watching Bale, I tried to soothe my heart, but the plane shook again and we tilted forwards sharply when the engine failed completely. As I was groaning, I held back my tears as best I could, grabbing Lizzie's hand.

'We're going down!' Alastor shouted. 'The rudder's jammed. I can't reach altitude!!'

'Bale!' I prayed when my husband suddenly vanished from his spot. 'BALE!!!'

After a few seconds, which seemed to take forever, the Devil appeared again in the middle of the plane, and then he rushed to Alastor.

'There's a remote control sigil at the top of the

roof!' he growled, noticing Alastor's disgruntled look. 'It's a spell!'

'Bale!' I screamed again when I felt my ears block as the fall rate increased.

'Sophie, calm down!' My husband was by my side, grabbing my shoulders and also putting his hand on Lizzie's crying face. 'Hey! Listen to me. I need you to calm down! The aeroplane has been subjected to a strong spell.'

'A spell?!' exclaimed my friend.

'Yeah, someone's trying to take control of it, and it's a very strong magic spell. I need you to stop the panic, Sophie,' Bale replied firmly, and I gulped, pulling back my tears and clutching Lizzie's hand harder. 'Good girl.'

'Sir!' Alastor shouted. 'I can't switch to manual control! The engine's on fire!'

'Wait a second...' Bale frowned.

'Sir!' There was no answer, and Alastor raised his voice, 'BALE!'

'I'll try to take control!' Bale responded by standing up in the middle of the plane again and, with a deep breath, closed his eyes. As he raised his hands up, Bale twitched his fingers, and I noticed the veins of his hands lit up with a bright-blue light. Tightening all his muscles, the Devil's body was covered entirely in blue flames as the plane began to rise. I breathed heavily and looked at the black smoke of one of the engines and once again turned my gaze to my husband, whose hands were shaking with a massive stream of energy. Sharply opening his eyes, Bale growled as if he was trying to lift the plane up high with his own hands, and maybe that's what happened as we began to level the course.

'Al!' Bale shouted loudly. 'Let go of the controls!!'

Letting go of the rudder, Alastor rushed towards us, kicking down the plane door and letting the cold air and the buzzing in.

'What are you doing, you moron?!' Lizzie screamed in panic.

'He can't do it!' Al murmured, and I looked at Belial's heavy breathing. 'The spell's too strong!'

'It's not just a spell,' answered the Devil, 'it's someone who feeds this spell with divine energy! The one that won't let me break this damn spell! Al, plan B! You grab Lizzie. I take Sophie!'

'What?!' Lizzie and I shouted in one voice, feeling the plane begin to fall down again. My legs trembled, and my whole body became numb with fear.

'Yes, sir.' My bodyguard nodded and took one step over the distance between himself and my friend, unbuckling her belt and grabbing the girl in his arms.

'Are you crazy?! WHAT?! NO!' The witch started to wave her hands, but Alastor held her up and came to the edge of the door. In a panic, Lizzie screamed in terror as he bent over and jumped out of the cockpit. Clutching her legs and hands to the demon, screaming in his ear and cursing all the gods and demons, Lizzie said goodbye to her life, promising that, if she lived, she would never fly again.

Alastor's strong body was sinking lower and lower, disturbing the clouds and rushing closer to the ground. Feeling her swift death getting closer, Lizzie embraced Alastor's neck more tightly, feeling a sharp jolt and strong vibration all over her body. Al's sturdy body fell to the ground with his firm legs standing, making the ground shiver and crack.

'Sophie, listen to me carefully!' exclaimed Bale when I tried to recover my breath. 'I need you to come to me!'

'Eh?!' I panicked. 'I…'

'Immediately!' he roared up, and I unbuckled my belt in fear, grabbing the seat and trying to keep my balance while the second wing of the falling plane was covered in fire.

'What do I do?!' I swallowed my tears, grabbed my husband and watched the smoke get in.

'Take your scarf,' Bale said quietly, looking ahead. I didn't even argue while pulling my silk scarf from my neck. Bale nodded, 'Now turn around and tie yourself to me with your back to my chest.'

'What?!' I looked at my husband incomprehensibly, but when I received a disgruntled look in return, I obediently got us together, tying a strong knot at the waist.

'Now, lift your hands and grab my collar. And whatever happens, don't let go of my shirt...' he whispered in my ear, letting go of his control of the plane and making it go down faster. Squeezing me tightly at the waist with one hand, Belial melted the floor underneath us with his other hand and rushed down, leaving the burning plane.

I couldn't even let out a scream. I clasped my back to Bale, grabbed the collar of his shirt with my hands, falling down with him and hoping for the best, though it felt impossible. Feeling his heated body behind my back, I suddenly felt a jolt and noticed the familiar black wings that swung up and slowed our fall.

It was terrifying.

Flying amidst the clouds, Belial and I were slowly sinking to the ground until the plane over our heads exploded, with many shards scattered apart and shining. I could feel my Devil fluttering and screaming in pain as the steel splinters of the plane cut through his wing. Having squeezed me harder, Belial, with his wounded wing, did his best to gently touch the ground, falling on the cold grass and groaning in pain while I untied myself.

I felt dizzy, hearing hysterical Lizzie, Alastor's worried voice and my whole gut growling inside from the panic I'd experienced, the fear and worry for the Devil screaming in agony...

I felt nauseous and ended up vomiting, covered in shivers and enveloped by a panic attack. Trying to control my breathing, I turned my head towards the screaming Devil.

I rushed to Bale lying on the ground as Alastor was looking at the glowing wound on his wing.

'Fuck, fuck!' murmured Bale, coping with the pain. 'Shit! Dammit!'

'I'm afraid it's broken, sir,' Alastor said sadly, and I was surprised to hear that from my bodyguard.

'Don't his wounds heal instantly?' I asked, remembering my husband's special abilities. Alastor sighed and shook his head while Bale continued to grunt.

'Normal wounds heal quickly, but he was injured by a shard of shrapnel that was affected by a celestial energy spell.'

'Is that why the parts of the plane were glowing?' asked Lizzie, getting down on her knees and wiping her tears while trying to use a healing spell for the wing.

Alastor nodded. 'Yes, it seems that our enemy has decided to step up, daring to go against us unexpectedly. A simple spell is nothing for the Devil, but if it was fixed by the divine energy of a celestial being like him, the wounds heal longer. It will take a day or two...'

'Can we call your people to pick us up?' I asked the tortured Bale. He just shook his head.

'I used too much energy,' he whispered, 'I'm on the verge. I don't want to go back to the city now, it's dangerous. Besides, until my wing heals, I can't take them away.'

'Well, what do we do?' I asked. I was nervous.

'My father seems to be in charge of real estate in the area!' exclaimed Lizzie. 'There should be a farm nearby for sale! The house, for all I know, is empty. Shall we stay there?'

'Al, ask my men to pick Lizzie and Sophie up. I'll stay here.' Bale got on his feet and swung about. The black feathers of the wounded wing were stained with blood, spraying on the grass , leaving a dark, bloody mark.

'I'll stay here,' I replied firmly, looking at the tired Bale who wouldn't argue with me.

I was tired. Scared. Angry. But determined.

Lizzie agreed to go home because she wanted to ask her grandmother about possible similar spells to understand what might be ahead of us. My friend vowed not to leave me in this struggle and to help find the truth, as she was now also the victim of the attack.

When we found the house, we broke into it. Alastor lit a fire in the fireplace and waited for one of Bale's employees to arrive, driving his car to the nearest suburb of Somerset to buy supplies for a night while we stopped there. Al needed to be at the crash site as police would soon be investigating. Waiting for my bodyguard, I asked him to go with Lizzie because I wasn't sure of her safety. Next to Bale, I was in little danger, and I didn't want to leave my friend alone after what I had experienced. Having agreed, Alastor promised to return in the morning.

Closing the front door and stepping into the living room with a full arms of bandages and cleaning wipes, I sighed and looked at Belial's wide back with wings down by the fireplace. As I squeezed my lips, I sat down beside my husband and looked into his tired brown eyes. With a slight smile, he turned his face to the fire and sighed.

'Sorry, I know they scare you,' he said quietly, twitching his wings. In silence, I turned my gaze to velvety black feathers. It wasn't that they scared me. It's just that the sight of these gorgeous wings made me remember that my life would never go back to the way it was. The glow of the fire in the fireplace gently sparkled on the moist feathers, and I slowly raised my hand with my fingers touching the fluffy edges. The wing shuddered, and for the first time, I experienced a slight childlike delight. 'It tickles.'

'I'll... bandage the wing.' I smiled in return, opening the first-aid box. Washing the wound with pure alcohol, I gently stroked the wing, spreading the feathers and bandaging the wound with a fracture, trying not to pull it down. 'Your wings...'

'Hm?' he said with his head turned to me.

'They're very beautiful.' I smiled again, seeing Bale squint in pain as I tightened the bandage. 'I like the black wings better than the white ones.'

'Really?' He smiled and closed his eyes. The wavy hair fell on his face, and his look softened.

'May I...' I said, 'look at the real you?'

'What for?' He spoke weakly, opening his eyes and looking into the fire again. It swayed as if comforting the Devil, and the firewood cracked, releasing a light spark.

'I want to get used to it...' Quietly, I answered. In silence, Bale never turned to me, but his brown eyes sparkled with amber until his pupils were beautifully golden, with the fire glistening and playing as if listening to his master. A light-blue haze of Hell's flame touched his dark hair, and two silver horns appeared, shimmering.

I shivered.

Sitting by the celestial creature, I looked at him silently from head to toe. He was truly beautiful, with a touch of beastly charm. Strong hands were covered in blue flames, and a light azure glow ran through his bulging veins. He was on edge. I saw it. Using a large flow of his energy, Bale needed to return to Hell. However, going there now, wounded, he would put himself and others in danger.

'Why is the road to Hell through a mirror?' I asked with interest.

'You're very curious, aren't you?' Bale laughed, and I pulled his horn unhappily. 'Hey! That hurt!'

'Don't be a smartass, you horny bastard!' I snorted. Laughing, Bale put his head on my lap and sighed.

'People often forget that all negative thoughts, hatred, anger and envy are present in them as internal demons,' he replied, 'and they do not need to go to Hell to know the Devil within themselves. All you have to do is look at your own reflection. The mirror never lies. It opens the door to reality and the world in which all lies are revealed.'

'Right.' I nodded, touching the wavy hair with my fingers and stroking it. 'And how do you get to Heaven?'

'There is a portal in Hell through which souls go to Caelum,' Belial continued, 'but angels like Raphael can go there without using it. All angels are given the Ring of Heaven for this.'

'Like yours?' I noticed the ring with the shiny red ruby.

'Yes,' Bale nodded, looking at his jewellery, 'my ring has a slightly different purpose now, but for the angels, it is the road to Silver City. All they have to do is turn the ring three times, and the portal will open right in front of them. The Archangels, though, have been doing without it lately.'

'Would you like to go back to Caelum?' I asked carefully, but Bale didn't respond to that question. Perhaps he has asked that himself many times.

'I love the human world.' He smiled weakly as he looked into my eyes. 'Heaven is but a page of my past. I cannot call it home. From the beginning, I felt uncomfortable there.'

'I wanted to ask you something.' I bit my lip, and Bale rose slowly, twitching his shoulder and spreading one wing.

'You want to know what I talked to the detective's wife about?' The Devil asked, and I got the creeps.

'Yes.'

'I can't give you the details because it's not just about her and me,' Bale replied, making me frown. 'All I can say is that she wanted to make a deal.'

'What kind of a deal?' I got on my feet and walked up to Bale as he leaned against the wall and threw his head back, clutching his fist with one hand and trying to cope with the increasing flow of his own energy. I noticed how the line of his blue flame reached the neck for the first time. He was losing control.

'She asked for the end of her torment.' Bale sighed. 'As she feared her son would do something foolish.'

'Michael?' I was staring at Bale in a puzzled way.

'He turned to me once, asking me to make a deal with him to save his mother.' I took a step back, looking down in disbelief. 'I almost agreed and came to this woman to see the one for whom the holiest person in the world wished to make a deal with the Devil. But…'

'She refused,' I finished for him.

'She wanted no such fate for her son and asked me to put an end to her torment.' Bale shrugged. 'I had great respect for this woman's sacrifice and fulfilled her request for free.'

'That's why Michael is so angry with you.' I smiled sadly, guessing what my dear friend was trying to tell me.

'He has many reasons.' Belial sniffed and made a growling sound when the glow of his blue flame became brighter.

'Can I help you somehow?' I turned to my husband, taking a step forward.

'Yes, go upstairs and lock the door,' he replied strictly, looking at me with his golden eyes, 'I can't help it. Alastor is not here, and you are not safe near me.'

'As soon as I feel threatened, I will do so.' I smiled sadly, letting my husband know that I would not leave him until I needed to.

'Sophie…' he begged, but I just took a step forward. Strangely, my heart told me that I was safe now. Something inside me was trying to break free again, taking control of my body as if pushing me to take a bold step. Was it my inner power that was trying to tell me something? Was there something that could help me ease the Devil's torment?

As I approached the fallen angel, I touched his warm flame with my hand and looked up at his worried face. He frowned and shuddered at the touch as if he was trying to hold himself back.

'I don't know what attracts us to each other,' I answered honestly, lowering my eyes and looking at the glowing veins on his neck, 'but this unfamiliar power inside me is trying to break out near you. It's what makes me reach out to you and give in to my sixth sense.'

'Please, Sophie,' Belial's voice was quieter, and I noticed his cheekbones become tense, 'I don't want to hurt you.'

'What if you won't hurt me?' I asked gently, looking at him again.

'My power can tear you apart by turning your soul into millions of pieces,' he whispered, glancing down at my lips. He contradicted himself and seemed to struggle with his own desire rather than with the growing power.

'Something tells me that's not going to happen.' I bent forwards and touched his lips with a light, barely visible kiss. My heart pounded, and my body trembled with fear. However, my mind refused to retreat.

I was desperate.

Without permission, I touched his lips again, squeezing his T-shirt harder and putting my hand on his belt, standing on my tiptoes, as he was much taller than me.

Belial gently touched my hair with his fingers. As he opened his lips, he drew closer to me. Pressing me harder against himself, he kissed me back, touching my tongue with his, making me sigh deeper.

Giving myself up to my lustful desire, I let go of my husband's shirt and stretched my hands further, putting my palms on his naked waist with my fingers under the top. His back was terribly hot. Excited, I made a light, begging groan. I felt as if I was consumed by the fire. As I detached myself from the Devil for a second, I whispered a couple of incoherent phrases as he waved his nose around my cheek and my neck, breathing in the sweet scent of my body.

'You smell like vanilla,' he whispered, and I chuckled. It must have been my constant presence in the coffee shop with baked goods.

Maybe it was the dim light of the warm fireplace that gave his body such a magical glow or maybe this moment was so tense. But God, I wanted him desperately. I wanted to touch him, all of him. I wished he would take me here and now.

'I...' my voice was barely audible, 'want more.'

'You're driving me crazy,' he breathed in my ear, making a chill run over my skin, and I pulled his T-shirt up, forcing the black-winged angel to pull away and tear apart the fabric to free his lush wings. The spark of desire glittered in his amber eyes. 'I won't be able to stop now.'

'I don't want you to stop,' I whispered, gently touching his bare stomach and sliding my hand to his belt again, raising my eyes and staring at him. He tucked his fingers into the hem of my dress, trying his best to not rip it off my body in a wild desire. Seeing the shining veins on his chest, I ran my fingers over them without resisting as he lifted me up, wrapping my legs around himself and carrying me closer to the fireplace, onto the soft rug.

I wanted to make love with this man.

Sitting on his lap and feeling his animal carnal impulse bulging, I smiled at my vulgar arousal. My thoughts have found a completely obscene, twisted shade. By letting Bale pull my knitted dress off me, I got rid of my underwear, presenting myself to the King of Hell completely naked, turned on and coveted. He attacked my lips, and we both drank each other in. Gently pushing me back, his hands trailed my legs up, to the hips and slowly, gently slid to my inner thigh.

'Are you scared?' He smiled, kissing my stomach and running his tongue from my navel to my chest. 'You could die.'

'I feel a mixture of emotions,' I replied, feeling a light electric wave when the Devil's hand and shining streams of energy touched my waist. 'I trust my instincts.'

'I should stop...' He raised his eyebrow right above my face.

'No, I want it,' I answered honestly, gently guiding my palm over his silver horns. Belial said nothing, putting his head down and kissing my lips again, sliding his hand down my thigh and not resisting the way I played my fingers with his hair. Gentle lips went down to my breasts, and I gasped when his strong hands squeezed my chest, playfully biting one of my nipples.

I could feel him grinding his hips harshly against me. He growled into my ear when my fingers trailed up and down the bulge in his jeans. Holding his desire, the Devil moved down, making me gasp when I felt his lips leave a kiss on my sex. His mouth was hot and wet, and it drove me completely insane. My fingers grasped into his locks, and he tortured me by sliding his fingers inside.

'B-Bale!' I moaned, arching my back and dying in pleasure. My whole body felt numb. His warm hands gripped my hips, and his tongue made rough circles, making my body shake. His grip became harder, and I arched to him even more, begging for that final wave.

He was teasing me. Tormenting me.

Feeling the passion and desire growing, Bale was quite convinced that I was completely relaxed and turned on, ready to allow him anything. I was clinging to him with my body, pressing my feet against the rug, so he finally decided to not torture himself and me anymore. Having detached himself from me, he lay down more comfortably between my legs, taking my hand in his and looking into my bright eyes. I was drowning in the boiling melted gold of his eyes, burning with desire.

'Hold on tight...' he whispered when I felt the pressure between my legs.

'Are we gonna fly?' I smiled, putting my other hand on his back, and touching the soft feathers of his wings. The Devil's true image played with my imagination, making the languid feeling at the bottom of my abdomen grow. Something magical and beautiful was about to happen this night, despite the result of this forbidden bond.

'You'll see...' he whispered, 'if you survive.'

'I'll risk it,' I moaned.

Waiting for a smooth, slow penetration, I gasped when he was inside me with one strong push. The hot wave passed through my veins, and there was a significant lack of air. Clutching my hands harder and wrapping them around Belial's neck, I began to eagerly swallow the air as he moved backwards, pulling out and pushing forwards again, deeper. Another hot wave passed over me, but more furious and faster.

'Ah!' I moaned, squeezing his hair in my palm and biting his shoulder.

'Fuck...' he trembled. Experiencing an electrical charge at my toe tips, I felt this incomprehensible feeling spread around my ankles, then around my thighs. With every penetration of the fallen angel, my moans and his animal groaning, hot breath, I felt something inside me explode as if blood was pouring into me like boiling water. My body was covered with a glowing shade as my veins swelled and filled with the Devil's radiant energy. I seemed to soak up all of his excess power. 'More... Take me!'

'Hell, I'll break you,' he said hoarsely, pushing in again. 'Damn... I've... been wishing for it for centuries!'

'Ah! Li...' Greedily swallowing air, I choked on my own moan, tilting my head back. 'Lior!'

When I heard the happy growl in response, feeling

that the wild desire of the fallen angel Lior was only increasing, I repeated his true name over and over again like a prayer. I was moaning for him, begging for this fire inside me, absolutely senseless for this man.

I craved him.

Scratching my husband's back and suffocating, I pushed him into me to get more energy, more power. I felt him growing even bigger inside, and lust completely wrapped me up. My eyes opened wide, shining brightly, as Bale squeezed me harder and speeded up the tempo like he was possessed. I could see the excited look in his golden eyes, but I didn't let him stop, begging him to continue. The tingling electrical charge in our bodies slowly merged, spreading energy evenly, and making our bodies shiver and shake.

Holding on to his neck and biting his shoulder, I felt dizzy. Moaning, pushing harder, I was already completely lost in time and space. I seemed to arrive in eternal euphoria as if I was drugged. As I continued to absorb all of the Devil's energy, I felt the blast within me approaching soon, making the movement coarser and wilder.

I was at the peak.

Realising that I would soon reach the limit, Belial pulled me to his knees, grabbing my waist and hips with his arms, helping me to sit up and go down again. He let me finish this wild dance myself. Feeling the freedom of action, I got my hands tangled in his hair and leaned my head back, moving away from him, pressing down again and again so hard that penetration brought a pleasant pain.

'S-Sophie... ugh.' Closing his eyes in pleasure and clenching his teeth, the Devil wasn't aware of how bloody beautiful he was right now. I wanted to devour him inside me, to feel his animal desire more. 'Fuck, you feel so good!'

More movement, one more thrust, and I could feel something exploding inside me, the flow of energy in my body trying to get out, and I squeezed the Devil harder. I could feel him tensing up, causing a light wave of energy to break out and making the mirror in the hallway crack and the room shake with an ultrasonic wave. Clenching me with all his strength, he growled in my ear while his wings lightly shook.

Falling on the rug, exhausted, we tried to get our breaths back. Feeling the tickling feathers behind my back, I smiled when Bale covered me with his wing like a blanket. An inexplicable desire to laugh suddenly enveloped me, and I laughed out loud.

'I'm glad I amuse you,' the Devil snorted at me, leaning on his elbows, and I just kept laughing, feeling an extraordinary burst of energy inside me.

'Tell me—' I laughed, calming down and pulling a fluffy throw over me '—will it be like this every time?!'

'I have no idea.' Bale smiled in response, brushing his wet sweaty hair back with his clawed hand. 'This is new to me, too!'

'Amazing...' I whispered, looking at my hands while they were glowing with white light.

'You're my starshine,' He smiled. As I turned to Bale, I stared at his palm in astonishment. 'You're not shining anymore!'

'Yeah, it's weird.' He looked at his hands. 'It feels like you've pulled the excess of my energy out of me.'

'Perhaps that's my power?' I shrugged my shoulders, and Bale only smirked. We didn't know exactly what had happened, but one thing was clear to us. Our future together still had a chance because I felt like I had nowhere better to go. Belial's brown eye colour returned, his horns were hidden, and only his wings remained as evidence that I had given my love to the fallen angel.

Feeling my husband's warm body behind me, I turned to the fireplace and pressed my back against him. Watching the flame fade away, I smiled gently and secretly wished that the light would get a little brighter and warmer. The flame flashed into a wild dance, making me wince and raise my head. Thinking that Bale had read my thoughts and fulfilled my wish, I turned to him, but the Devil's closed eyes and his silent breathing were evidence that he was already asleep. As I turned again to the fireplace, I gulped and bit my lip. I lifted my palm and moved my fingers, sincerely wishing to repeat the effect, and as if obeying me, the fire flared up again.

'No way...' I whispered with my lips alone when my bright glow slowly faded. Did I really draw a part of the Devil's power into me?

'Are you all right?' Bale mumbled, sleepy, holding me tighter.

'Yes,' I answered briefly, allowing his strong hands to hold me. Closing my eyes, I slowly plunged into a dream world, clutching the pendant my father had given me in the palm of my hand and recalling his last words.

'You are the key to the light! Remember, the deepest darkness holds the brightest of light!'

THE DEVIL'S SIGNATURE: THE ABIDING PACT

CHAPTER TWENTY

As I opened my eyes, I slowly turned my gaze to the extinct fire. When I was alone in the middle of the lounge, I pulled the fluffy throw on myself and took a few gentle steps towards the hallway, looking around and trying to find my husband. When I noticed his silhouette outside the window, I smiled slightly and opened the front door, shivering from the cold and glancing up into the sky.

The grey sky was covered with clouds, the morning air cooled down the skin and lungs, and in the midst of silence and calmness, light white snow fell slowly. Winter was an early guest this year. Wrapping myself in the throw, I looked at my fallen angel sitting on top of a bench by the gate, lowering his black wings and enjoying morning peace. I stepped barefoot on the cold snowy ground and noticed how it suddenly got covered by a narrow patch of green grass . The Devil didn't turn around and just allowed me to walk towards him on the soft grass provided by magical abilities. Thankful, I looked at my husband with a gentle smile on my face and felt extreme happiness for the first time in all these months.

Sitting down near Bale, I let him cover me with his wing, and we both stared into the horizon. Despite the cold outside, I was warm.

'I have to go back to Hell,' Bale replied quietly, noticing my surprised look. 'My wing is almost healed. And I have to stay there for a while...'

'Why?' I asked with interest.

'The balance of this world is unstable.' He frowned, and I gulped, trying to understand the consequences of this situation. 'It seems that our enemy is one step ahead of us again. I can feel the chaos approaching.'

'What are you going to do?' I looked down and glanced at my cold hands.

'I noticed that the number of rebellious demons and souls increased a long time ago. Someone regularly opens the door for them and increases their army. Recent events in the city are not the only ones. Azazel also told me of similar disasters in other cities. Our enemy is increasing the death toll to gain control of the souls. I feel a rebellion is approaching. I need to go to Hell to gather my own strength and prepare my people for increased protection and stop the upcoming war.'

'Can I help you?' I was genuinely curious.

'I don't want you to put yourself in danger—' he smiled softly '—just focus on yourself. Get some rest, open your dream gallery, and keep an eye on my company. I'll be away for a while, and I'll be back at some point. This isn't your war. It's happened before, when Heaven and Hell fought each other, bringing destruction to this world.'

'OK...' I nodded, sighing.

'And then we'll decide what to do.' Bale grinned, and I smiled. 'You know you don't have to choose this life. I would love to help you find the truth about your power if that's what you want. But if you prefer to leave it at the stage it is, I won't insist.'

'To be honest, I am keen to live a normal human life, and I am still afraid to follow the new path. But... my visions and what is happening are part of my life that I cannot ignore. I'd like to know what those abilities are. Maybe then I can find peace for myself.'

Bale agreed. 'I understand.'

'I want to see the world. It was always my dream.' I sighed as I looked up at the grey sky. 'I want to open a gallery, to study the art of this world, to look at the universe from a new perspective. Everything that has happened to me over the past six months has greatly inspired me. It seems that, for the first time, I am not afraid of change.'

'I will support you in any decision, Sophie—' Bale turned his head to me and smiled happily, and I looked at him with gratitude '—but still, I think that human life is more suitable for you. Even though we are attracted to each other by an unknown power, I wouldn't want to be a hindrance to anything in this life for you. I don't mind being just a chapter of your life, a temporary impulse that will make you experience something new and unusual. My work, my possible war and the world I live in don't have to be your concern.'

'Thank you for understanding.'

'Whatever you decide, you can always turn to the Devil.' Bale hugged me with one hand and with a smile. 'I will grant you any wish for free and without a deal!'

'How noble.' I rolled my eyes and closed them,

trying to catch this moment of harmony and happiness. I felt that this was the last time we would be so happy with each other. Whether it was my inner strength or my intuition, I knew that this trip to Infernum would be a long one for Bale. The happiness I have experienced in recent days is short-lived and not eternal. And my heart knew it from the beginning.

'How do I find you if I want to?'

Bale reached for my hand, touching my fingers and gently taking off my wedding ring, raising it before my eyes and showing me the inside of the ornament, on which I noticed the Devil's engraved name 'Lior' with a five-pointed star at the end of the signature. I'd never noticed that before. The autograph shone a golden spark, and I smiled.

'If you want me to be near you, turn your ring three times, and I will hear your desire.'

'The Devil's signature...' I whispered as I looked at the ring.

'It's an indestructible seal. This signature is eternal, and nothing can destroy the contract or any other document or object I have signed. It cannot be torn or burned,' Bale explained. 'This is an abiding pact, blessed by the universe itself. This ring is evidence of my soul becoming part of you.'

'Thank you, Bale.' I looked at my husband with kindness, and he smiled as he looked up again. 'My power was awakened by you. Tell me, if I distance myself from you, will my power disappear?'

'Perhaps...' Belial agreed and I nodded understandingly. Maybe it was for the best. I could be an ordinary human again if I decided to choose the future without Belial. But... I still wanted to believe that we had a chance to stay together. For me, it was love, and for him... even though he refused to accept it, my heart told me that Bale truly loved me. I didn't need proof or words, his actions spoke for themselves, and there was nothing more important to me.

'I like this house. It's quiet and cosy,' I tried to change the subject by looking back and glancing around me. 'I would love to return here someday.'

Bale looked at me gently and held his hand on my cheek, looking down at my lips and slowly approaching. Closing my eyes, I pressed harder against him, hiding my hands behind his back and touching his fluffy wings with my fingertips. Feeling his lips on mine, I forced all my thought to disappear, so I could fully indulge in this magical connection between us. The sun appeared slowly at the horizon, filling the grey sky with a pastel-pink tint and allowing the snowflakes to melt in the air.

Was it a passion between us? Were our feelings a temporary spark because of us wanting to get out of our tiring worlds for at least a second before returning to reality? Perhaps, in the future, I would grow old and tell my children about the beautiful dark angel that helped me love life again.

Maybe that was the end of my story.

As we drove down the deserted road between the hills and the fields, Bale and Alastor were looking forward to coming home. The time was still early. There were hardly any cars around. Bale asked my bodyguard to choose an empty path so he could stretch out a bit. Holding the steering wheel steady, Alastor slowed down, allowing his master to jump out of the car, making me swerve and quickly turn around, watching the strong silhouette of the fallen angel land on the road. As he scattered, Bale filled up his lungs full of air, spreading his beautiful black wings and rushing upward, swinging them.

I pressed into the back of my seat and raised my head up when Alastor opened the roof of the car.

Looking at the soaring angel above me, I laughed happily, like a child.

Hovering in the sky, Belial was gaining speed as he caught up with our car, even though Alastor was speeding. Soaring down, Belial flew like the wind over my head, rushing forward. I refused to let him out of my sight and stood up, waving at him and screaming excitedly. Alastor smiled softly, and I dreamed that this moment would never end.

Once above me, Bale grabbed my hands and pulled me up, holding me tight and heading up again. Hugging his neck, I looked down, enjoying the view of the green hills covered by the first snow, the colourful fields, and the blue sky. Losing myself in the clouds, I could not feel the cold air, as the Devil's hands warmed me to the bone.

I seemed to be lost in eternal flight and, for the first time in my life, I wanted to have wings. I saw the world as I had never seen it before. The feeling of freedom, harmony and peace completely enveloped me. The wind was playing with my hair, clouds were approaching my face, my body was in shivers, and I wanted to squeal with delight. I was suddenly wrapped in an unfamiliar joy, anticipation. It seemed to me that I was getting closer to my dream, to my goal. Manoeuvring in the middle of the clouds at almost the speed of light, Bale was circling the boundless blue heaven.

For a second, feeling weightless, I cried out when Belial let me go, but only to be under me and make my body fall right on his back. Clenching his shirt and climbing up, I sat on his back as if flying on a huge bird.

'Spread your wings!' sounded in my head, and I shuddered for a second, recognising the voice of my husband's consciousness. As I gathered my thoughts,

I looked at my hands clutching Bale's shirt, 'believe me. Just let go of me...'

Slowly stretching my arms like wings, I held my breath.

'Now, fly!'

I could feel the clouds with my fingertips, touching the skin with imaginary fluff. Completely surrendering to this flight, I flinched when the angel suddenly soared down. I only held my breath as I looked forwards to the opening of the boundless world we were flying to. Feeling weightless and free like wind, I took a deep breath, filling my lungs with cool morning air. It seemed like I was just falling into eternity, flying towards my destiny. For the first time in my life, I felt so free...

There was a push, and I grabbed his shirt again, watching Belial level his torso and almost slide on the surface of the water of the nearby river, creating a splash and mighty waves.

'Whoo!' I screamed when I heard him laughing. 'That's so awesome!'

☆

I watched Bale collecting his papers and putting them in a silver case with sadness. With a slight smile, he touched my forehead and gave me a light kiss as he moved away. Belial had to stop by his office and come back to Infernum later. I hoped I could escort him, but he said he would use the mirror in his office.

'It feels like you're saying goodbye...' I said to him as Bale turned around and smiled sadly. Why was my heart so lonely? Why was my whole gut trying to get out of place and go after him? However... I kept standing still and watching his wide back seem further and further away from me. He was going back to his world while I stayed in my own.

I was hoping to see him again.

Fully dedicated to the atmosphere of Christmas, I was immersed in daily worries. The café was overflowing with customers, and my mother gladly gave herself up to this fussy vibe, handing out mince pies and treating others to hot chocolate and whipped cream.

She sadly told me that the police department had officially closed my father's case, but I didn't grieve much. I knew the truth about his death, even though I couldn't find the killer. James often stopped by the café, watching me and looking for Michael, but I never experienced another flash of visions when Belial returned to Hell. I was a little worried about Michael, but I soon got a message from him that he was returning to London and would be happy to have a cup of coffee with me.

Lizzie enjoyed Roberto's sweet embrace, telling him about the new findings at her grandmother's antiques shop. The poor man only nodded, without the opportunity to add even a word in the midst of my friend's babblings.

My life slowly got back to normal. I missed Bale terribly, but the anticipation of the Christmas holidays and our upcoming meeting inspired me. It seemed like I had finally found my place in the world. My future wasn't defined, but now it didn't scare me.

Bale's return to Infernum seemed to have helped. I'd heard that the balance has been restored more or less from Alastor for several weeks now. There have been no dubious catastrophes, no evil spirits, and I noticed that my supernatural friends were pretty calm and not worried anymore.

☆

'Sophie, you seem very inspired by the upcoming holidays?' Raphael laughed when I closed the café door and tightened my scarf. The angel often walked me to my car with Alastor. We'd become very good friends, and I was happy to hear a couple of interesting stories about Bale's life in Heaven. Raphael always supported me during my time of grief and anxiety, not allowing me to spend time alone, and I was truly grateful to him for that.

'Bale will be back soon.' I smiled. 'This is our first Christmas together.'

'You do know that Jesus was actually born in spring, right?' Raf winked, and I just smiled.

'Traditions are sacred, even if they are borrowed from pagan beliefs, and I don't care much about details.' I shrugged. 'I'm not going to decorate a Christmas tree in April! '

'No imagination.' Raf sighed, and I only smiled. 'I'm glad you're happy now.'

'Thank you. I finally feel I'm in the right place, to be honest. Even though I still haven't found out the truth about myself, I don't think it's that important right now. I have a choice and am free to go my own way rather than following a fake script. It's a pity my dad isn't around to support me.'

'I'm sure he would have been proud of you.' Raf put his hand on my shoulder, looking at me intently. 'I knew him, and he was one of Caelum's best angels.'

'I'm glad.' My heart warmed from his radiant smile. He didn't even need wings to look like an angel. His grace, magnificence, inhuman beauty – all this made the soul take off in his presence, and all problems evaporate. Truly angelic grace...

He was very kind.

Driving through the busy streets of central London

with the dazzling Christmas lights, I involuntarily smiled as I noticed the silhouette of an angel on one of the festive trees. Strangely, it reminded me not of the Lord's messengers of Heaven but of the Devil himself. It may seem unusual to some people, but the blue shine of this Christmas tree ornament warmed my heart.

'You've been in a good mood lately, ma'am,' Al observed.

'Life seems to be getting better.' I nodded.

'I'm happy for you,' said my bodyguard, and I looked at the former samurai warmly. I hoped he liked my Christmas present. I have been searching for something meaningful for a long time, and who could have imagined that it would be at Lizzie's grandma's shop that I would find the most appropriate gift. A friend of mine helped me dig up an antique toy in numerous boxes, which looked like a wooden whistle in the form of a bird. As per her words, it was popular during the old era in ancient Japan. I was attracted to this toy with its simplicity and elegance, which Al could appreciate. Especially, I was hoping that he would appreciate a little flower at the bottom of this whistle – let it remind him of his little Hanako. Al had become a very close friend to me. He understood my sadness and my regrets and patiently allowed me to immerse myself in my own thoughts and experiences. Al never pressured me, and he was the support I needed. His softness and reliability became indispensable to me.

I watched a peaceful snowfall outside the library window as I turned my eyes to the fireplace. When I thought about it , I moved my hand, but the flame remained almost still. A slight disappointment touched my heart. The remnants of my power seemed to have run out. Now, more than ever, I felt like an ordinary human. Perhaps it was for the best.

Hanging a silver bauble on a Christmas tree branch, I smiled and sighed tiredly. I hoped Bale appreciated my efforts in his library, as I'd spent a couple of days parsing papers and cleaning up. Now, there was a tall tree near the couch. The room smelled of pine, just like him.

'Madam!' Alastor burst into the room, anxiously looking at me and making me jolt.

'Scared me!' I exhaled, grabbing my chest, and staring at the bodyguard. 'What's the matter?'

'Sophie, are you all right?' Raf showed up behind the demon, and I stared at both of them.

'I'm OK. Why are you panicking?!' As I watched Alastor's anxious look, I frowned and suddenly felt a cold sweat on my back. I didn't like that look from him. 'Al? What's the matter?'

'Master...' he whispered.

'Bale? What about him?' I felt panic building.

'I was contacted by Azazel and was told that resistance began at Infernum...' Al replied, and I looked at him incomprehensibly.

'How? Didn't Bale go there to get things under control?' I asked nervously.

'Sophie—' Raf glanced down '—Bale never showed up at Infernum.'

'What?' I whispered. 'But... how?'

'His deputy, Ifrit, is trying to keep things under control at the moment, but she's been less successful lately.' Alastor sighed. 'Ifrit believed that Bale was in this world and would soon appear, so no one suspected anything strange until Azazel came back here to pick up the signed documents without finding our master.'

'But... if Bale's not there, then where is he?'

Raphael pursed his lips and gave me an envelope.

With doubt in my heart, I took it and opened it, pulling out a letter with neat handwriting.

'Dear Sophie,

I hope you're OK. I'd like to apologise in advance for what you'll soon find out. Please believe me, if there was any other way, I would do anything to avoid it, but... I have to leave you. My happiness was sincere and I really felt alive by your side. I dared to hope for the best and I seem to have started to experience that forgotten feeling from which I fled for so long.

However, I have made mistakes in the past and must pay for them by taking responsibility.

In spite of my desire to be near you, I have to follow my duty and choose the safety of the entire human world over you. The balance of your world has been disturbed, and it is only my fault because I let my love for humanity distract me from my duties, and I eventually lost control of myself. It is useless to deny that I have no place in your world. Unfortunately, by my father's decision, I failed to fulfil my duties as I should have, and important changes will soon occur.

By order of my father, there will be a new ruler at Infernum, whose aim will be to restore the balance that I have not kept. In exchange for your safety and keeping the balance, I am forced to make a deal with my father and disappear, leaving the human world forever and dealing with the rest of my life in the other world.

I'm terminating our agreement and finally giving you the freedom you wanted so much. I think this is the best outcome for you and me because I will find peace and rest, as I wanted, after all the years that I have wandered between worlds. And you – after enjoying our short time together – can step forwards and become whoever you want. Achieve your goals, strive for the best and do your best to be proud of your life.

My company and everything I left behind is at your disposal. Even though I have not been able to find someone who puts you in danger, I have made sure that my people will protect you. I think that, without me, you will finally be left alone, and you will be able to fulfil all your dreams. Alastor will follow you everywhere, even if you decide to go to the other side of the world. I don't want any unnecessary fears to stop you in this life.

Thank you for accepting me and understanding. I will appreciate our friendship and this is an extraordinary time, however... we have to go back to reality and go our separate ways.

I'm sorry I can't tell you these words in person...
Bale'

As I squeezed the piece of paper, I stared at the floor, holding back my tears. I couldn't believe that all my hopes had collapsed like that. The divorce papers came out of the envelope, and I closed my eyes as I gathered my thoughts.

'Is it true?' I looked at Raphael. He nodded.

'Everyone in Caelum is already aware of the change at Infernum. The final preparations for selecting a new judge are underway,' he told me. 'I found a letter on his desk when I came to ask Bale what was going on.'

'Alastor, what do you say?' I asked with hope.

'I can't feel his energy, ma'am.' Al frowned. 'It's true that he's not in this world.'

'These changes were planned long before he disappeared.' Raf frowned. 'Sophie, did he say anything to you about this?'

I was about to say no, but then I suddenly realised the meaning of his previous words. 'Well... he hinted that our paths might diverge. He spoke as if he was sure it would happen. He insisted that I didn't have to worry about continuing with a simple human life.'

'He often mentioned that your marriage was temporary...' Raf nodded, and I sat down in the chair, looking at the letter signed by my husband.

'That was the deal from the beginning...' I smiled with sadness in my voice, scolding myself for wanting more from this contract. Bale had tried to be gallant and didn't push me away coldly but only gently mentioned that we weren't meant to live happily ever after. It was so naive of me to think that I could plan my future with someone like the Devil.

My heart was compressed with pain, and I began to feel the anger growing in my soul. It was so unfair. However, I had to accept the fact that Bale had been seeking peace of mind for some time after a long life as someone he never wanted to be. Perhaps it was time for him to do what he wanted to do – give up and just enjoy harmony with himself. He deserved it more than anyone else.

I was going the other way. My heart wanted more. Now I had this chance, and I had no right to let it go. My wish has finally come true. I was completely free, self-reliant and able to achieve my goals.

Apparently, my mother was right this time. Some answers we're not meant to get.

My story was truly... finished.

No matter how tempting the opportunity to reveal the truth about my inner power was, the desire to find answers is not always rewarded. It was time to turn the page and leave that extraordinary experience behind. I couldn't find my father's killer, but my soul was calm because I knew the cause of his death and could move on.

After exchanging few words with Raphael, who was supposed to go back to Caelum and follow his father's orders to help with the organization of the new rules, I collapsed into Bale's chair and ran my hand over his table.

'What will you do, ma'am?' Al asked sadly. He didn't seem to believe it himself and was very disappointed that he hadn't got a chance to say goodbye to his friend. I smiled gently and looked again at the letter, touching my husband's signature and holding back the tears that were stinging my eyes.

I sighed. 'I'm not sure, Al, but all the doors are open for us now. I want to open the gallery, just as I dreamed. Perhaps I can take a journey around the world and finally enjoy a new experience. Everything seems so unreal… I've wanted to go back to my life for so long, and now that I can finally do it… I'm in doubt.'

'You're scared,' said Alastor, smiling softly, 'and I can understand that. But I, ma'am, will continue my duty and follow you anywhere you wish. That's what the master wanted. And it is what I want…'

'Thank you for your devotion.' I stood up, headed for the fireplace, and threw the letter into the fire.

When I heard the door close and was left alone, I sighed and hugged myself as the flame absorbed the sheet of paper. Longing, sadness, regret – all this enveloped me. The realisation that I was free to move on with my life without Belial was frustrating but also worrying. I had no idea where to start.

Colourful baubles on the Christmas tree reflected the warm light of the fire in the chimney, bright lights danced in a slow motion, snow fell outside the window, and there was peace around.

A pendant around my neck sparkled in the light, and I smiled weakly, remembering my father's words. I was the key to the light – I wonder what that means. Not all dreams come true, and not all prayers are answered. We make our own destiny and are responsible for our own failures. Everyone has their own truth, their own answer to an important question, their own destiny. Our faith in ourselves is the key to happiness and truth, and no one can prevent it, not even the Devil himself.

As I turned around, I took a step forwards by planning a warm family celebration tomorrow night, unwittingly touching my wedding ring with my fingers. With a fleeting smile, I closed my eyes and suddenly felt my body shiver, and my thoughts suddenly became clear. When I took off my ring, I saw a familiar signature again and frowned. As I pressed the ring to my lips, I slowly turned to the fireplace and stared at the ashes from the letter.

An incredible rush of energy suddenly filled me up, and I smiled quite a bit. Everything suddenly fell into place. I rushed to the door and opened it, calling my bodyguard. Worried, he was immediately in front of me, and I cheerfully grabbed his shoulders, watching his perplexed look.

'Al!' I said enthusiastically. 'We're going on a trip!'

'Where to?' asked the man in surprise.

'Anywhere we want!' I said it with confidence. 'The world is open to us, and we are free to go! You were with Bale the whole time, weren't you?'

'Yes, ma'am...' He nodded.

'Perfect!' I exclaimed. 'I want to visit all the places he's been to! I want to see the world through his eyes, to experience what he has experienced! I want to be inspired and feel how beautiful this world is. Bale's love for the world was strong, and I want to thank him for the opportunity he gave me to follow in his footsteps. I've lived in a cage for so many years, and now, thanks to Bale, I am a free bird!'

Alastor smiled as he looked at me and took in my confident gaze. 'I think it's a wonderful idea, ma'am. I'm sure that's what he would have wanted for you. When do we leave?'

'Tomorrow…' I squinted, looking straight at my bodyguard, and he flinched for a moment, but then he lifted up the corners of his lips and nodded politely, understanding my desire.

He didn't need to hear it from me. He knew my plan.

When I let Alastor leave, I gazed around the library as if I were saying goodbye to it. Turning my look towards Bale's last portrait, I lifted my head up in a proud gesture, satisfied with the artwork he had taken as a gift from me, and I left the room, closing the door behind me. Taking a quick glimpse in the mirror on the wall, I took in my dark hair and deep charcoal eyes. The darkness within me was on the verge of breaking out.

With each step, I became more confident, and stronger. It seemed as if I had found my own wings and was flying towards my destiny. My smile slowly turned into a frightening grin, and I finally felt like something inside me lit up. I was filled with fire, and my desire for power rose.

'This is an indestructible seal. This signature is eternal, and nothing can destroy the contract or any other document or object I have signed. It cannot be torn or burned. This is an abiding pact, blessed by the universe itself.'

I don't have any special features, and if you pass by, you might not even notice me. Everyone is the hero of their own story, subject to the trials of destiny and difficulties. But this... this is my story. One about my life turning upside down in an instant and about fate throwing a burden on my shoulders that was beyond my control. But I coped... I accepted the challenge of fate and agreed to fight for my future. I didn't give up and I firmly decided to go all the way to the end, confidently searching for the answers to my questions, eager to see the world, to find myself and my purpose.

My name is Sophie Angela Mortis-Deemer. I live in central London, and I am the CEO of Infernum Enterprise corporation.

And I... am the Devil's wife.

ABOUT THE AUTHOR

Jane E.Elend is an artist, writer and fantasy book series author. The Divine series are a fantasy multiverse consisting of three different series.

As a Psychology graduate, Jane has spent the last decade creating a new world full of charismatic characters.

Jane was born in Estonia, leading her way to the United Kingdom where she started a new life with a passion for writing.

Jane works from home in Bournemouth, United Kingdom. She spends her time as a full-time employed single mother, enduring sleepless nights while working on her novels or art, including her graphic novel based on the series "The Devil's Signature".

Jane values a wicked sense of humour and takes pride in her quirky witchy lifestyle.

Visit Jane E Elend's official website for the book series:

https://www.thedevilsignature.com/

The Divine Series

The Devil's Signature

Book One: The Abiding Pact
Book Two: The Eternal Bond. Part I
Book Three: The Eternal Bond. Part II
Book Four: The Final Deal
Book Five: The Witch's Seal
Book Six: The Samurai's vow
Book Seven: The Blood and Ink. Part I
Book Eight: The Angel's Promise
Book Nine: The Messenger's Oath
Book Ten: The Heavenly Deceit
Book Eleven: A Soul Crusher's Lullaby
Book Twelve: The Blood and Ink. Part II
Book Thirteen: The Empty: A Hunt for Holy Grail

Spin Off

The Presence

BONUS

The Character Short Stories

The Bride of the Dragon Emperor

Book One: The Bride of the Dragon Emperor. Scales of Present
Book Two: The Wife of the Dragon Emperor. Scales of Past
Book Three: The Dragon Empress. Scales of Future
Book Four: The Empty: A Hunt for Holy Grail

The Wolf and the Dream Catcher

Book One: The Wolf and the Dream Catcher. Waxing Crescent
Book Two: The Wolf and the Dream Catcher. Waning Gibbous
Book Three: The Wolf and the Dream Catcher. Full Moon
Book Four: The Empty: A Hunt for Holy Grail

Printed in Great Britain
by Amazon